# CONSORT OF DARKNESS

*A Story of Nyx and Erebus*

## MOLLY TULLIS

The Bibliophile Blonde LLC

*For my goddesses, above and below.*

# A NOTE FROM THE AUTHOR

The beauty of mythology is how it transforms as it is retold, from generation to generation. *"Consort of Darkness"* takes place during the events of Zeus's uprising against his father, Kronos, a series of battles known as the titanomachy. This story includes original plot lines and mythological references that do not follow existing accounts to the letter.

*"Consort of Darkness"* is a Greek mythological retelling that contains graphic violence, swearing, and sex scenes.

# PROLOGUE

*"What hurts you blesses you. Darkness is your candle. Your boundaries are your quest." - Rumi*

In the beginning, there was darkness. It was not the absence of light, but its own living, breathing thing. The darkness encompassed the Underworld like a blanket; it wrapped up close and filled every crevice, crack, and corner. It wasn't cold or cruel—like you might believe—when it came to the pitch blackness. It was like slipping into warm water— slowly, then all at once.

In the darkness, Nyx was home.

))))

WE ARE BORN FROM SHADOWS, and we return to them when we die. The fear of this lightlessness is one that is implanted in us by men—by gods—who convince us that only wicked deeds happen in the obsidian depths. Far from being a place of eternal hellfire, it was only in darkness that Nyx found peace. There was no greater peace than the one that was known to someone who could embrace its depths, and no depths ran deeper than those of the Underworld.

In a time of gods, men, and titans, the rising tensions between the light and the dark were beginning to stir like the first words of a song. This was before the time of heroes — there was no Hercules, no Achilles, not a word had been whispered of Odysseus. The gods were nothing more than children, fighting amongst themselves as the world pulled and pushed through its adolescence. It was the titans who had the world in their iron-grip, who used the gods as errand-boys, generals, and playthings. In kind, it was how gods treated men.

The only beings as powerful as the titans were the primordials. The ones who had sung themselves into existence, who had birthed themselves from blackness and created their power alongside it. The most powerful of these was Nyx.

She existed before the titans, before the gods, before the concepts of man, earth, and time. Nyx had pulled herself from Chaos and existed in the blackness —giving it the guardrails that it needed. She saw the world for what it was, misshapen and deformed, and created a dimension in which life could prosper amongst death. She shaped the Underworld, poured Tartarus from her fingers, and birthed night into reality for the world needed its rest. From Nyx's womb came sleep and death, Hypnos and Thanatos, intended to equalize both gods and men and give them all the reprieve they needed when their souls grew weary.

The black depths of the Underworld were her doing, and the very boundaries of life were her creation. In the beginning, she was worshipped. Her gift of peace and obsidian and her feminine creation were all seen for the balance that they established in the world.

She was not alone. Nyx was night, but what was night without its cover? Not long after Nyx had pulled herself into existence, Erebus followed. He *was* darkness. While Nyx was the divine embodiment of night and all that it entailed, Erebus was action. He was primordial, an enforcer, the executioner. The final knell of sleep and death and the champion of the night. Nyx created the space for Erebus's darkness and the two were one. It was with Erebus that she had born Hypnos, Thanatos, and Charon. Before time immemorial, Nyx was known as the Consort of Darkness. Their passion for one another was woven into their very beings, running as deep as their power.

Over time, as the gods who existed in the sun grew nervous over her power, her name was wiped away. Dark tales were spun of the depths, striking fear into the hearts of anyone who heard them. Darkness was criminalized; the night became a time of fear and villainy, and life's balance deteriorated along with it, leaving the world to succumb to its excess.

The gods and the titans had started to fight, their squabbles threatening to overthrow the balance that Nyx had created. War was brewing, and it would take everyone with it. Erebus had begun to be tempted by the promises of the light, to be praised and celebrated like the gods, to be worshipped by man as they sat forgotten in the Underworld. Nyx had scoffed at such hopes, calling them foolish. Erebus recoiled.

Night itself and darkness incarnate were beginning to separate.

# PART I

Nyx watched the rolling waters of Phlegethon, the sound of the waves always calming her down. The Underworld was becoming too crowded these days. She found herself repeatedly retreating to Tartarus for some peace and quiet, where it was rumored to be so dark that the blackness wrapped around the land like a cloak. The rumblings between gods, men, and titans exhausted Nyx as she watched their reverence for death slowly eroding. All men wanted to live in the sun now. The gods all wanted to be exalted in the daytime.

Loneliness had been something that had never been a part of Nyx. She had created everything that she had ever needed in her life, everything that she felt the world had needed… and then, there was Erebus. The two of them were primordials who had called themselves into creation and ingrained their lives with each other. His darkness was an extension of her night. Her night was the home to his darkness. Recently, the struggles of the gods had threatened to drive a wedge between the two of them, creating a loneliness in Nyx for the first time in her long existence.

She didn't like how it felt. People always claimed that the

night was empty, that the absence of light was cold—it wasn't true. There was plenty of warmth and peace to be found in her blessed coverings, in the shade, away from the blistering sun. It was *loneliness* that was the true void. Only hers came without the darkness, not in it.

She was lost in her thoughts as she stared out at the river. A recent batch of arrivals to the Underworld had caused the Gate to get backed up and Charon was behind. The screeching of desolate souls had sent Nyx diving deeper to Tartarus. *There was a time when souls never minded dying.* Her thoughts were bitter. *They welcomed my children. They greeted Thanatos with a smile. Now, a few hundred years with these gods running around, and they cry foul.*

"Nyx."

The voice didn't break the silence, but it pulled Nyx from her thoughts. It echoed in her mind, ringing between her ears and making her heart beat faster. She sighed, readjusting herself on the riverbank, and refused to respond.

A moment later, the shadows on top of the water began twisting, morphing into something solid. They moved towards Nyx and curled at her ankles. She watched as the black tendrils wrapped around her legs.

"Erebus." Nyx's voice rang out in the depths. She fought to keep the smile off her face, even if their relationship had been... at odds, recently. The darkness chuckled in response.

"You're hiding from me," Nyx chided, sighing and looking at the skyline.

"I'm here." Erebus's voice echoed aloud this time, coming from all the shadows at once.

"You never let me see you anymore."

"You can see me."

Nyx rolled her eyes, standing up and pushing the shadows off her like she was dusting off dirt. "You know what I mean."

There was a heartbeat of silence, then two, then three. A slight breeze picked up as it began to spin in a small torrent, a black column of shadow appearing as a man stepped out of it.

He was bronzed with dark, curly hair nearly falling into his face. Even his chiton was black. The expression on his face was cautiously playful. Nyx's smile finally broke free.

"There you are, Erebus." Her voice took on a wistful tone.

"You sound like my mother."

"You don't have a mother."

Erebus only laughed quietly in response and took a few more steps toward Nyx, as though he was testing the waters. She raised an eyebrow, and he stopped where he stood. After eons together, they hardly needed words to communicate. They didn't speak verbally to one another for centuries until the humans had popularized it.

He knew that he had hurt her with his last attempt to push the issue with the god's growing contentions. Equally, it had wounded his pride that she had brushed him off so quickly. They had found middle ground to continue their *working relationship*, but the changing boundaries of their dynamic were slowly driving Erebus insane.

"Have you spoken to Hypnos recently?" Nyx shifted the subject. She spent more of her time with Thanatos in the Underworld, while Erebus often frequented Hypnos in the realm of men.

"He's well." Erebus shrugged, the pleasantries between them made him uncomfortable. He knew Nyx like he knew himself and speaking to her casually, without the traditional intimacy of their conversations, writhed in him like a bad itch. "Everyone sleeps eventually."

"And everyone dies eventually." Nyx's voice got sharp. "Yet, they fear it now. Thanatos is overrun. Do you know they pray to these other *gods* to keep him from their doorstep? Thanatos!"

"I know." Erebus sighed inwardly. He knew how badly Nyx was hurting over her children, especially Death, and how their reputation was being mutilated in Greece.

"He existed before any of those overgrown children. No better than the titans, all of them."

"It will pass. The realm of men is fickle." Erebus answered the same way that he always did.

"Yet, you want to join them in their squabbles." Nyx's temper found its way to the surface. "If it's so fickle, why do you care?"

If Erebus could have gone pale, he would've.

"That's different."

"Enlighten me."

"You don't enjoy the light as you have so often reminded us all." Erebus cursed himself as soon as he said it, knowing that he was pushing it a little too far. Nyx's power started leaking from her body, waves of black sparks rolling over her pale skin. Erebus rubbed his hands over his face and shook his head.

"Darkness—" Nyx's voice dropped, taking on a deadly echo that happened when her power was boiling up inside her. Erebus shook his head. She only called him *Darkness* when she was serious or… intimate. She had called him *Darkness* since time began and only referred to him as Erebus once mankind had started.

"I'm sorry." His voice was quiet, sincere. "I didn't come here to dredge this up once more. You know how I feel about this. The gods and the titans are on the brink of a war and that will affect the humans. They disrespect you these days with their insolence. *That's* why I care."

Nyx was silent. The only sound in Tartarus was the burble of the river behind them. She turned around, putting her back to Erebus as her eyes followed the water again. He watched her shoulders relax and her power slowly ebb away like the waves.

"I don't care if the gods respect me. I don't know why you care what they think, either. You're so eager to leave behind all that we've built."

Erebus sighed and took a few steps closer to Nyx, stopping when he was just out of arm's reach from her. He could feel the heat of her body rolling off her in the cool depths of the Underworld, pushing him a little bit more towards insanity. The tension between them was cleaving him in two.

"You spend a lot of your time now in Tartarus." Erebus attempted to redirect the conversation. "Would you not come up to Elysium? Asphodel? Spend some time at the Gate."

"Do you know what they say now about Tartarus?" Nyx turned around and faced him. Erebus saw the tears in her eyes.

"Not... Not recently." His voice got quiet as he realized once more that there was no escaping this topic between them.

"The gods say it is the darkest pit of hell." Nyx's voice was stone; her mouth was set in a thin line. Erebus watched as some of her power began rippling over her skin once more.

"It... It is." Erebus cocked his head in confusion as he looked down at her. "I thought that was why you liked it."

Nyx shook her head. "You don't *get* it. They say that like it is something to be afraid of. They're talking about Tartarus like it is the deepest pit of hell, the place where only the world's worst go. An eternal pit of fiery damnation...or something."

"They will learn eventually." Erebus shrugged, debating with himself over moving closer to Nyx still.

"My precious Tartarus," Nyx sighed, her voice tinged with notes of melancholy. "It's the darkest level of the Underworld, yes. It's not a punishment. It's peaceful. I built it, Erebus. I built it for the souls who were the most tired, the most traumatized."

"A refuge."

"Yes." Nyx blinked as a few tears fell.

Erebus struggled to keep his emotions off his face. *When was the last time I even saw her cry?*

"It was a sanctuary, and now, the gods have convinced mankind that only the worst souls are sent here. I can't understand why you want to do anything for those creatures."

She turned away from him once more, and Erebus felt defeat settle into his bones.

He had come here to try and move past their disagreements, but it was obvious to him now that if the surface world was in turmoil...so would Nyx and Erebus. He saw the appeal of cooperating with the gods and was tempted by the praise they received. He knew now with certainty that Nyx was turned off to the idea. She watched how the other gods had treated her, treated her *children,* and there would be no changing her mind.

Smoke and shadows began to pool around Erebus's feet again as he began to disappear into the mist, his human form evaporating to his primordial shadows. He looked at her once more before he vanished.

"It doesn't have to be so black and white, Nyx."

"Darkness and light always are."

))))

NYX WANDERED QUIETLY through the Underworld, abandoning her body in exchange for her primordial form. She moved through the fields like a rolling wave of nightfall, bringing with her waves of darkness. It wasn't the same as when Erebus was beside her. The blackness ran deeper when he was there, and it gave Nyx space to let her mind drift to the night. Now, it felt like she was pulling double duty. They had been able to continue working in tandem, but it was apparent that Erebus was still upset over her refusal to join the cause of the gods.

She wasn't obtuse. She knew what it was like to be worshipped by man. Before the gods and titans had begun to corrupt and run amok amongst the humans, the world had respected Nyx. They had loved her, worshipped her, even. She was the mother of death and sleep, the consort of darkness, and they had adored her for what she had created. Women prayed to her for safety in the shadow of the night and laid offerings at her temples for divine, feminine blessings. Her power was known for its all-consuming strength.

Then... the gods happened, and mankind was easily polluted. They stopped seeing Nyx as a goddess of creation in her own right and started seeing her as something to fear. It was the gods first. They had ransacked her temples and burned them, tossing her acolytes out into the street. Then the men forgot. Only a generation or two later, the women had forgotten too.

It hurt, yet she was not lost in her ego. Nyx moved on as normal, creating the Underworld and pouring more realms out for the souls that eventually all came through to her. Erebus told her that she needed to delegate. It was something that Nyx couldn't get comfortable with—all the realms of the Under-world were hers. When night fell, the entire world was her domain, too. Who else would she pass that off to?

Over the past century as the conflict had risen, a few of the less intrusive gods had found their way to her depths. Nyx was fine passing off parts of it to Hades, whom she found only *slightly* less annoying than his brothers. A few of the other gods that had followed him weren't terrible, either. Tartarus remained Nyx's. She wouldn't give it up to anyone, no matter how awful the humans now described it.

*Could they not let me have one thing?* Her thoughts turned petty, and she chided herself for it, moving around the Elysium border. *First, they came for me. Will there be no safe spaces left? A refuge! It is a refuge and yet, they run from the rest. They hide from it. They tremble in front of Thanatos, even Hypnos.*

*"Someone is always sleeping, Mother."* Hypnos's last words rang out in Nyx's mind as she thought of their last conversation when she asked him to spend more time in the Underworld.

Everything on Earth was making her nervous, a feeling that — like loneliness — was new to Nyx until this century.

Thanatos was stoic and calm. He had a presence that sucked up all the oxygen in a room, but instead of feeling oppressive, it felt gentle. It was as if he was removing all the necessary decisions from you and giving you the permission to *let go*. While it might be an unwelcome feeling to a young man in the middle of a sunny afternoon, it was an unparalleled comfort to those whose thread had been cut by the Fates.

Nyx's thoughts were never far from concern about Thanatos. Her son had always taken such pride in aiding the human world, and now she couldn't bear that the humans greeted him with fear on their faces.

## 2

A sphodel was noisy. It was a lot noisier than Nyx was used to in Tartarus, but if she wanted to see her friend, it was a necessary trip. The meadows were filled with the souls of man, those who hadn't completed any heroic deeds but didn't need the sanctuary of Nyx's depths. While it was called the meadows, that was slightly misleading as it stretched as far as the eye could see. Asphodel was one large meadow, but it included a wood and the rivers Lethe and Styx on either side.

She didn't mind the souls—they were often friendly and gave her warm smiles as she passed. It was the attention. Over the last few centuries, she had forgotten what it felt like to have all eyes on her. There was only one temple left dedicated to Nyx. It was in Litochoro, and she had shrouded it in permanent darkness to protect her acolytes. She viewed those women as her friends and could hardly remember what it felt like to be worshipped or to be looked upon with reverence. As she glided through Asphodel, she was reminded.

There was a fleeting moment when she thought she understood Erebus, until she realized that all he needed was to walk through the meadows; he didn't need to go to war to find worshippers.

*Gods.* Nyx shook her head as her thoughts raced. *They've gotten to Erebus and given him an ego. He used to laugh at the things those other men got up to.*

There had been a time when Erebus was more stoic, the silent sword to her commands. An enforcer under the cover of her night. She didn't recognize the primordial who had stood in front of her, begging her to go to battle with *Zeus.* Their stilted conversation earlier that day proved that there was no middle ground between them anymore, leaving a hole in Nyx's chest that was widening rapidly, pushing her to return to Asphodel and seek out her friend.

As Nyx moved towards the forest that ran alongside Lethe, she wondered what would happen if a primordial drank from its waters. Most of the souls that came to Tartarus sipped water from Lethe, the river of forgetfulness and oblivion, to remove the traumatized memories of their past lives. They would then go rest in Tartarus until they were ready to be reborn.

*If I just…*

Nyx almost gasped out loud, her own thoughts shocking her. She had never considered drinking the waters of Lethe before…but there was a growing panic in her body. There was a terrible sense of foreboding that crowded her mind, making it hard to see her own reason. She was nervous about losing Erebus.

*What would that… What would that even mean? Losing Erebus… He's… I mean, we're…* Even her thoughts were disjointed.

Nyx pushed the feeling from her mind as she wove in and out of the trees. There were less souls in this part of Asphodel, the human notion of *being afraid of the woods* apparently never went away. The air was thick with the scent of daffodils and narcissus. It calmed Nyx. Dark waves of nightfall slithered through the trees as she descended upon the middle of a small clearing, an elaborate stone home in the very center.

Nyx had always thought it pedestrian that her friend had wanted a homestead like a human, instead of simply existing in her goddess form. It was one of the only things different between them.

The home was built with bricks and wooden beams, and it was centered around a courtyard. The courtyard had a short row of columns and an altar, which never failed to make Nyx smile. She only had one temple left, but her friend always paid tribute to her, despite Nyx's many protests that it was unnecessary. A seashell mosaic was on the floor in the center, making a strophalos. The strophalos of Hecate.

The dark clouds gathered in a vortex above the courtyard, spinning down to the ground until Nyx stepped out of the inky mass in her female form. As soon as her feet touched the mosaic, Hecate walked outside.

"I didn't know to expect you today." Hecate's tone was warm, and she moved over to greet her friend. Hecate was Nyx's closest ally in the Underworld, both having an undying dedication to the human women of the world.

Hecate had long, dark hair with a scarlet tint that matched her deep red peplos. She wore a small diadem that was engraved with a crescent moon, which she never parted with. Her voice had an echo effect that always sounded like three people were talking at once: the maiden, the mother, and the crone. She tempered the effects of her voice around humans; however, she did tend to amplify it around human men when she was seeking vengeance.

"I needed to see you." Nyx's tone was laced with a concern that made Hecate's brows rise. She loved Nyx, but Nyx had never *needed* to see anyone. A thousand years ago, Hecate had to keep Erebus from plunging the world into a second ice age when Nyx decided to take an extended nap in the cosmos. She couldn't be reached and forgot to let her husband know her plans. The memories of it still gave Hecate a headache.

"Of course." Hecate nodded eagerly, extending her arm and ushering Nyx inside.

She may have laughed at her friend for wanting a human residence, but she had never been more grateful to see the warm hearth and settle into the coziness of Hecate's kitchen. The goddess of witchcraft was always brewing something that smelled delicious, and herbs hung from the rafters. Two large, black dogs were sleeping in front of the fire, and a few cats ducked out of the open window when the women walked in.

Nyx sat at the table and Hecate moved over to her cauldron, feigning busyness to put Nyx at ease. Hecate knew Nyx wouldn't be able to open up if she was staring at her. The silence stretched on for a few moments as Hecate moved around, grabbing a pestle and mortar, absentmindedly crushing some seeds. Nyx was unmoved, staring into the flames as dark clouds danced around her like a cloak. Hecate tried to keep her face stoic—Nyx was losing control if she was slipping between her human and primordial forms.

"Have you heard anything from Zeus recently?" Nyx finally broke the silence. If the question surprised Hecate, she managed to keep it off her face.

"I've heard this talk of overthrowing Kronos, yes." Hecate shrugged as though she was discussing the weather.

Nyx said nothing in response as she turned her attention back to the fire.

"Is that what this is about? Why do you care what Zeus is doing?" Hecate's voice took on a gentle, probing tone. One of her dogs picked its head up, looking at Nyx with an almost human-like stare.

"I don't. It's not about Zeus."

"Okay." Hecate's response was gentle, but her silence was resolute. She would listen to Nyx for hours but wouldn't push her to share. A few minutes went by before Nyx began again.

"It's about Erebus."

*Ah.* Understanding flooded Hecate's face. If there was anything that was going to rile Nyx, it would be Erebus.

"What about him?"

"He wants to join Zeus." Nyx's voice cracked for a moment, unleashing the hurt that had been building in her. That *did* surprise Hecate, and she stifled a gasp. She had also always known Erebus to scoff at the realms of the gods and titans. He was ancient and powerful—only Nyx surpassed him —and not easily stirred to emotional displays like the immortals.

"What are his reasons?" Hecate excelled at keeping her tone calm as she kept her questions short.

"He thinks helping Zeus overthrow the titans is the best way to regain the adoration of the humans. They've been making a mess recently."

Nyx wasn't making eye contact with Hecate; waves of dark clouds continued to rise and fall around her. Hecate forced herself to take a deep breath before responding.

"The...adoration of the *humans?*" Hecate's voice finally betrayed some of her confusion. Nyx nodded.

"He has noticed how they don't worship him and me the way they used to. My temples are gone. The humans are afraid of Thanatos. He wants us to move *into the light* as he keeps saying." She waved her hand around her face exasperatedly.

"Into what?" Hecate's composure finally snapped as she slammed her mortar down. At her sudden outburst, flickers of red power erupted over her skin. Both of her dogs jumped up, barking.

"I know." Nyx nodded with taut lips. "The *darkness*. He wants to be worshipped again and wants to do it with the gods."

Hecate paused and studied her friend, trying to comprehend what a blow this must be for Nyx to hear. Darkness was a part of the night. Any critiques that Erebus had about himself or the way the world saw him inevitably made it sound like he was criticizing Nyx.

"When did he bring this up?"

"The first time?" Nyx shrugged. "About a year ago. Zeus has been all over Greece over the past few months, garnering support."

"A year?"

"Yes. He approached me about it the other day, but we've...been a bit at odds since the very first time he brought it up." Hecate's heart broke. She had no idea that her friend had been feuding with Erebus for so long. A year was trivial to an immortal and nothing to a primordial, but the idea was still upsetting.

"You two haven't seemed out of sorts. I haven't noticed." Hecate moved around the kitchen counter and took a seat next to Nyx.

"We came to a bit of an...understanding. We've been working together, but that's it." Nyx flushed as Hecate's eyes went wide.

"You don't mean...?"

"I do." Nyx shrugged.

"You haven't...in a year?"

"No. I didn't really think that's what we were agreeing to, but he can't seem to look at me for longer than he has to."

"That *can't* be true!" Hecate shook her head fiercely, grabbing Nyx's hands in hers. "Erebus loves you. More than that. You two... You two *are* one another."

Nyx finally let a few tears fall.

"I think that's the problem now. He doesn't want to be."

## 3

Nyx stayed in Hecate's kitchen longer than she had intended, even though she wouldn't speak of Erebus anymore. The conversation drifted to mundane topics as Hecate kept a careful eye on her friend. If Nyx and Erebus's relationship had diminished to a working relationship over the past year, the repercussions could be disastrous. Hecate knew how much the world needed both night and darkness to merge. The primordials had been together since they engineered their own creations, and if they weren't together as a couple, there was little hope they'd be able to keep that hurt at bay.

"I should go." Nyx stood, the dark shadows of her power already blurring across her skin. Her feet had already started to dissipate when Hecate stopped her.

"Why don't you stay?" Her voice was hopeful. Nyx had never spent more than an afternoon in her home. Hecate knew that Nyx much preferred her primordial form, being in Tartarus, and didn't enjoy being in the human residence, but the situation was unprecedented. Hecate watched carefully as Nyx's feet became solid and her power vanished.

*Okay. Well, she's staying… That's good. But also, she's staying.*

*That's new.* Hecate had to struggle to keep herself from overanalyzing each of Nyx's moods. She knew it wouldn't be helpful, but she tended to jump to women in need of aid.

"I suppose that for a while—"

Nyx's voice was cut off by a crash in the courtyard. Hecate and Nyx were both on their feet and running out in a moment, trails of black and red power flickering behind them. It was still light out since Nyx hadn't departed to relieve Hemera, Goddess of dusk. One of the columns had been knocked over, and pieces of the heavy stone were scattered on the ground. The dust was still settling, and from it emerged a mop of blonde curls and the golden face of—

"Hermes, for *fuck's* sake," Nyx growled, sending tremors out from under her feet. Hermes's only response was a loud, jovial laugh as he shook some of the dust from his shoulder. Hecate rolled her eyes but couldn't suppress her grin entirely.

The dust settled as Hermes stepped over a piece of marble and crossed the courtyard to the women. He was taller than them, permanently looking like he had come from a beach somewhere in Greece. His golden chiton hung off one shoulder, and he perpetually wore pteruges, even though he was barefoot.

"You know I'm helpless when there are two beautiful women in once place." His smile was infectious as he winked at Hecate. He was smart enough to keep his flirting to a minimum around Nyx—only to a minimum, he couldn't turn it off.

"What are you doing here, Hermes?" Nyx's voice was cold. He was the opposite of Erebus in every way; she didn't like being reminded that regardless of their arguments, Erebus was all she wanted.

"One of these centuries, you're going to warm up to me, Nyx." He rolled his eyes playfully.

"I wouldn't hold your breath."

"That's okay." Hermes shrugged, devilishly nonchalant. "I can hold it for a very long time."

"You destroyed my courtyard." Hecate raised an eyebrow expectantly, trying to distract Hermes off Nyx before she swallowed him whole.

"I will fix it promptly, goddess." Hermes grabbed a hold of Hecate's hand and pressed it to his lips, getting a scoff from Nyx and a shake of the head from Hecate. "I did avoid the mosaic and the altar."

"Nyx would've killed you before the dust cleared if you had run into it."

"I am not *that* egotistical," Nyx snapped. "I don't even care if Hecate has the damn thing. I'm not Zeus."

"Ah." Hermes grew somber. "That is what I've come to talk to you about."

"If you're here to talk about Zeus, then you can —"

"Nyx." Hecate's voice took on its ominous echo. Besides Erebus, she was the only person who wasn't afraid to push back against Nyx. Nyx didn't respond but turned her head away. "Go on, Hermes. What have you come here to say?"

The god took a slow breath as if he knew that his message was going to upset them.

"Zeus has officially declared war on Kronos." Nyx snapped her attention back to Hermes, and Hecate let out a slow breath. Hermes bit his lip. "He formally requests..."

"*He formally requests?*" Nyx's voice was a deep, echoing baritone as she dematerialized into her primordial form in an instant. The night came down, blanketing Asphodel in darkness. The wind picked up, and thunder went rolling over the meadows. Hecate and Hermes stood immobile in the courtyard until Hecate waved her hand, bathing them in soft moonlight.

"That's a helpful trick." Hermes chuckled, breaking the tension.

"No tricks about it. Selene learned everything from me, got it?" Hecate gave him a small smile, but it didn't reach her eyes.

"Oh, I'll never forget."

"Now, tell me what you need to tell me about Zeus. I'll make sure that the Underworld gets the message."

"Well…" Hermes's voice dropped, and some of the gaiety left his shining face. "You should know that he's already spoken to Hades. Most of the gods, in fact. This is no longer chatter or wistful, chaotic thinking by a petulant Zeus."

"It's always a petulant Zeus."

"Fair." Hermes snapped his fingers. "It has happened, though. Zeus has declared war on his father." Hecate nodded, a sinking feeling growing in her stomach.

"I understand. Who has sided with Zeus?"

"Well, Hades and Poseidon, which we all saw coming." Hermes rolled his eyes as though it pained him to mention the brothers. He leaned against a column. "The rest of the gods have joined him, too."

"Mmm." Hecate ran her hands through the ends of her hair while Hermes stared unabashedly. "What have the titans said of this?"

"Themis and Prometheus have sided with Zeus."

"Then we really do have a war on our hands, don't we?" Hecate asked grimly. Hermes pushed off the column and went to approach her, placing a hand on her shoulder. As soon as he touched Hecate, her dogs came running outside, barking at the god until he yelped in surprise.

"Hecate!"

"Oh, they won't hurt a fly." Hecate chuckled, leaning down and petting the hell hounds until their tongues were lolling and tails wagging.

"I'm sure they won't hurt flies and women, but men seem to be in their own category." Hermes looked at the dogs sarcastically.

"Aren't they though?" Hecate's smile was wide as she sent the dogs back in the house, her expression changing once more. "What is it that Zeus needed to tell us, then?"

"Lots have been drawn. Everyone has chosen a side, whether they're titans or gods. Zeus will expect an answer from *everyone*." To Hermes's surprise, Hecate laughed.

"Has he gotten a response from any of the other primordials?"

"Well...no."

"He won't. If he expects one from Nyx, Zeus will be sorely disappointed."

"He wants her to fight with him."

"I'm sure he does. She's the most ancient of us all. That doesn't mean that it's going to happen." As soon as Hecate denied Hermes, dark clouds moved over the moon and covered the pair in the blackness once more. Hecate nodded as if she was agreeing with the night.

"I think you have your answer, Hermes."

Hermes shook out his shoulders and flexed his arms, gold dust appearing around him as he prepared to ascend. Hecate waved a hand again and brought the moonlight back.

"What about you, Hecate?" Hermes looked at her with a softer expression. "It's not going to be good if any of the gods defy him."

"Are you *threatening* me?" Hecate's voice dipped low as her red power flickered, the second and third head of the maiden and crone flickering on her shoulders.

"Don't shoot me!" Hermes tossed his hands up in defeat and kicked off the ground. "I'm just the messenger." There was a splitting crack as the earth shook, the moon going out once more like a candle. Hecate tried fruitlessly to bring back the soft light.

"Shit," Hecate cursed under her breath as she recognized the rolling current of Nyx's power threatening to choke Asphodel once more.

"Is it Nyx?" Hermes looked around in the dark.

"Yes. She's angry." Hecate shot Hermes a warning look. "Nightfall has come early in the mortal realm. That doesn't happen often, and it only happens when she's furious. It's best that you leave the Underworld… Now."

"You don't have to tell me twice. Remember what Zeus—"

Hermes was nearly knocked out by a blast of wind. There was an outpouring of darkness that extinguished even the lights of Hermes's and Hecate's power, leaving them both briefly choking on air in the courtyard. It only lasted for a moment until it passed.

"Was that also Nyx?" Hermes gasped, his eyes wide.

"No…" Hecate shook her head as her lips settled into a grim line. "*That* was Erebus."

"Do not start with me, Helios." Nyx stared the titan down then eyed the horizon. "You know as well as I do that there is a *balance* to this."

"You're the one who's picking a fight!" Helios shrugged, refusing to move. The sun was still out, and it should have set hours ago. The titan oversaw bringing it across the sky in his chariot each day but had grown tired of the confines of his role. Everyone knew that it was a pointless stand, and yet, he was determined to throw a fit.

"What are you trying to get out of this? More glory? It's always glory with men, isn't it? I've never understood that." Nyx shook her head. Her power began to unfurl around her, smoke and shadow dissipating. "This was futile, Helios. Now I'm going to be cranky."

The titan shrugged, the sun's rays intensifying behind him as waves of light and dark power rippled over the sky.

"Let's just say that I want to make sure you aren't getting rusty." Helios cracked a wicked grin, infuriating Nyx. Every few years, he threw a tantrum to get a good brawl out of it. Nothing made her angrier. It always messed up the mortal world for days.

Helios and Nyx crashed against one another in the heavens, flashes of lightning and columns of darkness pouring out of the sky. The mortal world ricocheted between night and day, being plunged into chaos. The tides changed erratically, and strange winds whipped over the land; people and animals alike began running for shelter as the earth itself seemed to spin. For a brief moment, it felt like the sun was being blown out like a candle. Yet, however quickly it had started, the battle was short-lived.

Nyx grew tired of Helios's games, and with one great shriek, she evaporated into blackness and swallowed the sun whole. She could suppress Helios's strength, but it took all her effort—until a cool, stoic presence moved through the eternal night. Helios screamed in outrage and tried to find his way through the black sky while the earth went silent. The weight inside of Nyx began to ease until it stopped entirely. Nyx's power amplified, and the sun nearly vanquished inside of her. Erebus. She should have known that he wouldn't miss a chance to piss off Helios.

"*Sorry I'm late.*" His words rang through Nyx's mind.

"*I didn't even miss you.*" Her response was playful in its tone.

"*Didn't even* need *me, did you?*"

"*I had it handled.*"

"*You did. Nice to have a little bit of help though, isn't it?*" Nyx could almost feel Erebus smiling at her. Yes, she would have been able to handle Helios by herself. Yes, it was infinitely easier to handle Helios with Erebus's perpetual darkness marrying her power. It was like he was the finishing notes; he turned her raw, primordial night into a song.

"*Let's finish this up and go home, Nýchta.*"

Nyx nodded, knowing only Erebus could see her in the onyx absence of light. Helios was still having a tantrum across the sky. With one nod, Nyx dissolved into dark masses of power and sent the sun flying over the horizon. Helios let out a frustrated cry as Erebus and Nyx listened for the sound of his chariot taking off after it.

"It will take him until dawn to find it." Nyx watched after Helios's retreating form, a bored expression on her face. Erebus knew better. She wasn't bored; she was tired. These skirmishes with gods and titans had taken an upswing. There was no being as powerful as her, but it was a burden keeping all the immortals in line when they rose.

"Perfect timing. Let's go home." Erebus sent her a soft smile that was equal parts devilish and endearing. It was a look that he had perfected. Nyx knew there was one thing on his mind, which was *exactly* what she needed. Nyx sent a current of power out over the mortal realm, securing nightfall and following Erebus back to Tartarus.

He was waiting for her in his mortal form when her feet touched the ground. Erebus walked over to Nyx and wrapped an arm around her waist, pulling her into his body and capturing her mouth in a wicked kiss. Nyx let out a soft murmur of surprise and immediately leaned into him, her hands going up to tangle in his hair. It was a patient embrace, one that was slow and coaxing as he eased her mouth open for him. Erebus always kissed her like he had all the time in the world.

"I love you like this," she admitted softly, pulling back to catch her breath. Erebus's arm was tight on her waist as he began rubbing small circles on her back. Her eyes started to roll back into her head at the soft caresses.

"I know. You know why that is?"

Nyx shook her head, and Erebus chuckled. It was a dark sound that made her stomach flip. He continued, pressing himself closer to her so she could feel how ready he was.

"It's because I'm stronger than you like this, isn't it?" Erebus's voice took on a deep, controlling tone that made her weak in the knees. She dropped her hands around his neck and pressed up against Erebus, muffling her response, as her hips rose desperately to meet him.

"What was that?" He turned his head until his lips brushed her ear. "You're going to need to use your words."

Nyx lifted her head. "Yes."

"That's right." A slow smirk grew over Erebus's face as he gripped Nyx's chin and tilted her head up to meet his. "It's nice to have someone stronger than you for once, isn't it?" His gaze was hot as his eyes met hers. It was all Nyx could do to nod, feeling her control slipping as she easily fell into their dynamic.

Nyx's submission was not freely given. Erebus earned it. She was more than willing to offer it up to him when she needed it. There were times when the weight of her primordial form was too much and only slipping into their mortal forms released the tension, where Erebus was stronger.

"Please, Erebus..." Nyx's voice was quiet, a soft tone that let Erebus know *exactly* where her head was at. He eased them both down onto the soft ground of Tartarus, smoke and shadows swirling. In a flash, both of their tunics were gone.

"Gods, you're flawless," Erebus groaned as he leaned down and began trailing kisses up her stomach.

"Don't remind me of those idiots right now." Nyx smiled, her grin quickly falling into a loud moan when Erebus bit her ear.

"My apologies. Let's make sure you're entirely focused on me, yeah?" His voice was dark and teasing, and it made Nyx's toes curl. Erebus's hand slipped between her legs, and he gently parted her with his fingers. Nyx's legs fell open at the touch, exposing herself to him as he started a slow pace that was driving her insane.

"*Please* don't tease."

"I'm sorry..." Erebus pulled his hand away. "I know you weren't telling me what to do. Were you?" He almost sat up entirely and Nyx found herself nearly shrieking to pull him back down to her.

"No, no, I w—wasn't!" She was breathless, and Erebus's laugh was sinful.

"I didn't think so." Erebus started circling her clit slowly, smirking at how utterly drenched she was for him. Nyx's breath was coming in short pants as she lifted her hips up to meet his fingers, praying for more. He loved watching her like this—so undone at only the smallest of touches, so *eager* for him to possess her, to wear her out until she couldn't remember anything but his name.

As she was distracted and focused entirely on his fingers, Erebus sat up and flipped Nyx onto her stomach. She let out a sharp cry at the loss of contact.

"Erebus!"

"I know you like it like this…" His voice went straight to Nyx's core as she trembled. "You can't get enough of me taking you, feeling me all over you. Isn't that right?" She let out a soft moan, and any last remnants of her control vanished. Erebus's leg slid between hers, knocking Nyx's knees wider as he pulled her waist up.

"Yes—I l—love it." The words stuttered out of her.

Erebus let out a low growl, the sound of Nyx calling out to him amplifying his arousal. He leaned back briefly, surveying the sight in front of him. He was in awe every time the most powerful primordial in the universe whined for *him*, needed *his* dominance to get out of her head.

Nyx made another pained noise, attempting to clench her thighs together to get some friction.

"Be good." Erebus gave her a sharp smack on the ass, making Nyx whine. "You know you're only allowed to take what I give you." Before she could respond, Erebus grabbed her hands and pinned them behind her back. Nyx arched immediately and pressed back into his touch.

"Y—yes!" Nyx's moans were nearly pitiful as she pressed up against his hard length. Erebus growled and moved his other hand to her waist, still pinning her wrists.

"It's okay," he said, sounding full of teasing sincerity. "Don't worry. I'll will give you what you need."

Nyx opened her mouth to snap at him but was cut off as Erebus sheathed himself inside of her entirely with one thrust. Their moans mixed as Erebus began moving, his grip tightening on her as he picked up a nearly merciless pace. Nyx dropped her head to the ground and succumbed completely to him, her limbs feeling weightless as she relished the heat and the stretch of her walls around him. They were already on edge and hurtling towards release within minutes of being surrounded by each other. Their souls had been entwined since the dawn of time, and whenever their bodies followed suit, it was like coming home.

Erebus felt Nyx clenching around him and knew that she was on the edge. He bent down, pressing his chest to her back and keeping her hands at her spine.

"This is just for me, isn't it?" Erebus's voice was breathy, and he pressed a kiss to her temple. "Only I get to see you like this, with your hands pinned at your back... letting me do whatever I want..."

Erebus released Nyx's wrists and reached up to grab one breast, pinching her nipple until Nyx let out a scream. He felt her shaking underneath him, screaming into the void as she came.

"*Fuck*, Erebus!"

Feeling Nyx around him was all it took, and Erebus was releasing inside of her, seated to the hilt as he collapsed against her back. His thrusts slowed down to a stop, and with a heavy exhale, Erebus lay down and pulled Nyx to his side. Nyx's eyes fluttered open as she curled around Erebus's body on instinct.

"How are you, Nýchta?" Erebus raised an eyebrow at her as he took in her smiling face.

"Divine, Darkness... But I do have a question." Nyx traced a finger up Erebus's chest.

"Hmmm?"

"You didn't bribe Helios to start shit, did you?"

Erebus's laughter brightened up Tartarus.

## 5

After ensuring that Hermes had his answer, Nyx went back to Tartarus. She wasn't interested in hearing anyone else's opinion of the impending war. If Zeus had declared war on Kronos, there was only one person who might be able to change Nyx's mind.

*Gaia.*

The mother of Earth.

She currently resided deep in Tartarus's depths, resting so far below the surface that only Nyx knew where to find her. Aside from the primordials who had created themselves, each god and titan owed themselves in some way to Gaia. Kronos was her son; Zeus was her grandson, and no one had watched the skirmishes of immortals like she had.

Nyx never liked to disturb those who rested in her sanctuary. If anyone had a reason to be there, it was Gaia. When Gaia's husband, Uranos, had begun imprisoning some of their children, she tried to reason with him. Uranos was concerned that one of his children would overthrow him, but Gaia didn't see why that warranted such a strong reaction.

Uranos responded by continuing to capture their children, now imprisoning them in Earth's own depths—in a part of

Gaia. She was taunted with the cries of her own sons and daughters, unable to see the sun and wasting away in the universe she had built for them.

Gaia had gone to her remaining children and asked for help in overthrowing their father. The only one who responded was Kronos. It was another few years of bloody battle, but eventually, Kronos emerged victorious. Yet, in a tale that had existed since the dawn of time, Kronos took advantage of his mother and drained her of her power.

Gaia was outraged. In a cruel twist of fate, she learned too late that it was Kronos that Uranos was afraid of. She tried to call out to the remnants of her husband, spread all over the Earth, but she was too late. Gaia apologized to the dying breaths of Uranos. He was unable to respond, but to let her know that he forgave her, Uranos cursed Kronos.

Kronos would one day be overthrown by one of his sons like he had done to his father. Gaia took solace in this and retreated to Tartarus, mourning the husband she lost and the son who had plundered her.

Nyx knew that Gaia still heard everything that happened on the Earth's surface, for better or worse. Gaia was able to tune it out in Tartarus, but Nyx had a suspicion that she had been listening ever since Rhea was able to smuggle Zeus out from Kronos's grasp. For the first hundred years of his rule, Kronos ate his children as soon as they were born, afraid of Uranos's curse. Zeus survived infancy, and then somewhere in Tartarus, Gaia sat up straighter and waited to watch the family legacy unfurl—sons overthrowing their fathers.

No one would change Nyx's mind except Gaia. If Gaia said that this was a war that was worth getting behind, Nyx would. It was as simple as that. Nyx saw a camaraderie in Gaia, both primordial and more ancient than some of these newer gods could even comprehend. There was a growing fear in Nyx's stomach when she looked at her relationship with Erebus that they were soon on their way to becoming

another cautionary tale, like Uranos and Gaia. Rhea and
Kronos.

*Can the powerful fall in love?* Nyx's thoughts were preoccupied
as she landed softly in Tartarus, choosing to walk in her human
form to where she knew Mother Earth rested. *Powerful men fall
in love all the time. Is it love or do they enjoy their bounty and move on?*

*Can powerful* women *ever fall in love?*

The answer was all around Nyx in Tartarus's depths where
Gaia slept — *no*. Something cracked in her chest, and she
approached the Mother with tears in her eyes. The hills in
front of Nyx began to move and shift slowly, morphing into the
form of a sleeping woman in the blackness. She was taller than
Mount Olympus and stretched high above Nyx, dark eyes
blinking open.

"Nyx." Her voice was tender, soft, like a mother embracing
a child. "You come to me crying, child, while I rest in your
depths. Have I taken advantage of your sanctuary?" Gaia
moved as if to sit up and leave.

"No, Mother!" Nyx's voice was almost panicked, and she
wiped at her eyes. "I have come to seek your council."

"I'm not sure what on. There is nothing that I can do that
the Goddess of Night cannot."

"You flatter me, Mother. I have come to ask you about...
Kronos."

The silence was loud. Nyx could have sworn that she saw
the hills rise a little higher up into the sky as if Gaia grew
larger to defend herself from the threat of Kronos's name.
When the silence stretched on a little too long, Nyx raised her
hand in a respectful gesture and prepared to leave.

"Wait, Night. I shall answer your questions. Then, you
shall leave me to another century of sleep, unmolested."

"I oblige." Nyx nodded her head and evaporated into her
primordial form, her darkness spreading over Tartarus, so she
might speak to Gaia as equals. "Zeus has formally declared
war on Kronos."

"I have heard this."

"I have denied your grandson's request to join his cause."

"Do you join the cause of Kronos?" Gaia's voice dropped lower, the hills that made up her body began to shake with anger.

"No, Mother," Nyx snapped in response, her own voice thundering across the Underworld skies. "I have joined no cause. I told the gods and the titans that these battles will never end. It will always be son revolting against father. It will never end."

"You are wise." Gaia nodded in agreement. "For what do you seek my council?"

"Erebus has expressed a desire to join Zeus."

"Ah." There was a small earthquake in response as if Gaia was stretching out her limbs in exasperation. "Men will always go to other men in the time of their ego's needs."

Nyx's heart sank. "This is what I fear. You hear all that happens on Earth, Gaia. Is this worth my attention, for the human's sake, as Erebus claims?"

There was another great swath of silence.

"It is another one of the many battles that men will have. Whether they are titan, God, or primordial. Menfolk will never stop. Zeus was always going to revolt against Kronos. My husband's curse has come to pass." Gaia paused once more before continuing as if she was chewing on her words and evaluating their toxicity. "This war will determine the immortal's struggle for power for the next millennia. Whomever arises, will stake their claim on Mt. Olympus for the rest of Greece's history."

Nyx felt her heart stop. *Was I wrong to rebuke Erebus so? This doesn't seem like it's a passing fleet of patricide.*

Gaia could hear her thoughts in the Earth.

"Take heart. While this may determine who takes ownership of the Grecian skies, the balance will never be more important. The darkness, death, night incarnate... These things must always remain the same... so the world can withstand the bickering of fragile gods."

"What... What of Erebus?" Nyx cursed the catch in her voice when she asked, thankful that she wasn't in human form.

"I cannot speak to the future of souls. I only speak of what will happen to Earth. For that, you must seek the Fates."

"I understand. Thank you, Mother." Nyx's heart was no lighter as she prepared to depart to Asphodel.

"Hear me once more, Night, before I return to the depths of your sanctuary for a hundred years." Nyx paused. "These are, indeed, the whims of men and gods. You are not wrong to avoid the skirmishes of my family. There will be more in the future, and this one, while large, will be no different. But if you fight... everything will fall before the darkness."

There was a large creaking sound as if a thousand trees had snapped in half, and the hills flattened out in front of Nyx. In an instant, the landscape in front of her had plateaued. Gaia had returned to the center of the Earth to wait out the war of her sons and grandsons.

Nyx took a deep breath, struggling with the weight of what Gaia had confirmed for her.

*Maybe Gaia has the right idea.*

## ❧ 6 ❧

The earth shook as the stones came crumbling down, sending shockwaves through the ground. The temple that stood there had once been a sight of great pilgrimage, a testament to the power of the darkness and the balance of life. The pine trees around it whistled when the wind blew in from the water, carrying the smell of salt and sun. By design, it was when the sun set that the temple really shined, the white stones glowing in the blackness like a constellation come to earth. It had been crafted slowly, painstakingly, to be the most beautiful when the sun had set. A long foyer, flanked with columns, lead into an open-air dome that celebrated the sight of the moon and stars above it. They said that the power of the darkness kept the rain from falling in the temple even when it was pouring outside.

The smell of incense always flooded the clearing and the woods around it, letting the nearby villagers know the priest-esses were at work. Tapestries sewn from purple and black hung down from the altars, bodices of the goddess made from black stone offered up gentle expressions of acceptance. In the very center of the great temple was its altar, always being attended, lit with fire as flowers, kindling, and oil were thrown into it to keep it fed. The mosaic floor held an alternating pattern of lunar shapes, the cycles of the moon etched into a circle around the atrium. Behind the altar was the temple's shining glory, a statue of black marble that was over seven feet tall, the only one that existed of the night in her human form.

It fell the hardest.

Hera watched it hit the ground with a sick sense of satisfaction. Priests toiled on her behalf, pulling the banners from the hanging rafters and toppling statues and busts. Yet, it was the sound of the heavy brass altar falling that sounded like a death knell as it hit the broken pavement. The fires from the temple had spread around them, catching the nearby trees, and creating a burgeoning wildfire.

The temple fell around them in pieces—looters already descending on the borders of the wreckage—and the holy space was no more. Its former acolytes were huddled together on the corner of the clearing, watching with tears in their eyes in horror as their sanctuary vanished in moments.

"What are we going to do?" one of them cried as she gripped her sisters.

"Nothing. We are no match for the strength of these men."

"They should be worried about their own heads. Who believes that they can desecrate a temple of Nyx and get away with it?" The priestess shook her head in disbelief.

"They are priests of Hera." Another woman, the newest convert, shook her head. "Nyx does not have the power that she once did." The priestess's eyes flashed cold.

"Watch your tongue." Her voice was like iron. "These are new gods. Man has only just begun to worship them, and they will fall prey to the fickle follies of their new idols."

"Then where is she?" The convert challenged, taking a step towards the priestess. "If the goddess of the night cared, don't you think that she would have put a stop to this?"

"Do not question the will of the gods," another acolyte cut in.

"Nyx is not a *god*." The priestess cut them all off with a glance that could start a fire. "She *is night*. I will not question that, no more than I will question why the sun rises. We will begin again…" Her voice trailed off as two priests ambled over to where the woman was standing. The priestess turned to face them, her head held high despite her disheveled appearance. The other acolytes hid behind her. These were the priests of the new gods, who carried swords and wore armor, unlike any of the priests that the women had known before. Men had found religion.

"What shall we do with them?" one of them asked, chewing his lip as his hands rested easily on his sword. There was an expression in his eyes that the priestess had seen too many times for comfort.

"You heard Hera." His companion shrugged, unsheathing his sword. "Kill them all."

)))

NYX'S SCREAM echoed throughout the deepest parts of the Underworld. It shook mountains and made rivers stop. The very firmaments of darkness trembled, and the world alternated between day and night.

When she heard the first stone fall, she watched with growing annoyance. Hera was petty. Nyx knew Hera would come for her temples on the warpath for popularity. It wasn't until she saw Hera's lackeys pull their swords that she went hurtling towards the Fates. She beseeched them and tore at her hair, threatening to plunge the world into darkness, but even Nyx knew that she was not to interfere with their will. Yet, the Fates respected Nyx's authority and power over all of them, and they knew that Hera was to blame. They cut the acolyte's strings of life before the women could be defiled, letting them slip into the Underworld like falling asleep.

In the mortal world, with their weapons drawn, the priests approached the women and watched as they fell to the ground before anything could touch them… dead. They felt a cold burst of air and left with their own stories to tell—that Nyx had pulled her acolytes from them at the last minute. She had come after all.

Nyx was at the gates of the Underworld to greet them. She ushered their souls from Charon under the blanket of her black-ness, cradling them in her warmth and keeping the bright lights of Asphodel from their tired eyes. A great wave rolled over the mead-ows, and Nyx took her acolytes to Tartarus. She pressed kisses to the brows of her faithful, thanked them for their work and devo-tion, and brought their lips to Lethe. Their memories of Nyx and their faithfulness expunged, and she wept as she turned them over to the night to recover. It was all that she could offer them now.

As she wept and watched their disappearing spirits, the darkness amplified and circulated around her as Erebus took a mortal form. He stepped out into Tartarus, looking up into the sky and peering around at Nyx's immaterial form.

"Come to me, *Nýchta*."

Silence.

"Come to me." His voice dropped lower, sending a ripple of authority out into the abyss. The night responded to him as it personified, Nyx materializing in front of him. Her eyes were wet as she looked up at him through tears.

"Erebus…" Her voice cracked as she stepped towards him. "T–Those women… They t–trusted me…"

He took a few steps toward Nyx and embraced her, his arms wrapping tightly around her body as she curled into reflexively. It was one of the reasons he coaxed her into a human form, where she could feel small—like her burdens could be carried by someone else. By him.

"It's *not* your fault." His voice was unforgiving as he leaned down, whispering the words directly in her ear and squeezing her tighter to him. "Hera made a command, and the Fates followed through. We'll never know what for."

"I should have protected them! I s–saw the temple was f–falling..."

"You don't give a damn about buildings." Erebus interrupted her, pulling back and cupping her face with his hands. He let his thumbs stroke her cheeks with a gentleness only Nyx would ever see from darkness incarnate. "As soon as those women were in trouble, you did everything you could."

"It wasn't e–enough!"

Erebus's heart broke as she collapsed against his chest, and he moved his arms around her back. He hated seeing her like this. Nyx was one of the most powerful beings in existence, and she doubted her own abilities half the time.

"It was. The *Fates* intervened as much as they dared out of respect *for you*. For *your* acolytes, they pulled them from the mortal coil and delivered them to you."

Nyx didn't respond, confirming for Erebus that he had made his point. After he waited a few more moments, he maneuvered them down onto the ground. Erebus pulled a tree of shadow from the earth and leaned against it, letting Nyx shuffle between his legs and lay against his chest once more. His hands traced patterns on her back and played with her hair, resuming small ministrations all over her body to keep her calm.

There was no one who knew Nyx like Erebus, who was able to help bottle her power, refill her reserves... In those moments, she wasn't beholden to the title of night incarnate. She was simply the consort of darkness, at peace at his side. Nyx could surrender her soul and every bit of her tension to him, knowing that he would tend to it with care until she had the strength to pick it up again. Such was the burden of powerful women and the demands the world thrust upon them, the price for daring to be both feminine and strong.

Erebus didn't know how much time had passed when he saw Nyx's feet begin to evaporate. Slowly, ever so slowly, she succumbed to her immortal form like she was waking up from a dream. He followed suit, disintegrating into darkness until the two of them were one in the cosmos of Tartarus.

*"Hera will pay."* Nyx's voice echoed only in Erebus's mind.

*"Now is not the time to go after these gods."* Erebus cautioned, preferring to watch and wait.

*"I care not what they do to temples, affairs of state, or how they seduce man. Hera will pay for calling for the death of my acolytes."*

*"Nyx, Hera is young. She is impulsive."*

*"And I'm stronger than her."*

Erebus went to speak, but there was a small crest of power that rang through the darkness. It was subtle but existed, nonetheless.

*"One of the gods calls us."* Erebus chuckled, ever amused by how they thought they could call upon the titans. *"Shall we indulge them?"*

Nyx only laughed, and night and darkness went rolling over the Underworld to Mt. Olympus.

Once they had arrived, Nyx and Erebus assumed their mortal forms and descended from the black clouds that trailed them. They leisurely walked up the stone steps leading to the top, Erebus taking his position trailing Nyx's righthand side.

Mt. Olympus had become a recent home for the new gods, setting up dominion where they could watch the mortal world —and each other—with ease. Only the Underworld was safe from its vantage point. The columns started above the skyline, beyond human's view, trailing up towards the great hall that Zeus had commissioned for himself. In the future, he'd influence the Acropolis in Athens to look like his hall on Mt. Olympus.

"Do you think he's compensating?" Erebus murmured so

only Nyx could hear. She turned around and raised a brow at him, encouraging him silently to behave. The torches were lit as the pair moved silently through the entrance, passing facade after facade that had been engraved with tributes to Zeus.

*Interesting that he has decided to remove Kronos from his own mythos.* Nyx took in the murals and paid special attention to how Zeus viewed himself. *A lot can be determined from how he tells his own story.* She was pulled from her reverie by a great, booming voice from deeper inside the Acropolis.

"Nyx! Our goddess of the night. I'm so glad you heard me, all the way down in the Underworld."

Erebus groaned, making no attempt to hide the flagrant roll of his eyes. The pair stepped into the main hall, greeted by a gathering of the new gods. Zeus had seated himself on a throne of his own creation at the head of the room, his legs spread out wide and one hand stroking his beard. The rest of the gods stared openly, not used to the sight of the dark titans. They gawked as if they were strange animals. The only one who nodded in recognition was Hades.

Nyx fought the impulse to shove them all into blackness immediately and watch them cry in confusion. Instead, she plastered on the face of a diplomat, smiling internally at the knowledge that she and Erebus only *appeared* less powerful in their mortal forms.

"Luckily, your voice is powerful, Zeus." Nyx let the words slide out of her like honey, watching the transformation over Zeus's face as he lapped it up. *How pitiful,* she thought.

"Indeed!" He laughed gaily, clapping his hands together and sending a roll of thunder through the room.

*Adorable.*

"Now…" Zeus looked between Erebus and Nyx. "It seems to me that there has been some… unpleasantness of late, involving my dear wife."

Nyx dropped her smile as her face turned to stone and her thoughts grew violent. *How dare he beckon us to this charade? He acts like Kronos or Chaos, some king of these new gods, and he wishes to get ahead of the massacre Hera ordered.* Black clouds began gathering around Nyx and Erebus's feet. A collective gasp rippled through the crowd assembled.

"Yes." Nyx's voice had taken on a deadly echo as it dropped, her titan form beginning to crack through. "Although, if you call an attempted massacre merely some *unpleasantness*, then we might really find ourselves in a situation."

Zeus swallowed thickly, looking to Erebus as if he was going to negate her. Erebus merely shrugged, ruffling the curls out of his face and smirking.

"Indeed." Zeus let his hands drop to the armrests of his chair. "I've hidden Hera for the time being. I didn't know what she had planned. She knows that she has overstepped. We would appreciate your... forgiveness when it comes to this matter."

"Forgiveness?" The black clouds rose from Nyx's feet and began curling around her legs. "Hera set out to destroy a temple in my honor and demanded my acolytes be *murdered.*"

"— and she feels bad about that," Zeus cut in, waving a finger in Nyx's face. Erebus's eyes got wide as he looked at Zeus, mainly in shock that the new god had grown so bold. A deadly silence settled over the crowd.

One heartbeat.

Two.

Three.

Nyx smiled.

She vanished.

Erebus laughed.

The gods screamed as the hall was plunged into blackness, flames being swallowed up by the shadows. Nyx evaporated into her titan form and sent all of Mt. Olympus into nightfall. Erebus was only a moment behind her, following her around the hall and amplifying the night with crushing darkness.

"Hear me now, Zeus." Nyx's voice was the sound of power and it reverberated off the stone, coming from everywhere and nowhere all at once. "You claim that you had no knowledge of what Hera was going to do. This is my gift to you—the gift of knowledge. May you and Hera have a special tie of spousal privilege. Everything you do, Hera shall know. Everything she does will ring in your dreams."

"Nyx!" Zeus's voice was laughably quiet compared to hers. "You would dare curse a god—"

Erebus's dark shadows circled Zeus until he choked, cutting off his threats.

"I do not *dare*," Nyx continued. "To dare implies audacity. There is nothing audacious about what I say to you now. So, it shall be. May you both be cautious of causing the other any... unpleasantness."

The finality of Nyx's words echoed around the hall. As soon as it had descended, the night evaporated. The torches were relit, and the gods stumbled around the room, trying to find one another as they got accustomed to the light of day once more. Erebus and Nyx were gone. Zeus leaned back on his throne, too stunned to speak. He had tangled with the titans and lost. Somewhere, hidden in Greece, the knowledge of Zeus's long string of infidelities began running through Hera's mind—and she shrieked.

Back in the Underworld, Nyx and Erebus's titan forms intermingled in the sky and caressed one another in the depths.

"I thought you said you didn't want to tangle with the gods?" Nyx prodded, wondering why Erebus had shown a change of heart.

"I didn't..." Nyx could almost see him shrugging. "...but I will never defy you in the presence of others, *Nýchta*."

Nyx's heart swelled, and she pulled them both further down into hell, letting the darkness crush them both into one.

## 7

Nyx left Gaia in the depths of the Earth, moving silently back towards Asphodel. She needed to follow up with Hecate and see how the conversation with Hermes had gone. Nyx could sense that Hermes had left but was curious how Hecate had gotten him to leave.

*Damn trickster.*

When she stepped through the gates to the witch's home, she noticed that the columns were already repaired.

*Well. At least Hecate forced him to have some manners.*

"I did make Hermes clean up his mess before he left," Hecate spoke from inside as she sensed both Nyx and her thoughts. Nyx didn't respond and walked quietly inside the house, stepping into the kitchen, and saying nothing as she sat herself once more in front of the fire. If there was one constant in the world, it was Hecate's kitchen. The fire was always full, the smell of rosemary and pine, the ever-present movements of Hecate at her worktable.

Hecate noticed her friend's somber expression and once more said nothing as Nyx entered, resuming the work that she was doing at her table. It was becoming a common tableau that frightened Hecate. Nyx, who was so full of energy, consistently had the air of someone who had already been defeated. It was utterly unlike her. One of her dogs came up and sniffed at Nyx's hand before making a pitiful whining sound and settling at her feet. There were a few more moments before Nyx spoke.

"Did Hermes have anything else to say?" She turned and looked at her friend directly for the first time.

"Nothing of consequence." Hecate shrugged it off, putting down a bundle of herbs that she had been wrapping. "Erebus was looking for you, though."

"Was he?" Nyx cursed her heart for skipping a beat. "Did he come here?"

"Darkness rolled through shortly after you left." Hecate gave her friend a playful smile. "It nearly scared the chiton off Hermes. I don't think he had ever felt Erebus in his truest form." Nyx couldn't help but let out a deep, all-consuming laugh at the image.

"Not many people have." She grinned, the thought of a terrified trickster cracking her facade and forcing a smile.

"Hermes got your response, don't you worry. Although, you'll likely have to contend with the fallout."

Nyx waved a hand in front of her face as though that was inconsequential. "I'm much more concerned about the fallout with Erebus. If that hasn't already happened." Hecate's expression softened. She moved silently over to where Nyx was sitting, sliding next to her and wrapping her up in her arms. It wasn't often that Nyx allowed herself to be embraced—a position that was typically reserved for Erebus entirely—but the dawning that he wasn't an option broke her chest open. Nyx fell into her friend's embrace and cried.

It was sometime later when Nyx pulled herself from Hecate, lost to the wave of loneliness that she had never experienced. Her face was somber, the telltale darkness appearing around her feet as she prepared to leave.

"Do you know where he went?" Nyx couldn't meet Hecate's gaze.

Hecate was overcome with the impulse to roll her eyes. She knew that the pair were going through some things, but Nyx could find Erebus in a heartbeat. She could sense him, wherever he was in the world. Nyx was denying herself if she wanted to pretend that that wasn't true.

"Find him," Hecate said simply, standing and walking back over to her worktable. She picked up another jar without a care in the world, and Nyx knew that she had been dismissed. One of the reasons that women prayed endlessly to Hecate was for her defensive, loyal spirit to the feminine souls across existence, but she also refused to let them sit needlessly in their suffering. Nyx nodded, giving one of Hecate's dogs a scratch on the ears, before she dissipated in a wave of shadows and disappeared from the kitchen.

"Show off." Hecate chuckled, hoping that Nyx pulling some of her old tricks was a good sign.

))))

NYX LANDED IN ELYSIUM, keeping an eye on the horizon. It was still quiet in the tall grasses; the great heroes of man had yet to populate it. Asphodel was noisy with the souls of the departed, and she couldn't imagine speaking to Erebus in her sanctuary of Tartarus now. The truly evil souls ceased to exist at all upon their death, a fact that man would never be able to comprehend. It was one of the reasons they so easily believed Zeus's new lies about Tartarus.

It was here, in Elysium, that Nyx waited for Erebus. She assumed her mortal form and let her hands run across the fields of narcissus, the blooms brushing up against her legs.

She was lost in her thoughts when the sky dimmed, flickering like a dying fire, as blackness wrapped around itself, and

Erebus touched down. His face was unreadable. He stood a good ten feet off from Nyx as if the distance was going to have any effect on buffering their conversation. Both were dressed in their traditional black, Nyx's chiton longer than Erebus's and tangled amongst the flowers. Her face was stoic as she looked upon him, trying to forget the feeling of his curls running through her fingers. The wind picked up around them as if it sensed the confrontation.

"You look well." His voice was always warm when he looked upon Nyx. It was like a reflex, and he couldn't help it. Nyx let out a sad, small laugh.

"I look *well*. Is that what we have deteriorated to?" She ran a hand up her arm as if to self-soothe. Erebus caught it. He knew her tells, even if she didn't admit them to herself. At this moment, she was every inch the titan of the night, not the woman who once gave him permission to cradle her. He reacted appropriately.

"I will always respect you, Nýchta."

Nyx laughed harder, but it was a cruel sound.

"Tell me, why does that feel like a downgrade?"

Erebus said nothing, neither moving towards her nor shying away. It was the consistency in him that had always drawn her to the darkness, and the fact that he was the only being in existence who had never had a glimmer of fear when he looked upon her at full power. In fact, it was the opposite. He helped her power sing. The existence of the darkness was there to amplify the night; the eroding of their relationship felt like a phantom limb.

"You were looking for me," Nyx said quietly, but her words cut through the grass. Erebus couldn't help but notice that she had resigned herself to only speaking to him out loud. The mental connection that they had shared was cut off.

"I was." He shrugged, crossing his arms over his chest. "I heard that Hermes was here, and I knew that would make you uncomfortable—"

"The *gods* do not make me *uncomfortable*, Erebus," Nyx snapped, turning to face him head-on. She welcomed the rush of anger that came over, letting it consume her sadness. It was so, so much easier to be angry. Erebus fought the urge to call her out, but he resigned and held up his hands in surrender.

"Noted. I heard that Hermes was here, and I wanted to know what he had to say."

"As if you don't know." Nyx's lips thinned out into a grim line. She had a suspicion that he was speaking to all the gods.

"I don't." Erebus sighed again and tried his best to remain patient. He knew that her walls were up and getting indignant would solve nothing.

"Zeus has formally declared war against Kronos. He is demanding that all the gods and titans pick a side. Hopefully, his side." Nyx watched Erebus's expression, which did seem — to his credit — shocked.

"I was unsure if he would ever do it." Erebus looked off into the sky, searching for something as Nyx watched his mind race. He turned to her, taking a step closer as Nyx took a step back. "I'm sure that you answered for us?"

"I wouldn't presume your answer, Erebus," she snapped, and he struggled to keep a lid on his own temper.

"I still defer to you, Nýchta." His voice was softer, quieter, as he let her name fall from his lips. Erebus let the rest of his own guard slip, his face turning over in an expression of soft wanting. He knew that his best attempt at getting through to her was to show vulnerability first... *I'll show you mine if you show me yours.* His thoughts were full of longing. The silence stretched on between them, and Nyx's expression was unreadable.

"I told him I would not be joining. I did not speak for you." The subtle declaration that she had not taken a stand on behalf of both night and darkness was damning. Erebus was rocked with the revelation that they had become separate entities in her mind. He prayed that her heart had not yet suffered the same fate. Nyx spoke again.

"What happened? When Hera first attacked my acolytes, I wanted to put the gods in their place. You wanted to wait. What... What's changed?" Her voice cracked.

"I did wait." Erebus sighed, attempting another step towards Nyx. "I waited five hundred years. I am tired of their squabbles now; they need to end. The humans no longer have respect for us. Now, our best plan is to join the gods and accept their help in restoring our reputations." He paused and Nyx seemed unfazed. "What about you? You wanted respect. It was why you went after Hera."

"*Don't* twist my words!" Nyx spun on Erebus, pointing at him and taking a few more steps in his direction. "My concern was for my women. Not buildings or altars or honor. I was content to let that *burn.* I watched, too. I've come to see that these *are* nothing but squabbles. You cry out for respect, Erebus, but I think you're just *bored.*"

"Bored?!" Erebus roared back in return, and both dissipated immediately into their spaceless forms. Thunder and lightning rolled around in Elysium as crests of nightfall crashed against waves of darkness. The smoke and shadows of Nyx and Erebus were *fighting* each other instead of coexisting.

"I am not bored, Nyx," Erebus yelled again, the sound echoing off the boundaries of the Underworld. His voice immediately softened. "You still can't recognize what it looks like when someone wants the best for you."

The darkness evaporated, leaving a thin layer of dusk over Elysium, and Nyx came collapsing down into her mortal form like a tornado. As the shadows cleared, she lay in the field of narcissus and wept.

## 8

Nyx was still sitting in Elysium when she felt currents of power rolling through the ground. Erebus had left. It took all her willpower to shut it out and keep herself from going to him. She didn't know how long she had been lying in the grass when the presence of other gods caused the dirt to tremble. The earth beneath her pulsed with it. Nyx knew that in the Underworld that meant one thing: Hades.

Hades had taken to the Underworld like Poseidon to the sea and Zeus to patricide. Nyx and Hades had a careful arrangement, one that was full of respect but carefully devoid of familiarity. There were particulars to his job that she did not want, and he knew that she was composed of something greater than him entirely. This amicable distance had suited them until she began to learn that he was going along with Zeus's rumors that Tartarus was a place for the gravest of sinners. Nyx was content to continue to watch this play out among the weaker immortals but did not forget where Hades's chips had fallen.

Nyx allowed herself to slip away into shadow as she felt gods approaching. While gods could always sense one another's presence, her abilities as primordial were unmatched. It wasn't long until Hades and Poseidon appeared together, walking in Elysium.

Poseidon looked—admittedly—like a fish out of water, looking around as if he was trying to gauge where the closest river was. He preferred a dark blue himation, draped over one shoulder, that appeared ready to be thrown off at a moment's notice. His hair was perpetually curly with salt and seawater, the gray curls stuck to his temples as his beard looked permanently wet. His skin was tanned and red from the water, laugh lines and crow's feet deeply set into his face. Poseidon had the potential to look incredibly kind or incredibly cruel based on the level of warmth he allowed to slip into his gray eyes. There were bands of silver around his wrists and ankles, inlayed with mother-of-pearl and bright coral, and he preferred walking barefoot. While she couldn't see it, Nyx knew that his beloved trident was somewhere hidden on his person.

Nyx's gaze shifted to Hades, who talked animatedly next to his brother. Hades was always dressed the same way, with a black chiton that went to his ankles and black leather sandals. He had secured a silver brooch at his shoulder—a new development—and Nyx eyed it cautiously, always wary of men and their trophies. He kept his beard much shorter than Poseidon's, more of a permanent shadow across his jaw, and kept waves of black hair off his forehead with a leather band. Nyx knew by mortal standards, Hades was incredibly wealthy, controlling—governing—the Underworld and all its metals and gems. It was for that reason, he surprisingly never wore any, which until now had been a valuable merit in Nyx's mind.

Both gods made striking figures as they stopped in the grass, and Nyx could see how the humans had started to fall to these gods. They were everything that humans were—they had mortal forms, flaws, hubris, and pride. Who would not want to look upon their deities and see themselves reflected? Nyx stopped, quieting her thoughts as she let her shadows slip closer to them. She listened.

"I don't know why you have any doubts, Poseidon." Hades shook his head, looking at his brother in a way that could only be described as challenging.

"Ha! Doubts! You misread caution for a character flaw." Poseidon shrugged it off, flicking his hand through the air. "You've always been the impatient one."

"Impatient one! Don't confuse me for Zeus. I have nothing but time — death comes for everyone."

"That's Thanatos," Poseidon corrected him, raising a brow. "Be careful that you aren't the ones overstepping your bounds, not Zeus."

*One point for Poseidon then.* Nyx's thoughts strayed towards violence as she overheard Hades take claim to her son's work. *Hades would do well to remember that he merely governs here. He is not darkness or death, my husband and my son.*

Nyx surprised herself as she fiercely defended Erebus in her mind before shoving down the thought. Now was not the time to fall prey once again to her ever-changing feelings about Erebus. *Except your feelings aren't ever-changing.* She interrupted herself. *That's your problem. You know how you have always felt for Erebus. How you always will...*

Nyx's thoughts were cut off as she heard Hades's reply.

"My apologies, dear brother." The words were saccharine. "Don't let Amphitrite or Pontus hear you talk about the sea then."

"We're getting off track," Poseidon snapped, water gathering around his temple like a damp halo.

"Easy there, you might splash someone." Hades rolled his eyes at the watery signs of Poseidon's temper, knowing that he was limited in the Underworld. "We're here to talk about the other brother, anyway."

Poseidon eyed him, knowing that the charlatan attitude was a part of who Hades was. He was old enough to not take it personally.

"I do have my doubts." Poseidon looked past Hades and

into the fields around them. "Do you really think that this will be different from every other war we've ever had?" The question gave Hades pause.

"We have had a lot of them, but Kronos is a threat to us all. He's eating his children." Hades looked at Poseidon with a raised brow as if challenging him to counter that point.

"So they say. We made it out alive."

"Only because of Rhea."

"Have you gotten her take on this?" Poseidon crossed his arms over his chest. "This whole thing could be because someone cheated." Hades groaned loudly.

"I'm not getting into a war alongside Zeus because someone *cheated*. We'd never stop."

"It's an important clarifier." Poseidon held up his hands to feign innocence. "We've been pulled into skirmishes with Zeus's extramarital affairs for the past five hundred years."

"About that," Hades scowled, "Do you think Nyx had any clue what she was unleashing when she cursed Zeus to not be able to keep secrets from Hera?"

*Absolutely I did, you fool.* It took all of Nyx's primordial strength to keep her from laughing in the darkness around them. *There is nothing I do that I do not understand the full weight of, which is something that you gods can never understand.*

"Most likely."

*Poseidon, I don't despise you.* Nyx grinned from the ether around the gods.

"That's not the point." Poseidon began again. "I have already pledged my allegiance to Zeus, you were there. I will ride this thing out. I simply need to know if this is some sort of dalliance or if there is a real issue at the core of it."

"Everything with Zeus is technically some sort of dalliance." Hades smirked, an impish look taking over his face.

"I don't want to hear what you two get up to, corralling women." Poseidon immediately looked repulsed.

"Don't lump me in with him." Hades's voice got dark.

"Every one of my participants is willing. Next time you're on the mortal realm, drop by a temple of mine…"

"Stop," Poseidon snapped, rubbing his temples. "You know, someday, you are going to get your attitude handed to you by a woman. When you come crying to me about it, mark my words, I will laugh."

Hades waved off the thought but changed the topic, nonetheless.

"To answer your question, I believe this has merit. Kronos *is* eating his children and the mortal realm is in chaos. If we can overthrow him and establish some sort of order, everybody wins." Hades shrugged as if he was suggesting a dinner menu and not a war of immortals.

"Everybody but Kronos and the titans who have sided with him."

"There are always losers in a battle like this, Poseidon. I didn't think that you would be the one to care for them."

"I don't." Poseidon shrugged, looking at Hades with a deadly look in his eye. "But I will not be the god who gets caught on a technicality. There are too many powers at work in the world, Hades, and you would be mindful to watch your wicked tongue."

Hades nodded, his mood somber for once, as he took note of Poseidon's words.

"It is settled then?" He eyed the god of the sea. Poseidon took a deep breath and then nodded, extending his hand out to his brother.

"It is settled. I have already chosen my side with Zeus, but hear me again… I will fight with him against Kronos."

As the two gods shook hands, the binding effect of their power rippled once more through the fields. Nyx fled from her atmosphere around them, a sick taste in her mouth, left by men, gods, and their prideful ambitions.

## 9

Nyx abandoned the Elysium fields, leaving Hades and Poseidon none the wiser that they had been watched. They began walking once more through the grass, strategizing and pouring over the lists of gods and titans who had chosen a side.

"Who in the Underworld is unaccounted for?" Poseidon asked his brother, arching an eyebrow as he mentally ran through its inhabitants.

"Everyone." Hades seemed annoyed. "You know I don't control them."

"You certainly act like you do."

Hades cracked his knuckles and a ripple of power spread out from around him. "I *mind* them. They mind me. If you have any grand ideas, *you* go tell Hecate what to do and see what happens." Poseidon held up his hands in surrender.

"Pass. She has not claimed a side yet?"

"She won't. Nyx has said no, which we all anticipated, but Zeus remains bent on getting her to side with him."

Poseidon made a low whistling noise. "Everyone would be wise to leave the primordials well enough alone. Especially

Nyx. We know enough about the darkness under the water to understand that there are some things that should stay there."

Hades laughed. "You're speaking of Erebus now."

"They are the same."

"Not as of late." Hades looked like an old woman with a secret. Poseidon raised a brow, dreadfully curious but much more cautious than his brothers of tangling with primordials.

"Then we're all in trouble," Poseidon snapped instead of giving into the gossip. "Those two pulled themselves into existence for one another," he said, pointing a finger at Hades, "and if Zeus is trying to get in between them, it won't work. What is his obsession with Nyx anyway?"

"It *has* worked." Hades's voice had a different, softer tone to it, almost one of regret. "In regard to Nyx…"

"Zeus knows that she is the only being alive that is stronger than him." Erebus's voice rang out in the air, deep and amplified, causing both gods to turn around in shock.

Rolling, black clouds gathered above them. Hades and Poseidon watched as they spun down towards the ground, touching the earth, and Erebus emerged from the column of smoke and shadow. Hades let out a low whistle.

"Neat trick."

Erebus growled, ripples of shadow pouring out from him and snaking around Hades in a threat.

"Shall I show you an even better one?" Erebus hissed. "You gods need a sound reminder of who you are dealing with."

"Darkness." Poseidon nodded his head in respect and soundly elbowed his brother. "You'll have to forgive Hades. He's forgotten how to consort with other people. He spends all his time with the dead." Hades narrowed his eyes at his brother but shrugged in agreement.

"You will both be careful of how you speak of Nyx's name. As for Zeus, he's afraid of her. His life has been ruined by the curse she put on him five hundred years ago. He knows that should she choose to fight with Kronos, it's over."

"What say *you?*" Hades pushed.

"You've heard my piece." There was a guarded air to Erebus as he watched over both gods. He didn't trust either of them, even though he wanted to convince Nyx to join their ranks.

"We have heard you defend Nyx." Poseidon nodded. "No one negates her power. We have not heard what you have to say."

Erebus studied them both. In perpetuity, he had never spoken publicly or privately against Nyx. There might have been things that they disagreed on — time immemorial was a long time to be alive to agree on everything — but they discussed those matters between themselves. Erebus loved Nyx like there was nothing else in the world. In his world, there wasn't. He didn't mind being the amplifier, the muscle, the enforcer, to her divine will. The idea of speaking out against her, even disagreeing with her wisdom, in front of others was one that had once been abhorrent to him.

The world was changing. All he wanted was to see her restored to the place of respect that she deserved. There was a time before this current slew of immortals when Nyx was revered above all else — Hecate, too, when he thought about it. Now, there was nothing but bullish men shoving their way through and pulling their whiny wives alongside them. Zeus had always known what Hera had intended to do when she set out to ruin Nyx's temples; anything that praised Hera reflected well on him. It broke Erebus's heart to see his children shunned, Thanatos feared and Hypnos brushed aside, and Nyx disregarded like an ancient bogeyman.

The slow desecration of all her temples, followed by spreading rumors of Tartarus, all contributed to public opinion. It was calculated. Erebus *knew* that. No matter what Nyx wanted to say, he wasn't blindly playing into Zeus's hands. If they could join this battle and end Kronos, it would be an opportunity for the world to see them once in the light. There would be temples resurrected to Nyx again, to her honor and glory, the safety that she could provide. That she *did* provide. Erebus was falling prey to the one thing that any righteous man so often did—a nearly blind need to safeguard his family, no matter how strong they were.

"Nyx has spoken," Erebus said again with a finality in his tone that gave no room for debate. Hades prodded again.

"You agree with her then?"

"I did not say that." Erebus shook his head, fixing his glare on the god of the Underworld. "You would be careful not to push me or my words." Shadows rippled out from around Erebus, making a flicker of fear appear in Hades's eyes once more.

"Tell us what you think, Erebus." Poseidon encouraged, coaxing his voice to sound like soft waves. Erebus felt a deep part of him, the part that had always belonged to Nyx, cracking. He had been without her intimacy for well over a year now. The need to be heard and understood was creeping through his ichor.

"If this goes according to plan, I'm sure you would have a more permanent place in Zeus's pantheon." Hades shrugged, gauging Erebus's reaction. He seemed unimpressed on the surface, but there was a slight shift in his eyes. "As would Nyx," Hades added on. Erebus's eyes glowed brighter.

"Better her than Hera." Poseidon rolled his eyes, not in jest, but genuinely believing it.

"I... I see some merits in the idea of overthrowing Kronos." Erebus chose his words carefully, refusing to say outright that he would support Zeus.

"As we all do." Poseidon nodded. "Let it be understood between us that there is no love lost for our other brother."

"He's a prick." Hades's mouth twisted up into a smirk. "In case anyone was curious as to where I stood."

"We always know where you stand, Hades." Poseidon gave his brother a playful shove. "You never shut up about it."

The camaraderie between the two sent another pang through Erebus. He didn't want to find himself enmeshed with them, not remotely. It drove him to the end of his wits when he thought back to what it had felt like when he and Nyx had never been separated.

"Join us, Erebus." Hades's tone was once again somber. Poseidon looked at him with wide eyes, shocked that he would defy Nyx and directly invite Darkness to the fight.

"Careful, Hades." His warning was laced with the ferocity of deep riptides.

"I live on the edge."

"Listen to your brother." Erebus's voice had dropped once more, a shadow pouring out from his body and wrapping itself tightly around Hades's throat. "You do not understand what you ask of me. None of you understand what Nyx is capable of."

"You are afraid of her." Hades stuttered the words out as the shadow tightened.

"I respect her." Erebus's form was threatening to break apart in shadows, his eyes turning entirely black. Poseidon took a few steps back, in awe of the torrents of power that were spilling out of the primordial. "*You* couldn't begin to understand what it is like to respect and love, God of the Underworld."

"Do not—"

"You will do well to remember I called you the God of the Underworld. Not of death, of night, or of darkness. Tend to the lands we have given you, Hades, and keep my wife's name out of your mouth." Hades opened his mouth to speak, and the shadows answered, wrapping tightly around his throat.

"We've heard you, Erebus." Poseidon raised an arm to avoid the death of his brother. "You may want to overthrow Kronos, but we will let Nyx's answer be yours. Be well."

Poseidon held his breath, hoping that the respectful farewell would settle Erebus.

He watched on as the shadows snuck their way down Hades's throat, snaking around him until they were coming out of his ears and mouth. Hades choked, Erebus making a dreadful growling noise before he erupted in a rolling thunder-clap. Darkness exploded all around them, sending both Poseidon and Hades to their knees.

The blackness dissipated as soon as it had come, leaving the gods shaking on the ground in the soft light of day. Erebus was nowhere to be seen.

"Well." Hades coughed and slowly stood up. "It seems that Erebus is having some doubts."

## ❧ 10 ❧

Erebus shook off the rest of his temper and went looking for Nyx. He had sensed her presence in Elysium when he arrived, yet she was nowhere to be found when he spoke with Hades and Poseidon. Their words bounced around in his head as he thought about all the things they had to say. Both brothers didn't seem that they were overly eager to be involved with Zeus; Erebus didn't love that part of the plan, either, but it seemed necessary.

Everything had escalated since Hera first began ransacking Nyx's temples. Erebus's heart was being caved in two as he thought about each moment that he was spending apart from the Night. He wanted her to be respected, worshipped. Even if she didn't care about that, he needed the whole world to see what she brought to them. The rest of existence would be nothing without her. Erebus moved as shadows through the Underworld, descending into Tartarus, where he knew she would be.

Once more, he descended in his mortal form as he touched down, wanting to bear himself out to his wife—so she could see the expressions on his face when he spoke to her. Whatever was happening between them, this chaos, the unknown... It needed to end, tonight. Erebus had arrived in the blackness with metaphorical olive branches around his shoulders.

"Nyx…" His voice was quiet, barely above a whisper, but he knew that she heard him. She was everywhere; she was the ether.

Nyx appeared in front of him in a whirl of wind, but only Erebus could sense her. She kept her intangible form.

"Erebus." The word was noncommittal and sent a pang of sadness through his chest. Nyx's unwillingness to appear in her corporeal body was another message.

"The gods were here." He knew that she was aware—she knew everything that happened in the Underworld—but it felt like something they needed to discuss.

"I know."

Erebus struggled not to roll his eyes. He wanted to try and find some common ground. When Nyx's walls were up, it was a tough act to try and penetrate.

"What did you think of what they had to say?"

"Did you speak to them?" Nyx's voice was quick. She had left Elysium willingly and had turned a blind eye to the gods after her departure. Now, she was morbidly curious if Erebus had joined them.

"Yes." Erebus nodded solemnly, knowing that it would likely anger Nyx, but he insisted on not hiding anything from her. An awkward silence settled over them.

"Did they try once again to convince you to join their cause?" He could hear the tension in her voice, as though she was struggling not to crack herself.

"They did. I told them of your answer."

Silence.

Erebus could almost *hear* Nyx's surprise.

"Of my answer?"

"I told you once that I would never speak against you to another god, man, or immortal. That is still true. No matter what is happening between us, Nyx."

"You mean it?" Nyx's voice took on another tone, one that was almost hopeful. The darkness began to whirl around Erebus, and he dared to pray that she would appear in front of him. He wouldn't be able to breathe if he knew that she didn't have the space to be vulnerable with him, the space that she had grown into needing more and more over the years.

"I meant it then and I mean it now, Nýchta." Erebus couldn't resist the use of her nickname.

"What did you tell them?"

The atmosphere spun a little more, and he could almost see her feet.

"I told them the truth. That I saw some merits to Zeus's approach, but I respected you. Your answer was enough for us all…" His voice was honest—raw—and for once, he didn't stop the burgeoning tears. He needed this. She needed to see him like this.

The whirlwind touched the earth, and Erebus saw the edges of Nyx's body beginning to come together. He continued.

"I reminded Hades of his place. Well… I nearly choked him out." Erebus stopped and couldn't help but laugh at the memory. "I left Hades and Poseidon in Elysium. I gave them no further answer other than what you had said. When you speak, you speak for me, Nyx." There was a soft sound from the clouds, like a breath catching. Nyx had almost materialized entirely in front of him.

"Will they try and convince you again?" Nyx's question hung in the air between them. Erebus knew why she was asking. If he was honest with her, then he knew that he should say yes. If he said no, she would surely know the truth anyway. This was a complicated matter, and everyone was going to be pitching for their sides until the conflict was over. He breathed deeply, knowing that there was a lot at stake based on how he answered her question.

"Yes. They will. The brothers will undoubtedly only focus

on the fact that I said I saw *some merits* to the idea of over-throwing Kronos."

Nyx materialized. Her eyes were bright, and she found herself eagerly pouring over Erebus's face, searching for any sign that he was lying to her. When she found none, it was like a dam had broken.

Night and Darkness went colliding into one another, seeking a refuge in one another's arms that they had not found in over a year. Their collision sent rolling waves of thunder over the entire Underworld, causing Hecate to look up at the sky with a smile from her courtyard. Hades chuckled from his throne room, momentarily distracted from flirting once more with the Fates. Thanatos and Hypnos grimaced, knowing the sound of their parents. The fields of Elysium and meadows of Asphodel were drenched in blackness, a rich, endless obsidian wave that blanketed everything under the earth. There was a peace in the void that had been absent from the Underworld since Night and Darkness had begun to separate, now crashing into one another once more with abandon.

As soon as they came together with a driving force, both Erebus and Nyx immediately vanished once more into their boundless bodies. In those forms, they could be completely enmeshed in one another, and they ceased to ask where one of them ended and the other began. The night was all consuming and the shadows of the darkness cradled it, stretched its power out even farther. Nyx and Erebus were one body and they wept from the pleasure of their homecoming.

It was not perfect, but it was home.

Erebus had denied a direct request from the gods; he had been honest with Nyx about his thoughts and intentions. Most importantly, he had refused to speak against her wishes. This mattered to Nyx most of all, that any discussion they had between the two of them could get as calamitous as it needed to, but to the world, there should never be any known separation between the two.

Nyx took the two of them hurtling deeper and deeper into Tartarus where their tears of joy and cries of pleasure could only be heard and amplified by their shadows. She wept... and wept... and wept... that her safe place had come back to her.

They both went crashing to the ground, and the air spun with how quickly they transcended into their physical bodies. Erebus was on Nyx in a second, his hands tangling in her hair as he pulled her to him.

"It's been too long." His voice was guttural and sent goose-bumps erupting down Nyx's skin. She molded herself to him, pressing as close as she could, as though she wanted to disappear once more into him.

"I know." Nyx's agreement was quiet, spoken against Erebus's lips as he kissed her. There was nothing tentative about it; both poured their frustrations and tensions into the embrace. It was all teeth, tongues, and desperate breathing as Nyx's hips began canting up against his. Erebus growled and their clothes vanished as he lowered them down to the earth. Nyx lied down against the soil of Tartarus, feeling it ground her as Erebus's shadows began pouring from his body. They covered them both like a blanket, caressing, pulling, *touching*. His hands started trailing down her body as he kept kissing her. Her temple, her jaw, her neck...

Nyx fought to keep her eyes open as she tilted her head to look at Erebus. It was her favorite sight in all the cosmos. His dark curls were starting to stick to his forehead with strength, the tanned, taut lines and muscle of his body corded and tense. She knew by the way the muscles in his thighs and ribs twitched that he was already close, but so was she. Erebus seemed content in that moment to soak Nyx in, to keep roaming his hands over her body as he kissed down her centerline, like he needed to convince himself she was real. His hips ground down into hers and she felt him, hard and ready against her, and decided that Erebus was taking too long.

Nyx threw one leg around Erebus's waist, and in one svelte movement, rolled them both over.

"Fuck—" Erebus let out a loud groan and let his head fall back, settling his hands behind his head.

He stared up at Nyx in adoration, one hand going to her waist and the other going up to caress her breast. Nyx settled her knees on either side of his hips and rocked against him, causing another strangled groan from Erebus.

Nyx sat up a little straighter and guided him into her, moving slowly until he was seated deep inside her.

"Ohhh…" Nyx's voice was breathy, and she adjusted, this angle the only way that she could take all of him. He couldn't speak, trying to slow his breath so it wouldn't be over before it had even started.

Nyx began moving her hips, riding him slowly until they were slick with sweat and gasping for air. He moved his hand from her breast to her chin, gripping it and forcing her to make eye contact with him. They stayed like that for a few desperate moments, saying everything they couldn't say out loud with their eyes and their bodies as the earth itself started to shake.

Erebus growled, moving up to a sitting position and gripping her waist tightly. He began thrusting up into her, taking control from underneath her, his movements wild and frantic. Nyx was overpowered immediately as she threw her hands around his neck, leaning down and biting his shoulder as he fucked her.

"Come on, Nýchta…" Erebus turned his head and whispered to her, his lips dragging across her ear. "Finish for me. Let me know how much you missed me. I want to *feel* it." His voice took on a dark, authoritative tone that left no room for argument. His hand dropped to her clit, making slow, intense circles that contradicted the wild rhythm of his hips. The combination was devastating, and with Erebus's words in her ear, Nyx raked her nails across his back and lost herself to the sensations.

As soon as he felt her coming around him, Erebus was done. He thrust up into her one final time and held her there, reaching their climaxes so intensely that they exploded into their primordial forms—the waves of pleasure so intense that it ripped them from their own bodies.

Neither of them knew how much time had passed when they came to their senses. Erebus materialized first, conjuring a shadow tree once more as he leaned back against it. He propped one knee up and kicked his other leg out wide, an invitation. Nyx slipped into her body once more like breathing, long, dark hair flowing down her back. Erebus's smile was downright devilish as he ran a hand through his hair, pushing the sweaty hair off his temples.

Nyx grinned softly and gracefully slid down to the ground, sliding between his legs like a ship desperate for port. She rested her head on his chest, toying with the folds of his chiton on his shoulder—which had somehow reappeared. Erebus sighed, a deeply contented sound, leaning his head back.

"That was…" Erebus whispered as he turned and kissed Nyx's forehead, his lips lingering there.

"*Everything*," Nyx smiled. "But I can't say that I'm willing to go through losing you again, no matter how short a time." She tightened her grip on his arm.

"Agreed."

"Promise me something…" Nyx's voice was somber once more. Erebus tensed for a moment, desperate for their moment to not be taken away from them after all this time.

"Anything." His answer was honest.

"Promise me, you will let this fade away. There is to be no more talk of this damned war between us, Erebus."

He was silent—not because he didn't want to make that promise; he would fall on any sword she placed in front of him right now. Everything was so volatile amongst the immortals in that moment, he might break that promise without realizing it or if new information came to pass.

"Nyx," he stroked her hair gently, "I will defer to you. I always have. That will never change... but I cannot promise that a topic like this will never come up again. Especially if it plagues everyone we know and the world that we live in."

"I'll build a new world," Nyx growled, and black magic flickered across her skin. Erebus pushed it away with warm strokes of his hands, keeping her temper down.

"I have no doubt it would be one that I would love to live in, but you would miss the human souls you care for." Nyx harrumphed in response, and Erebus couldn't resist a chuckle at the sound coming from such a powerful, cosmic being.

"We'll see." She accepted her answer in its wisdom. "I don't have to like it, though."

"You don't." Erebus leaned down and kissed her forehead. "If I may ask... why don't you want to be part of something bigger than the darkness?"

Nyx's whole body went still. She picked herself up off his chest, staring at him with an intense gaze.

"Bigger... than the darkness?" Her voice was incredulous.

"I digress," he raised his hands in surrender. "That was a poor word choice. Why don't you want everyone to see the greatness of the darkness?"

"Why would I want to be bigger by the human's standards? I am already all-consuming. Who I am, what I am, what we *do*, Erebus... They will never be able to change it. How can you be bothered what the fly thinks of the wolf?"

"Humans are afraid of the darkness now." Erebus shrugged. "It does not bother me. It pushes me to the end of my wits when I hear how they are afraid of our children or how they don't respect you—"

"You respect me," Nyx cut him off, grabbing hold of his face with her hands. "That is all I need." She began pleading with him, tears once more springing to her eyes. "Don't you understand? *You* are all I need. Please don't make me lose you to chase the adoration of *gods*." She spit the last word out like a poison.

Erebus stared at her with shock, until his hand came up and grabbed the back of Nyx's head. He pulled them together, the kiss untamed from the very start, causing Nyx's body to curl into him on instinct. When they finally broke apart, he nodded.

"You are all I need, in this life and the next, through time immemorial. When immortals die and humans live forever, when we are all swallowed up by hells even unknown to us, we'll always be there in the darkness, Nyx, and that is all I need or could ever want."

Erebus pulled Nyx down to the ground, and they poured their adoration out on one another until the shadows came between them, begging for a rest.

E rebus and Nyx were pulled from their slumber when a ripple of power went through the Underworld. It could hardly be sensed deep in Tartarus, but nothing escaped Nyx when it happened on her domain. The couple shifted with a groan, annoyed at the intrusion.

"It seems that Zeus is going to ask us personally," Erebus said with a raised brow, sensing the god's call.

"I doubt that it will be an ask." Nyx rolled her eyes, standing up from where she had been nestled into Erebus's side. "Shall we?" she asked Erebus as she began to slip away into her primordial form once more. His answering laugh was rich and mischievous.

"You know how much I love watching you work." He grinned, and the shadows overtook him, collapsing his form into shadows.

"Then this will be fun." Nyx's response echoed through the dark skies as the thunder hid their laughter. They made their way undetected through the Underworld, over the mortal realm, and stepped down into their bodies at the base of Mt. Olympus once more.

There was a somber attitude over the mountain; the torches

that were normally lit up the path to Zeus's palace were extinguished. Typically, whenever Nyx had to visit, you could hear women laughing and Dionysus raiding the wineries to descend to Greece from miles away. This time, there was silence. Nyx turned to look at Erebus, who shrugged to acknowledge the silence and agreed that it was strange. He stepped a little closer to Nyx, and his shadows wrapped around him, materializing into a sword at his belt. She chuckled, feeling his protective instincts behind her.

"I'm sure that isn't necessary." Nyx's smile was teasing as they crept higher up the mountain, not so secretly enamored with once again having Erebus at her back.

"The Night's Sword, remember?" Erebus leaned over her shoulder from behind her, whispering it in her ear in such a way that made her blush.

"You say that as if I could forget who gave you that title."

"You are not a forgetful woman."

Nyx turned, a devilish glint in her eye, and pressed him up against the mountainside. A dagger of black magic and starlight appeared in her hand as she pressed it up against his throat with a wink.

"I'm not a woman at all, Erebus." Her voice was like velvet and smoke. "I'm night." Erebus smiled in response, shuffling slightly against the wall.

"You're going to have to warn me before you pull a blade on me," his expression was mischievous, "Or I'm going to need to cool down before walking into a court of other gods." Nyx let the dagger vanish as her head fell back in laughter.

"Let them be intimidated." She moved up the steps once more. By the time the couple had made it to the top, it was desolate. There was no one moving about, and the general chaos of Mt. Olympus was nowhere to be found. Nyx moved confidently forward, taking in the scene with a calculating eye as she disappeared through the front steps of Zeus's hall. Erebus was a step behind her when he felt a cool hand on his shoulder. He whipped around, hand on his sword as his shadows flew out from him only to see Hades stepping out from behind a column.

"What are you doing, Hades?" Erebus's voice was distrustful. "Other than lurking around on Zeus's front steps and hiding behind columns, that much is apparent."

The Lord of the Underworld shrugged, dusting a shadow off his robes. His expression was unreadable, which was rare. Hades was a god with very little to hide, even though he took his privacy very seriously and very seldom appeared stoic.

"I'm trying to let you know what you are about to walk into." His brow furrowed as he crossed his arms across his broad chest, half exposed.

"You're trying to let *me* know. Not Nyx." Erebus's tone was dark, but Hades only rolled his eyes.

"Yes. We know what Nyx will say. You, on the other hand, said that you saw some merits to overthrowing Kronos."

"I did say that," Erebus deadpanned, not inviting any more room for conversation. Hades shifted his weight between his legs. It was unnerving—even for Erebus—to see him so off his game.

"Zeus is going to try and give Nyx an ultimatum," Hades hissed, leaning in closer as the shadows pushed against him. "Do you understand what that means?"

"Do *you?*" Erebus's shadows exploded, wrapping all around the front steps and securing Hades to one of the columns. He struggled to keep his voice down as he leaned in, a breath away from the God of the Underworld's face. "Zeus has gone mad. Nyx will side with neither Kronos nor Zeus, and an ultimatum cannot sway her."

"He doesn't seem to understand that," Hades hissed, the shadows tightening around his throat once more. "Zeus assumes that if she isn't going to side with him, that she is going to side with Kronos."

"She doesn't want to be involved at all." Erebus's voice

dropped to a growl and the power in it reverberated off the stone columns around them. The darkness crept closer and closer to the edges of the steps, threatening to spill over and consume Mt. Olympus.

"This is happening. Accept it. You both cannot hide your heads in the sand."

"We aren't hiding." Erebus let the shadows tighten around Hades ever so slightly. "You lot are the ones who are insisting that we repeat ourselves over and over. We are not joining this fight."

"I see we're using the royal *we* again, aren't we?" Hades' voice dropped to a lower tone, even though it still couldn't match the God of Darkness. "No more trouble in paradise?"

Erebus's power threatened to pull the columns down as he stepped forward, fisting Hades's chiton in his hand. He ripped the god towards him, letting his shadows obscure Hades's entire body in blackness.

"Keep Nyx's name out of your mouth." Erebus's features began to blur as his body rapidly dissolved into shadow and reformed, flickering like a candle. Any of the bravado that Hades had shown slipped away as he watched the primordial begin to lose control.

"You could join us, you know." Hades switched tactics and let the charm slide into his voice. "Join us, join my brothers and me. You would have a place on Mt. Olympus. Temples would rise in your honor—agh!"

Hades was cut off as Erebus's other hand came up and soundly punched him across the face, slamming him back into the marble.

"Temples like the one that Hera has destroyed?"

Hades coughed, spitting flecks of golden ichor onto Erebus's sandals.

"I'm only the messenger," Hades spat out. Erebus growled.

"I'll let fucking Hermes know he's been replaced." He stepped away, his shadows recoiling immediately and dropping

Hades to the stone floor. Erebus didn't look back at him as he stepped inside the great hall.

If anyone had heard inside what had happened between Hades and Erebus, they didn't show it. Nyx was already standing in the center of the crowded room. She was partially in her mortal form, her calves disappearing into a cloud that looked like the night sky. It rolled and curled where her feet would be, spreading around her like water. It created a rather terrifying but beautiful illusion.

The rest of the gods were scattered about the hall, some of them sitting at banquet tables that lined the walls. Zeus sat on his throne, with Ares on one side and Poseidon on his right. If Nyx had noticed that Hades wasn't there, she hadn't commented.

"There is your better half." Zeus looked up from where he had been staring at Nyx, acknowledging Erebus. Nyx said nothing, refusing to comment on the fact that Zeus was incapable to comprehend she was more powerful than Erebus. Erebus said nothing, refusing to honor it with a response.

"You were saying?" Nyx brought the conversation back to the matter at hand.

"Yes." Zeus waved his hand in the air like he was swatting at flies. Ares looked calm, always capable of turning off his temper when he knew the time wasn't right. His helmet was nestled under his arm, and he absentmindedly tapped it with his other hand.

Poseidon, by comparison, looked more anxious. Only Nyx and Erebus could likely tell; his facade was polished enough that it would fool the other gods. Yet, his eyes shifted a little too often, and he was conjuring shapes of water in midair as if he wanted to distract or distance himself from the conversation. The ends of his tunic were wet, leading Erebus to believe that he, too, had been summoned last-minute and walked out of the sea.

"The time has come..." Zeus's voice boomed throughout

the hall, the sudden burst in volume causing some of the other gods to jolt to attention. "...for the two of you to pick a side. You both know by now what we are up against."

*He is insane.* Erebus stood behind Nyx, shaking his head. *If he thinks that he can put an ultimatum on primordials. On Nyx? On me?*

Nyx said nothing, her expression one of net neutrality. She turned her head slowly to one side as a saccharine smile slipped onto her face. The night sky at her feet turned stormy, small rolls of thunder and flashes of lightning ricocheting off her legs.

"God of lightning," she purred, taking another step towards Zeus. "Why don't we have a word in private?"

It was not the response that Zeus had been expecting. His face seemed to pale, if only for a moment, as he watched the illusion at Nyx's feet. The flashes of lightning seemed to mock him, to remind him that everything that happened once the Sun had set was her domain. Even the weather. He was cornered. Zeus was vying for a position of king of the gods and if he refused Nyx's request, he would seem weak. He was not dumb enough to not accept small miracles; he knew that if she wanted to, Nyx could likely end the discussion—if not the war —right there in his throne room.

"Of course." He clapped his hands once, loudly, letting larger bolts of lightning spark out from his hands.

"Let's not whip them out and measure, hmm?" Nyx eyed his light show with discontent, letting the clouds at her feet fade away as she stepped down onto the tiled floor. Zeus could only manage an embarrassed chuckle as he looked away.

"Dionysus!" Zeus snapped at the god, who was lounging on a bench with a young man in his lap. "Do me a favor and have the wine poured when we return." Dionysus had the least amount of care when it came to politics, his cheeks ruddy and blonde waves cascading down his neck. He didn't bother looking up at Zeus or giving any indication that he heard him, other than to snap his fingers. All the cups in the room began overflowing and Erebus had to take a few steps back to avoid the puddles of wine.

"Great," Zeus muttered and rolled his eyes, flicking his wrist towards a door behind the chair. He stood and disappeared into it, beckoning Nyx to follow him. She turned around briefly, giving the slightest of nods to Erebus before she walked across the room and disappeared after Zeus.

As she ducked through the doors, she saw that they were in a quiet antechamber of some kind. It was relatively small, only two small benches and a hearth in the middle of it, but it was richly decorated. Tapestries of deep purple hung from the ceiling and the tiles on the floor were all inlaid with gold and mother-of-pearl. The far wall had a low table, already filled with jugs of wine that had overflowed at Dionysus's command.

"A small office." Zeus flashed her a winning smile, answering her question as if she read his thoughts.

"I could only wonder why you'd keep such an... intimate room prepared, so close to your throne." Nyx kept the smile plastered on her face, the threat apparent in her words. Neither of them had forgotten her curse and the centuries of chaos that had followed suit. Zeus gave her a polite nod, but his features were strained.

He sat down on one of the benches, extending his hand out as he offered up the second bench to Nyx. She walked around the fire, her feet once again disappearing into shadows and black clouds, before sitting down.

"Nyx," Zeus grinned, "I'll spare you the speech —"

"Lucky me."

Zeus coughed, his nervousness becoming more apparent. "You know what we're doing and why. I would implore you to join the cause."

"*Implore* me?" Nyx laughed, her dark eyes flashing in the firelight. Her black robes seemed to come alive, patterns of stardust and obsidian magic flickering across the folds. "Interesting. A mere moment ago, in front of the others, you were demanding that I pick a side."

"A show, you know." Zeus squirmed. "The other gods... They need someone to lead them when this is all over. You know..." He was repeating himself, thoroughly flustered. Nyx savored it. She knew that he would never truly give her an ultimatum; he couldn't. Her power outlasted him in every way. The only reason that she had requested to get him alone was for her own enjoyment in watching him squirm.

"You're a fool." Nyx raised an eyebrow and cocked her head to one side as if she was studying him. Zeus's eyes snapped up to hers for the first time, and a little bit of fight appeared in his eyes.

*Ah. The pride. You can always get a man to lash out when it's their pride.*

"I would think that you still owe me a little bit of respect. We can at the very least, chat as equals."

Nyx exploded in an array of dark clouds, stars and magic flooding the small space, as her eruptions of laughter echoed around them. Zeus's face got redder the more that she laughed, and he stood, both of his fists shaking.

"You listen to me, Night —"

"No." Nyx silenced him in a moment. Her voice dropped an octave, reverberating around the room in its command that left no room for argument. Her magic slipped down Zeus's throat, making it look like he was drinking tar. "You will listen to me, *Zeus*. You and your other gods are nothing. You spend all day looking at man and convincing yourself that you are great... but look at me, Zeus. Gaze!"

Her magic poured out of his eyes, and the God of lightning wept black tears. He gagged and sputtered, black spit getting caught in his beard. The night continued to spin around him.

"Are you so great now? God of lightning?" Nyx laughed, and it shook the room as she caused lightning bolts to streak across the ceiling. Zeus grew even more enraged, struggling to stand to his full height. When he finally did, he unleashed one great bolt of power and sent it up into the clouds around him.

Nyx's power caught it and fizzled it out, like damp fingers pressing out a candle. Zeus's eyes got wide in horror as he stumbled backward and fell over the bench behind him. Nyx's dark power was still pouring from him as he struggled to catch his breath. She watched for a few more seconds... before it all vanished. In an instant, the night sky had disappeared from the room, and it was returned to its previous state. Nyx stood, in mortal form, politely in front of Zeus without a single hair out of place. Zeus was still lying flat on the floor, coughing up the remnants of black power that tinged his skin. Nyx flicked her ebony hair over one shoulder and straightened out a fold in her tunic.

"Erebus and I will be taking no sides." Her voice was as calm and pleasant as if she was discussing the weather.

Zeus could only nod in agreement as he sat up, staring at her with wild eyes. There was a hatred beginning to brew there as he promised himself that he would not suffer such an indignity again. Nyx ignored it and turned on her heel, going towards the door.

"Oh, and Zeus?" She turned back around and gave him a smile that was dripping with the sweetness of ambrosia. "If I catch word of you ever sending your brothers to talk to Erebus again, I will feed you to Kronos."

Zeus opened his mouth to scream... but Nyx was gone.

# PART II

Nyx stepped out of the antechamber. The rest of the gods were none the wiser. They barely looked up from their side conversations and their wine, only seeing Nyx walk down the steps in front of Zeus's throne. There was no expression on her face. She carried a look of such neutrality that they assumed nothing had come of the conversation with Zeus. It was only Poseidon who took another close look, his gaze flickering between the primordial to the doors that she had closed behind her.

Poseidon sighed deeply, throwing a glance at Erebus. Erebus was entirely focused on Nyx as she crossed the room to him. The pair avoided touching one another, but the way she stood near him betrayed their intimacy. Both began moving seamlessly towards the door, falling in stride with one another. Their movements were synchronized without effort and as they began fading away into their primordial bodies, the very lines that defined them blurred. The gods watched as Nyx and Erebus left, their eyes only then scanning back to where Zeus had disappeared to. When he did not appear, they resumed their gossip and their indulgences. Zeus did not come back to the throne room for the rest of the day.

Erebus resisted asking Nyx what had happened. The fact that she had walked out of the room without the Lightning God said enough; he knew anyway that it wasn't possible to force Nyx to change her mind. The sun was already setting, and Erebus followed as they didn't go back to the Underworld. Nyx was getting ready to bring nightfall.

It was an incredible sight. Erebus knew that if the mortals could ever watch it—and see it the way that he did—it would certainly change their minds about exalting these child-gods. Nyx was moving through the skies, only the slightest outline of a body apparent in the clouds. Her form was a dark outline against the fading, pale blue sky. She shook her hair and stars began pouring out from it. Stardust and sparks came tumbling from around her shoulders, circling her with light that could only exist in darkness. Her eyes slowly turned white with moonlight. Nyx blinked constellations from her eyelashes, her diamond tears turning into the greatest of stars in their universe. Erebus watched in perpetual awe as Cetus, Centaurus, and Scorpius emerged where she wept and went galloping into the sky. The constellations, one-by-one, took their place in the heavens. They were still barely legible against the dusk, but Erebus could see them. He could see every part of Nyx as she transformed.

Nyx's hands went to her face as she wiped away her tears, flicking them away as they descended as shooting stars back towards earth. She rolled her shoulders back as if easing some unknown tension, and darkness began rippling from her body. It poured from her womb, from her breasts, and split her back —and Erebus watched once more as Nyx gave birth to nightfall. The blackness started tracing across the sky like an oil spill, soaking and drenching the earth. Nyx's face contorted in a silent scream as her power spread all over the cosmos, pushing enough strength from her body to cover the entire world in night. The blackness kept going, the edges pushing over the horizon.

The stars and constellations were still settling into position as nightfall finalized, the last of the light chased away. It was in these few moments in the total obsidian atmosphere of new night that Erebus listened. In her nightfall, it was the sounds that he sought out. The sound of humanity as they released a collective sigh, as fires were stoked, and people went to rest. The sound of mothers relaxing as children fell asleep. The sound of animals, plants, and even the rivers beginning to slow down and release their pent-up heat from the day back to the sky. A collective sigh back to the heavens.

Once the dust had settled, only then did Erebus summon to look up at Nyx. She didn't look tired, not remotely, but rather bored. After nightfall, she always looked energized but now she just looked bored. The last of her black magic was unfurling around her in wisps of smoke as if she had just been on fire. Nyx blinked a few times, the moonlight leaving her eyes as they returned to normal.

"Nýchta?" Erebus moved towards her in the sky, extending a wave of shadows towards her. There were still a few holdouts over the earth, the last lights of evening, and Nyx always sent out one final wave of power to finish the job. She blinked a few times and looked up at Erebus. There was something in her expression that he couldn't place. She wasn't tired—the concept was laughable—but there was something in her gaze that made Erebus question what had happened in the room with Zeus.

"Can you finish the job?" Nyx nodded out towards the horizon, where the last embers of daylight were floating around the Helion's dust trail. It took all of Erebus's strength to not react visibly. She took such pride in her work, Nyx hardly ever asked Erebus to tuck in the final elements of nightfall. The last time that she had was the day that Hera destroyed her temple and she wanted to get back to her acolyte's souls.

"Of course," he kept his smile warm, "I would be happy to." Nyx nodded and Erebus moved towards her, pulling Nyx into his arms before she could protest. He felt her soften slightly as he pressed his lips to her brow.

"I'll finish up. We'll talk later. Go see Hecate." Erebus winked at her, knowing that Hecate was the only other person who Nyx would talk to. He rightfully assumed that bond had only grown in the year that their relationship had been further estranged.

Nyx gave him a soft smile, kissing his lips once and disappearing in a cloud of starlight. Erebus watched as the last of the light faded and exploded, a dark wave of shadow, and grew... and grew... and grew... until he blanketed the earth.

))) ))

THERE WAS A SOFT BREEZE, and Hecate looked up from where she, predictably, had been working at her kitchen table. This evening, the kitchen smelled like cinnamon and rosemary, and her dogs were asleep in front of the fire. Her home was a sacred space, and she possessed the innate ability to know whenever anyone arrived on the property. There were no footsteps as the black energy moved down the hall towards the kitchen, affirming Hecate's suspicions. She smiled when she felt Nyx's presence and knew that things had improved between Night and Darkness, but there was a tense atmosphere around Nyx when she entered the kitchen. Hecate knew about Zeus's summons, and with the energy that Nyx was radiating, she was now surprisingly concerned about how the meeting had gone.

Nyx said nothing, half in her primordial form and appeared to Hecate as a torso and a head, obscured by dark clouds.

"I assume the meeting with Zeus went well?" Hecate didn't

let the silence permeate as something within her urged her to get Nyx talking.

Nyx took her normal seat at the table and enveloped the air around her with a black mist. One of Hecate's dogs picked up its head and sniffed the air before lying back down, seemingly just happy that Nyx's lack of legs now meant it didn't have to move.

"These gods are going to push me over the edge," Nyx snapped, her magic flaring. Hecate raised an eyebrow and put down the small bowl she had been holding.

"What happened?"

"Zeus tried to give me an ultimatum in front of the gods."

"Ah." Hecate couldn't keep a smile off her face. "How did you respond?"

"Aptly." Nyx paused. "In private. However, I find myself wishing that I had left that reminder for him in front of the rest of his lackeys."

"Only you would call a room full of immortal gods *lackeys*."

"They're a nuisance. What does immortality matter to me?"

"You forget *I'm* a goddess." Hecate chopping a bit of rosemary.

"And *you* are nothing like those animals." Nyx made a little sound of disapproval and waved her hand in the air in boredom, settling into her body as the dogs shuffled away from her feet. Hecate opened her mouth to speak when there was another rumbling in her courtyard and her smile got wider.

"It's been a while since I've been lucky enough to have both Nyx and Erebus in my kitchen at once." Hecate kept her voice at a normal level but knew that he could hear her as he entered. Erebus's booming laugh echoed in response. He stepped into the kitchen, matching Hecate's grin as he moved over and kissed her cheeks in greeting.

"Darkness." She raised an eyebrow and looked towards Nyx. "Do *you* want to tell me why Nyx is sulking in my kitchen?"

"I'm not sulking," Nyx protested, resting her chin in her hand. Erebus went over to where she was sitting on the long bench, pulling Nyx into his side and letting his arm fall around her shoulder. Hecate couldn't help but suppress a chuckle. There were only two people in existence who were able to cajole and touch Nyx in such a casual, intimate way, and they were both in this kitchen. She never got tired of seeing Erebus's effect on Nyx.

"There's a little bit of sulking." Erebus looked at her with a small smirk. "You also had me finish nightfall, which is one of your favorite things to do."

"You finished nightfall?" Hecate put both her hands on the counter and leaned towards the pair. "Tell us then. What happened with Zeus?"

"I felt your power in the throne room." Erebus nodded in encouragement. "Zeus didn't return, either. All the gods know that your will was executed."

"They aren't going to leave us alone," Nyx sighed. Her expression turned to Erebus and got tense. There was a subtle look in her eyes that made Hecate feel like she was suddenly involved in an intimate moment. "*Especially* Poseidon and Hades. I know that he cornered you outside."

"Then you know what my response was."

"Wait." Hecate threw her hands up in frustration as flickers of red magic burst from her fingertips. "What did Hades say?"

"You know that he's already joined forces with his brothers."

"Clearly." Hecate's voice grew tense, and her eyes narrowed in Erebus's direction. "Is he bothering you about it?"

"Easy, Auntie," Erebus raised his hands up and laughed. "He's just being Hades. Yes, he pulled me aside before I could enter the hall and pressed the issue."

"What did he say?" Hecate began stripping the rosemary branch forcefully, her eyes not leaving Erebus.

"The same things he's been saying." Erebus tried to be placating. "It's okay. You know I'm more powerful than he is."

"I don't worry about *power* when it comes to Hades." Hecate rolled her eyes. "I'm more powerful than he is, too. Everyone here would do well to remember that."

"If you want to steward the Underworld, I've been offering to give it to you for years." Nyx shrugged, "You know how I feel about him."

"I will not be a steward of anything." Hecate said, her lips pressing into a thin line. "I'd rather focus on the women who need me. Besides, you know the Fates love him."

"They love to *fuck* him," Erebus cut in. "There's a big difference."

"Careful." Nyx's tone was foreboding. "They're the Fates, Erebus. In some way or another, we all answer to them."

"Which is why I'm not lying." He turned to her and raised an eyebrow, his smirk widening. Nyx rolled his eyes but couldn't completely hide the corresponding laugh on her face.

"Erebus. Hades is brash and cocky, but one thing he isn't… is stupid. He's smart enough to know that you and Nyx are primordial. If he is pressing this issue on you, there's a reason. Something else is afoot."

Hecate looked at him, the whites of her eyes beginning to expand and glow. Nyx sat up a little straighter, and Erebus met Hecate's gaze. Power, an ancient one, filled with the wills of witchcraft and the essence of Gaia far beneath them, began to seep into the room. It started pouring from the walls in a red mist, slowly filling up the room, as pots, bowls, and containers that filled Hecate's apothecary also started to overflow with it. The dogs sat up straight, staring back at their master with the same blank expression.

"What's happening?" Erebus turned to Nyx, whispering as he looked around the room. The cauldron hanging in the fireplace started to boil over inexplicably and smell of cinnamon.

"She's channeling." Nyx nodded, a soft smile coming over

her face. "You forget that Hecate is not simply some diviner of potions, my love."

Hecate's voice began to slip in and out of its echo, as the heads of the crone and maiden appeared on her shoulders.

*"LISTEN NOW, God of darkness, Goddess of night.*
  *Be careful to dissuade yourselves from Zeus's plight —*
  *If what we caution is what comes to pass,*
  *The night Nyx fights will be her last."*

THE KITCHEN DESCENDED INTO CHAOS. Hecate's trance was broken, and the physical manifestations of her power receded back through the walls, into cups, under lids. The dogs immediately laid down and began to whine; only the boiling cauldron remained. Hecate blinked twice as her vision cleared, as she grabbed her head and the maiden and crone disappeared. Erebus jumped to his feet with a shout, his brow furrowing as he panicked over the ominous prediction.

"What does that mean? Where does it come from?" He crossed the kitchen in two bounds while his gaze went wild and roamed over Hecate as if she was hiding the answers on her person. He was frightened, not angry, and as Hecate came to, she saw the terror in his eyes. Nyx remained painfully stoic at the table.

"I know not where it comes from, Darkness," she said quietly, shrugging, her voice tired. "Sometimes straight from Gaia. Other times... a bigger presence."

"What's bigger than Gaia?" Erebus's eyes went wide, dumbfounded.

"The conscience of women." Nyx spoke up from the table. "Every womb, every breast, every female spirit in existence. Past, present, and future. *That* is what Hecate channels, and it includes Gaia. It is not even only her."

"What does it mean?" Erebus stepped back over to Nyx, his hands going to her cheeks. "I... I can't... I can't imagine it..." He felt his chest beginning to separate as he dwelled on the thought of an existence without Nyx in it.

"It doesn't matter," Nyx cut him off, turning her head slightly to kiss his palm. "I won't fight. Besides... I don't fight in the night, Erebus. I *am* the night."

Nyx and Erebus remained with Hecate a little while longer as they waited for the atmosphere in the kitchen to settle. Hecate busied herself with making a strong pot of tea— *"Something I always drink when I have visions"*—as her dogs headed outside. Erebus could hear them moving in circles around the house. He heard a rumor that they were the souls of men and a god that were cursed; the dogs would show up at Hecate's door and would stay with her, until one day they walked off into Asphodel and never returned. The goddess of dogs was one of her many titles, so Hecate never noticed anything surreal about an ever-rotating roster of canine companions.

Erebus watched Nyx's expression as she stared once more into the flames, watching them as they curled around the cauldron in Hecate's hearth. He nudged her gently, letting a shadow slip free and curl underneath the table, around her ankle—out of sight. Or so he thought.

"I can see that, too," Hecate chuckled as though she were a mother who was supervising teenagers. Nyx chuckled softly, her eyes not leaving the flames.

"Let's go," she murmured quietly, breaking her gaze to look

at Erebus. He nodded, turning and giving Hecate a respectful nod.

"We appreciate it, as always." His voice was somber as he studied the expression on Nyx's face. There was something that hadn't been there before Hecate's prophecy. She hadn't reacted as strongly as Erebus did, but it was obvious that she was affected.

"Don't think too much on it," Hecate read both of their minds as she raised an eyebrow in their direction. "You know as well as I do those prophecies always mean something very different when they come to pass."

"It's more the *come to pass* part that I'm worried about." Erebus couldn't help but let a little frustration slip into his voice, even though he knew it wasn't Hecate's fault.

"It doesn't matter." Nyx looked between her husband and her friend. "We aren't getting involved." Her eyes flickered to Erebus, where she studied the look in his eyes. There was nothing there but sincerity, yet she found that she still questioned his motives when it came to the matter at hand. He was searching for something, searching for glory—Nyx had too much experience with men whose appetites had been whetted for power.

"We aren't." Erebus's tone, however, was resolute. "It would cause too much chaos to the mortal realm as you illustrated."

Hecate watched as Erebus's eyes and tone seemed to be playing games with one another. Whatever synchronicity these two had found before coming into her home, the prophecy was threatening to shatter it. If it hadn't already.

"Let the humans and men fight in the light." Nyx sighed and looked out the small window in the kitchen. "When they close their eyes to greet rest and darkness—it will always be us, Erebus. I don't know why that isn't enough for you."

"It is!" He turned to face her on the table bench, some of

the color draining from his face. "Where are you getting that from?"

"It's written all over your face." Nyx sighed again, eyeing him for a few moments before she turned her gaze back to the fire. "You could still be swayed."

Hecate said nothing, busying herself once more with a kettle in front of her, seamlessly distracting herself as to not appear like she was eavesdropping even though the conversation was happening in her kitchen.

"I don't know what else you want me to say, Nyx." Erebus shook his head in frustration, running a hand through his hair. "I told you about Hades and Poseidon. You know that I'm not lying."

"You're not telling the truth, either. This war still tempts you."

"I never lied about that! I said that I would defer to you. I did." The shadows around Erebus began to smoke as though he was slowly turning up the heat in the atmosphere. Stars began flickering and smoldering in Nyx's hair as their power began to recognize one another and push back against the argument.

"You still don't see my point." Nyx's voice was cross as it took on a deeper baritone, echoing in the kitchen.

"I don't have to!" Erebus threw his arms up in frustration. "Don't you see that? I trust you. I said I wouldn't defy you to others and I didn't. Do you really think that you can't trust *me* because I don't agree on everything you say?"

"No." Nyx shook her head, poking Erebus in the chest. "*Do not* misquote me. This isn't about agreeing with me. If you *see Zeus's point* at all, then yes, we have a problem." Storm clouds began gathering around Nyx's feet, sending soft rolls of thunder echoing off the tiled floor.

The burst of wind caused the fire to flicker as Hecate gracefully pretended there wasn't an atmospheric argument between two primordials happening in front of her (nothing could run Hecate out of her workspace). When Nyx's voice broke over the din, it was with a crack of pain that struck Erebus in the chest.

"Never in a millennium would *my* Erebus have found any common ground with that child." Her voice cracked. "And it frightens me." She stood, stepping away from Darkness and bringing her power under control.

Erebus followed suit, his shadows disappearing, as he watched as Nyx slipped out without a word. There was something in his chest that began to crack. He had done everything that she asked... hadn't he? She went down the hallway and was gone, leaving Hecate and Darkness standing in the kitchen. Hecate seemed un-phased by the quick exit.

"I don't understand." Erebus turned to Hecate, who only shrugged.

"She's frightened for the first time in her long existence, which is a terrifying feeling all of its own."

"What could *she* possibly be frightened of?!" Erebus tossed his hands up in the air and sat back down on the long bench.

"Are you that daft?" Hecate finally snapped, some of her calm resolve slipping as she slammed her hands down on the counter.

"Nyx is the one thing in this universe that I might understand as well as you... and I don't have a clue what you're talking about." Erebus sighed deeply, knowing that Nyx was already well on her way to Tartarus. Hecate's expression turned uncharacteristically grim once more.

"Do you? Do you understand her?" There was a twinge of warning in her voice.

"I've told Nyx I won't side against her. What could she be afraid of?" Erebus's tone deepened, some of his shadows circling around his legs again.

"Losing *you*, you idiot!" Hecate snapped, rushing out from behind the counter and putting her hands on her hips as she glared at Erebus. "You don't see that?"

His expression darkened immediately.

"Because we had a fight?"

"A fight!" Hecate scoffed, red sparks shimmering off her fingers. "You call abandoning Nyx for a *year*, a fight?"

"I didn't abandon her!" Erebus stepped towards Hecate, darkness flickering in the kitchen. "I did my job, and she did hers. We still worked together—"

"Is it true that you didn't go to her bed that whole time?"

"What does *that* have anything to do with it? Is there nothing private with you damn gods?" Erebus's voice dropped to a growl.

"If a man isn't fucking his wife, I have questions." Hecate rolled her eyes, her temper already dissolving as she looked at him with a stare that would make even a primordial shiver. Erebus's jaw clenched.

"It was best… for a while, if—"

"Stop." Hecate raised her hand and silenced him, shaking her head. "I don't want to know. You need to understand that it's not only your actions but your intentions. Yes, you sided with Nyx, but how could you not see that your sympathies to Zeus hurt her?"

"Sympathies! They're not sympathies. I only think that it would be—could be—good if we… you know…"

"Do go on. You're making such an eloquent point that I'm enraptured with your cause," Hecate deadpanned, her gaze nearly withering a man as ancient as time itself. Erebus shook his head.

"I'm not going to do this again. Nyx will understand. I am not going to do anything to separate myself from her."

There was a tense silence that settled over the kitchen as Hecate continued to stare at Erebus with an imperceptible look in her eyes.

"She's worried she's already lost you, Erebus." Her voice softened. "You've waxed so much poetic," Hecate waved a hand in the air, "about wanting to be *in the light*… It makes her question every moment you've spent in the darkness together. Between the two of you—"

"It's a lot of darkness." He sighed, rubbing his hands over his face. "How? How could that make her question everything that we've built together?" Hecate shrugged, finally taking her stare off Erebus and grabbing a jar from her apothecary table.

"I'd say 'she's human' but that isn't true. She's a woman though and a strong one at that. It's the way of strong women to be prepared for the day that a man can't accept their strength anymore."

Erebus said nothing, sitting down once more at the table as his mind ran in a million different directions. He had been convinced that they had gotten over the worst of their issues together, but Hecate's prophecy had dragged everything back up to the surface. Things that he didn't even know were there. He was embarrassed that he hadn't considered the effect that his intentions would have on Nyx. Everything Erebus symbolized was action. He had never had an issue with Nyx consuming him, bringing on nightfall, giving him a place to operate in the darkness. The idea that he had different allegiances now, even if he didn't act on them, would hurt her... Of course, of course they would.

*As old as the universe, only ever been with one woman—and I still find a way to mess it up.*

"Erebus," Hecate snapped him out of his trance.

"Yes?"

"You certainly aren't going to solve your problems sitting in my kitchen." She looked towards the door. "Nyx thought you were right behind her." Erebus shook his head as if he could rattle his thoughts free, and stood quickly. Hecate looked him over once more like she was analyzing his intentions, and Erebus went after his wife.

))))

Nyx waited in Tartarus, knowing the moment that Erebus had followed. He hadn't followed her as soon as she left Hecate's home, and she figured the goddess had a word or two reserved just for her consort. She waited, keeping her eye on the horizon in her corporeal form as she felt him materialize around her.

"What else did Hecate say to you?"

There was a tone in her voice that felt distant, aching. It struck something in Erebus, and he wondered if that prophecy was all that it took to send them both careening once more towards division. He watched as rogue stardust settled on her shoulders, wondering how often the cosmos she contained felt like the weight of the world. His shadows flickered around him in response as if they anticipated the weight of her absence.

"She loves you deeply." Erebus shrugged. "Your friend."

"She does." Nyx turned to faced him and there were tears in her eyes. "Do you?" The question was singular and defiant; it rocked Erebus once more to his core.

"I know I've hurt you." His brow furrowed as he took one small step forward, giving Nyx plenty of time to retreat. When she didn't move, he took another step forward. "You must understand, anything that I feel about joining Zeus, it doesn't mean that I don't love you. Love us. Love *this*."

He took one step closer. The tears broke on Nyx's cheeks.

"This whole thing frightens me," she shook her head, "Gaia has told me to stay away from it. We've all heard Hecate. It's not about power…"

"What is it?" Erebus's voice was pleading, begging for some insight into what was happening in his beloved's head.

"*We're* primordials," Nyx sighed, tossing her head over her shoulder as her voice got angry. "If Zeus is overthrowing Kronos, some titan, in a power grab, do you really think he won't try to come up with a plan to get *us* under heel?"

"He wouldn't dare!" Erebus's voice rose, his shadows flaring out from all around him and immediately flocking around Nyx as if protecting her from an invisible threat. Nyx looked at them with a small, wistful smile.

"I shouldn't be upset..." she said softly. "You've agreed with me, but feeling that you don't want this, that it is only a matter of time until you give in..."

Erebus crossed the remaining distance between them and pulled Nyx to his chest, his hand going up and tangling in her hair. He led her to the crook of his shoulder, letting his body wrap around her like armor as she shook with silent sobs.

"Nýchta." Erebus's voice was a quiet, gravelly whisper as he turned to her ear. "I'm so sorry. I don't regret a moment with you. How could I? Everything I do is for more moments with you."

"This does not need to concern us." Nyx pulled back from him, something wild and untamed in her eyes as she gripped his face. "Who have you become?"

Erebus's eyes went wide as her panic washed over him, feeling the anxiety rising in Nyx like a wave of her own power. A wave that she wasn't in control of. He watched her for another moment, afraid to breathe while she searched his eyes. Another moment passed and before he could let her worries consume her, Erebus leaned forward and kissed her. There was something panicked about it, rushed and frightened, an embrace that was frantic and fearful as if every second they had was already stolen.

For the first time since time, Erebus and Nyx found no comfort in their intimacy. It was like an aftertaste, a memory or recollection of a feeling that was quickly fading—something already gone.

## ❦ 14 ❦

Erebus left before sunrise. He knew that Nyx heard him leave but couldn't summon the courage to acknowledge it. Something in them had cracked, and he didn't know how to fuse it back together. Whether it was the prophecy or a break that had been brewing between them, he didn't know what could save them. If Nyx felt like their relationship was that tenuous, that *fragile*, then he was out of ways to convince her otherwise.

The Underworld was still dark, and Erebus felt Nyx depart Tartarus not long after he left. She hadn't come looking for him. Slowly, methodically, from where he sat in between the realms, he felt his darkness come back to him. Shadows rushed over the grass and disappeared at his ankles while waves of black clouds rolled over the meadow's skies. He watched and recognized Nyx in her primordial form from a distance, ushering nightfall back under her breast, tucking stars into her hair, and descending the moonlight back into the depths. It was a long time before Erebus moved, watching the sun rise, wondering what the purpose of darkness was without night.

Skies moved when primordials and immortals navigated their way through the world. Not a cloud moved in the Underworld when Zeus crossed the border and began walking the fields, looking for Erebus. Erebus didn't move. He waited, eternal in his patience, as he knew that the dogged god would find him eventually. It was no surprise what Zeus was after, and it was a conversation that Erebus was all too willing to avoid.

It was impossible to miss Zeus as he rounded a hilltop and saw Erebus down below, on the banks of Styx. Only Dionysus made a louder entrance.

"Erebus!" Zeus clapped his hands together, a thunderclap disrupting the solitude that Erebus was licking his wounds in. He didn't acknowledge the god's presence with anything but a subtle nod, refusing to even look in his direction. Zeus watched the back of Erebus's head as he walked down the slope, unable to keep the scowl off his face as the golden-boy facade cracked. He was *over* these primordials and their temper tantrums.

When Erebus sensed the god was next to him, he turned, looking at the saccharine smile that Zeus had plastered on his face. To anyone else, it would be genuine—charming, even— but Erebus's desire to smother the grin off Zeus's face had him pulling back his shadows before they followed through.

"Zeus." Erebus's face was expressionless. "What brings you to the Underworld?"

"Can an immortal not visit the realms as he pleases?" The reply was both a quip and a challenge, putting Erebus on edge. There was nothing he hated more than the passive aggressive word games of the gods, of their oaths and promises that said one thing and meant another. He was much more prone to blunt statements and swift action, and why wouldn't he be? He had the power to back it up.

"An immortal, maybe. Are the gods immortal? Seems too soon to tell." It was Erebus's turn to smile. To Zeus's credit, only a flicker of emotion passed over his face.

"I'd like to speak to you about that, actually."

"Your mortality? I'd love to discuss it." Erebus couldn't

resist. The frustrations of the past year started bubbling up to the surface, a slick, white-toothed grin of an ancient predator slipping across his face. Zeus fought back a shiver at the feral look in the ancient's eyes.

"This affects all of us, Darkness." Zeus used the Greek title that man had picked up over the past few centuries. It didn't inspire the severity that he had hoped as Erebus only raised an eyebrow.

"Does it?"

"Yes," Zeus sighed as though he was repeating himself to a child instead of a primordial, older and more powerful than he was.

*The gall on him, though...* Erebus's thoughts were violent. *He certainly does believe his own mythos, which is impressive for a god who created half his own stories.*

"I'm waiting with bated breath."

Zeus took a step closer to Erebus and looked him dead in the eye, his mouth tightening into a thin line. It was the most severe that Erebus had ever seen Zeus; most of his expressions were laced with some bought of comical anger or mischief.

"We need you. This confrontation with Kronos is getting closer every day. You know this, and I won't repeat to you the severity of the situation we find ourselves in."

"The situation *we* find ourselves in?" Erebus couldn't help but push. This entire situation was Zeus's fault. He wasn't going to allow the child-God to push a narrative where he was the victim. Zeus threw up his hands in mocking frustration.

"However we got here, we're here now."

"No." Erebus's voice was resolute. There was a timbre in his voice alone that rivaled all the thunder Zeus could manufacture. "How did we get here, God of lightning? If you want me to join your cause, be direct about it."

Zeus stared at Erebus, his brow darkening. There was an anger to Zeus that made Erebus understand why man and other gods were afraid of him; why they had so willingly fallen under his heel. It had nothing to do with his ability to lead, whether he was the most powerful or even the most likable. No. Zeus's secret was much more nefarious than that—more dangerous than all the demons in the Underworld. Zeus was *volatile*. His face twisted, and any traces of niceties fell away. What remained was an angry man, lightning crackling between his fingertips and smelling like smoke. What he didn't understand was that there was nothing Erebus loved more than the scent of conflict and scorched earth.

"My father has had his time." Zeus spoke and his voice had transformed, devoid of true power but loud. Loud enough to hide its insecurities from anyone but a primordial, who had seen everything since the day that they had created themselves.

*Interesting.* Erebus let his eyes wander over Zeus's body, watching as Zeus almost imperceptibly shifted his weight nervously from one leg to the other. *Do you not like feeling scrutinized? What is it like, being on the other end of a power dynamic where you don't know what the other man will do?* Erebus kept the thoughts to himself, but his shadows reacted once more, reading his subconscious thoughts like commands. They slipped out from under his chiton, curling around Erebus's strong legs before sliding over to Zeus.

Zeus could only watch in horror and pull his hands away as the shadows gripped his fingers, extinguishing the lightning like candles.

"Erebus—"

"You do not speak honestly," Erebus growled, tired of Zeus's games. He made no effort to recall his shadows as more of them poured from him, wrapping around Zeus like hungry dogs. The blackness licked at his arms and his legs, winding around his waist as they pushed at his back. Zeus's face turned from anger to panic as he began pulling at the shadows like they were flies he could cast off. Every time he tried, his hands went through the shadows, and they tightened their grip.

"Stop this," Zeus roared, the last of his control shattered.

His face was red, and his beard was flecked with spit as he yelled at Erebus, a sound that was possessed like that of a dying animal. It was not the noise of a powerful god but a weak man or a lame predator. He attempted to lunge for Erebus, but the shadows around his ankles snared, causing Zeus to fall to the ground in a tumble of blackness. He landed with a cracking noise as weak bolts of lightning shot out of him and singed the grass around his body.

"You do not speak honestly," Erebus repeated himself, bending down on one knee and leaning over Zeus's face until he was next to the god's ear. "I will have nothing to do with liars and cons, Zeus. Mark my words—watch your back. It's dangerous to play power games when you only have a *god's* share."

As if to spite him, there was a strike of lightning, and Erebus and the shadows were gone. Zeus waited a breath, then two, before sitting up slowly. He was alone on the hill in Asphodel.

*I guess it's time for another approach.*

)))

A DAY PASSED. Erebus did not seek out Nyx, nor she him. He knew that Zeus had not left the Underworld. Instead, he had gone straight to Hades. There was something about having Zeus in his realm for more than a few hours that was off-putting. He knew that there wasn't brotherly love lost between Zeus and Hades, but the fact that Zeus had spent the night as his brother's guest was...unusual.

Erebus would never say that his relationship with Hades was *bad*; it simply *was*. Nyx had long decided to let the god take management of the Underworld, carefully putting Thanatos,

Hypnos, and Hecate alongside him. Hades was many things, but he wasn't weak-willed. If he had decided on something, then there would be no going back. There had to be something in it for him if he was allowing his brother these war-games.

It only took a shift in the wind, and Erebus knew that they were on the move. There was a subtle shift in power, a reallocation of sorts, and Erebus grit his teeth as he realized Poseidon was sliding through the rivers of the Underworld. The brothers were all here, together. And they were coming for Erebus. He made no move, continuing to stare out at the banks of the river while he waited. The darkness started to ebb from Erebus, causing pockets of night to cover the sky above him. He made no effort to reign them in, but as he was lost in his thoughts, there was a sudden wave that broke the surface of the water.

Poseidon stood up slowly, his body morphing from the foam of the current as he became corporeal. Droplets of water fell down the folds of his tunic, dripping down the bracelets on his wrists. His eyes were serious, creased, as though he was already angry as he glanced around the pockets of blackness in the atmosphere that Erebus made no attempt to control.

*An excellent start to this meeting.* Erebus felt walls going up around his thoughts.

"Erebus." Poseidon's tone was respectful as his feet hit the shore, even if his expression was cautious. "My brothers are coming."

Erebus knew that he was on edge, but he didn't appreciate the warning—as if he didn't know everything that happened in the Underworld.

"I'm aware." He raised an eyebrow, a silent challenge to Poseidon as he called his shadows back to him. They wrapped around him like a torrent, quickly vanishing into Erebus's body as the sky cleared. If the show of power affected Poseidon, he said nothing. His expression was calculating.

"They want you to join with Zeus." The god of the sea had

a warning tone in his voice as if there was something going between them unspoken.

"I must say... I've never felt so wanted in eons of my existence."

"That seems like it would be a blow to Nyx." Hades's voice cut through the tension between Poseidon and Erebus, only to immediately add to it. Erebus turned, eyeing both gods that walked towards him. Hades seemed unbothered as if this was something that he did every day. Zeus, on the other hand, looked like he hadn't slept all night. Erebus supposed he'd hadn't, so far from his sparkling Mt. Olympus and lying down with the dogs of the Underworld.

*Woof, you bitch.* Erebus's own thoughts surprised him with the childish animosity that they held for the God of lightning, but he garnered that they weren't unwarranted.

They were dressed casually. They had not shown up in armor or anything else that would convey a war council. Erebus rightfully assumed that they wanted to be disarming. Hades's head-to-toe black flowed over the ground, mimicking shadows and providing sharp contrast to Zeus's white. They looked like two utter opposites: Hades dark-haired and smirking easily, Zeus blonde as the sun and agitated. Poseidon was somewhere in between the two as they came to flank their brother.

"What a family reunion." Erebus's voice dropped to a growl as he stared at the brothers. They were only gods, but they were the three most powerful gods. He felt his shadows began to unfurl from him once more with an unholy desire to drown them all. Maybe set Poseidon on fire.

"Erebus..." Zeus's voice was calm, coaxing. It was a new look for the boy-king. "We need you." Erebus felt his eyes go wide. Had he not sent Zeus away yesterday after he had refused to accept any responsibility?

"Do you? It seems that you have been a busy man,

recruiting people from all over the realms to join your patricidal crusade."

"Now, you insolent—" There was a sudden flush in Zeus's face. Lightning crackled on his fingertips and the atmosphere exploded in power. All at once, it seemed like each of the men lit the fuse that they had been nursing. Darkness enveloped the meeting as lightning struggled to break through, and waves began crashing angrily against the river's shore. The Underworld responded to Hades's power, the ghosts of the unclaimed clamoring leagues behind them at the borders of Styx. Chaos descended as the elements raged against one another until darkness choked them all out. Not a word was exchanged between the gods and the primordial.

Erebus waited until it was silent, and he pulled back his shadows. The brothers looked a little more frazzled, but not entirely shaken. Hades, especially, had a smile that was threatening to split his face in two. Poseidon looked cautious, tense, as if this was a situation that he had been trying to avoid entirely. Zeus looked like an angry—no, a petulant—teenager.

"Call me *insolent* one more time…" Erebus's voice reverberated through the air as his eyes glowed white, shadows threatening to spill from him once more. "Speak your piece and be gone."

"Listen here," Zeus started, his face flushed, when he got a sharp elbow in the side from Hades. Poseidon threw him a warning glare as the river picked up behind them. Zeus sighed deeply before he started again.

"We need you, Erebus. I know that you don't like me." He held up his hands in surrender. "Look beyond me, though. Kronos is threatening all of us. He is eating the rest of his children."

"You are scared of him." Erebus stated the fact, repeating it for no other reason than to remind everyone of Zeus's insecurities out loud.

"We all should be." Zeus nodded. Erebus was shocked,

even if he didn't show it, to see Zeus admit his failures out loud. "Think of Nyx." There was a pang that went through Erebus's chest at the mention of his consort.

"She has given her answer, and where she goes, I will follow."

"You have said that." Poseidon's eyes went to Zeus in a sharp reminder to keep his mouth shut. "We do not wish to come between the two of you, but don't you want to do what's best for her?"

"What's... What is best for her?" Erebus's voice lost its edge.

There was something inside of Erebus that had begun to shatter. He didn't know what to do to fix his relationship with Nyx anymore, and these past two days, he had been afraid that there was nothing that he could do. There was only one thing that could ever bring Erebus to his knees...and it was Nyx.

There was a subtle glance that went between Hades as Poseidon, something unspoken that even Zeus missed.

"If you agree to this, to fight with me..." Zeus sucked in a deep breath as if the next part pained him. "I'll see to it that all of Nyx's temples are restored. I will personally oversee it myself. Every human man shall know that no offering goes to me that is not doubled to the primordial herself."

The silence was deafening.

Erebus waited.

His heart felt like it was going to beat right out of his chest.

The shadows threatened to spill out from him, begging to be released as they pushed against his veins.

*This, this... this is what I could give to her. This is what I could bring to Nyx, to my beloved, to see her once more at her glory, to give her all that she deserves.*

Erebus's thoughts homed in on this as a solution to his problem. He was a man, after all, and when presented with a course of tangible action that he thought could help his beloved, he would take it. He would fight Kronos if it meant fighting his truest enemy—the space between him and Nyx. Hecate's warnings and Nyx's wishes were drowned out by the idea.

"How do I know that you mean this?" Erebus fought to keep his voice steady, but the brothers knew that they had struck a nerve. Zeus nodded, tugging a ring off his finger, and tossing it to Erebus, who caught it in one smooth motion.

"The gods gave me that ring to solidify my position once this mess with Kronos is over. It holds some of the power of each of us, including myself. You can hold on to it until the battle is over and my word has been fulfilled."

Erebus was studying the ring, assessing its power, and did not see the panic in Poseidon and Hades's eyes. They turned to one another behind Zeus's back, their emotions betraying that *something* was not going to plan. Neither Zeus nor Erebus saw it, blinded by their ambitions and personal objectives now at stake with the war at hand.

The skies darkened suddenly, and everything went quiet. All the god's attention was on Erebus as he looked up from the ring.

"You have a deal, God of lightning."

## 15

Another loud crash in the courtyard didn't break Hecate's concentration. She was sitting at her kitchen table, her gaze lost in the hearth as the flames danced in front of her eyes. She knew all about the meeting between the brothers and Erebus; there were very few things that Hades could do that could avoid her foresight. The primordials were another story, but she knew enough to be concerned. Hecate only turned towards the door when her dogs started barking, a mop of curly-blonde hair peeking through the doorway.

"Hermes," Hecate deadpanned with a roll of her eyes, keeping the grin off her face. "Do you always have to renovate my lawn when you show up?" Hermes's laugh was infectious as he stepped entirely into the kitchen, sidestepping around the dogs with his hands raised.

"Hecate, O terrifying one, you do get more ravishing every time I see you." The trickster had a smirk on his face a mile wide as he leaned down to kiss her cheek. Hecate didn't respond, but she also didn't move, allowing him to embrace her.

"If you are going to flatter me, Hermes, please use lines that you don't use on other goddesses."

He chuckled and sat down at the table across from Hecate, sliding onto the bench.

"You wound me!" Hermes made a show of clutching animatedly at his chest. "Who else do you think I would call *terrifying*?"

"Hera." Hecate answered quickly, raising an eyebrow. "For very different reasons, I would imagine."

"*Very* different." Hermes's good mood seemed to vanish as he rolled his eyes at the mention of her.

"What can I do for you?"

"You cut right to the quick!" The grin was back, and Hermes leaned forward across the table, capturing Hecate's hands in one of his own. "But if that's an open offer..."

It was Hecate's turn to laugh as she pulled her hand back. "It wasn't."

"Oh, you are coming for me today, aren't you?" Hermes shook his head in mock disappointment. "What's a god to do with you? What would your acolytes say?"

"They pray to me to deal with men like you." Hecate pointed at Hermes. "*Especially* men who can't forget one of Dionysus's parties a hundred years ago."

"You've kept me going ever since then, you witch." Hermes winked at her devilishly and sobered up quickly. He didn't respect many of the gods, but he respected Hecate, and he knew when her tolerance for banter was up. "Alas, as much as I'd love to reminiscence in *painstaking* detail, there are things unseen... so here I am." Hermes leaned back, crossing one ankle over his knee, and gesturing around the kitchen.

"God of the unseen, yes," Hecate fought the urge to roll her eyes, "Everyone seems to be using this shift in the regime as quite the power grab."

"Things unseen, messages, tricks..." Hermes shrugged, "You can't say that they aren't all very fitting."

"Mm." Hecate's voice was noncommittal as she returned her gaze to the flames while she continued to speak to Hermes. "Do you want to elaborate? It is the Underworld, after all. 'Things unseen' is hardly distinctive."

Hermes opened his mouth when there was a low rumble of power that swept through the house. Hecate jumped to her feet, the heads of the maiden and the crone flashing on her shoulders. The power rattled the jars on her shelves and caused a cloud of mist to gather around their feet, disembodied faces peering at them through the fog. Hermes blanched as though he had eaten something unpleasant, relatively unused to the power of the Underworld. The very walls seem to vibrate with it as the light from outside dimmed.

"Hades," Hecate's voice echoed as red power flickered across her skin, "Rein it in or don't enter my house." White light began to take over her eyes until they glowed. Her dogs began to bark, running out of the room with their hackles raised. A moment later, Hades appeared in the doorway, gray, lifeless power erupting over his skin and sucking all the air from the room.

"Goddess." Hades's voice was smooth as silk. "You know I mean no disrespect."

"You know better than to enter my house with your power out," Hecate growled, her voice dropping in pitch once more. Tendrils of red power started pouring from her skin as her three-headed appearance solidified.

Hermes sat down with an amused look on his face, snapping his fingers occasionally to add his own spark to the flames…literally. A slow grin slid over the God of Underworld's face.

"I told you she was a *sight*," Hades said, full of approval, calling out to someone else. Confusion flickered over both of Hecate and Hermes's faces, and a moment later, all Hades's power vanished from the room with a wave of his hand. The three gods stared at one another, Hecate nearly growling before she settled herself and her heads disappeared.

"Well." Hermes clapped his hands together. "This has certainly gotten more exciting."

"What do you mean by this, Hades?" Hecate moved around him and stepped over to her workbench, immediately pulling herbs from their jars and preparing a kettle.

"He means that I've been underestimating you." Poseidon's rich, salty voice filled the room as he stepped in behind his brother. He looked suspiciously dry, and therefore, rather uncomfortable, one hand fidgeting with his coral cuff. The God of the sea had been under the earth for well over a day and he was ready to be home. Hecate nearly snarled, dropping the cup that she was holding.

"Am I meant to host every *fucking* god in the pantheon in my kitchen? Might I remind you that none of you were invited?" Hecate's anger picked up like wind, blowing through the room as her dogs came running back in, growling at both brothers. Hades and Poseidon jumped away from their snapping jaws, dodging to the side. Hades growled back. Hermes sat at the table, still unmoving, his eyes going back and forth between all the gods like he was watching a sporting match. Poseidon, ever the most stoic, bowed his head in respect.

"I apologize for my intrusion... and my brother's." He slapped Hades on the back a little too hard, wiping the smirk from his face. "As for Hermes, well, we've all been apologizing for him for a while."

"Hey!"

Poseidon broke the tension and Hecate's anger faded, leaving a no-nonsense look on her face.

"What can I do for you all?" She stared at each of the gods with a look that made them whither slightly. "The sooner you tell me, the sooner that you can all leave my house."

"I was on my way home, and we were implored to ask you, once more, if you had thought about joining Zeus." Poseidon held his hand up and cut Hecate off before she could shout in outrage once more. "I know. I know. Trust me, intuitive one, I'll do you no more disrespect by asking."

Hermes cocked his head to the side, watching Hades and Poseidon closely. There were tricks and messages aplenty between them, and he was determined to find out what they were.

"You didn't come to the Underworld with your brother to ask *me* again." Hecate's voice was devoid of emotion, making it even more threatening. Poseidon shrugged.

"Well, Hades is always…"

"Not Hades. Zeus. He was here. Do not coax at me with your respect, Poseidon, and then attempt to lie to me in the same breath."

"Hecate—"

"I will dry you out like a fish out of water," she snapped, her patience threatening to cave with all the gods in her kitchen. Hades's eyes went wide as he took a step back, nudging Poseidon forward with his shoulder. The brothers had more power than Hecate, especially combined, but Hecate wasn't just about power. She was about intuition, witchcraft, and revenge; her battles weren't fought with one-on-one power. No, the death blow often came after people had thought they had won, or she had forgotten. She had cultivated a reputation for handling men, both mortal and immortal, who had trespassed against the innocent. Neither Poseidon nor Hades were interested in ending up on her never-ending list.

Hecate was still standing at her counter, and she took a step in their direction.

"Zeus was here. He summoned both Poseidon and me to his side to speak to Erebus again." Hades shrugged and Hecate's power began to bubble over, red sparks covering her skin like freckles. "Now, Poseidon was just leaving."

He needed no more exit, and Poseidon gave a short nod in respect before slipping out of the kitchen. There was a rush of air that smelled like seawater, and the remaining gods felt his presence leave the Underworld. Hecate already knew what had happened, and the tangible flickers of her power only grew stronger.

"First, you come into my home—all of you, uninvited—and you ask me to join Zeus?" Her gaze pinned both Hades and Hermes to the wall.

"Leave me out of that! I made no such request," Hermes whined, crossing his arms over his chest and positively sulking. Hecate continued, nearly shaking a finger at Hades.

"Now you're going to tell me that the three of you cornered Erebus once more."

"I…"

"Don't tell me," she snapped once more, busying her hands with the pot long forgotten. "In fact, I need the both of you to get out of my house or I'll curse the private bits of you that you *do not* want cursed."

Hermes's eyes got wide, and he nodded, an uncomfortable grin sliding onto his face.

"Well," he said, standing and clapping his hands together, "once again, it's been fun. Wonderful getting to see all of you, but that's not a curse that I'm willing to tempt. Hecate, you give men nightmares, me included." Hermes leaned over the counter, in an outrageous act of bravery and kissed her cheek once more. "Never change."

Hermes walked out towards the door, clapping his hand on Hades's shoulder before he leaned in and spoke in a voice only Hades could hear.

"I don't know what you and Poseidon are planning, but I could always bring you a message from Cain if you're looking for advice."

Hades snapped his head towards Hermes with a growl, but the messenger was already down the hall, laughing to himself and running a hand through his gold hair. There was a moment of silence before Hades cautiously took another step inside the kitchen. Hecate had crossed the room and was tossing a few different herbs into the fire, watching as the flames and smoke sparked in different colors. There was a tense atmosphere in the room as the imprints of all the god's power still hung in the air. Hades noticed that there was something on Hecate's face that looked tired, if not just annoyed. She went about her work methodically and hoped that by ignoring him, he would get the hint.

"I believe you were dismissed." Her tone was final, and Hades fought the urge to roll his eyes.

"Erebus is on the way. I thought it would be helpful if I were here for this."

Hecate stood slightly and sat down on the workbench at the table, running her hands over her face.

"When all of this is over, I am going on a very, very *long* vacation from the Underworld."

Hades gave her a soft smile, something indecipherable washing over his face. "You would deserve it." If Hecate had a response for him, there was nothing apparent on her face and nothing was said out loud.

"Here he is."

Hecate sat up straighter, looking towards the door. Only a moment later, a whirlwind of shadows appeared, spinning into the mortal form of Erebus. He blinked a few times, looking back at Hecate and finding himself surprised at Hades's presence. Erebus was tired, and it was written on his face. He carried with him the weight of a man who had been pulled in too many directions.

"Oh, um, hello, Hades…" His tone was sheepish, some of his normal confidence gone, and he ran his hand through his hair nervously. Hecate stared at him like a mother who was waiting on her son to confess his sins.

"I already know," Hecate quipped, leaning her back against the table as she turned her gaze once more to the flames. "You can drop the act."

There was total silence in the kitchen.

Hecate was more than willing to let the men stew in it until they cracked. Hades looked over to Erebus with a shrug as if asking *'what did you expect?'* Erebus's shadows were moving under his skin, desperate to break out and push him from this mortal form. He was uncomfortable enough without being in the bounds of a physical body, which he often only enjoyed with Nyx. The only sound was the snapping of the fire, which continued to change colors and send out different sparks of magic. Hecate stared at them as though she was studying them, and honestly, she was.

It was another few moments before Erebus caved. He sighed deeply, a heavy, fatigued sound that went far beyond the situation they all found themselves in. For a moment, it filled Hecate with pity. She knew that Erebus wasn't anything like the gods; he was just a man, faced for the first time in his long existence with the idea of life without Nyx. But... gods, were all men this *stupid* when it came to women?

"Erebus." Hecate broke the silence, her heart softening for him just an inch. She turned to face him, sighing when she saw how sad his eyes were; they held so much hope that this was somehow the right decision. "It's a battle of gods, not primordials. You'd do well to know that you are bigger than this. If you cannot see it, maybe, you aren't."

The last of the hope left Erebus's eyes.

## 16

Nyx didn't react when Erebus had woken up and slipped away without saying anything. They both knew that there were things unsaid between them. The night that they had spent together, regardless of what had been said out loud, carried too many unspoken fears.

Erebus was afraid that Nyx thought their relationship, after millennia, was fragile. Nyx was worried that if he had been tempted by the gods once, Erebus would be again. If he saw any benefit to stepping into their pantheon, *doing his business in the light,* then how could he love the darkness they shared anymore?

So she let him go.

There was a rumbling in Tartarus as Nyx stirred, dredging herself up to the meadows. She felt like there was something in her that had calcified, burying her heat deep down in her chest. A melancholy had taken up presence in her heart that she had never experienced before. It was a rare thing to break the heart of a primordial.

*If this is what these mortals experience, no wonder they weep and bleed for the attentions of Aphrodite.*

Nyx hid herself in the skies, wanting to keep away from

prying eyes. There was no one that she wanted to see and no one that she wanted to perceive her. When she was in this form, only Erebus could detect her presence. A small part of Nyx's heart admitted that she was only traversing the Underworld in this form to get Erebus's attention. The rest of her heart ignored it.

As she circled over Asphodel, there was a shift in power that got her attention. There were very few gods who had enough of a presence to make Nyx pause, even if it was just for a moment. This was three gods. She knew Hades's signature immediately, but the other two took a second. As soon as she had identified them, a snarl crossed over her invisible face and a surge of anger went through her.

*Zeus, Zeus, Zeus... What a bold little mouse to come into the den of the cat. Do you really think that passage with your brothers would save you?*

Nyx had a short temper and a broken heart, variables which had proven disastrous for women for centuries. The wind had picked up, signaling the arrival of Poseidon in a mortal form, and she let herself float down to the stratosphere as the gods came into view. There were four figures standing on the banks of Styx in a stand-off.

*Just as I thought. Zeus, Poseidon, Hades... Erebus!*

If she had been in a mortal form, Nyx would have released a shriek that could've drowned a siren. The personifications of her heartbreak began to rage against the cages of her body; her borders were liquid and amorphous as magic threatened to choke the sky. Before she plunged the entire world into obsidian, Nyx managed to take one shaky breath and get closer. She watched in utter horror as Zeus pulled a ring off his finger and tossed it to Erebus.

Erebus caught it.

Erebus inspected it.

Erebus nodded.

Erebus left.

Nyx was paralyzed as she saw the gods depart; the deal was made. In that moment, she was an amphora running over with ancient, cosmic power. It leaked out of the cracks in her chest, threatening to drown the world in perpetuity as she leaned down over Asphodel. A great, silent shriek suffocated the rest of the peace out of her body as it threatened to cripple Nyx mid-air. Erebus had gotten into bed with her, encouraged her, swore his fealty to her... and went out to meet Zeus the very next day, accepting his terms.

*Then let there be a war, Erebus, if you so desperately want one.*

Nyx's thoughts turned wicked and vile, thoughts of an eternal night and a blackness that could end worlds consumed her. She struggled to keep her rage contained, desperately trying to conjure images of her acolytes, of bystanders and civilians, those who would suffer if she unleashed her pain on the world. How often do men break hearts and leave the pieces for women to pick up, to cut themselves against, only to strike them down for crying out when they bleed?

*If you were me, Erebus, you would have surrendered to your shadows with this pain and bathed us all in them...*

There were too many thoughts in Nyx's mind as her body was ripped apart through the sky and pulled in each of the four directions. She could hardly focus enough to bring herself back into one form, until a singular thought cut through the static in her soul.

*The Fates.*

Nyx took a deep breath. Then two. Then three. She felt the pieces of her beginning to reassemble from where they had been thrown across the sky with her rage. Slowly, she stepped down to the earth, her feet solidifying on the dirt, in the footprints of Erebus. The rest of her body followed suit and once she was fully corporeal, Nyx set off on foot to keep her power in check.

The Fates sat up a little straighter, making note that Nyx would be early.

))))

"Sister!" The voice was light, melodic, as it rang out through the cavernous hallways.

"Yes, Lachesis?" Clotho's voice was echoed in response.

"Will you get Atropos and meet me in the great hall? It seems—"

"Nyx is here early."

"I'm already in the hall!"

The three voices of the Fates rang out in one song as they constantly talked over one another. Far from the old spinsters of legend, the sisters were impossibly beautiful and lithe. They prepared themselves for the age of the gods by camouflaging their true appearances whenever they were paid a visit, knowing all-too-well how beauty would cause the downfall of many a god. The only souls that they did not hide themselves from were Nyx, Erebus by extension, and Hades—simply because it would be too much work to glamour themselves constantly from those who lived in the Underworld. Clotho especially didn't mind seeking Hades out every once in a while when her sister's company grew too predictable.

The Fates lived in a large estate between Tartarus and Elysium, out of reach from anyone who was sent to either heaven or hell. Their loom was held in a center courtyard, protected on all sides by the estate's walls. More importantly, it was protected through layers of enchantment. If anyone other than the sisters dared to cross into the courtyard and manipulate fate, their existence and memory would dissolve entirely. It was an oblivion that no soul could be recovered from, no matter if they were immortal.

Nyx approached on foot, which confirmed for the sisters

that she was as distraught as they had foreseen. The front door opened to the great hall, making it easier for them to greet guests and keep those guests far from the sister's weaving. The roof was covered in large, wooden beams, and there was a large basin of water in the very center, painted on all sides with glyphs in a language that pre-dated everyone in the room, including Nyx. Swirls of incense smoke curled up towards the ceiling and disappeared as painted tapestries of events future and past hung down from the ceiling.

Along the back wall of the room, sat three floor cushions, each threadbare cotton and worn around the edges. They were the opposite of thrones, simple resting places, where the Fates sat to pass judgement and hold discourse as a reminder that there was nothing simultaneously as simple and resolute as the word of the sisters. There were temples in Greece that were not as carefully designed or reverent in their layout.

It was into this hall that Nyx stepped, pulling on the heavy oak door without announcing her presence. There was no point, and she knew that, having a long, respectful relationship with the Fates. She had never once come to them in a panic, begging or pleading for them to change course, except on her acolyte's behalf. To only cry about destiny once in her long, primordial life showed an acceptance and doggedness about Nyx that the sisters had long admired. Each of them was now seated on the floor, soft smiles making their way across the sister's faces in tandem as the primordial stepped fully inside.

"It's creepy when your faces move at the same time." Nyx raised an eyebrow, a smirk of her own appearing on her face. She made her way across the tiled floor, gliding as if her feet had disappeared back into the ether. The sisters sat up a little straighter, eyeing her for a second before they broke into laughter.

Each of the Fates stood up and went to meet Nyx, the Goddess of night and the sisters meeting in the middle of the room. They kissed one another's cheeks and stroked each other's hair, finding that rare form of companionship amongst powerful women that knew too well what awaited them in the world of gods and men.

"What troubles you, Nýchta? Tell us," Lachesis inquired, tilting her head to the side.

"Tell us."

"Tell us." The sisters echoed one another. Nyx took a deep breath and felt her tears quickly threatening to fall. She hadn't anticipated that all it would take was one question, asked with care, to make her break.

"You already know." Nyx tried to laugh it off with a wave of her hand, her eyes going to the statues that lined the walls. "I don't know why you want me to rehash it."

"We need to hear it from you."

"Hear it from you."

"Hear it from you." The trio once more nodded in agreement. Nyx sighed, looking between the sisters before landing on Atropos.

"Erebus has agreed to join Zeus and his brothers in this war on Kronos. I want nothing to do with this. Now... Now he's gone behind my back and joined them. Is there..." Nyx paused, cursing herself for how weak she thought she sounded. "Is there any hope for us?"

She searched the Fates' faces for pity and breathed a sigh of relief when she saw none. They looked at her with concern, maybe with even a little solidarity, but there was no pity to be found in their soft gazes.

"The night and the darkness will always have to be together."

"Always have to be together."

"Always have to be together."

Nyx fought back a grimace as she heard the words repeated thrice. It was hard enough reckoning with the betrayal in her chest, hearing *'together'* just once sent another twang of something uncomfortable down her spine.

"How?" Nyx's voice grew a little more desperate as she scanned the sister's faces. The longer that you asked the sisters questions, the vaguer that the answers became. Their eyes had begun to glow white, and they lost some of the expressiveness of their faces as they succumbed to their trances. The sisters who Nyx had greeted as friends were gone, and the Fates, who were abysmally detached from everything and everyone, had taken their place. The smoke from the incense scattered around the room began to inexplicably pick up, filling the room with rosemary.

The sister's eyes were now completely white, glowing with an intensity that made Nyx and all her darkness want to back away. Their expressions were gone. The Fates' bodies began to levitate a few inches off the floor, moving through the air until they had filed in a straight line in front of Nyx. They opened their mouths, one voice ringing out through the hall although their lips didn't move.

"LISTEN NOW, *God of darkness, Goddess of night.*
  *Be careful to dissuade yourselves from Zeus's plight —*
  *If what we caution is what comes to pass,*
  *The night Nyx fights will be her last."*

NYX'S HAND flew up to her face as she felt a cold chill go down her spine and a wet, creeping panic settled into her bones. It made her want to shake out of her mortal form and desperately hope that those feelings of increasing anxiety would stay trapped in its anatomical prison. Her thoughts began to pick up in intensity and her mind raced, wondering what it could possibly mean that the Fates were issuing her the same warning as Hecate.

What was she supposed to do? Erebus knew that she

couldn't fight. If she entered this war, if she sided with *Zeus's plight*, then somehow… it would kill her.

She knew that prophecies had a way of being cryptic, especially one that was repeated by the Fates, but as she raced through any potential double meanings, Nyx found none. The Fates were quiet, still hovering in their trance state, and Nyx felt herself breathing quickly. She had never come face-to-face with fear in such a tangible way. Combined with the loss of Erebus in her mind, Nyx was convinced for the first time in her long existence that she might already be dying.

"What does that mean?" Nyx shrieked again, tossing herself down at the feet of the Fates. She bowed to the sisters, weeping on the floor as her tears soaked the mosaics underneath her. Her face was pressed up against the cool stone while she screamed, her voice nearly going out at the desperation. Nyx sucked in one sharp breath, gasping for air, only to let out another strangled cry—one that was so loud, so full of power and heartbreak, that all the windows in the great hall shattered. Glass went flying all around the room as nightfall swept in, dark waves of clouds pouring in the room like water.

The Fates didn't move as they answered her question.

"*Listen now, God of darkness, Goddess of night.*
   *Be careful to dissuade yourselves from Zeus's plight —*
   *If what we caution is what comes to pass,*
   *The night Nyx fights will be her last.*"

Nyx bellowed, her body exploding into a million pieces as she erupted from within. Her mortal form was gone and only the primordial goddess remained. She rose to the rafters, filling the entire great hall, as she stared down at the floating figures of the Fates.

"Have I not already died?" Nyx screamed, her voice deep

as it echoed over the entire Underworld. "Is this not already my final night? Is this not the pain that any mortal feels upon death, ten times over?"

The Fates said nothing, but the glow started to diminish from their eyes as they sank back down to the floor. Nyx paused and took in a shaky breath, looking around the room as the sisters pulled themselves from their unified trance into their individual bodies. The great hall had been destroyed, remnants of Nyx's dark power all over the room and glass covering every square inch of the floor. Even the tapestries had been shredded at the sound of her shrieks. A deep, profound embarrassment overcame Nyx like she was coming off a high.

Nyx eyed the open, broken windows and decided that she didn't want to be present when the sisters regained their consciousness. She dissipated and slipped out of the room like smoke, disappearing entirely in the skies of the Underworld. She made it back to Tartarus and began winding down, down, down...so deep into the center of the Earth that no one would ever be able to find her.

## 17

**N**yx didn't know how much time passed in the depths as she let herself bleed out of her edges until she was one with the blackness. It couldn't have been more than a day; her duties would pull her from her solitude to usher in nightfall. She knew that there was no heartbreak that could transcend her responsibilities.

*That's the problem… isn't it? What if the source of your heartbreak is the one who sends your darkness out into the world?*

She groaned at the idea of pushing Helios out of the sky without Erebus behind her. It could be done, that wasn't the question, but it would pull her focus. Her attention would be ripped from the stardust and the moon's tears, entirely pinpointed on dragging that blanket of obsidian across the sky. There would be no artistry, no intuition, and even the constellations wouldn't shine as bright. There was no being alive as powerful as Nyx, picking up Erebus's mantle wouldn't diminish her, but it tore her from her essence. It would turn her into both the judge and executioner, neither job being done entirely to completion.

There was a soft ripple of power in the darkness that pulled

Nyx from her thoughts. Her breath caught as she peered out into the void, waiting to sense or to see who had managed to find her in the deepest parts of the world. Even Hades, God of the Underworld as he claimed, couldn't sense her here. Yet, there it was, a soft song of power that echoed throughout the sky that stuck to it like tar.

*Erebus.*

Nyx should have known that only he would ever be able to find her here. When she hid in the darkness, there was no place that Erebus wouldn't be able to follow. Her heart leaped in her chest as she recognized him, only to curse herself a moment later for her weakness.

"Nýchta?" Erebus's voice was melodic. It was always amplified and its most resonant when it was in the depths, calling out to her. Nyx felt her soul twist at his call and kept her mouth shut, entirely unsure what to say, even though she knew he could sense her, too.

"Nýchta." There it was again, softer this time, but closer and no longer a question. Nyx watched as Erebus descended into his body, a peace offering of sorts. He stood there in the darkness, peering out into it as if he could see her, and she knew that he could. Even as she was barely more than ether, Nyx knew that he was the only person who would always see her. *Could* always see her. Regardless of the form that she took or how deeply she retreated, only Erebus would be able to bring himself to her. She waited for a moment and watched him standing in the deepest pit of Tartarus, unperturbed and patient. A deep well of fresh heartbreak spread in her chest as she forcibly reminded herself that this was the man that had betrayed her.

She replayed the scene of Erebus and Zeus over and over in her head, refusing to take her attention off it, until the pain was swallowed up by anger. Only then did Nyx follow suit and dropped down into her body.

"Erebus." She answered him coldly, taking one step towards her lover, stardust dripping down her dark hair like water. She stopped a few feet short of him, her face settled into a stony look. Nyx studied him closely, taking in his expression. He was in the same black clothing that he always wore; his hair was curling around his temples as if he had been running his hands through it too often.

Erebus sensed this and held his hands out by his sides; something about his reaction only infuriated Nyx further. She sucked in a breath, preparing to cast him out of the Underworld, when he spoke first.

"I need to tell you. I need you to understand..." Erebus's voice cracked, and his eyes filled with tears as he stared at Nyx, watching each movement of her face as if he was predicting her next steps. The sadness that poured from him startled Nyx, her brow furrowing as she watched him. She had expected a petulant Erebus, maybe even an angry or stubborn Erebus, but not *this*. He looked like he was ripping himself in two from the inside—in that moment, Nyx realized that chest-cleaving sorrow was the only thing that they now shared.

"Tell me what, Erebus? What do you think that you could possibly *have kept from me?*" Nyx felt herself melting into hatred, and she did nothing to stop it. Erebus's eyes got wide as he realized that she knew.

"N-no, look...you must believe me. I wanted to tell you myself. I've come to tell you myself."

"Say the words," Nyx growled, taking a step towards him as the heat in her veins began to spark, flickers of black magic running up and down her arms like goosebumps. Her hair started to levitate, shooting stars like fissures hanging off the ends and electrifying the air around her. She stared at him with an unholy halo of black and purple magic illuminating her head.

Erebus's shadows reacted on instinct, not recognizing the

threat as his consort, and began shooting out of him at all angles. Tendrils and tentacles of black, thick smoke poured from his body, rushing around the couple, forcing them in the center of a tornado of shadows. The wind created by the current pushed the two of them even closer together, brows furrowed and ancient, primordial power clashing in the eye of a storm. It was lucky that Nyx had retreated to the deepest circle of Tartarus. If this confrontation had taken place anywhere else in the realms above or below, it would've caused utter destruction.

"Say the words," Nyx screamed, her finger flying up to Erebus's face as she accused him. "If you were bold enough to do it, you should be bold enough to *say it!*"

Erebus growled, his eyes growing even darker as his body went tense. His lip curled in a snarl as he took another step closer to Nyx, leaving no space between them. If either one of them moved, they would be touching.

"I've joined Zeus." His tone was factual as if he was reporting on the weather and not betraying Nyx with every step he took towards her.

"Get out of my sight." Nyx dismissed him with a wave of her arm as she felt herself preparing to strike. The words rang around in her head, and the only thing that she could see was Zeus tossing Erebus his ring.

"Do you not want to listen to what I have to say? Or do you want to have a tantrum and ask questions later?"

"Listen," Nyx shrieked, comets falling from the hem of her chiton. "Listen to you like you said you would listen to me?"

"Circumstances have changed!"

"Oh, *enlighten* me, Darkness!" Nyx started laughing manically, her eyes beginning to go black.

"Everything that I have done, I have done for you!" Erebus's voice dropped lower as he grabbed Nyx's wrist, pulling her finger out of his face. "Have you considered trusting someone for once in your long life?"

"Trust! You want to talk to me about trust?" Nyx attempted to pull her wrist free but only managed to pull herself closer to Erebus. They were both breathing hard, swirls of dark magic and shadows circling around them.

"I do since you can't seem to trust a single decision that I make."

"It's not your decisions I don't trust. It's your logic behind them!"

"Have you really started to believe I don't want the best for you? What would be so terrible about knowing that I'd go to war for you? Die for you?"

Nyx recoiled as if she had been struck, her chest heaving as she grit her teeth. Erebus refused to let her budge as one of his arms dropped around her waist, anchoring her to him. He leaned down and closed the distance between them until his lips almost grazed hers. There was pain in his eyes, so apparent that it almost overrode Nyx's anger. She battled the crippling desire to comfort him like she had always done.

"I'll repeat myself. What would be so terrible about knowing that I'm going to war for you?"

"You could DIE, Erebus!" Nyx screamed, finally letting her tears fall as power crested uncontrollably around them. She laid it out on the table, pushing aside her concerns about Zeus and the human world, terrified that the prophecy might extend to him, too. Erebus pulled back only briefly in shock, staring at the brokenness on Nyx's face as she struggled to contain herself. She opened her mouth again to speak, but Erebus closed the gap between them, crushing his lips to hers, silencing them both.

It was a nearly hurtful embrace, as they poured all their pain into the kiss. Nyx let out a small cry of surprise before she threw her arms around Erebus's neck, running her tongue along his lips in silent invitation. He wasted no time opening himself up to her, both devolving to tongues and teeth, clashing

and pushing against one another with their pain that masquer-
aded as hate.

Erebus's hand moved up and tangled itself in her hair, gripping it tight and pulling until Nyx broke the embrace and
stared up at him. They were both breathing heavily, staring at
one another with a hundred things unsaid and a thousand
miles between them. Neither one of them were able to reign in
their power, and it continued to ebb around them, cocooning
them in a torrent of shadows and a storm of shooting stars.
Erebus looked down at Nyx's expression, watching how
starlight caught in her hair as his shadows weaved in and out
of their legs.

"Do you think even death could keep me apart from you?"
Erebus's voice was low and barely intelligible over the din of
the storm around them.

"When darkness dies, Erebus, where does it go?" Nyx's
eyes were full of tears as she stared at him.

In lieu of an answer, Erebus wrapped his other arm around
her waist and pulled her to him once more. He kissed her
again, losing himself in the embrace as if he could commune
entirely with her through the undying need that he had for her.
Nyx's arms went from around Erebus's neck to gripping his
shoulders, feeling his body tense and flushed behind her fingertips, desperate for more. She squeezed him again, still furious
but unable to contain her desire for him and deciding she
didn't want to.

Nyx pulled away from Erebus as if she had been burned,
realization pooling in her gut like a stone. He had betrayed her,
but she still wanted him. There would be time for her to hate
herself for it later.

"Nýchta?" Erebus asked quietly, leaning down and
brushing his forehead against hers. Nyx shook her head.

"Don't… just… don't."

"Maybe we should…" Erebus stopped, his grip on her loosening but unable to let go of her entirely. His eyes were searching but Nyx was resolute.

"No." Both of their powers were still unyielding, the storm around them increasing to a fever pitch as Nyx tugged Erebus down to the ground with her. She threw a leg over his waist and settled herself on top of him, grinding her hips down in one movement that made Erebus's mind go blank. Anger bled between the two of them until it was indistinguishable; Nyx dragged her hands down his chest until she tugged the folds of his chiton off.

Erebus groaned, tossing his head back as sweaty curls stuck to his forehead. His hands crept up Nyx's legs until he gripped her thighs, his hips moving on their own accord as he bucked up to meet her. Nyx leaned down and captured Erebus's mouth in a kiss once more, Erebus letting out a low grunt as she bit his lower lip until it bled. Nyx licked it up before sucking his lip into her mouth, driving her hips against him as she went nearly mad feeling his hardness against her.

She let out a soft whine, one hand going to her own peplos until she bunched the fabric up around her waist. Erebus sat up so they were face to face, Nyx sitting up straighter as she slowly sat back down over Erebus, guiding him inside of her. Erebus's teeth ground together as she went tortuously slow, her head falling back as she adjusted to him. They sat there for a single moment, both suspended somewhere in between an all-consuming need for one another and hatred; the latter of which was something neither of them had ever felt when looking at one another. It was the kind of hatred that could only come from heartbreak, the kind of anger that could only incubate alongside intimacy.

Something silent passed between them and the storm broke. Lightning flashed about them as shadows went spiraling, comets raining down between them as constellations came to life in the dark skies. It was like being caught alive in the middle of a cosmic upheaval. Erebus growled, wrapping his arm tighter around Nyx's waist, and flipped them over. He braced his hands on either side of her head, and she let out a cry as he shifted inside her.

"Nýchta," he growled, the nickname now sounding like a threat.

"Move, Erebus," Nyx hissed back at him, her lip curling as she raked her hands down his back. He let out a low grunt and pulled out completely from Nyx, making her whine at the loss, until he pushed forward and buried himself inside of her. Her head fell back in a silent scream as Erebus laughed darkly, his own mirth getting choked off by a groan as Nyx clenched around him. Erebus picked up a grueling pace, pistoning his hips into her as she drove her body up to meet his thrusts. There was nothing considerate or tender between them, each pull and push accentuated by harsh grips and biting teeth.

Nyx tried to keep herself together as if she didn't want to give him the satisfaction, but there was nothing she could hide from him. Erebus growled, dropping his hand between them and pressing up against her in slow circles until she came with a startled cry, black magic pouring out of her fingertips and hair. Erebus thrust himself between her thighs once more, shadows blanketing the darkness as he collapsed against her. He stayed there for only a moment, catching his breath until the atmosphere between them shifted and he rolled off her. Nyx winced at the loss of him but turned away from him, nonetheless.

The magic faded. The power receded. The storm calmed down around them. Erebus finally felt his heart rate drop, and he sat up, peering into the depths of Tartarus. All the starlight was gone…and so was Nyx.

Erebus was alone and naked on the cold ground, something having been severed inside of him.

Nyx had left, leaving a trail of fading stardust on the ground. Erebus stared after it until it faded completely, leaving something glinting in the blackness. He stood and took a few steps, adjusting his chiton as he went, before leaning down and picking the shining object up.

It was Nyx's pin, the brooch that she wore on her shoulder. It was inscribed with the ancient names of both darkness and night, featuring a carved image of them working together.

A sick realization settled over him. Nyx had denied Erebus.

## ❦ 18 ❦

When Nyx slipped away from Erebus, she left Tartarus and didn't look back. Her brooch had made a sickening thud on the ground and left a corresponding crack in her chest. She couldn't do it. Even when they had pulled one another down to the ground and given in to their need for each other, the only thing that she could see in Erebus's eyes anymore was betrayal. The crest had fallen off her shoulder, and her mind only wondered if Erebus were to wear it, would it match Zeus's ring?

Her mind cried out that anything that had ever existed between them was dead, but it wasn't that simple. What did death even mean to a couple like her and Erebus? The thing that always existed between them was their existence, the way they had pulled themselves from starlight to be with one another, birthed themselves into existence, designed to fit the other's purposes. Nyx designed the lines of her body to give him harbor, and he had crafted his shadows to bow to her will. The pain inside of her chest threatened to break her into dust, and she toyed with the idea of retreating beneath Gaia or exploding herself into stars.

Nyx walked until she could go no further, finally letting

herself slip free of her mortal body. She had held onto it for longer than she normally would, feeling like it was the only thing that could hold her together. The wind picked up, and she dissolved into the sky, becoming endless, moving across the horizon until she crossed out of Tartarus. The lights of Asphodel warmed over her skin, and Nyx sighed in relief. She would have felt her cheeks grow hot with shame as she realized that leaving the darkness behind had brought such relief.

She touched down once more, hidden amongst one of the many groves in the meadows, sliding down an oak tree like smoke and pooling at its roots. She wanted to feel small. She waited, anxiety pooling under her skin like ants and finding herself unable to focus on anything. Finally, she sprung up in her human form again, finding solace in the physical action of breathing. Nyx leaned back against the tree and sank back down, burrowing her fingers and toes into the dirt. Her countenance was only just coming back to her when she heard a twig snap in the distance behind her.

Nyx moved slowly, knowing that whatever was lurking in the forests of Asphodel couldn't possibly harm her. She stood up and sent her power out in a wave through the topsoil, evaluating who it was. Her power ran up against someone, someone whose power sang like hers. She broke into a smile. *Thanatos.*

Nyx said nothing but pulled her power back, stepping out from behind the tree and waiting. A few moments later, a grinning Thanatos stepped into the small grove, a serene look on his face. If there was one thing that Nyx had always envied her twins, it was peace. Both Thanatos and Hypnos were slow to anger, always calm and always transcendent. It was hard to get worked up over anything when your job was either to sleep or to die.

Thanatos stood taller than his mother when he took mortal form, with hair that was even darker than his father's. It was an inky-black color that almost looked blue in the light, if you could ever catch him there. His hair was cropped shorter than most of the gods', sticking up from his head at odd angles. The only visible difference between Thanatos and Hypnos was that Hypnos's hair was longer and always tied up with a piece of cord.

Thanatos didn't wear a chiton in his mortal form, either, further distinguishing himself from the rest of his immortal brethren. He wore hoplite armor, missing a weapon and a shield because what would death need with a weapon? His presence stilled everything around him, no matter where he went. Thanatos was nothing if not fair, but he was merciless. Once a decision had been made and the Fates had called their shot, there was nothing a mortal or a god could do to avoid his touch. Nyx didn't know if she had ever heard him raise his voice. He was gentle in his absoluteness but ruthless in his execution. He had his brother Hypnos's touch with a lethal edge. Thanatos was the God of death.

"Mother." Thanatos smiled warmly, crossing over to her and extending his arm. He wrapped it around her shoulders in a short, warm embrace before kissing her cheek respectfully. "I thought I might find you here."

"You thought you would find me in an unnamed grove in Asphodel? Really?" Nyx raised an eyebrow at her son. "You betray yourself. Be honest." Thanatos didn't blush but simply tilted his head to the side, nodding once in defeat as his smile dropped.

"I've sensed the disruption between you and father. We all have. Whatever argument you just came from nearly broke the mortal world in half." Nyx's eyes went wide as she took a step back in shock. Thanatos never held a punch.

"We were... We were deep within Tartarus." Nyx defended herself. "I never would have argued with your father like that if we thought it would affect..."

Thanatos held up a hand and cut her off. "I'm not

concerned with it." The smirk crossed his face once more. "It keeps me busy."

Nyx sucked her teeth once and looked at her son with a chiding expression. "What an awful thing to say." Thanatos's expression was unrepentant.

"It's true. Who cares?"

Nyx fought the urge to roll her eyes as she collected herself. "Was that what you came to tell me, then?"

"No. There was a moment today... briefly..." Thanatos struggled with his words, something that Nyx had never seen before. "Where the bells called for you, and you were on my list. I came straight here to see if you were okay. You are my mother, after all." He smiled softly, devoid of any teasing or malice. Thanatos looked at Nyx more closely, seeing the confusion and exhaustion behind her eyes. Her power felt different... until he realized that it was because it was decoupled from Erebus's.

Nyx found herself fighting back tears as she cursed her human body and the shock that was running through her. What could it mean that Death had almost come to collect her? The prophecy had only stated that it was certain if she fought with Zeus. Nyx quickly bottled up her questions and stared at her son, refusing to break in front of him.

"What, did you and Hypnos flip a coin?"

"No, he wanted to go see Father," Thanatos deadpanned.

"Well. I am here. Your father is in Tartarus, presuming. He has... He has decided to join Zeus." Nyx scanned her son's faced for any reaction and was not surprised she didn't see one. He didn't react to much; he was too far removed from the mortal world, let alone the games of gods.

"This angers you?" Thanatos asked inquisitively, his tone genuine. Nyx nodded.

"I asked him not to." Her voice was hardened and resolved but full of chaos and the remnants of her calcified heart. "He did it anyway. Then he had the nerve—" Nyx was cut off as

Thanatos reached out and pulled her to him, tightening his arms around her once in a warm embrace. He let go only a moment later, pulling back and bracing his arms on his mother's shoulders.

"You'll figure it out." He sounded confident. There was a glimmer in his nearly black eyes that was undetectable. Nyx looked at him in surprise, and he only shrugged once more, taking a step back. She could hear the bells in the distance that cried out for her son. Death stayed busy.

"You're very certain of this." Nyx studied him as if he hid the secret somewhere on his person, backing away to depart to the mortal realm once more.

"I know what death feels like. I know what it smells like." Thanatos stopped, his voice going cold but somehow gentle in its resolution. "There is a part of you that has died, but it hasn't won out yet."

Nyx felt the blood leave her face as she stared after her son. "What does that mean?"

"It means, luckily, you aren't on my list today." Thanatos disappeared into the wind as the sound of bells grew louder and stopped altogether, the God of death swept up in his never-ending duties. Nyx almost screamed in frustration as she felt rage rising in her once more, faced once again with a problem she couldn't solve and half-answers from those she trusted most.

Nyx's power crested with each wave of anger that pulled at her limbs until she burst into the sky, ripping down the light with it. She was tired of crying. She was tired of being upset. She was tired of feeling afraid of the dark. All of Nyx's powers began swirling through the skies of the Underworld, soaking up the clouds until dusk was painted across the horizon. She let herself expand... expand... expand... anchoring her essence into every crevice of the Underworld in a way that she had not allowed herself since her creation. The souls began shrieking in confusion as the Underworld was plunged into an eternal wave of black and purple magic.

*Let there be night.*

))) )

EREBUS SAT in darkness until Hypnos roused him from it, pulling him back from the edge of the world. He watched a few hours later as the Underworld descended into night, feeling something churning in his stomach as he felt the sky change over to something else entirely. This was night, an eternal night, and there was nothing for him in it. He could sense from the way the power moved through the atmosphere that there was no call to him and no grace for his darkness. No, this was Nyx bringing about nightfall on her own, and it was clear that Erebus wasn't invited.

There wasn't a place for him in the Underworld, especially in this dusk that Nyx had created. Erebus made his way to the edge of Asphodel, following Styx all the way up to Charon's crossing. Hypnos and Thanatos were the twins, and Charon was Nyx and Erebus's youngest son. *Youngest* always meant something entirely different to the immortals.

Charon was waiting at the edge of the pier, leaning against one of the wooden supports. He was the most solemn of them all, which was quite the accomplishment when your parents were the primordials of night and darkness, and your twin brothers were sleep and death. He wore a long, gray tunic, with hair that was curled like Erebus's, and thick arms that were corded with muscle from the near-constant rowing. The edges of his tunic were always damp, and he never wore sandals. There was something blank permanently etched onto his face, even though Erebus knew that beneath it was a subtle kindness that calmed down each soul he encountered.

"Father." Charon grinned, clapping his hands together in greeting.

Erebus went to return the embrace, when he stopped in his tracks at the edge of the pier. He watched as the waves crested behind Charon, who glanced over his shoulder at the commotion. There was a whirring of water that turned into a small cyclone above the surface, which deposited a very stoic looking Poseidon on the pier.

"I can't say that I expected to see you here." Erebus raised an eyebrow at Poseidon, taking a step towards him. "Although I guess you are never far from water."

Charon looked like he was going to laugh but held it in, keeping a steady expression on his face as he studied Poseidon. The god ignored Charon entirely, sidestepping him and walking with urgency to close the gap between him and Erebus.

"Listen to me." Poseidon's voice was dark and stormy, and there was something in his eyes that made Erebus's shadows start to appear. He stopped short of Erebus, both eye to eye as shadows met the waves behind them.

"I'm all ears," Erebus growled, feeling threatened by the chaos that the god had brought to his door.

"Everything is not as it seems." Poseidon shook his head. If Erebus knew better, he would say that the god seemed paranoid. "Whatever you do, do *not* trust Zeus. You've chosen this side, and it's something I hold myself responsible for—"

"You are hardly *responsible* for me, Poseidon. You'd do well to remember who's the most powerful one of us."

"I am trying to own up to my part of this if you would listen. Damn it!" Poseidon took a step back and cursed under his breath. He took a deep breath and looked over at Erebus once more. "Zeus is assembling his allies in the mortal realm, at the base of Olympus. War is starting. Your presence has been requested, and I'm trying to warn you." Poseidon's voice dropped to a low hiss, and Charon visibly perked up as he listened in.

"You're here to warn me that Zeus is a tricky bastard? That's hardly new information," Erebus snapped, already annoyed with how many people were trying to insert themselves into his affairs.

Poseidon shook his head. "He's a bastard, but he's not to be underestimated. I'm warning you now, Erebus. Whatever happens… do not trust Zeus."

E rebus stared Poseidon down, looking at Charon over the god's shoulder. There was something sinking in his gut and making him unsettled. He was already tense after his fight with Nyx, especially paired with the eternal night that she was plunging the Underworld into without him. Poseidon wasn't one for idle threats. He might have been partnering with Zeus, but there was something in Poseidon's eyes that made Erebus wary.

"I'm serious." Poseidon's voice dropped and he took another step towards Erebus. The waves of Styx started to pick up behind him, sensing the god's anger. "There is no going back now, but whatever happens, do not believe a word that he says."

"What is this?" Erebus snapped, his shadows rising with the water. "Did you not convince me that this was a good idea? Now you think I'm going to fall to Zeus's side like some lap dog?"

Poseidon only shook his head. There was an expression on his face that Erebus couldn't quite place, looking somewhere between regret and frustration. Charon watched on, unmoving, occasionally looking over his shoulder at the waves. Potentially wondering how much work was waiting for him on the other side of the river the longer that he watched.

"No... no, I don't think that. I only wanted to warn you. There is more than one war at foot, Erebus, and you'd be wise to think about what matters most to you. Whatever it is... keep it at the forefront of your mind."

"Now—" Erebus's voice was exasperated as a shadow wrapped itself around Poseidon's ankle.

"Enough." Poseidon shook his head once and dislodged the shadow, the waves erupting behind him. In the dark of the Underworld, they looked like clouds, crashing and breaking the surface. "I've said enough."

The God of the sea turned and walked back down the pier, giving Charon a respectful nod before he stepped off the edge. Erebus nearly chased him down, but he was gone in an instant. Poseidon disappeared among the water, and it immediately calmed down as if he was an offering it had been waiting for. Erebus paused for a moment, attempting to dissect all the different thoughts running through his head.

He stood there, in the center of the pier on the river Styx, staring out into the abyss. For once in his never-ending existence, Erebus didn't know where to go. He knew that he needed to follow Poseidon and join the other gods and immortals at the base of Mt. Olympus. But Poseidon's warning stuck in his mind on loop. What mattered most to him? It was Nyx. He could answer that without a moment's hesitation and leaving the Underworld with things the way they were broke him.

Charon walked over to Erebus, clasping his father on the shoulders and bending down to meet his gaze.

"Are you having second thoughts?" Charon's voice was smooth, quiet. He had a way of speaking that acted like a balm. Erebus shook his head.

"I've agreed to do this and I will." He stood up to his full height, rolling his shoulders back. "Poseidon is right, though. I

can't leave just yet. I need to speak to your mother again."
Erebus sighed as if he knew he was headed out on a fool's
errand. Charon only nodded, his face impassive—passing
judgement was never his job. He looked over Erebus once
more, sucking on his teeth and resigning himself to whatever
conclusions he came to with a small shrug.

"If you need a ride to the other side, you know where to
find me." Charon walked away without another word before
sliding into his boat and pushing off from the pier. He did it so
quickly and gracefully, if Erebus didn't know any better, he'd
call Charon a ghost. By the time he had blinked, his son was
gone, and Erebus was off to find his wife.

He dissolved out of his mortal form immediately, letting his
form crash into an explosion of shadows. He sent them out in
every direction, scouring and combing through the Underworld's blackness. There was an uncanny feeling as Erebus's
power mixed with the eternal night, and he only paused for a
moment to wonder what peril this was causing the Underworld's other residents. He hardly noticed it. What he did
notice was how it felt so ill-fitting now, that his shadows could
be pouring through the obsidian waves and feel displaced. It
was true, then. He hadn't made a mistake earlier. Nyx had
tossed the Underworld into night and brought the darkness
with it, leaving no space for Erebus. She might as well have
exiled him.

*Unless that's exactly what she was attempting to do.*

Erebus's inner monologue was unnecessarily cruel although
it may have been correct. It didn't take long for Erebus to find
Nyx, however, somewhere beyond the horizon of Elysium. The
fields of Elysium were still empty, giving her some semblance
of peace outside of Tartarus. He materialized once more,
calling his shadows back to him, not wanting to show up in
front of her once more and appear confrontational. Erebus
knew that she was in the ether above him, could see her ethe-
real form just barely outlined in the darkness and the clouds,

so he waited. The primordial God of darkness sat down in the grass fields of Elysium... and waited.

Time was a difficult concept to an immortal. There was no way to tell how long Erebus waited. He was lost in his thoughts, staring off at the blades of grass as they moved, entombed in the night that had not once ceased. Finally, there was a shift in the wind, and a small column of black smoke poured down from the open skies. Erebus waited with bated breath... and Nyx stepped out of it. She kept her distance, not moving towards him, her expression perfectly blank as if she was etched out of stone. Nyx was barely hanging onto her mortal form, her hair drenched in starlight and her peplos tied with strands of moonlight. She took Erebus's breath away.

He stood on shaky legs, letting his shadows envelop him, wrapping around his shoulders and pooling around his feet.

"Nýchta," he pleaded, Erebus sounding broken and small. He looked at her with a lump rising in his throat, his eyes filling with tears as he reached a hand out towards her. "I love you. Please... There has never been anything for me but to exist as an extension of you. No part of me can survive without the magnitude of you as my home. I know you're angry, but please...listen to me. I'm doing this for you. Everything I have ever done, in each lifetime I've lived, is for you."

Erebus felt the crack in his chest grow wider as Nyx stared at him, unmoving. Her eyes glowed entirely white, and comets shot out from her fingertips, her body composed of an entire nocturnal ecosystem and radiating with power that Erebus knew no one alive or immortal could match. She stood, unmoving, transfixed, as if he was talking to a marble statue in a temple. Erebus had never felt more mortal, pleading with an unmovable god as his pleas fell on stone ears.

"Please..." Erebus tried again, dropping to his knees as he buried his head in his hands, pulling on his own hair until it hurt. "I must go. I have to see this through. I cannot stand the thought of those gods running amok and sullying your good name. I... I just..."

Erebus's voice trailed off as he looked up at Nyx with tears running down his cheeks. He sucked in a sharp breath and shook his head, standing. She didn't move.

"I love you. Regardless of day and night, of darkness and of light, no matter what the gods say, or the Fates decide... I love you. Whatever you believe my motivations to be, know this, I did it all for the love of you." Erebus's voice cracked, barely above a whisper, but he got it all out on a choked breath. He managed to look at her once more, but he didn't see Nyx there anymore, the Consort of Darkness. He saw a cosmic, primordial goddess as she stood there among the stars and the moonlight. She was a powerful, other-worldly creature... utterly lost to him.

Erebus turned on his heel and left, never once looking over his shoulder. If he had, he would have seen the mother of night drop to her knees and cry. Nyx cried until starlight poured from her eyes and washed down the hills of Elysium, mixing with the waters of Styx.

Darkness and Night were no more.

》》》

IF YOU LISTENED CLOSELY, you could hear how noisy Hecate's kitchen was. Although the Goddess of witchcraft moved silently, the fire popped in the hearth; her dogs shuffled aimlessly around the table; water boiled and spilled over in her kettle. She was where she could always be found, in her kitchen, the center of her home, still recovering from the intrusion of all the gods. She didn't blink when the Underworld was plunged into endless night, rather, she had expected it. The separation of Nyx and Erebus was going to cause greater problems then Nyx proving a point with eternal darkness.

*Although I can't imagine how taxing that is.* Hecate rolled her eyes as she continued to have a conversation with herself—she was always the best company. *To perform two jobs at once. Even if she is the most powerful of us all, that wasn't what she was made for. They were made for each other.*

Hecate knew that Erebus should know better, but she understood where he was coming from too. Men were blinded by their love, determined to fix whatever they could. He saw the world disrespecting his wife, and he wanted to correct it. Nyx saw an impudent child-god making a power grab, and she wanted Erebus to stay far from it. Which mattered more... who could say. Hecate was deep in concentration muddling together dried lavender and water when she sensed an arrival in her courtyard. Only a moment later, a deep, distressing wave of power ran through her home, and Hecate sucked in a sharp breath at the pain it carried.

*Oh no.*

She wiped her hands on the folds of her tunic, stepping around from her counter and waiting. Nyx appeared in the doorway in her mortal form, sagging against the frame as if existing was a great effort. As soon as she laid eyes on her friend, she burst into tears. Hecate was on her in a moment, pulling Nyx to her chest as they both sank to the floor. Nyx tossed her arms around the goddess and screamed, her body convulsing with the weight of her sobs. Hecate let out a deep sigh, rearranging them both gently on the tile and running her hand through Nyx's hair.

They sat there for a few minutes which felt like an eternity as the energy of Nyx's pain washed over Hecate in waves until Nyx quieted. She let out small, gasping breaths every few seconds as she tried to catch her racing heartbeat. Hecate pulled back slightly so she could see Nyx's face, cupping it with her hands. All she could see was the heartbroken expression of a woman, something that Hecate was well-versed in. She wasn't a primordial, but Hecate understood this kind of all-consuming sadness more than anyone; it was what her acolytes prayed to her for.

"Great one," Hecate sighed gently as if she was coaxing a babe and not the most powerful being in existence. "What pains you like this? Surely it is not Erebus?" Her mind raced as she wondered what else could have caused their fight to escalate so intensely.

"It is only Erebus," Nyx wailed, beating her hands against the floor. Hecate made no move to stop her, knowing that Nyx couldn't *really* hurt herself in mortal form.

"What happened?"

Nyx shook her head, and it took her several tries to get the words out. "He came to me. He told me he loved me… but… but it's not enough. He won't go back on his word, and he's going to leave for Mt. Olympus."

Hecate sighed, leaning her head down to rest it on top of Nyx's, and squeezed her closer, waiting a few more moments as she tried to find the right thing to say. The separation was going to kill Nyx and Erebus before any war did. The eternal night in the Underworld could only last so long until other immortals started asking questions. If Nyx continued to act out in heartbreak, chaos would erupt if she took this to the mortal realm. There were already rumors that Helios had heard of what was happening in the Underworld and was not happy. The gods and immortals were gathering at the base of Mt. Olympus, and tensions were high enough.

"Nyx…" Hecate started slowly. "Do you not realize that Erebus only wants to bring you into the sun so the world might feast upon your glory as he does?" She held her breath when she finished, worried that she might have stepped too far in defending Erebus. Nyx didn't respond for a full minute as her breathing evened out. When she spoke, she didn't look up or attempt to make any eye contact with Hecate.

"I don't care about the attentions of men. I only care about Erebus... who could find me in the dark."

"That's why he has gone." Hades's deep voice echoed through the kitchen, causing Nyx and Hecate to snap their attention to the hallway. Hades stood in the entrance to Hecate's home, down the hall from where they sat in the kitchen's doorway. His dark frame could barely fit. Tendrils of smoky power evaporated off him as he looked at both women with a solemn gaze.

Nyx sucked in a breath and then jumped to her feet, moving before either Hades or Hecate could stop her. She went screeching down the hallway and exploded into her primordial form, waves of power sending shockwaves through the house. Hades barely had time to throw his hands up over his face before Nyx barreled into him, sending both tumbling into the courtyard.

Hades landed with a sickening thud on the mosaicked tiles, and the impact sent cracks in the floor all the way to the edges of the courtyard. The columns shook and the altar spilled over, sending water all over them both. Nyx was barely holding onto a human shape at all, her eyes fully white with rage and power. Hades sputtered and coughed a few times to clear his vision, looking up at the primordial on top of him. Nyx had her hands around his throat as she sat on his chest, her heels digging into the ground and cracking through the stones. He was smart enough to not fight back, knowing that he was no match for Nyx, but waves of gray and black smoke cascaded from him in self-defense he couldn't control.

Nyx shrieked, a sound that shattered the windows in Hecate's house, sending the jars in her kitchen flying to the floor. She seemed to realize what she was doing, and in a moment of clarity, growled and let go of Hades. Nyx's body detonated and utter darkness fell upon the courtyard, constellations being flung all over the walls of Hecate's home like mud splatter. Hecate could sense her back inside the house.

Hades waited for a full five minutes before he dared move, sitting up slowly. He found Hecate standing in the doorway, looking out at her destroyed courtyard with a slow shake of her head.

"You thought you could come convince her of this? Again?" Her voice was admonishing, barely above a whisper, but Hades caught every word. He shook his head slowly before he sat up and rested his arms on his knees.

"I thought I could *remind* her that Erebus loves her." He shrugged, now seemingly unaffected, as if nearly being destroyed by Nyx's power was another normal afternoon.

Hecate studied him, turning her head gently to one side, as she peered deep into his soul. When it came to matters of the heart, she specialized in the vengeance of scorned women, but she could see into a man as well as Aphrodite. There was something at the core of Hades… something warm. It was hidden behind a deathly cold exterior, but it was there. Something was amiss when it came to Poseidon and Hades plotting with Zeus, but whatever was going on, it had bothered Hades enough to come and try to convince Nyx that Erebus loved her. Hecate could only shake her head, turning on her heel and disappearing inside to tend to the primordial in her kitchen.

*What was going on?*

## ✄ 20 ✄

Nyx filled every crevice of Hecate's home, refusing to let Hades drive her from the comfort of her friend's hospitality. It was the only place that she felt like she could breathe; no God of the Underworld was going to take it from her. As she waited in Hecate's kitchen for Hades to leave, she began to fume as she felt the tendrils of his power around the property.

*What else could he possibly have to say?* Nyx's inner monologue growled, causing small shockwaves to shake the kitchen. She was undetectable as she floated above the kitchen table, only traceable by the glimmers of her power. There was too much rage rippling under her skin to keep herself contained in a mortal body. It would be all too easy to listen into the conversation happening outside, but she refused. Finally, she felt Hecate *and* Hades making their way towards the kitchen, sending another shockwave of sharp anger through Nyx. When they walked through the doorframe, Hecate had a warning glare on her face.

"Listen to him." Her words came out sharp as she raised an eyebrow. Nyx attempted to drop her racing heartbeat, slowly materializing out of the air into her body once more. Hecate gave her a warning stare as she took in the waves of black and purple power that erupted under Nyx's skin, betraying her thin temper.

Nyx tossed her hair over her shoulder, her black eyes staring down Hades as he stood at the door. Even though she had thrown him to the ground outside, he hardly looked put out. Hades stared back at Nyx, unafraid but also unchalleng-ing, running a hand through his dark hair before scratching his beard absentmindedly as if he had all the time in the world to make it through this conversation. His own power, actualized as gray smoke, curled around his broad shoulders like a mantle. Nyx let out a sharp breath through her nose as her brow furrowed.

"Is there something else that you wish to say to me, Hades?" At the sound of his name, shooting stars shot out from under the hem of her tunic like sparks. Every wall in Hecate's home creaked again as it bowed under the weight of a primor-dial and a god barely able to contain their powers.

"Nyx..." Hades's voice had changed, dropping lower and carrying a severity with it that even Nyx had to recognize. "Erebus loves you. You need to try and understand what we're trying to do—"

"If one more person tries to tell me what I *need* to do, I will wipe them from existence." Nyx stood, not abandoning her body but letting it grow taller until she grazed the ceiling. Her hair whipped around her shoulders as the kitchen began to shake. Any jars or pottery that had not already been knocked off their shelves went tumbling to the floor. Even the fire started to leap higher as it consumed the kettle sitting above it entirely.

"Don't do it..." Hecate warned, feeling her power rise in response to the threat to her hearth.

"I am trying to *help* you!" Hades's control finally snapped, and he stormed into the kitchen. He let his god-form overtake him until he was eye-to-eye with Nyx, his eyes glowing gray and his body tense. Gray shadows wrapped themselves around his chest and arms, visibly trembling with restraint. Nyx only growled in return as a black hole appeared behind her, slowly beginning to expand. Hades remained unmoved as his hands tightened into fists at his side.

"Try me," Nyx hissed, her voice beginning to echo and sounding utterly inhuman as the humanity bled from her eyes. "Do you want to see where the God of the Underworld goes when he dies?"

Hades roared in response, and there was a sonic boom as the two immortals collided into one another. The house began to shake as tiles fell from the roof and cracks appeared in the walls.

"Nyx," Hecate shrieked, crouching down behind her counter and holding on for dear life as jars and herbs went flying into the portal. "Stop this!"

Her pleas landed on deaf ears as Nyx and Hades unleashed the full torrents of their powers on one another. There was no scenario in which Hades could overpower her, but Nyx remained cautious that if she simply ripped open the universe to consume him, there would be collateral damage.

Hecate gripped her counter and hauled herself up, her hair whipping wildly around her as the power in her kitchen threatened to destroy it. She peered over the edge as she watched both Hades and Nyx try to rip the other apart. They had dissipated entirely into their god forms, clouds of gray and black smoke, and only when they moved forward to strike would their faces appear amongst the chaos. Hecate stared, partially in awe and partially in disbelief, at Nyx as stars began to orbit around her.

She was a terrible sight, and it was in that moment that Hecate understood the full extent of why Zeus was afraid of the Goddess of night. There was a black hole behind Nyx, framing her body as her long hair stuck out at all angles in a perverse halo. Beacons of purple, black, and blue magic would combust from her in waves as stars and comets shot out from the folds of her garments. Wind whipped around her, containing all the sounds of the night, wolves howling and owls shrieking. Nyx's eyes were completely white, and her lip was curled back in a snarl, as she stuck a hand out towards Hades. Dark tendrils, like tar, shot out from the ends of her fingers and pierced through the clouds until they disappeared.

Hecate didn't need to wait to know if they hit their target. Hades emerged from the other side of the kitchen with a shout. He ripped the shadows off him, and Hecate could see red marks, like claw marks, across his half-naked chest where he had been struck. He might have been outgunned, but Hades would not go down in his own realm without a fight to the very end. His eyes were now pitch-black and wild, something utterly calm in the very center of his gaze, something...dead. Any warmth that Hecate had sensed in Hades was now gone. His hair was matted to his forehead with sweat and gray shadows still wrapped around his biceps like an extension of his body.

Hades launched himself towards Nyx, snarling like one of his own beasts of hell, cocking a fist back as he did so. A wave of gray smoke filled the entire kitchen, momentarily snuffing out Nyx's cosmic light show. It was so thick, it took a moment for Hecate to catch her breath. Hades came crashing down right in front of Nyx, slamming his fist into the ground, causing the one of the exterior walls of the house to come crashing down. The impact sent out a shockwave of cold power that instantly froze everything around it. It was so cold that it burned hot. It took Hecate a moment to realize that the absence of warmth caused by Hades's power was the absence of *life*.

"You want to know where the God the Underworld goes when he dies?" Hades snarled, and his voice echoed throughout each corner of hell. He picked his head up as Nyx shook frost off her shoulders, the black hole growing behind her as it now threatened to take the kitchen table with it. "You can't kill what's already dead, Nyx."

Nyx let out a guttural scream, her hand shooting forward and wrapping around Hades's neck once more. She leaned down and stared at him, their powers cascading against one another, merging and opposing like oil and water.

"There are things far worse than death, *Hades*."

Hades stood to his full height, shaking his shoulders as he stared at Nyx. Neither of them moved, and Hecate held her breath, still anchoring herself to the kitchen counter. The portal behind Nyx had stopped growing, but it was still threatening to pull the whole house in on itself. Some of the light faded from Hades's eyes as he cocked his head to the side, slowly coming back to a mortal form as he waited. As quickly as he had lost control, Hades seemed to regain it as if he had remembered why he was there in the first place. The warmth that Hecate had sensed in him returned.

"You're experiencing it now." Hades acknowledged, his voice quiet as Nyx tightened her grip on his throat. "For what it's worth, I am sorry."

As soon as he said those words, a switch flipped in Nyx. Her eyes went wide, and the white power seeped from them, her dark irises slowly coming back into focus. She shrunk down to her mortal height and released her grip on the god. The black hole behind her began swirling in a clockwise direction until it caved in on itself. Without removing her gaze from Hades, Nyx waved two fingers in the air and everything that the portal had consumed came crashing down from the ceiling onto the floor, which effectively broke all the jars, pottery, and furniture that had disappeared.

Hecate stood to her full height with a relieved sigh and a roll of her eyes. "Thank you. I'm so glad you thought to return my things after you nearly ripped a hole in the universe in my kitchen." She leaned against the counter and tried to catch her breath, both Hades and Nyx still staring at one another.

They had regained their human bodies—Hades looking like he had emerged from a fight with the Nemean lion, and Nyx giving off the appearance of someone who had walked out of the center of a hurricane. A broken expression crossed Nyx's face, only for a second, but it was enough that both Hecate and Hades saw it.

Hades sighed, rubbing the back of his neck with his hand as he looked up at the ceiling. "No one wanted it to be this way. If you believe anything that I say, please believe that." Nyx nodded but said nothing, wrapping her arms around herself as if she'd never be warm again. When she turned and looked at Hades, a little flicker of power danced in her eyes again.

"Resolve this. End it. Quickly." There was a reverberation in her voice that sent chills down Hades's spine, and he knew that the next time Nyx lost control, she'd take the everyone with her. "Or I swear, Hades, I will swallow the entire world in night."

Hecate couldn't help but utter a sharp gasp, her hand flying up to cover her mouth. She knew that Nyx was hurting, but she never thought that her friend would threaten the balance of the universe. It was the one thing that she always strived to protect. Hades studied Nyx once more before he gave her a curt nod of recognition. There was another moment of silence in the kitchen before Hades turned on his heel, walking towards the door with his hands up. When he got to the door-frame, he stopped and called out over his shoulder.

"Nyx, tell me this… what is night without its darkness?"

The primordial had been staring down at the ground and whipped her head up as she snapped in response.

"Perpetual."

Hades shook his head. "Unbalanced." He was gone before Nyx could offer any rebuttal. She sank down in front of the fire, which miraculously was still going strong. Hecate said nothing, knowing Nyx would start speaking when she wanted to. For the rest of the afternoon, Nyx didn't move. She sat in front of Hecate's hearth and mourned, dying a thousand deaths over. By the time the sun had set in the mortal world, she had not let her night release its grip on the Underworld.

Hecate moved around quietly for the rest of the day, slowly reassembling her kitchen and her apothecary stores. If there was anything that she held sacred, she knew not to disturb a heartbroken woman who had fallen at her hearth. Was Nyx not sitting in the very place that woman prayed to Hecate from all over the world? Hecate didn't know if Nyx had chosen that spot instinctually or randomly, but it was sacred; Hecate would not disturb her if she was in front of the fire.

Luckily, reassembling clay and brick was easy for a goddess, and Hecate was making quick work of the repairs to her home. She was about to start work on her missing exterior wall when there was a bright flash of light like a falling star. Hecate jumped back with a small shriek, her hands going to her hips.

"If there is one more surprise today, I swear that I will hex the next uninvited person into my kitchen!" She grabbed the closest thing to her—a broken branch of rosemary—and tossed it at Hermes's body. His golden mop of hair poked into the kitchen, the grin on his face ever present.

"Goddess of moonlight," he crooned. "Are you finally remodeling to add that second bedroom for me?"

Hecate scoffed, "As if you would stay there." Hermes burst into laughter as he stepped over the foundation stones and into the house.

"It's true, Goddess of the scorned. If you let me under your roof, I'd spend my time pleading to get under—"

"Oh, stop," Hecate cut off Hermes before he could make a crude remark. "Don't use my titles. I'm subject to flattery."

"You said to not call you anything that I call the other goddesses." Hermes shrugged, leaning against the counter and picking up a random jar and sniffing its contents.

"Are you here for a reason, Messenger?" Nyx interrupted them, her voice sounding like stone. Hermes's head snapped up to where she was sitting, noticing her for the first time. His expression shifted as he stood up a little straighter, nodding once.

"Indeed."

"Out with it then." Nyx stared into the flames, keeping her back to him. Hermes looked at Hecate, as if for permission, and she nodded at Hermes to continue.

"First blood has been drawn."

Nyx paused for a second, her shoulders going tight as she didn't remove her gaze from the flames. The tension was palpable; even Hecate didn't move as Hermes studied their faces for a response. Then her shoulders relaxed, dropping back into the same stoic position that she was in before.

"What does that mean, Hermes?" Hecate let out a long sigh, pushing some of her hair back from her face. For an immortal, she felt like she had aged a decade in a week's time. She leaned her weight against the counter and looked at him.

"The war has started. Zeus drew first blood. He struck down Atlas, and after that, Kronos sent the titans after Mt. Olympus."

"How do the god's fare?" Hecate's brow furrowed at the idea of all the titans going after the god's sanctuary.

Hermes shrugged, tousling his hair as he hopped up and sat on the tabletop. He was the picture of nonchalance, completely at odds with the news that he was delivering.

"They're all fine." Hermes waved off the concern as if it was a trivial question. "Everyone is planning their next move, you know, the gods and all."

"*We're* gods, Hermes." Hecate rolled her eyes, stepping away from him and returning to refilling some of her jars that had been misplaced.

"Trust me, Goddess of serpents, that's something I'll never forget."

"You could seem somewhat more concerned about this, is all." There was another aimless shrug from Hermes as he leaned back on his elbows, much to Hecate's chagrin. If her kitchen wasn't already half-destroyed, she would've forced him off the table.

"Everyone is using this as some sort of power play. You should hear what each of them has planned, the second someone else has their back turned." The look in his eyes was positively gleeful.

"You're terribly worried about the outcomes of this, clear-ly," Hecate deadpanned once more, entertaining Hermes more than anything else. She cast a quick glance over at Nyx, who was still zoned out and staring at the flames of the hearth. Hermes only laughed, his head rolling to one side as though he was sunning himself in the kitchen and trying to find his best light.

"What can I say? The gods are plotting. It means a lot of tricks and a *lot* of messages. I'm in heaven."

"At the moment, you're in hell. In my kitchen. Which you keep finding yourself in... without an invitation."

"So you don't want any updates?" Hermes sobered for a moment and looked at Hecate, then over at Nyx. As mischie-vous as he was, he wouldn't keep bringing updates from the mortal realm if they weren't wanted. Hecate let out a soft sigh, and her gaze drifted over to Nyx too, who still hadn't moved. They both knew that she heard every word, but there was something in her that had cracked wide open; she was like a sieve, currently unable to hold onto anything happening around her.

"I'll know." Nyx's voice cut through the kitchen even

though her tone was quiet. There was a weight to her voice that was final. Hecate looked over at her friend, trying to evaluate what could possibly be running through her head.

"I'll take that as a *no* then," Hermes grinned as if any answer would have satisfied him.

He pushed himself up off the table and leaned over the kitchen counter, kissing Hecate on the cheek quickly. She gave him a sharp glance but couldn't keep the grin off her face entirely. Hermes was a shameless flirt, and he'd never let her forget the only night that they shared at one of Dionysus's revelries, but he had a secret code of ethics that not many of the gods knew about. It served him well if everyone thought he was translucent.

"Is that all it takes with you? One night at Dionysus's?"

"Maybe you've always been it for me, Goddess." He raised his eyebrows shamelessly.

"I've seen you try to fuck a tree, Hermes."

"Hey! Her name was Didyma."

"You should be careful with the nymphs, anyway. You know how Pan gets." Hermes waved her off as though she was warning him that it might rain.

"He's got a one-track mind these days."

Hecate grabbed his arm and tugged him over to her. She leaned in, knowing that Nyx could hear them if she wanted to, but Hecate was betting that she was otherwise occupied.

"Let *me* know," Hecate's voice was firm. "I need to know if —" She was cut off when the entire kitchen was plunged into darkness. It was different from the endless night that Nyx had forced the Underworld into. The light of the moon was gone; the stars were diffused, and it was as black as pitch. It almost flickered, momentarily bringing the soft lights of twilight back, until the darkness would consume them once more.

"What is this?" Hermes looked around, trying to find the doorway to exit the house. Hecate let out a sharp gasp as her hand came up to cover her mouth, taking a step away from the hearth.

"It's... It's darkness and night. They're... They're fighting with each other." She looked over towards the fire.

Nyx was now staring straight ahead at the mantle, muttering curses under her breath, while her hands glowed white-hot. She was completely enveloped in a trance, putting all her focus on keeping the Underworld entombed in night — night that she controlled, including the moon, the stars, the clouds of a purple sky. The darkness fought back, but it was two steps forward and one step back. Nyx overpowered it each time, but it kept coming back. Finally, the moonlight shone through the cracks in the wall, and it seemed like the darkness wasn't coming back. Nyx let out something like a strangled moan, slumping over in front of the fireplace.

"Nyx!" Hecate shrieked as her face went white. Nyx narrowly missed falling into the flames, her mortal body shuddering once. She kept making that awful sound, somewhere in between a groan and a cry, something that sounded like a death knoll. Both Hecate and Hermes ran over to her, Hermes pulling her up into his arms and away from the fire. Hecate leaned forward and pushed Nyx's hair off her face, both studying her expression and trying to figure out what was wrong. Her eyes rolled to the side as though she couldn't focus on anything in front of her before they fluttered closed.

"Has this ever happened before?" Hermes looked down at Nyx, all the usual gaiety gone from his eyes.

"No," Hecate whispered firmly, her eyes flickering over to the mess of her apothecary contents. If they hadn't been strewn all over the floor when Nyx opened a literal black hole in the kitchen, Hecate would be able to whip something up to help rouse her. She was racking her brain for a solution when Nyx moved in Hermes's arms, blinking her eyes open. As soon as her vision came into focus and she realized that she was leaning against Hermes, she jumped to her feet.

Hecate and Hermes stood up quickly, both extending their arms out to help steady Nyx. She waved off their attentions and buried her face in her hands before taking deep, slow breaths. It took a few more minutes before she straightened up, rolling her shoulders back and blinking tears out of her eyes.

"What happened?" Hecate asked softly.

"Was that what primordials call a lover's quarrel?" Hermes chimed in, poking his head out from behind Nyx's shoulder. Hecate's mouth dropped a little as she looked at him, making eye contact with Hermes and giving a little shake of her head.

Nyx said nothing, still nearly catatonic as she opened her mouth like she was going to say something. It took a few more moments to finally speak, her voice sounding hollow.

"That... That was Erebus." Nyx stepped away from Hermes and Hecate, sitting down at the kitchen table. They waited for her to continue, already having assumed that it had been Erebus.

"Go on..." Hermes encouraged her again, and Hecate rewarded him with a sharp slap to the back of his head.

"Ow!" he yelped, jumping a few feet away from the goddess. Nyx ignored them both as she rubbed her hands over her face in an attempt to self-soothe.

"He's left the Underworld, off to join the gods. The night has no darkness and *that*," she waved her hand in the air, "was me locking down the nocturnal balance."

"Oh, Nyx..." Hecate's face softened even further as she crossed the room to go to her, sliding in next to her on the bench. She slid her hand over Nyx's and waited for her to continue.

"What...? Sorry, someone fill in the one god who doesn't live in the Underworld." Hermes piped up, hopping back up on the counter and looking at both women on the table. Nyx only looked up at him, her face making room for exasperation next to its exhaustion. She said nothing and stood silently, pulling herself away from Hecate's grasp.

"Don't go..." Hecate seemed to sense her friend's motives. Nyx said nothing in response and quietly slipped out of the kitchen. Her presence didn't leave the house entirely, meaning that she had simply retreated to one of the other rooms. Hecate turned on Hermes and gave him a withering stare.

"You don't think she's spread thin enough as it is right now, Hermes? I know your default setting is not solemnity, but you would think..." Her voice rose in pitch as her temper rose, crossing the kitchen to poke him in the chest. The god held his hands up and shook his head rapidly.

"What happened? What do you mean that darkness and night are *fighting* each other? How does that even..."

"I'll tell you how," Hecate snapped again, turning her back to him as she looked around the kitchen for something to keep her hands busy. She grabbed a cracked pot holding a rosemary plant, sitting down at her table and beginning to run her hands aimlessly over it. Her magic sparked to life, slowly, as she trailed red sparks over the rim. She channeled her magic absentmindedly and began to fix the pottery at a glacial pace. "Nyx is the night and all that it entails. I don't think people truly understands what that means. You hear *night* and you think *darkness*."

"Sure." Hermes shrugged. "But that's wrong?"

"No." Hecate shook her head, moving her hand faster. "It means the night sky, the constellations, the moon, the planets that shine their brightest at dusk, the purple clouds, the weather, the creatures of the darkness—"

"*Creatures of the darkness* as in the creatures of the Underworld?"

"In part. It also means the owls, the snakes, the predators that make their home on her domain."

Hermes's eyes got wide as he slowly started to tally all the things that that entailed. "Those exist on the mortal realm." Hecate only nodded in response and kept going.

"There is no god or primordial who reigns over their realm

in such totality. Even Helios is the God of the Sun, not the god of day itself." Hermes's eyes grew impossibly wide, and he paused, raking his hands through his hair and tugging on the curls. He let out a low whistle.

"No wonder Zeus is afraid of her... Why he downplays what she can do." His gaze landed on Hecate, and she let out a dark chuckle.

"He's never seen the full extent of her power. I haven't, either. None of us have. There has never been a time in time immemorial that Nyx has unleashed entirely."

"You didn't answer my question." Hermes looked at the door where Nyx had left. "How are night and darkness fighting one another?"

Hecate nodded grimly, as though she had been hoping that her previous answer would suffice, and she could avoid this question. She looked at the pot in front of her and startled, seeing that the cracks were fixed, and the rosemary had started to grow incorrigibly with her magic. She rolled her eyes and pulled her fingers back quickly, tucking her hands in her lap. Hermes could sense that she was anxious about the answer, and he didn't push. It took another few minutes until Hecate took a deep breath and continued.

"Erebus is the darkness. Nyx, clearly, can manipulate and control the darkness, too, but it takes all her focus. While she manages all the auxiliary parts of the night, too, we can all see that darkness is its most recognizable trait."

"Right, so they make quite the pair."

"Indeed." There was something in Hecate's voice that Hermes couldn't place. "But without Erebus managing the darkness *with* Nyx, it becomes too... all-consuming. It drowns out the moon, the stars, and it becomes so overwhelming that even the owls could lose their way."

Hermes let out a low whistle, thinking through what it would look like if apocalyptic darkness covered the world instead of *night* as they knew it.

"So…" Hermes continued, "Erebus leaving the Underworld means he's refusing to work with Nyx… so she's…"

"The definition of being everywhere at once. With Erebus refusing to work alongside her, inhabit the Underworld and make their trip to the mortal world once a day, it means Nyx is stretched thin keeping the blackness in line while giving space for the rest of the night's creatures."

Hermes shook his head and jumped off the counter, crossing the kitchen to Hecate. "What do we do? Can Nyx do that?"

"Of course she can." Hecate raised an eyebrow at him. "Trust me, her power isn't what we need to be concerned about." Hermes's face contorted as he tried to piece through his confusion again.

"Then what's the issue?"

"Ignorant man," Hecate hissed, her temper flaring as she fought the urge to throw her newly fixed pot at him. Hermes took a step back as if he could read her intention. "Always so willing to let women do the work for you."

"Hey—"

"Shut up," Hecate growled, her voice taking on a deep baritone echo as her power flickered to the surface once more. "Think critically. Yes, she can do it, but consider about how exhausting that is. It will consume her. What happens to all of us when Nyx gets fed up and simply retreats to the cosmos?"

Hermes felt all the ichor rush from his face. Hecate nodded in mock sincerity as she watched realization sweep over Hermes.

"Darkness would…"

"Consume the world," Hecate finished for him, a tight feeling in her chest only deepening.

"Well… fuck."

E rebus left the Underworld quickly after that. He couldn't stay there a moment longer when the essence of Nyx was woven into the very fabric of the horizon there. He even opted to cross over Styx in his primordial form; he couldn't imagine looking Charon in the face after that. After a few thousand years, the father and son relationship eventually evened out to one of equals, and no one wanted to be on the other end of a judgmental stare from the Ferryman. Judgement wasn't his job, but when he felt it necessary, it was harsh.

So one of the most ancient beings in existence fled his home under the cover of his own darkness. He knew that Nyx would feel it and would have to rush to correct the balance and that sent another stabbing pain through his heart. It felt like a rock in his stomach, an acrid, sour taste filling his mouth as he crossed Styx and the border of the Underworld. As he climbed upward, the light began growing stronger and felt like it was constricting Erebus on all sides. His heart twisted in his chest like there was a vice, tightening and tightening with each treacherous step forward—and away from Nyx. More than once, he considered abandoning everything and running back to her. His thoughts would drift to how he had already betrayed Nyx and he better push on. He would fight to see her glory restored and only then would he come home, with something to show for it, with proof of his love.

When Erebus emerged from Cape Tenaron, Poseidon and Hades were waiting for him. They had told him they'd meet him at the apex of hell and would go to Mt. Olympus. Cape Tenaron opened into a small meadow, where the brothers were standing, framed by daylight. Erebus took some small comfort in the fact that it didn't look like Hades was any happier above ground either; he was dressed in his usual black but shifted his weight and simultaneously looked bored. Poseidon, on the other hand, was more serene as you could smell the coast from the meadow. He was barefoot as always, his coral adornments shining brighter in the sunlight. Poseidon could immediately see that something drastic had happened in the brief time since he'd left him at Charon's pier. He tilted his head in respect.

"Darkness."

"Hardly," Erebus muttered under his breath, self-consciousness spreading through his veins in a way that he had never known. He messed with the folds of his chiton and then clapped his hands together once, like he could frighten away the darker thoughts clouding his mind. "Well, let's get going then."

The brothers were wise enough to say nothing, all of them dissipating into the wind and sweeping up into the heavens on their way to Zeus. As they moved over Greece, Erebus took note of the little pieces of night that seemed to have escaped the Underworld. It wasn't drastic—only he could notice it. A shadow that appeared where it shouldn't, a star that was a little too bright for midday. He was distracted, and before he knew it, they had arrived at the foot of Mt. Olympus.

The three immortals descended to the stair steps, materializing once more. Erebus felt another pang in his chest as he remembered the last time that he had been here. He felt nothing as he wound up those gleaming steps, a cold feeling rushing over him as Zeus's pantheon came into view. The one thing that he did notice, however, was how quiet Zeus and Hades were being. Erebus knew *he* was conflicted about his decision, but spending more than a few minutes with some of the trio without a spat or a friendly jest was unheard of. He filed that information away, realizing that he was once again entering a world of politics. Erebus froze his expression and let some of his shadows trail out behind him, refusing to enter the god's court as anything else than a primordial.

Hades pushed the doors open to the grand hall, producing a loud shout as his personality flipped. The doors flew open and banged against the walls, Hades's laugh echoing off the rafters and mosaicked tiles. All the gods, and a few select titans, were milling around the room as if they hadn't even moved from the last time that Erebus was there. They all turned at the commotion, but as soon as they saw Hades, most of the immortals turned their attentions back to their side conversations.

"Hello, Olympus," Hades's grin was almost lecherous, his eyes raking over the gods closest to the door. In this case, it was Aphrodite and Apollo. "You get prettier every time I see you." Erebus watched in slight awe as he saw Hades slip into his role of the quick-tongued charmer.

"Which one of us?" Apollo laughed loudly, looking... shiny. That was the only way to describe him, a lyre tossed over the crook of his arm for no apparent reason other than he was Apollo. He wore a shorter tunic than the rest of the gods, partially out of vanity, Erebus was convinced.

"Do I have to choose?" Hades turned his head to the side, a soft expression in his eyes contrasting the devilry in his smile. It was a deadly combination and Erebus was beginning to understand that some of Hades's mythos wasn't mythos at all. Apollo's laughter broke his thought process.

"Have you ever?" He grinned in response.

"Why would I want to?" Hades quipped right back, and he

leisurely departed Erebus's side for Apollo and Aphrodite's company.

Erebus watched Hades grab Aphrodite's hand and press a kiss to it out of the corner of his eye. Erebus turned and looked at Poseidon, who had also watched the interaction and gave Erebus a soft roll of his eyes. He tilted his head to the side, indicating that Erebus follow him, and they both walked off to the side. Erebus stood close to Poseidon as they surveyed the room. The gods were a cliquey bunch.

Zeus was nowhere to be found, but the gods intermingled amongst themselves in small groups of two or three. Erebus could nearly smell the backhanded dealings and alliances that were being made over each cup of wine. The only person who seemed to be moving effortlessly around the room was Hermes, who flicked about the gods, popping in and out of conversations like breathing. There was a small spark of light that caught Erebus's eye, so minuscule only he could see it, as it called out to him. There was stardust on Hermes's feet—just a little.

*Nyx.* Erebus's heart soared at the faintest echo of her presence. Hermes had just come from her presence; stardust would fade quickly in the mortal daylight. He had half a mind to go inquire after her, but he knew that Hermes would likely play up the separation between them or use it as currency. He held his tongue. Erebus turned to Poseidon.

"Who do you normally talk to at these things?" Erebus ran a hand through his hair and felt his shadows slip a little farther away from him.

*Fine. Spread out, let the gods be warned.* Erebus's encouragement to his shadows only spurred them on. Poseidon looked to Erebus and then down at the shadows, chuckling softly to himself.

"No one. I listen to my brother wax poetic about the new world order while I wait to get back to the sea."

"Has Zeus always been…" Erebus trailed off, turning his

back to the crowd and engaging Poseidon in a more private conversation.

"Been Zeus?" Poseidon gazed at Erebus and after a second, started laughing. It was a rich baritone that made the lines on his sun-drenched face stand out. There was something wild about Poseidon, something in his eyes, that Erebus knew the other gods—not even Zeus or Hades—could replicate completely. Erebus felt the humidity in the air around them rise slightly as the water in the atmosphere amplified with Poseidon's mirth. He clapped a hand on Erebus's back, the heady weight of it nearly jostling Erebus forward, unprepared.

"Yes," Poseidon continued, chuckling as his laughter died down. "He's always been this way. Ever since we were children."

"Why do you think that is?" Erebus scanned the room once more, confirming that Zeus hadn't shown up. Poseidon only shrugged.

"It's who he is." There was something in his tone that gave Erebus pause. Poseidon said it as if there was no hope, no changing that fact, as if he had resigned himself to it. It seemed like a heady feeling to have about Zeus's antics. What didn't Erebus know?

Poseidon leaned in closer as if he was going to say something when an ear-splitting giggle cut through the air.

"Poseidon! Darling, you've made it."

The God of the seas immediately pulled back from Erebus and sighed, his eyes fluttering closed for a moment in a look of total disdain. Erebus turned around to find the source of the cacophony and was face-to-face with Hera.

It took him a minute to place her, and if it wasn't for the surprise, he would've likely attacked her on the spot. His shadows, however, were quicker and almost immediately flared to life around his legs and wrists. Hera was standing in front of him, her peplos dyed a bright pink color, with massive, coifed brunette curls flipped over one shoulder. If it wasn't for the deadly look in her eyes contradicting the saccharine smile, Erebus would have had to admit that she was beautiful. The sharp planes of her face left no room for debate, even as her lips pursed forward. Hera looked down at Erebus's shadows and let out a small *hmph*.

"I guess I should be thrilled that you've joined my husband's cause," Hera said it out loud like she was reminding herself. She eyed Erebus's shadows like he had brought an unwanted dog in with him.

"Are you and Zeus still together?" Erebus quipped, cocking his head to the side in impressive mock curiosity. The barb landed, and the grin melted off Hera's face, her lips tightening into a thin line.

"Funny you should ask. How's Nyx?" Hera spat right back, the news of their separation had spread fast and was only confirmed when Erebus arrived alone. Erebus fought to keep his shadows restrained after they stood in darkness for a just a moment. Poseidon immediately stepped in front of Erebus and gave Hera a small smile.

"Hera," he said it respectfully in greeting. Erebus watched with a twisted sensed of awe how quickly Hera's face morphed. She lit up with a thousand-watt grin, her manicured hand coming to rest on Poseidon's arm.

"Poseidon, I'm *so* happy that you could come. Thank goodness, too, we need all the *gods'* power that we can get." The way that she emphasized *gods* let Erebus know that she wasn't too thrilled his power was involved. There was a wiggle to her eyebrows as she took another step closer to Poseidon, who immediately took one step back.

"It's what is best for us all," he said diplomatically, gently removing her hand from him. His statement pledged no unnecessary allegiance to her or Zeus, Erebus noted. Hera only deflated slightly before looking over to Erebus.

"I'm glad that *some* of the immortals have a sense of responsibility for the mortal world," she jeered, her face twisted up in nasty contempt.

"Shouldn't you be more concerned with Zeus's sense of responsibility for the mortal world?" Erebus grinned at Hera as he watched her face go red. "Let me rephrase. Shouldn't you be more concerned with Zeus's sense of responsibility for mortal *women?*"

Hera sputtered audibly as she opened her mouth to retort but was cut off by Poseidon's chuckle. Her expression quickly turned to one of betrayal as she realized he had joined in. Once again, she recovered quickly.

"Poseidon, I'd love to discuss some recent... matters with you, of a sensitive nature." There was a singsong quality to her voice that Erebus could also assume wreaked havoc on human men and probably most of the gods. Poseidon only raised an eyebrow at her in response, letting her continue. "If you were to come by my chambers this evening after the banquet..."

Poseidon cut her off with a quick shake of the head. Hera's face didn't fall like Erebus expected but quickly morphed into a disappointed but calculating expression.

"For the last time," Poseidon snapped, leaning in towards Hera with a growl, "I am not going to fuck you to piss off my brother. If you want to play mind games with Zeus, you'll need another pawn." Hera's eyes got wide, but she recovered her composure quickly, rolling her eyes as all touches of softness and wile left her face. She simply turned on her heel and walked off. Poseidon let out an annoyed sigh and looked at Erebus.

"Everyone here is playing a game. I mean *everyone*. The Underworld is different, it's..."

"Better?" Erebus replied with a remorseful tone as the gravity of his decisions kept rolling over him in waves. Poseidon shrugged.

"More straightforward. We all know you're the most powerful one here." Poseidon gave a little wave of his arm, gesturing at the great hall and all the gods gathered within it. "I'm not saying this to belittle that. But if there is anything that you're not used to, it's the mind games that take place in Olympus."

Erebus opened his mouth to respond when Poseidon's eyes flickered behind him. He turned around to find him face-to-face once more with another god; this time it was Athena.

"Erebus!" she cooed, grabbing his arm in a way that nearly mimicked Hera's. "It's been *ages*."

"I don't think we've ever had a conversation," Erebus dead-panned, looking down at where she was holding onto him until she dropped her hand. Athena only smiled.

"Then I think we should change that, don't you?" She took a step closer, and Erebus looked at her with disdain.

"You can't be serious right now." He let out a dark chuckle, one of his shadows curling around Athena's ankle and tugging her a few steps away from him. She let out a small cry of disgust and tried to kick the shadow off her like she had stepped in mud. When it dislodged, Athena looked up at Erebus with a furious expression.

"I can't believe you'd even care about Nyx, of all the immortals," she hissed. "They say she turns souls to stone in Tartarus. Stone! How can you not even give mortals peace in death?" Erebus's face contorted in rage, and he stepped forward, feeling his power beginning to ripple under his skin.

"Where did you hear that from?"

"I—"

"That's enough." Poseidon stepped in between them. "Athena, get lost. Erebus, let's go." He turned and grabbed Erebus's shoulder, walking them both outside to get some air. As soon as the doors shut behind them, Erebus let out a roar of frustration and ran his hands through his hair.

"Can you believe that? What the hell is her problem! Goddess of *wisdom*, are you kidding me?" Poseidon only shrugged.

"I suppose she thought it was wise to get a primordial on her side before a war."

"By insulting my consort and making feeble attempts at seduction?" Erebus spat and looked at Poseidon in bewilderment, who slowly nodded his head.

"Yes. That's how everything works here. I promise insulting someone's wife and flirting with them would work with every god in that room."

Erebus groaned, leaning his back against a marble column and staring up at the heavens.

"What have I gotten myself into?"

## 23

I t was barely dawn when Erebus watched Helios depart from Mt. Olympus, sleep having evaded him all night. He had sat around with Poseidon in the great hall for another hour before he couldn't fake interest anymore. Every interaction seemed fickler than the last; he had started to pine for the honesty of the Underworld. There was no need for pretense when the trappings of the mortal world had been stripped away. Each of the gods had slipped away to spare rooms, dark hallways, and corners of Olympus at all hours of the night. Erebus had observed them all from the darkness, sitting on the side steps of Zeus's pantheon, watching as night fell and studying its essence. It felt different. This was Nyx working alone, and it pained him.

He watched as the gods played their games under the nocturnal cover, in awe at how little they perceived the night around them. It meant nothing to them, like it was always guaranteed and Erebus struggled with the idea that it wasn't.

*I wonder if it's still night in the Underworld.* His thoughts turned to his consort, to how she was handling his absence, or if she cared at all. Erebus watched the retreating darkness with a sense of unfamiliarity and confusion as he pushed himself up off the steps. He had to get out of there. It had only been a day, and Mt. Olympus was stifling him. His gaze turned out over the valley from the steps of Zeus's temple where he was hiding, and Erebus made an impulse decision to visit the mortals below. Typically spending his time in the Underworld, he wasn't used to being so close to the lives of man. As he slipped away and began the long walk down the mountain, he shed parts of his immortality as he went.

Erebus was in his body, and he let some of his more betraying features fall away, each step he took making him appear more mortal. His hair stayed dark and curled at his brow but lost some of its luminescence. A dullness took over his eyes. The slight gleam to his skin faded away as though blood ran through his veins, not ichor. By the time that he had finished his descent, he looked like any other mortal man — albeit a devastatingly handsome one.

It was a short walk to Litochoro, and Erebus was utterly lost in his thoughts, distracted as he turned his head over his shoulder to look up at Mt. Olympus disappearing into the clouds behind him. He passed men and their carts on their way into the square, the occasional woman sitting beside him. Erebus was distracted by every couple, each person he saw in a subtle act of intimacy. It seemed to hit him in the chest. He tried to distract himself as he stared at the olive trees and the red dirt road, studying intently how it clung to his sandals when he walked.

Before long, he glimpsed the great archway marking the town's furthest borders, sentries walking up alongside the wall. There seemed to be more than usual, spears in hand, swords at their hips, even a few archers kept their eyes on the winding road as it disappeared into the horizon. Erebus turned to a man beside him, hauling a handcart full of fish.

"There seem to be more guards than usual here, no?" He raised an eyebrow, his gaze flickering from the top of the walls to the fisherman. The man looked up, squinting against the early morning sun before shrugging and dropping his gaze back down to the ground.

"Best keep your eyes down, son." The man's voice sounded like the sea, his skin red with years in the sun. "The gods and their fathers are at each other's throats."

"What does that mean?" Erebus pressed again, his voice dropping to a whisper as he leaned closer. They were approaching the gates, and he picked up that the man didn't want the sentries to overhear him. Or maybe he was worried the gods themselves were listening in.

*That would be a valid fear.* Erebus let out a shudder to think of what would happen if Zeus overheard a mortal disrespecting him when he was in a bad mood. *God, it's easier when everyone's dead.* Erebus felt another homesick pang for the Underworld go through his heart. The fisherman's eyes got wider, and he shook his head.

"You're not from around here, are you?"

"No…" Erebus wondered if he had been caught until he recollected that there was no reason for the man to think that he wasn't from simply… far away.

*A lot farther than you'd think, fisherman.*

"I'm from Delphi," Erebus lied smoothly, letting some immortal charm flicker over his face to smooth over his deception. "I'm here to see my mother's family, and I've heard nothing of what you speak of."

The fisherman immediately nodded and some of the worry lines disappeared from his face.

"Zeus has declared war on his father. Kronos destroyed some villages a few miles over. You know when the deities start throwing stones, their priests are even more willing to *increase* their sacrifices to appease them, to get the wars to end." Erebus couldn't keep the shock off his face as he sputtered, struggling to keep his voice down as they were only a stone's throw from the entrance to the city.

"You don't mean the priests are sacrificing mortals, do

you?" It was the fisherman's turn to be surprised, an awkward laugh taking him over.

"Mortals? You might not feel it now, young as you are, but we're all mortals here. And no, of course not, but if you attract any attention, you're more likely to have your lands or crops taken in tribute." He rolled his shoulders back and cast a look at his handcart as if he was making sure that a priest hadn't commandeered his haul while they were talking.

"Does anyone stand up to them? Who do you pray to?" Erebus felt his temper rising. Everything that he had believed, that joining this war would be good for Nyx and good for the mortals, was starting to feel like more of a lie.

"You best drop that line of questioning. Zeus, Kronos—this is a tale as old as time. Then again, I didn't go chasing after my father with a fishhook as soon as I could walk. I don't know how they do things in Delphi, but welcome to Litochoro. There's one rule: avoid the attention of the gods and those who act as an extension of their will."

The fisherman scoffed and picked up his pace, not looking at Erebus and walking double-time to get away from him. A sick feeling washed over Erebus and stayed there, settling into his bones; this wasn't how it should work. The gods were becoming increasingly vindictive, and their priests were, too. How were the people praying? Was there anything left that wasn't uncorrupted? Erebus walked under the archway and through the gates of the city, a cacophony of noise rising around him as he did so. The guards barely gave him a second glance as if they could sense that Erebus was more powerful than they were. He studied the main square, taking note of the stone and mud brick buildings, thatched roofs, and where smoke was rising to the heavens. He was now consumed with an idea, with one destination in mind. All he needed to do was follow the smoke.

The first few turns that he took only brought him to butcheries, other markets, or homes where people had their fires going in the middle of day. He politely declined stopping or eating at each one as he noticed mortals tripping over themselves to offer him hospitality.

*This might not be as good of a disguise as I thought. I wonder if the devout have a sixth sense for when they're in the presence of the ones they pray to, but who prays to Darkness anymore?*

Erebus's own conscience was silent for a moment until his heart answered.

*Nyx did.*

He promptly ignored the swift hit of heartbreak that threatened to pull him under or cause his shadows to unravel. Erebus ducked into an alleyway, watching a cat scurry away from him and a scrupulous-looking man flee. Under the cover of the building's shade, Erebus let his shadows unfurl. *Go. Find me the solace we seek.* He encouraged them all, his shadows whispering in response as they flooded out from him. Erebus leaned back against the stone wall and felt sweat beading at his brow, the release of letting his shadows go after keeping them hidden —for no matter how short a time—feeling like dipping in cool water on a hot day.

It didn't take long for his shadows to report back to him, and he was off, weaving through the streets and behind houses. The further that he went into the city, following his shadows as they flecked over doors and entryways, the less populated it became. The walls of the city began to press into him until Erebus was on a side street, barely wide enough to accommodate him, covered in shadow from the two-story buildings on either side of him. Wherever his shadows had found their target, it was hidden. Erebus turned a sharp corner and nearly ran into the door, shorter than he was and painted black. Two sticks of incense were sticking out of the dirt in front, their sweet, cloying smell drafting up to the heavens.

*This can't be it?* His confusion was palpable but was met with an outcry from his shadows, which insisted that this was the place. Erebus didn't think about it again as he knocked once. He was met with silence, only a sudden breeze drifting down the hidden street. As he raised his hand to knock again, the door swung open in front of him.

Erebus was face-to-face with a middle-aged woman, with graying hair curled into a knot at the base of her neck. She wore a simple black shift, a metal belt going around her waist. Her sandals were plain, but well made, and she carried herself with a maternal energy that had even Erebus straightening up a little taller.

"Can I help you?" Her voice wasn't unkind, but she eyed him with a sense of scrutiny.

"I've come to pay respects, priestess." Erebus bowed his head. There was a beat of silence. When she spoke again, the woman sounded both shocked and angry as if he had brought up something painful from long ago.

"No son of Zeus has paid tribute to the Goddess in a century."

Erebus bristled at the accolade that she used for mortal men and at the neglect the temple had suffered.

"Then, by your honor, I shall break the drought and water the altars of your temple," Erebus spoke formally, only then daring to pick his eyes up as he looked at the priestess. Her eyes narrowed as she leaned forward over the threshold as though she was studying him for the first time. There was a spark of recognition in her eyes, and she stepped back with a gasp.

"Only one... man... has ever beheld the goddess with the reverence that we have."

Erebus couldn't help but let a soft smile fall over his face. Some of his power flickered in his eyes, and his shadows curled around his bicep like arm cuffs. The priestess's face paled, and she gasped, her hand flying up to her face as if she could throttle the disrespectful sound.

"Oh —" She knelt as if to bow, and Erebus leaned forward, gently catching her elbow and shaking his head.

"That won't be necessary, Priestess." His voice was soft as his features flickered, more of his godlike attributes returning as ripples of dark power moved over his skin. "I meant what I said, if you'd allow me to pay my respects."

"O–of course." The woman kept her head bowed as she stepped aside, her eyes only flickering up briefly to meet his. Erebus stepped over the threshold and walked inside and shut the door behind him. His eyes took no time to get used to the darkness.

The room opened, revealing a two-story space that was meticulously cared for. He could see how the hidden nature of the building and its discreet door had kept it safe over the years. The floor was tiled simply, but exquisitely. He recognized marble stones and mother-of-pearl which had to have cost a mortal fortune to bring from Crete. It created a luminescent effect like walking on moonlight. The ceiling contained heavy rafters of dark wood, a tapestry hanging from each beam. They depicted stunning illustrations of the cosmos, of constellations and the moon phases. The golden threads shone in the dim lightning, giving the overall effect of a night sky.

It was the very center of the room, however, that took Erebus's breath away. At the head of the long hall, standing taller than a human man, was a statue made of impeccable white stone. There were only a few fires in the space, casting it in such a light that it looked as though it was glowing from within. It was impeccable craftsmanship, so well done that even a primordial like Erebus had to admit it. The expression on its face was so lifelike, so full of emotion, it looked like it was going to start breathing. In front of the statue was a small, circular altar, filled with a small moat of water around the center where the temple's eternal flame was lit. More sticks of incense and their wispy tails of smoke dotted the halls, filling the room with the smell of night-blooming jasmine and rosemary.

"Welcome," the priestess had walked up quietly behind him, "to the last temple of the Goddess of night."

Erebus's voice was filled with holy reverence as he looked up at the statue's stone eyes.

"It's Nyx."

## 24

The priestess nodded, sensing Erebus's emotion as she took a few steps back towards the doorway. Erebus walked forward, his eyes fixated on Nyx's stone expression. He made it to the front of the altar when he turned and looked at the woman.

"How long have you kept watch over this place?" he asked with a gentle invitation in his voice, beckoning her to his side. His voice was barely over a whisper. The priestess stepped forward and sighed softly, joining him in looking up at the marble depiction of the primordial.

"My entire life. It has been the only home that I have ever known."

Erebus startled and looked down at the woman, seeing only adoration in her eyes.

"I didn't... I didn't think that was possible. Hera..." he trailed off at seeing the pain in the priestess's eyes at the mention of Zeus's wife.

"Yes." Her answer was clipped, but Erebus knew that the anger wasn't directed at him. "Hera took over all of Nyx's temples roughly a century ago. This space contains the remnants of all that survived, brought here by any of the devotees that could escape. The tapestries came from a temple in Thermopole. The altar was plucked from the ruins in Ephesus, so on and so forth."

"This is... the only temple to Nyx left." Erebus let the statement wash over him like a wave as he fought the impulse to go back to Olympus and slaughter both Zeus and Hera. He had known that her temples were dwindling. It had motivated him to fight with Zeus, but he had assumed that most of them had fallen to the whims of mortal men. He didn't realize how calculated the attack on his consort had been by the queen of the gods.

*This was a mistake.* The truth rang out between Erebus's ears, and he felt nauseous. The priestess continued.

"My mother was a child at the infamous attack on the temple in Delphi where Nyx pleaded to the Fates and cut the acolyte's strings of life before they could be assaulted. My mother hid and then married herself off to a fisherman to avoid any further persecution if Hera's servants discovered she had survived."

"How did you manage to get here?" Erebus turned and looked at the woman with a confused expression, trying to unravel the story of the last temple they stood in.

"My father was a greedy man. He never paid homage to Poseidon and boasted he could plunder from the sea without repercussion."

Erebus visibly grimaced and the woman laughed, a bright sound that startled him.

"Exactly. Luckily, I take after my mother." The priestess stepped away from Erebus and began walking around the perimeter of the room, re-lighting incense as she spoke. "In the end, it wasn't Poseidon who went after my father. It was Amphitrite, who acted in respect of her husband and drowned my father's boat. My mother was pregnant with me at the time."

Erebus couldn't help but chuckle. "I've met Amphitrite. I'm not surprised." The priestess laughed again and nodded.

"I can't say I blame her. My father didn't have a great reputation in the village and had debts. There were some unsavory characters who felt that the only way to get what they were owed was through my mother." The priestess's expression tightened, and Erebus knew that she wasn't talking about her mother working off the debt.

"I'm sorry," Erebus offered, but she held up a hand.

"There is no need. Nyx heard that one of her acolyte's last descendants was pregnant and in peril, and she came up from Tartarus." Erebus felt himself freeze. The priestess stopped moving around the room, pausing and looking up at the statue as she finished her story in a reverent tone.

"Nyx arrived in the village not a moment too soon. There were already men at our door, but she turned off the stars and the moon. They couldn't see and stumbled over one another. Nyx hid my mother under the cover of nightfall and refused to let Helios rise until my mother had safely made it all the way here. To the last temple."

"You were born here?" Erebus looked at the Priestess and back up at the statue of his consort. She smiled and nodded, a proud expression crossing her face.

"I was. When my mother arrived, there were only two other women here. They raised me here. Now..." Her voice trailed off as she looked up to the rafters, a wistful expression on her face. "I am the only one left."

Erebus was struck dumb, staring around the massive hall as he reeled with the revelation of the priestess's story. He didn't know that there was only one priestess left. The *last* priestess. He wasn't surprised that Nyx had moved hell on earth—quite literally—to get a woman to safety. This was why he was doing this, wasn't it? She deserved all her temples restored...

"I would disagree." The priestess's voice cut through Erebus's thoughts as he turned to look at her.

"I beg your pardon?" Erebus blinked rapidly as he stared at the small smile that appeared on her face.

"The reason you have come to Zeus's side. Nyx doesn't care for any of this." She waved at her surroundings. "I suspect I am only still here because it's where I am at peace. The only thing the Goddess wants is… those she loves, close to her."

The words cut through Erebus like a knife as he felt an anger rising in him, a few shadows pooling at his feet. He quickly subdued them and repressed the harsh reaction, not wanting to unfairly unleash his pain on the mortal woman.

"You speak with her often, then?" Erebus realized that this priestess might have a better line to his consort than he did these days. The woman gave a small shake of her head.

"I do not. She does not care much for the rituals of mortals." She did not sound upset. "I speak with Hecate when she makes an appearance. The women of the Underworld are very invested in one another and the few women topsides who do not care for the world of Zeus." She laughed as though there was an inside joke that Erebus was missing. He gave a small shrug, resigning himself once more to the ways of women smarter than him.

Erebus gave one long look at the marble statue of Nyx, looking in her eyes as though she was there.

"I'm afraid I've made the gravest of errors," he breathed the words out like a prayer, a solemn oath said in the last temple of his wife. The priestess's smile widened as she looked at him, nodding in agreement.

"I believe your talents are also best served in the Underworld, God of darkness." She dropped into a polite half-curtesy, using his formal title for the first time.

"What is your name, priestess?"

The woman's eyes got wide as she looked up at him.

"Makaria." Her voice was barely a whisper when she said it.

"Makaria," Erebus repeated with a nod of his head, his lower half beginning to dissipate into shadows. "I will never forget the service you've shown my wife."

Erebus swept up in his own darkness, blowing out the remaining incense as he disappeared, leaving behind a stunned priestess.

))))

HERMES LEFT Hecate's kitchen quickly after the harsh realization that they were all playing a very different game than they thought. Zeus and Kronos were the least of the immortal's problems if Erebus and Nyx were unable to come together. He had sensed the gods gathering in Zeus's great hall and departed quickly, speckles of stardust on his winged heels. Hecate sighed, feeling like she had aged a century in the past few days.

*Immortals have too much time on their hands.* She shook her head back and forth, leaning down to give her dogs a pat before returning to the utter chaos that was her kitchen. It didn't take long, using her power, to reassemble everything the way it had been before Nyx and Hades unleashed inside her house.

*Next time, power struggles must happen outside.* She grumbled, preening once the last jar went back into its nook on the shelf. Hecate grabbed a mortar and began working out some of her frustrations, the fire sparking up higher in her hearth once more. She had only a few minutes of respite before there was a shift in the winds, a new wave of power rumbling through her home.

*For god's sake.* Hecate nearly growled, slamming down the mortar with a crack and feeling her power ripple down her arms. The triple head of the maiden, mother, and crone flickered on her shoulders. *Whoever is trying to disturb me once more —*

"Oh! Clotho!" Hecate startled out loud, cutting off her own thoughts. She stared in awe as Clotho, then immediately followed by Lachesis and Atropos, appeared in her kitchen. They materialized in a shimmer like a fine mist, grim expressions on their faces. Hecate didn't know the last time that she had seen the Fates leave their home, leave their loom unattended. Had that ever happened?

"It did happen once," Atropos read her thoughts and responded out loud.

"Happened once."

"Happened once." Her sisters repeated her, and Hecate sighed, her hand flying up to her chest, rubbing a spot on her sternum absentmindedly as her mind spun.

"I assume that you are not here for me." Hecate looked towards the doorway, half expecting Nyx to appear from the room upstairs, where she had been resting.

"You assume correctly."

"Correctly."

"Correctly."

Hecate steeled herself, not used to the ominous way that the sisters spoke as one unit. She pushed the mortar far away from her and looked to her dogs, who were staring at the Fates with their tails tucked.

"I have spoken to her, and Hades tried to convince her as well," Hecate prefaced their conversation. "We have tried to let her know that Erebus still loves her dearly." The Fates shook their heads.

"It is not enough."

"Not enough."

"Not enough."

*Not enough what?* Hecate put up a glimmer of power around

her mind, knowing that it likely couldn't keep the Fates out, but they might sense it and give her some privacy. *He doesn't love her enough? Or she isn't doing enough?* Before Hecate could open her mouth to respond, Nyx did appear in the doorway. There was an unreadable expression on her face, and only the top-half of her appeared in its mortal form. It gave off the appearance of someone who had only gotten half-dressed in the morning.

"Sisters." Her voice was quiet and full of regret. "I believe that I owe you an apology for the damage I did to your home."

*What damage is she referring to?* Hecate had to fight to keep her face stoic. *Who else in existence could cause damage to the Fates' home and get away with it… unless that's what this is about?*

It was Lachesis who turned to Hecate. "That is not what this is about."

"…not what this is about."

"…. What this is about." The sisters spoke again simultaneously as they turned their attentions back to Hecate.

*So much for the mental privacy.*

Clotho turned to look at Nyx, her sisters following her gaze as they refocused their attention on the primordial. Clotho's eyes began to glow white, Atropos and Lachesis following suit. It was Atropos, who started speaking, her sisters' voices echoing her.

"It's dangerous for you to be away from Erebus, Nyx." As each sister repeated the words, the temperature in the kitchen seemed to drop another degree. Hecate looked over and saw frost beginning to creep in the panes of her windows. It took a lot to make a shiver go down the Goddess of witchcraft's spine, but a warning from the Fates, who had left their loom to issue it, would do the job.

"What would you have me do?" There was a twinge of anger to Nyx's voice, as though she hated hearing his name but refused to raise her temper at the sisters. This time, Lachesis kept talking.

"You ask yourselves what you are without the other. Why do you separate yourselves at all? You are one together."

"One together."

"One together."

The echoing of the sister's voices hit a little harder, making the void in Nyx's chest expand a little bit more.

"I cannot forgive what he has done." There was a resolute quality to Nyx's voice that made Hecate's shoulders fall as if she was resigning herself to the fate of the world.

"Be near him. Your powers must work together. Go to the mortal realm and ensure that you can work together." The sister's echoing voices extinguished the fire in the hearth and froze over Hecate's windows entirely. She watched with a heavy sigh as tears fell down Nyx's cheeks.

"That's it then? There is no hope for... *us*? It is for the good of the humanity that you seek me out, to tell me to put aside my heart and the wrongs done to me?" There was no malice in her words, only heartbreak, even though the words were harsh. The Fates only nodded in sync.

"There is no hope for us, or you are only here to tell me to abandon all loyalty to my heart?" Nyx's voice rose as her chest heaved, looking at the sisters for clarification. At that moment, Hecate knew that Nyx wasn't going to get it. It wasn't in the sister's nature to clarify what they had spoken. As soon as she guessed it, the sisters began to fade.

"NO!" Nyx screamed, lurching forward from the door frame as if she could grab one of the sisters before they disappeared. The triplets had faded entirely, and Nyx fell through the mist they left behind. She made no effort to catch herself as she collapsed on the floor of the kitchen, burrowing her face in her hands. The primordial looked up at Hecate, tears running now freely down her face as she cried in earnest.

"Why won't they just take my heart with them into oblivion?"

## 25

E rebus made his way back to Mt. Olympus with one thing on his mind—Nyx. After speaking with Makaria, the last of his illusions of grandeur had depleted, and he was filled with the all-consuming desire to be next to her once more. He was in his primordial form, hurtling over the landscape and winding up to the top of the mountain as fast as the wind. Erebus would let Poseidon and Hades know that he was leaving as a courtesy and depart. It felt like there was a countdown clock in his chest, ticking endlessly and driving him to a near point of insanity to get back to the Underworld.

When he arrived in the great hall, most of the gods were still flitting about, sharpening their swords or drinking excessively, depending on how they chose to prepare for battle. The mood was vastly different to what it had been when he left, even the inebriated gods had a more serious attitude about them. Erebus spotted Hades first, leaning up against a column with a goblet in his hand that looked untouched.

*He certainly does know how to keep up appearances.* If there was anything that Erebus had learned over these past few weeks, it was that there was no point in making any assumptions about the God of the Underworld.

"Hades." He got the god's attention as he materialized in front of him. "What's happened?" Hades startled at the sudden appearances of Erebus but recovered quickly with a grim smile on his face.

"Rumor has it that Kronos is striking at dawn, which means we're all now striking at dawn." He rolled his eyes, and Erebus could sense the contempt rolling off Hades in waves. A chill went down Erebus's spine, but he ignored it.

"Where's Zeus? I'm leaving." He shook his head and held up his hand at Hades's shocked expression. "I don't want to hear it. I never should have come here. We all know it." There was something that changed on Hades's face, but he seemed to decide against voicing it.

"He's in his receiving room." Hades nodded in the direction of the small chamber behind the self-declared throne. "I'm sure he'll have something to say about this, Erebus."

Erebus rolled his eyes, his shadows curling up around his frame and wrapping themselves about his limbs.

"I'm not afraid of Zeus."

"I didn't say that you were. I didn't even say that you should be. I've warned you to not underestimate him, and that's what I'm reminding you of now." Hades's voice was firm but understanding, and he didn't try to talk Erebus out of the confrontation. Erebus gave a short nod and stepped away, crossing the hall to where Zeus was hiding. Some of the other gods moved out of his way when they sensed him coming, power stronger than all of theirs's coming off him like a frequency.

Erebus pulled opened the door to the receiving room and cursed. Zeus was leaning back on a bench, a nymph sitting astride him and undulating her hips while Zeus gripped her waist. The angle blocked Erebus from seeing the most offensive bits, but there was no mistaking that he was catching Zeus at a rather occupied moment.

"Hera is *outside*, for fuck's sake," Erebus hissed, slamming the door behind him.

The nymph startled, turning around and letting out a little shriek at the sight of Erebus. He turned on his heel to give her some privacy while the rapid readjusting of tunics rustled in the room. After a few moments, the nymph scuttled past Erebus and slipped out silently. Zeus hadn't said a word, and Erebus turned around, raising an eyebrow.

Zeus was still leaning back against the wall, a smug expression on his face without the hint of remorse.

"Look, Erebus—"

"I don't want to hear it," Erebus cut him off as his shadows picked up in intensity. "There are a lot of gods out there that are fighting for you, however, and they won't be too pleased if they end up with a shrieking Hera on their hands. Just a thought for keeping your troops satisfied, *general.*" His tone was undoubtedly mocking, but Zeus only shrugged.

"What about keeping a general satisfied?" The leer in his eyes was even palpable in his voice, and it made Erebus want to vomit. He refused to answer.

"I'm leaving, Zeus." His voice was definitive, and the god's expression changed immediately. Erebus watched as Zeus's face morphed from shock, to anger, to disbelief, before trying to quickly recover and plaster a placating expression on his face.

"Erebus, you wouldn't imagine leaving on a night like this. On the eve of a battle? A primordial, such as yourself—"

"I'm not battle-hungry or starved for glory, so don't try the same approach on me as you would Ares."

Zeus tilted his head to the side in acknowledgement, and Erebus watched as he changed directions, a true charlatan.

"A primordial, such as yourself, would never miss an opportunity to prove his love to his consort, no?"

"This is no way to prove my devotion to Nyx. I was wrong about that when I agreed to this. I won't say it again. I'm only telling you now as a favor." Erebus was resolute, standing at the edge of the room near the door. He struck an imposing figure even when he was materialized as a man, shadows smoking around him. Everything about him was darkness, from the color of his chiton to the blackness of his eyes. Zeus sat across the room from him, white tunic nearly glowing and gray hair shining in comparison. The two of them squared off like the forces of light and darkness themselves. He could see Zeus running calculations in his eyes as his expression remained stoic. When Zeus opened his mouth to speak again, Erebus wasn't prepared for the angle that he tried.

"You know that Nyx is too powerful, Erebus." Zeus's voice was harsh and cold, his brow furrowed. He was no longer trying to cajole Erebus into staying with any promises of grandeur or good-will. Erebus couldn't keep the shock off his face.

"I'm sorry... what?" He visibly recoiled a step in surprise, his mind going a million miles a minute. *He can't be serious. Nyx is more powerful than him, than all of us. The angle is that she is too powerful?*

"She threatens all of us." Zeus waved his hand in the air. "She threatens the balance of our world. How can we survive with the knowledge that she might plunge us all into darkness at any time?"

"You should be more worried that I will plunge us all into darkness for a comment like that, Zeus," Erebus growled, taking a step towards Zeus while his shadows spread out over the entire room like spider webs. The shadows covered the walls like veins, pulsating with power and trapping Zeus within the net. Zeus paled slightly, holding his hands up.

"It's a thought, Erebus. How long do you think she'll be content in this world? How long until even you bore her... unless you already have?" Zeus's voice dropped lower, not in anger, but in a devilish, coaxing voice. Erebus felt the knife twisting in his chest and fought to keep the hurt off his face.

"She'll have me until the day she decides she doesn't want me." There was a resoluteness to Erebus's voice that seemed to echo through his shadows and shake the room.

"What happens when she's tired of this world? When she grows annoyed with mortals? She could swallow the world. No one deserves that much power—"

Erebus was on Zeus in a second, tightening his hand around the god's throat. He leaned in, his voice dropping an octave as his lip curled.

"You should be very fucking careful what comes out of your mouth next, Zeus," he hoisted Zeus up by the neck, slamming him into the wall. His shadows swarmed the god, weaving across his body and pinning him there. Erebus released his hand, and Zeus sucked in a gasp.

"Erebus, this is—"

"War?" Erebus finished for him as he spat at Zeus's feet. "You don't know the meaning of the word. I will promise you one thing, if you follow me, or you bring the slightest hint of harm to Nyx's door…" The shadows tightened around Zeus, absorbing every bolt of power that attempted to flicker off the god's body. "I will redefine *war* for you." Erebus finished with a shout, turning on his heel and storming across the small chamber. His shadows recoiled immediately to follow him, letting Zeus fall to the ground with a thud. The god sat there, seething, as sparks flew off him like a dying battery. The door opened and slammed as Erebus left.

*This has only just begun, Darkness*, Zeus thought to himself, running his hand over his neck and letting his mind drift to images of Nyx and Erebus, imprisoned forever.

The sound of the chamber door slamming shut echoed over the great hall, causing most of the gods to turn and look at the source of commotion. They were met with the sight of Erebus, glowing with dark power, nearly vibrating out of his body. His shadows were still trailing along behind him, weaving and interlocking across one another like a dark, malicious veil. Hades and Poseidon were deep in conversation in a dark corner of the room, eyeing the departing Erebus but making no move to stop him.

Erebus left and was on the steps, his feet beginning to disappear as he prepared to descend back to the Underworld, when a low voice got his attention.

"Erebus." He hadn't expected anyone on the steps of the colonnade and turned around in surprise. He couldn't see anyone on the landing, and the doors to the great hall were closed. Erebus's feet reappeared as he walked up the steps, looking around one of the columns.

"Erebus." The voice said again, coming from behind him this time. Erebus spun around, and there was the source of the voice, stepping out from the shadows.

Erebus nearly took a step back in shock. In all his long years of existence, he had never seen or spoken to the god in front of him. Erebus could only identify him through the process of elimination. There was only one god that he had never met at least once. He didn't recognize him, which left only one possibility.

*Hephaestus.*

Hephaestus wore a shining Corinthian helmet of bronze, which only revealed his eyes, mouth, and a great, black beard. The metal seemed to glow, each rivet and seam fused with utter perfection. He expected nothing less from the great blacksmith. Hephaestus was taller than Erebus, with a barrel chest and arms and legs like tree trunks, a casualty of the trade. He was shirtless, a thick, leather apron covering most of his torso over roughly-sewn trousers—unusual for a Greek. Parts of him were covered in soot and ash, but there was something in his eyes that glowed like a forge. Erebus paused over the combination of a helmet and an apron, until it dawned on him that

Hephaestus was likely hiding his scarred face from view. There were silver rings on a handful of his fingers, each of them looking like they had been cut from one solid piece of metal.

"Hephaestus," Erebus finally recovered his voice, nodding his head once in a sign of respect as he stepped forward. The god's expression was utterly unreadable under his helmet, but his voice sounded like embers.

"I have a warning for you." Hephaestus's tone was clipped like he had something urgent to say and wouldn't waste any unnecessary words. Erebus stepped closer as his brow furrowed. He had never met the god before, and now here he was, removed from his forge under the mountain with a warning for him?

"I have been told many a time over the past few days to not underestimate Zeus." Erebus shook his head. "I don't need another vague warning."

Hephaestus shook his head.

"I don't mince words. You do need to be wary of Zeus. This war is not only about Kronos." Something tightened in Erebus's chest. He could have assumed that there were ulterior motives; every god in the great hall behind him had a different motive for the war.

"Other than overthrowing his father and legitimizing his claim as king of the gods?" Erebus fought the urge to roll his eyes, but it was replaced with a cold chill when Hephaestus nodded once.

"Kronos isn't the only threat to Zeus." Hephaestus's hand went to the sword at his side, which had been partially covered by the heavy apron.

"Everyone is in some way a threat to Zeus." Erebus pushed for more information. "He isn't winning a popularity contest anytime soon, no matter what he may think."

"Listen to me," Hephaestus snapped, his voice raising. "This isn't about fickle fighting amongst the gods. Zeus is worried about *you*. Even more so, Zeus is worried about your wife."

"Nyx?" Erebus felt anger rising in his chest. "She's more powerful than him. He's always been threatened by her. There's nothing he can do about that."

"He's going to try," Hephaestus warned, shaking his head slowly as if he couldn't believe that Erebus wasn't understanding the severity of what he was getting at.

"You're going to need to be more specific." Erebus crossed his arms over his chest, feeling impatient that this was holding him up from going home. "I've already told Zeus that I'll have no part in this war."

Hephaestus cursed sharply, shaking his head.

"You shouldn't have done that. You should stay here." The shadows began swirling around Erebus once more.

"I'm getting really tired of *gods*," he spit the word, "telling me what I should and should not do."

Hephaestus sighed, looking over his shoulder before turning back to Erebus and leaning in.

"Zeus wants to overthrow Kronos, but he's planning on taking you and Nyx down in the process. The both of you."

The anger in Erebus's chest amplified as he felt his power beginning rippling underneath his skin, the urge to go and rip the God of Lightning's head from his body threatened to overtake him.

"He *what?*"

"I know. Most of the time, I would ignore it but it's real. He wants to throw Kronos in Tartarus and imprison you both there with him. This crusade is a war on you and Nyx as much as it is on Kronos."

Erebus sat frozen for a second before running his hands over his face and letting out a long sigh.

"Then why ask me to fight for him? Why ask Nyx to? How does he even plan to do this, anyway? He can't overpower us."

Hephaestus shook his head. "Maybe he thought if he won

you over, you'd be easier to control. It would work out better for him if he got you both to fight for his cause instead of fighting you himself," Hephaestus grunted, a displeased and ornery sound. "He can't overpower you. He aims to trick you. I'm not sure of all the details, but I do know that he wants you and Nyx locked up in Tartarus."

"How can you be so sure?" Erebus pressed, leaning in and trying to look the god in the eye.

"Because..." Hephaestus let out a long sigh, "he asked me to build something to help him."

## 26

E rebus's shadows unfurled at the admission, swirling around the pair until they were hidden in darkness.

"Subtle." Hephaestus was unmoved, leaning against the column and crossing his arms over his chest. Erebus made a disgruntled noise and spoke through gritted teeth.

"He asked you to build him something to *help* him?" He stepped towards Hephaestus, who didn't move.

"He did. He wanted a set of chains made that would keep even a primordial incapacitated. I think that's why he wanted you and Nyx to join him. Then he could keep a better eye on you, maybe use them when the time was right." Hephaestus's face furrowed as he chewed over the words, thinking out loud about what Zeus's plan was. Erebus calmed down slightly, the shadows fading but not disappearing entirely. He was convinced that Hephaestus was there to help him.

"He didn't tell you what the plan was for them?"

"No." Hephaestus shook his head, looking frustrated. "Only that he wanted me to build them. I'm only guessing."

There was a moment of silence between the two of them as the rest of Erebus's shadows faded.

"I need to get back." Erebus took a step away and turned to go back down the steps.

"Wait," Hephaestus followed him, taking the steps two at a time, "Erebus, I think you need to stay." Erebus turned around and looked at the god, confusion marring his features.

"Stay? You just told me that Zeus wants to capture me, capture Nyx, and you think that I should stay here and fight for him?" Hephaestus nodded, his eyes seeming to glow a little bit brighter beneath the helmet.

"I'm supposed to deliver the chains to Zeus this evening. It's why I'm here. I think you need to stay, keep an eye on him. He won't stop until he's found a way to imprison Nyx."

For the second time that day, a cold chill went down Erebus's spine. He searched over Hephaestus's face, trying to find something that would let him know if he had other intentions. It only took a few days on Mt. Olympus to understand that everyone had their own motivations. Hephaestus's face was somber even if Erebus couldn't read his expressions very well underneath the bronze that covered him. The god was right. If Zeus was planning something, he wasn't going to learn what it was by leaving; if there was a plot against Nyx and himself, Erebus needed to make sure that there was a way to stop it. How could he stop a plan if he didn't know what it was?

*Forgive me, Nyx.* His heart dropped in his chest. *I promise, I wish I was coming home. I don't want to be here anymore.*

"I'll stay," Erebus muttered under his breath, rubbing his hand over his face. Hephaestus nodded, clapping his hand on Erebus's shoulder in an unexpected gesture. Erebus looked up and met the man's gaze. "Zeus is going to cause all hell to break loose — literally — if he attempts this."

"I know." That was all that was said between them. Hephaestus turned, disappearing back inside the pantheon, to go update Zeus on the creation of his weapons.

*Fuck.* Erebus wanted to kick something, and he fought the

greater urge to plunge the world into darkness. He wanted to go home. He was a simple man, at the end of the day, who wanted his wife. As soon as he had his moment of clarity, that there was nothing he needed more than to be back in the Underworld, Mt. Olympus found a way to keep him reeled in.

*Mark my words.* Erebus looked around at the shining acropolis around him. *I am only here for one reason and that, this time, really is for her.*

He watched as the sun began to set on the horizon, catching the final rays reflecting off the back of Helios's carriage. He sat on the steps as night descended, waiting to feel the comfort of its embrace around him. The sky turned darker, and the stars slowly flickered on as if on command, but there was something missing to it. It seemed incomplete, without its duality. Erebus sat there for the rest of the night, watching each second of darkness pass him and feeling empty.

By the time the darkness started to fade, there was a small commotion escalating in the hall behind him. Erebus sighed, looked out at the horizon one more time, and rolled his shoulders back. He turned around and opened the door, stepping inside the chaos once more. All the gods were bustling about with a frenzied energy, strapping on breastplates and sharpening weapons in the same place that they had been drunk the hour before.

In the center of them all, stood Zeus. He stood taller, even with the fading imprints of Erebus's grip around his throat. Erebus wondered if he was the only one who could see the marks. He was dressed in heavy armor, gleaming in the morning dawn in such a way that Erebus was sure it had been handed to him directly from Hephaestus. He scanned the crowd and found the blacksmith, leaning up against a wall, apart from the group. The rest of the gods paid him no mind, only Zeus's gaze fell directly on Erebus. His brow creased, and he stared at the immortal, not sure what to make of Erebus's commitment to stay. Zeus gave him a short nod, acknowledging his presence and making no other comment. Erebus said nothing in return, only exchanging a steely gaze and feeling his shadows running under his skin like a current.

He understood now why the gods were falling in line under Zeus. Or, at the very least, why they were letting him play this part while they concocted their own schemes. The God of lightning was standing tall, his shoulders pushed back, his graying hair and beard giving off an air of authority that Erebus knew was intentional.

*I don't even have gray hair.* Erebus did a mental eye roll. *Everything about him is carefully crafted and for all the effort, it might not take much to crack that facade.* The wheels began turning in Erebus's head as he moved off to the sides of the room, spying Poseidon and Hades deep in conversation.

The gods saw him coming and quickly stopped talking, temperate smiles crossing their faces.

"We heard you were leaving," Hades remarked, not unkindly. Erebus saw something in his eyes that he couldn't place... regret? Hades almost looked like he had hoped Erebus left.

"I've received some new information." Erebus shrugged, a knowing glance going between the three gods. There was a beat of silence and then a loud, booming laugh from Poseidon. It nearly shook the entire room, a truly joyful sound that was wildly out of place in a hall of angst-ridden gods on the brink of war. He clapped Erebus on the back.

"Now you're talking like an Olympian!" Erebus couldn't help but join in the laughter and an easy smirk slid back into place on Hades's face. The brief reverie was broken by a loud clap, Zeus calling the attention of all the gods in the room. The ambience in the room got heavier, everyone turning to look at him.

"As you all know, my father's reign of terror has gone on too long. We've lost too many siblings..." Zeus paused dramatically, looking around at each of the gods. "Too many to count.

Now it's time that we release this titan's grip on the world. For us, for men." He unsheathed a sword and held it up in a mock salute, with one grand gesture that made Erebus's stomach turn. The gods let out an echoing cheer, furor taking over them.

Erebus scanned the crowd and pressed his back up to the wall, flanked on either side by Poseidon and Hades. Each of the gods had a different glimmer in their eyes, some sort of secondary emotion that they were hiding. They cheered when Zeus encouraged them, jumping into his morale building "back and forth" but it didn't consume them. This had the potential of going in a million different directions once everyone's motivations came bubbling to the surface. Erebus was pulled back to the moment, listening to Zeus's comically booming voice.

"We go forth!" Another set of cheers, no one louder than Ares, who was the only one who had a genuine smile on his face. The gods cleared a path for Zeus, who went barreling through the center of the room as they all filed out after him. Erebus exchanged a look with the brothers on either side of him, who nodded, and they all begrudgingly set off, bringing up the rear.

"This is happening now, isn't it?" Erebus cocked an eyebrow, the only god who didn't have any sort of weaponry strapped to his side. They stepped outside, jogging down the steps.

"Did you tune out that entire speech?" Hades only laughed under his breath in response.

"Are you saying you listened with rapt attention?"

"I listened enough to understand that, yes, we're currently marching into a battle with Kronos. Which is an important detail to miss," Hades quipped back, unsheathing a bident from somewhere in his robes. Poseidon's face split into a wide grin, giving Hades a playful shove on the shoulder as he held up a trident.

"It looks like mine is bigger, brother." He winked and Hades smirked in response.

"You know it's all in the technique."

"Are you trying to lecture *me* on making waves?"

Erebus couldn't keep a small smile off his face. Their good-natured ribbing was rubbing off on him. He missed his family; he missed Nyx. The more time that he spent on Mt. Olympus, the more disconnected he felt and how estranged he was from the rest of the gods. He had never had any reason to stay connected to them, and he wasn't convinced he would now. Still, seeing the warmth between the two brothers—even as they descended into war—made him painfully aware of the hole in his chest.

The gods begin to scatter, some taking to the skies, materializing on mounts, leaping into the back of chariots. Erebus watched as Poseidon appeared on his left in a chariot made of water, pulled straight from the atmosphere. Hades was on his right, black clouds billowing out around him like smoke and obscuring his feet. They approached the edge of the mountain and peered out over the valley, getting the first glimpse of their battlefield.

Across the short valley, at the base of Mt. Olympus, Erebus could make out the line of Kronos and his sovereigns. Erebus had never seen Kronos up close, but he could identify him standing at the back of the lines like a general. Erebus couldn't help but turn around and notice that Zeus had taken up a similar position, letting the other gods rush down to the frontlines first. Kronos stood over eight feet tall, a massive sword hanging from his belt as he yelled out commands. The gods, Erebus included, had crested over the last peak and were now rapidly descending the side of the mountain to meet the titans on the field below. As Erebus felt the wind rushing past his face, he dissolved in the winds, taking his primordial form and a thick, powerful wave of dark shadow drenched the mountain like an avalanche. His gaze rapidly moved over the front line of titans, studying where he would make his first move.

Erebus's eyes landed on Menoetius, the titan of violent anger and rage. He was nearly as tall as Kronos, with long, wild brown hair and an unkempt beard. His mouth was twisted open in rage as he screamed into the skies, his fists shaking with two large clubs in his hands. Erebus had heard of his cruelty, and he had found his target. He crashed down on the grass, sending a crack through the earth's crust that went hurtling straight for the enraged titan. Erebus let out a resounding yell in return, a web of shadows hurling out from him in every direction before centering on the titan.

Erebus pushed off from one foot and leaped towards him, two massive xiphos made of impenetrable shadow appearing in his hands.

"Menoetius," Erebus yelled, vanishing into thin air before reappearing right in front of the titan's face. The titan roared, swinging his club with full strength towards Erebus. He saw it coming, willing himself to go as translucent as his shadows as the club swept right through him. Menoetius let out a massive shriek, spit flinging from his open mouth as he swung again.

"Erebus," he grunted, taking a step forward as he continued swinging his clubs, "Fancy sees you topside!" The words were a taunt, Erebus could tell, which he ignored as he continued to draw the titan further and further into the fray. Menoetius was easily consumed by his anger, entirely focused on the cause of that anger, which was solely Erebus.

As he dodged and parried, Erebus kept an eye on the scene around him. While he had engaged Menoetius to keep such a furious titan off the paths of the other less powerful gods, the armies were evenly matched. The titans had monsters on their side, devoid of critical thinking but outlandish in their size and cruelty. The gods were often limited by their surroundings, as omnipresent as they might claim to be. Erebus only caught sight of Athena, plunging a lance into the heart of a cyclops, and Hades, laughing and pulling his bident off the neck of another nameless titan. He had drowned out the sounds of the battle raging on around him, only for all of it to come crashing down on his senses at once. The sounds of clanging metal, the war cries of angry gods, the bellows of titans, screams of the injured.

"Watch out!" Poseidon's voice broke through the din like a wave, shocking Erebus to his senses. He turned around and saw Menoetius, now holding a wicked, curved blade and swinging it down at him. It took only a second for Erebus to call down a curtain of darkness around them, blinding Menoetius as he screamed and began swinging the blade wildly. Erebus, with perfect vision in the dark, took the xiphos and thrust them both upward through his neck. The titan made a sick, gurgling sound as he fell with a thud that expanded the crack in the earth.

Once he heard Menoetius fall, Erebus pulled away the blackness and took in quick stock of his surroundings. There were other felled titans in the valley, their bodies like massive boulders now dotting the landscape. The ones who remained were hurtling back towards Kronos's side, who was staring down Zeus with a murderous look in his eye.

"Let's go, Darkness." Apollo whipped past him in his chariot, a shining grin on his face. "It looks like we've all done our jobs for the day." Erebus nodded in response, not moving his gaze from Kronos as he followed the other gods in their retreat. They had won for today, but the titans had underestimated them. That wouldn't happen again.

The next battle wouldn't go in their favor as easily.

## 🜚 27 🜚

The retreat to Mt. Olympus was tense, even if they were walking away with a victory. Erebus almost immediately evaporated, dissipating into shadow and smoke as he rolled over the battlefield. He caught glimpses of the other gods as they made their way up the winding path, none of them looking particularly cheerful. Even Ares and Athena were walking side by side and had their heads bowed in deep conversation. Zeus was nowhere to be seen.

*So much for first on the battlefield and last off.* Erebus's thoughts turned violent once more, furious that Zeus was harboring plans so bold as to capture him and Nyx. He felt his shadows curling around the very edge of the universe and had to throttle them under control to keep from plunging the world into blackness. The rest of the gods slowly filed into Zeus's pantheon, no doubt waiting to debrief and drink—the emphasis on drink. Erebus took a few more minutes to calm down, waiting until he was sure that he wouldn't go after Zeus on sight. The last of the gods to go inside were Zeus and Poseidon, both wearing expressions that were muted, their weapons hidden on their person.

Erebus had to nearly coerce himself back into a mortal

form, his feet landing on the steps of the great hall. He moved double-time, a swiftness about him, as he tossed the double doors open. It had the impact that he was hoping for—the doors swung with a massive thud as they hit the walls, shadows pouring in the hall and collecting around Erebus's feet. He walked into the room slowly, power ebbing off him in waves that made every other god in the room take notice.

The primordial looked around, seeing most of the gods had cups either half-raised or halfway to their lips. Zeus sat on his throne at the top of the room, a furious look on his face. It was clear that he had been in the middle of a toast and Erebus had ruined it with a rather dramatic entrance. Erebus made no motion to speak to any of them, his black eyes grazing over the room with a stare that made even Ares shiver for a moment.

He found Hades and Poseidon, still together, standing off to the side. Hades had continued sipping his wine with a smirk on his face while Poseidon was holding his cup at his waist, untouched. Erebus moved seamlessly towards them, taking up position and crossing his arms across his chest. He looked up at Zeus and nodded once. The message was clear. Zeus had been interrupted by Erebus's late arrival and had now been given the *permission* to continue. His face turned so red that it looked like he was about to explode. There was a coughing sound as Apollo cleared his throat, and it shocked Zeus back to his senses. A smooth, serpentine grin slid back across Zeus's face as he raised his glass, finishing his toast.

Poseidon leaned over and muttered to Erebus, "Did you really think that was wise?" His tone of voice showed no judgement or contempt over the decision. Erebus shrugged and Hades had to fight to keep from laughing, chewing on his bottom lip.

"I think it was time that Zeus remembered he's not the most powerful one in the room."

"I don't think he's ever forgotten." Poseidon raised his glass and took a long sip as if the gathering now officially required alcohol to get through it.

"If we're going to whip them out and measure, please keep me out of it." Hades leaned over, laughing quietly from the side. Erebus shook his head in disbelief but grinned nonetheless. He turned his attention back to Poseidon, his expression sobering as he glanced back at Zeus.

"Maybe it's time to remind everyone *else* then." Erebus's voice was resolute. "I'm not here to play games anymore. Whatever politics are afoot, especially whatever you two are planning..." Erebus pointed his finger at the brothers. "I'm not doing it. I'm here to keep Zeus in line, see this through, and go home."

The brothers stared at Erebus quizzically before analyzing one another. Their plans had only ever been spoken out loud between the two of them, but there was a chance that Erebus had picked up on the undercurrent between them. Something had changed in Erebus, too, his motivations shifting just enough that they knew he knew something.

"What have you learned, Darkness?" Poseidon posed the question carefully, running a finger on top of his wine glass. Erebus turned to study him, the immortals sizing each other up. There had been a tense camaraderie between them up until that point; he knew that the brothers had been planning something, but he didn't know what. He was concerned that the brothers were now involved in Zeus's plot to trap him and Nyx. Hephaestus had only warned him off Zeus, but how would he know who Zeus had confided in? Erebus took a deep breath and decided. He could overpower anyone, if it went that badly.

Erebus let his shadows slip out a little more, curling around Poseidon and Hades's feet in a subtle warning. He leaned back against the column so he could address them both.

"Hephaestus warned me that Zeus had him make...a

weapon." He paused and studied their faces, pleased to find genuine confusion there.

"A weapon? Zeus uses his own lightning." Hades muttered in confusion, turning over to look at the god, who was in an opposite corner and arguing with Hera. Erebus nodded.

"He wanted a weapon that could restrain even primordials." Erebus's brow furrowed as he said it, anger rising in him once again with unparalleled fury. The shadows tightened around the brother's ankles until Poseidon slapped him on the back.

"Um, Erebus—"

"Oh, fuck." Erebus looked down and pulled back the shadows, nodding as they retreated. "Sorry. That's what I was told. A weapon to restrain a primordial." Poseidon was gripping his wine glass so tightly his knuckles had gone white, and Hades was shaking his head in disbelief.

*To their credit, if they knew anything about this, they're impeccable actors.* Erebus evaluated both and listened to his shadows as they snaked around the god's bodies. *There must be something else that they've been planning.*

"He couldn't possibly mean to defeat you?" Hades's voice was incredulous, a tone that Erebus had never heard him take before. He nodded. Poseidon cursed.

"He means to capture you? That's why he pressured you to be here? Is that why he pressured us to recruit you so terribly?" Poseidon turned to Hades for conformation.

"No," Erebus let out a long sigh. "I'm afraid his ambitions are worse than that." There was a heartbeat of silence before both brothers had to fight to keep their voices down, exploding in an array of whispered curses. The oldest curses, Erebus noted with a mental grin, invoked his ancient name.

"Capture Nyx... He's lost his mind." Hades shook his head, bewilderment covering his features.

"That's why you're here." Poseidon nodded solemnly, some

of his composure coming back into his face. "You're making sure that doesn't happen."

Erebus sighed deeply, not removing his gaze from Zeus, who had moved on and was now leaning against a wall and shamelessly leering at Artemis.

"Exactly. Hephaestus warned me."

"Is he making that weapon?" The realization dawned over Hades. "It would be suicide if he admitted that he could create something like that."

"I'm not sure. He didn't tell me. He warned me that he had been commissioned to do it. I would imagine that he's stringing Zeus along...but I can't be sure."

"Did you warn Nyx?" Poseidon put his hand on Erebus's shoulder and turned him towards him. "Surely, you've told her about this?"

Erebus eyed the hand on his shoulder and then raised a brow at Poseidon.

"Did I send *a warning* to Nyx?" He shook his head. "There is no warning her of anything; she doesn't know the meaning of the word."

"Why not at least tell her what you know? Let her know that is the reason you're staying? Erebus." Hades looked at him and shook his head. "Do you think you need to prove yourself because you came against her wishes?"

The targeted question made Erebus's heart skip a beat; he kept it off his face. Hades was right, but there were other reasons why Erebus hadn't told Nyx immediately of what he had learned.

"Zeus has spies everywhere. He'll know if I leave Mt. Olympus, even if I go in smoke and shadow. Everyone knows that Nyx and I haven't been speaking since I arrived. If I suddenly ran off to the Underworld and then reappeared, it would cause concern."

"Do you think?" Poseidon raised a brow as he looked out over the crowd of gods, now getting increasingly drunk as the evening wore on. The toasts kept coming, albeit somewhat prematurely, since they only had one win under their belt and the confrontation was far from over.

"I know so. Everything here is about politics. I know it, you know it. It would spark enough of a rumor mill if I went back to the Underworld that it might spook Zeus. He's only going to attempt this if he thinks he has the element of surprise." Erebus turned around so he faced both brothers. "Now, what is it that you two have been up to this whole time?"

There was a millisecond of a glance exchanged between Poseidon and Hades, but it was Hades who motioned for Erebus to follow him. The three gods silently filed out of the hall, using a side door that would hopefully get less attention. The gods were drunk enough that there was a good chance no one would see them leave, but on Mt. Olympus, someone was always watching.

The three immortals made it outside into the cool night air, the sweet reprieve of light filling Erebus's lungs with a sense of longing once more. He would never again take the feeling of rolling over the nighttime sky with Nyx for granted. The freedom that it brought him, the expansive breath of the universe that they got to call home when they descended. Hades led them down a paved road, amongst the other residences that some of the gods kept there, stopping in front of a black door.

"My ambassador residence, if you will." Hades ushered them inside. The house wasn't huge, but it was beautifully built —a residence for a god no matter how small it was. The stone was all black with a fire pit in the center, low benches surrounding it.

"You spared no expense." Poseidon rolled his eyes as he sat down, Hades and Erebus following.

"I live in the Underworld, you know that. I only took Zeus's offer to piss off Hera, that she'd have less room next door. And you're one to talk, you don't even have a home up here, water boy."

"Water boy?"

"Please," Erebus groaned, pinching his nose in frustration as he sat down. "Can we get back to the point?"

Both gods nodded, coughing and clearing their throats. It was Hades who spoke up. He looked Erebus dead in the eye and gave him a grin that was positively *deadly.*

"Poseidon and I have been planning on killing Zeus."

Erebus's eyes got wide as he nearly fell back over the bench until Poseidon scoffed.

"Don't be so dramatic." His expression was bored as Hades started laughing to himself.

"You aren't planning on killing Zeus?" Erebus leaned forward, his voice dropping to a whisper. They might have been safely inside Hades's only territory on Mt. Olympus, but it wasn't a chance he was willing to take.

"No." Poseidon shoved Hades. "We are planning on *over-throwing* Zeus, however." Erebus's expression didn't change as he went back and forth, studying the two brothers.

"You can't be serious. I mean... I can't say that I'd object but... you can't be serious?"

"We most certainly are." Hades shrugged in response.

"What about the other gods? Hell, the only reason I haven't done it is because of the chaos that it would cause." Erebus felt his heart beginning to race as he thought of the possibility. Poseidon was solemn as he stared into the unlit fire pit. There was something in his eyes that let Erebus know the god was serious.

"We've spoken to enough of the gods that they won't challenge us. They won't support us, either, but that's going to have to be enough." Erebus nodded as he mulled over the words.

"It's true. The two of you are the most powerful next to Zeus."

"Would you join us?" Hades asked directly. Poseidon cut off Erebus before he could respond.

"There would be an entire domino effect if a primordial got involved. No. You and I both know the best way to make this work is to write it off as a conflict among the gods. Among *brothers.*"

The three immortals fell silent as they sized one another up. There was a certain amount of trust between them now, everyone in possession of one another's secrets. Yet, there was a hesitation there, too. Maybe it was the air on Mt. Olympus, but it made everyone question everything.

"What were you planning on doing?" Erebus asked after a beat of silence.

"Casualties happen during wars." Hades's voice was slick, the famously charming God of the Underworld making his appearance. He had a grin that slid over his face that was positively lethal; he'd known that this was coming, and he had been planning for it. Erebus said nothing as his gaze flickered over to Poseidon, who was supporting himself with his arms on the bench as he leaned back.

"It's true. Who knows what will happen? Who knows how many witnesses there will be. Everyone will be so…"

"Occupied." Hades finished for him, sounding positively gleeful now. A comfortable silence fell between the trio as they stared off into the night sky and pondered over the roles that they had to play.

Outside, Hermes disappeared from the window.

## ❦ 28 ❧

After the Fates had left, Hecate helped Nyx get off her floor and took her to one of the guest rooms. She knew that Nyx would be more comfortable in Tartarus, but she didn't have the strength to get herself there. Even Hecate couldn't breach the boundaries of the sanctuary if Nyx didn't will it. It only took a little bit of prodding from the Goddess of witchcraft and Nyx stood, rolling her shoulders and wiping at her eyes as if nothing had happened. Hecate watched with sadness as Nyx packed up her emotions and filed them away; the missing clarity from the Fates had been the last straw. She was no longer occupied with getting an answer or trying to decode any additional meanings in her broken heart —enough was enough. Nyx prided herself on the ability to know when to walk away, and it seemed like that time was now.

Hecate opened the door to the guest room as she stared after Nyx with a keen eye, the transformation on her face both impressive and baffling. Nyx's eyes had dulled. The sadness had fallen away from her face, leaving only a stoicism that could only be found in someone who knew who she was. Any traces of her heartache were gone.

"Nyx…" Hecate's soft voice broke the silence between them. "Are you sure you're all right?"

"I will be." Nyx straightened her back and tossed her hair over her shoulder, letting some starlight fall. Her power was glistening underneath her skin, giving the appearance that she was glowing in the dark.

"Are you sure?" Hecate pressed again, taking another step towards her. Nyx simply sat down on the bed and gently dabbed at her eyes as if she was removing any final traces of her own tears. "If I recall correctly, you did just ask the Fates to haul your heart into oblivion." Nyx's gaze snapped to Hecate, a flicker of rage going over her smooth features before she settled.

*Ah.* Hecate bit her lip. *It's almost impressive how quickly she can bottle it up.*

"I did," Nyx admitted with a sigh as though she was committing a crime. "It was not the first time in recent memory that I may have overreacted."

It was Hecate's turn to feel her blood heat. "Overreacted? You can't be judging yourself that harshly. You and Erebus, you're…you're the same. You've never been separated like this. You're doing the work for the both of you—"

"Stop." Nyx's voice had dropped an octave, echoing with the timbre of her power. It sent a chill down Hecate's spine. "It would be in your best interest to not finish that sentence."

"You've never been through a break-up," Hecate deadpanned, pursing her lips as she scoffed. "Do you know who prays to me? A lot of women going through break-ups. This might be the one thing I know more about than you, Nyx." She was watching Nyx bury her emotions with an efficiency that terrified even her, and she had seen some of Greece's worst break-ups. Nyx's face flickered as she lost her grip on the cold stoicism she was holding onto.

"Do not lecture me," Nyx hissed. "Erebus and I are no more. We've broken up. I may have overreacted…"

"Overreacted!" Hecate threw her hands up in the air and scoffed. "You're judging your own emotions right now because you don't like how vulnerable they make you feel. In case you weren't aware." She crossed her arms over her chest and stared Nyx down, who's expression had gone from angry to blank.

"I said it would be in your best interest to not complete that sentence." Nyx's voice had taken on a grave severity that echoed throughout Hecate's home and made the windows shatter. Hecate watched on as Nyx carefully put away each emotion, every fraction of her broken heart, as if she could stop experiencing them if she didn't acknowledge it.

"Stay here as long as you'd like." Hecate shook her head, her voice sounding tight. She paused once at the doorframe, not looking behind her as she spoke. "You can carry both the darkness and the night, but you are the essence. The rest. He is the action, the tangible expression of what you are." The silence hung between the goddesses like tar before Nyx broke it.

"I don't know what you want me to say to that."

Hecate sighed, "If you need space or time, I understand. Don't hurt yourself further by ignoring Erebus's presence or pretending like he doesn't exist. That action is a part of you, too."

Nyx was stuck musing over Hecate's words as she disappeared, her footfalls getting quieter as she retreated to her kitchen. Nyx laid down and curled her feet up, making herself as small as she could. Everything about her existence was so big, so powerful, so all-encompassing. There was something utterly freeing in having Erebus as the mechanism for which her power went out into the world. Her capabilities were vast, but there was truth to Hecate's words. She wouldn't be able to manage both the night and the darkness if she ignored who Erebus was completely; she would have to embody the parts of him that made them successful.

*How am I expected to forget him if I need to think of him every time there's nightfall?* Nyx cursed, wrapping her arms around herself. *Gaia had the right idea after all. Men and their foolish notions, their dreams of grandeur... He sacrificed everything we'd ever built the moment he was promised power. What's a primordial like Erebus going to do with power lavished onto him by* gods? *They can't compete...*

Nyx's thoughts were wild as she felt them spinning further and further out of control. She had trapped herself in her body, now unable to focus for more than a second to disseminate. There was a crawling feeling, a rushed anxiety, making her feel nauseous as if there were ants running under her skin. Her breathing was coming in hurried, labored gasps as she fought back tears with a strength that made her feel like her heart was going to pop. It would only take a moment to vanish into her power and lose herself into the night, but she couldn't keep her mind still enough to accomplish it.

She rocked on the bed, keeping her voice muffled, somehow more embarrassed by the idea that Hecate would find her than the notion that she was having an anxiety attack. It was a new sensation to her, like loneliness, that had her pulling at the bedclothes for relief as sweat broke out on her brow. Her long, black hair was dulling, waves of white light dripping off the ends of it like water. The sight paralyzed Nyx as if she was losing her own power by the second. Her limbs trembled and hands shook, purple and black clouds appearing and reappearing in her vision. Time began to run together until Nyx was able to breathe and sat up slowly.

The light outside the window was dull, making Nyx curse under her breath and disappear into her immortal form. The sun had gone past the horizon, yet night hadn't fallen, leaving the Underworld and the mortal realm in a confusing sense of dusk. Nyx spread out over the heavens, pulling darkness along with her and painting the sky with stars. The quiet peace of night trailed her as she blanketed the Underworld; Nyx was tempted to turn around and throw herself into her own shadow, chasing that sense of tranquility.

As night fell throughout the Underworld, slowly dripping into Greece, Nyx wrestled with bringing the darkness along with her. Her power was all-consuming, and she fought the urge to plunge the world into an apocalyptic blackness. Nyx struggled as she rolled over the sky, hanging the stars and shaking the constellations from her peplos, feeling tears fall from her face. They turned into shooting stars and dropped down towards earth, her breaking heart coloring the horizon with nighttime hues of blue and black. Then there was the darkness. The deepest part of her power fought with it, tempting to soothe her pain by destroying the world in it. There was no balance, only anger and power.

"I'll defy fate!" Nyx screamed, her voice covering the heavens and shaking the moon itself. She struggled with her power and the darkness, keeping them both in check, so that neither one got the upper hand. Finally, when she had spread out from one edge of the earth to the other, she dropped like a stone to the Underworld. Nyx was a bright, streaking light that fell beneath the earth's surface, causing a streak of brilliance that stood out against the night sky across Greece.

When Nyx landed in the Underworld, she had come back to her body and fell on the grounds of Tartarus. It was quiet. Nyx was breathing rapidly, trying to slow her heart rate down as she laid there, unmoving. Her senses finally came back to her, and she sat up slowly, embracing the depth and its stillness.

*Maybe it is time I slept.* Nyx's thoughts turned to Gaia below her. While her thoughts were off in the cosmos, there was a flicker of power that reached out to her. One that she knew anywhere.

"Thanatos." A warm smile lit up her face as she sat up, the first genuine smile that she had in days. A thin veil of smoke appeared in front of her, and the God of death stepped out. He looked perpetually refreshed, like he lived somewhere in between perfectly asleep and freshly awake. His power had a calming effect that spread out in the air around them both.

"I heard you arrive," Thanatos said quietly, but it crossed the silence between them. Nyx closed the gap and felt a gentle relief in being in the company of his stoicism.

"Did it sound like death?" Nyx asked only half-heartedly, struggling to keep her emotions bottled up. Thanatos said nothing, tilting his head to the side as he studied his mother. When he broke the silence, it was with a gentle question and a nonjudgmental, neutral expression on his face.

"What do you think death sounds like?"

Nyx took a step back in surprise, furrowing her brow as she tried to make sense of the question. She shook her head and refused to answer.

"Is this what you ask people when you collect them? When you show up to their bedside, is this what you say?" Her response had no effect on Thanatos, and he simply shrugged again, leaving space for her to respond.

"I don't know, Thanatos. I can't imagine what it sounds like."

"Then why do you think you sounded like death?" His voice was clear as a bell, cutting through the silence and making Nyx's jaw drop. She floundered for only a second, Thanatos being one of the few people who could cut to the quick of her.

"Maybe I feel like it." Nyx sighed after a moment, turning away from the piercing gaze of the God of death. There was a calmness in him that at times unsettled even her.

"I know what death feels like." Thanatos shrugged simply, readjusting the shoulder of his chiton. "You don't feel like death." Nyx fought the impulse to roll her eyes as she looked back at him, now feeling her anger well up in her once more. There was a conflicting tide of emotions within her, as though her body was intrinsically pulling her in two different directions. Part of her was hellbent on a cold rage, while the other half wanted to slip away into the darkness that was missing from her. Nyx knew who she was and was confident in her power; how strongly she reacted to her own heartbreak made her question her own identity.

*How much can a heartbreak define you? What does strength mean if you are crippled by the loss of love?*

"There's no love lost between you." Thanatos's voice cut through Nyx's reverie, and she realized that she had said the last part out loud. She sighed, looking out over the deep horizon of Tartarus. The shades in the distance moved about peacefully as if they were in constant stages of a deep meditation. It was an existence that Nyx found more and more alluring.

*There's an ache in my bones at the idea of keeping the ultimate balance of light and dark equal on my own. What does power mean if you struggle with it constantly?*

"You don't have to do it alone." Thanatos tilted his head as he looked at her with encouraging eyes as if he wanted her to verbally excise more of her demons to him. Nyx nearly cursed at the idea she had spoken out loud again. Thanatos, on the other hand, looked like he wanted to laugh.

"You look like Hermes right now. Is this that amusing to you?" Nyx scoffed as she crossed her arms across her chest as if she could barricade her inner self off from him.

Thanatos shrugged, "Souls aren't the only thing that I take with me when they've died." He waved a hand aimlessly in the air. "Thoughts, emotions, feelings. All these things have a life cycle all their own and sometimes, they, too, must die."

"When did you become so…"

"Old?" Thanatos finished for his mother, mirroring her as he crossed his arms with a wink. "Sometime in the last thousand years, probably." Nyx let out a small laugh at that, shaking her head at her own intensity.

"Go on then." Thanatos encouraged, looking at her once

more with a peacefully serene gaze. Nyx let out a long breath and stared at him.

"Even if it's about your father?"

"Especially if it's about my father. Tell me. What's burdening you so badly that you think needs to die?"

"It hardly seems fair for a mother to put that on her son."

Thanatos's expression changed to one of a slight mocking.

"I think we became peers sometime over the last millennia. Besides, we're gods. I was born this way, and you know this is my specialty. Are you not going to let me show off?"

Nyx couldn't help but laugh a little harder than that. It was true. All her children had been born the way most gods were fully formed and in ownership of their power. There had never been a time when she had played house with a kitchen full of children. When she looked up at Thanatos, there was nothing but a calm acceptance in his eyes as if he knew what she was going to say.

"What burdens you so terribly?" he prodded her one more time.

"If I have learned anything these past few weeks... Thanatos, I will always, always love Erebus."

## ❧ 29 ❧

The sunrise that morning was blood red as if Helios was prophesying across the sky. Erebus looked up at it with a tense feeling building in his chest, standing near the edge of Mt. Olympus. Eventually, Hades and Poseidon had meandered back to the great hall, keeping up facades with the other gods and politicking their way through another round of drinks. Erebus had been unable to send himself back into the fray, unable to force himself to go through another perilous evening dodging glances from Zeus and advances from Hera. The never-ending gossip of the gods drove Erebus to the brink of his own insanity. He was unable to fathom those who made conversations that said nothing at all.

Erebus looked out over Greece, feeling an intense urge to release himself upon the earth and cover it with darkness. To stretch himself thin, from edge to edge, until his very soul was painted on the dirt and cried out to Nyx to join him. He felt a crescendo beginning in his stomach, chills traveling down his spine as his thoughts turned to the God of lightning.

Zeus had commissioned a weapon to capture his wife forever, locking her up in the very sanctuary that she had created for man. Zeus's precious, precious mankind. Erebus denied the bloodlust building in him as his shadows began dripping from him like sweat, turning his skin transparent and his veins black. He stood on the precipice of his sanity, struggling mid-transformation from his mortal body and god form. Even his brain wrestled with itself, a more primal, ancient part of Erebus threatened to take over—the primordial God of darkness, who was without modern language and political sensibilities. The ancient deity who preceded every soul living and every immortal god, who consumed worlds with his darkness and drank light from the wounds of traitors. His thoughts turned to the monsters and titans he had swallowed, when his mind was full of nothing, nothing for eons, except the scent of his beloved and the reminder of her touch.

Standing on the very edge of the mountain and of his grip on reality, Erebus sank to his knees and gripped his hair as he fought not to cry out. That ancient part of him was winning. That immortal would swallow the earth in darkness and would never let it see light again.

"What is this?" Erebus bellowed, his voice shaking the earth beneath him as power rolled out of him like a steady, incessant base. He felt like a caged animal, having believed the gods and cared for the attentions of men, now forced to play their games. He was overcome with a longing for a time before there was any other existence. Erebus rocked on his knees as his shadows spread, curling around him and bleeding from his veins. It gave him the appearance of a man possessed, covered in his own black blood as it trailed up his arms. Erebus felt the last of his control slipping away, his vision ebbing as he nearly surrendered himself to his own power when a heavy hand clapped down on his shoulder.

"God of darkness." It was Poseidon's voice, aged and salt-coated, that broke through Erebus's confusion. He blinked several times and looked up, blinking at the solar flare behind

Poseidon's head. It took a few moments before the God of the sea's features came into view.

"Poseidon." Erebus choked his name out with a sigh, sitting down and dropping his head to his knees. "What is happening to me?" The god sat down next to him and looked out over Greece.

"The same thing that happens to all of us, in one way or another. You see it in men all the time."

"Do tell." Erebus encouraged drily. Poseidon only smiled, the lines around his eyes and lips growing more prominent.

"There's a moment, a reckoning... maybe a fight pushes it along. But every man who's loved a woman, primordial or mortal, finds a moment of separation when they realize they didn't leave a wife behind—they left part of themselves, too." Poseidon's eyes grew somber, as he continued staring out at the valley below like he was looking for something.

"That sounds like someone speaking from experience."

"It is." That was all that Poseidon offered on the subject before he stood, carefully dusting his hands off on the folds of his tunic. "Zeus has called for us all. Kronos spilled first blood this morning."

Erebus leaped to his feet, a scowl covering his face as he looked down at the valley below.

"How is that possible? I've watched Greece all morning—"

"It was Prometheus," Poseidon said quickly. Erebus sobered. "It looks like he left last night to broker peace with Kronos and the other titans. They didn't know he wasn't an official envoy and sent him back to Zeus rather...unofficially."

Erebus didn't stop to think about what that meant. Both immortals turned and joined the other gods, who were filing out of the temple with Zeus at the helm. There was a somber attitude over them all. It was as if now this had become real to them, only now had they realized the lives on the line...as if only now, they realized that even an immortal could die, even a god could bleed.

Poseidon and Erebus slipped in the menagerie, spotting Hades up ahead, his expression grim. Zeus turned around, raised his hands, and the procession stopped.

"We have now seen firsthand what Kronos is capable of, now is not the time for us to divide into factions, my friends." Zeus's voice was loud, but it lacked authority. There was a hidden meekness in his words. He pleaded with the gods to not abandon him; he begged for their subjugation with each syllable. It rippled out over the immortals gathered with him, who were prepared for war, but their dedication leaked from their faces. "If you support me now —"

"Support you *now*?" It was Apollo who spoke up, his normally shiny face contorted in frustration. "What do you think we've been doing?"

Zeus hesitated for only a moment.

"If anyone speaks out against me, they are trying to separate us —"

"You've already separated yourself." It was Ares, his shoulders back as if he was perpetually ready for a confrontation. "I haven't seen you take up arms once." His hand slid smoothly down to the hilt of his sword.

"I was simply..."

Zeus's voice was cut off as a sudden cacophony rose from the valley below. Nearly all the gods turned to look at once, immediately pulling weapons from sheaths and taking to the skies. Erebus took one glance down below, and his shadows unfurled around him. Kronos was advancing, taking advantage of the early morning light and the shock of returning Prometheus's body to Mt. Olympus. The array of titans had expanded. Erebus cursed under his breath as he saw their ranks had filled out with the monsters of hell.

Half of the gods had already met them on the battlefield, streaking down the side of the mountain with violence in their eyes.

"Erebus." Hades was at his ear. "If you hear me call for

you, respond." Before Erebus could comprehend what that meant, Hades was gone. Only moments later, he was locked in combat and thrusting a short blade in between the ribs of a titan.

Erebus released his shadows, and they exploded out from him, running down the mountain like infected veins. He grappled with the weight of his power as he felt them like phantom limbs, coming up around the ankles of titans and the necks of monsters. There was a nearly collective sigh of relief and a fresh battle cry from the gods as they advanced against their opponents with the assist. Zeus struggled with a nameless titan, who managed to deflect every charge of lightning, when he watched in horror as shadows snaked up the titan's leg. The titan dropped his shield and began screaming, clawing at his own leg until there was blood, like the shadows were *burning* him. It didn't stop at his leg and soon shadows were pouring from his nose and mouth. The titan's hands went to his throat as he dropped to his knees, spasmed, and died.

It was a fearsome sight — Erebus, the God of darkness and all his elemental power, shadows pouring from him like a never-ending well. The whites of his eyes were gone, and there was a current around him like a live wire. He was everywhere and nowhere all at once, standing at the precipice of Mt. Olympus as shadows drenched the battlefield.

Zeus was furious. He turned on a heel and nearly shot up the mountainside to crash into Erebus. He had never seen this before. None of the gods had. There was Erebus, the nearly full extent of his power dominating every blade and power in Greece. Zeus's spine ran cold as he realized that this wasn't even the full extent of what he could do, if he plunged them all into darkness. And greater than Erebus, was Nyx.

Kronos seemed to have the same realization; his face contorted in rage from across the field. He opened his mouth and yelled something that Erebus couldn't decipher as he studied the titan. He was wild, standing tall with a tunic that went to his knees. There was one sword at his side and another in his hand, his eyes wild and barrel-chest heaving with anger. He was yelling commands, something, someone... calling for something... Erebus felt his control slip slightly as he tried to decipher what Kronos had called out for. There was a sudden shriek that cut through the air, slicing above the sounds of war, and Erebus's eyes went straight to the source of the sound. It was Nike, her face frozen in a panic as her arm extended out towards the horizon.

*Shit.* Erebus desperately tried to find the source of her anguish. *It can't be good when the Goddess of victory is terrified.*

He didn't need to look long as there was a massive impact, and the earth shook.

Then another.

Then another.

A massive figure appeared at the edge of the valley, standing so tall that it nearly blocked out the rising sun. His arms nearly hung down to his knees, his back hunched over and torso a mottled mass of muscle and disjointed bone. His torso descended into a writhing mass of tentacles, slipping over one another and propelling him across the landscape with a shocking dexterity. Each time one of the great limbs hit the ground, it shook. Leathery, rotten wings stretched out behind him, claws as long as a man on the end.

*Fuck.* Erebus hissed, his eyes scanning for Poseidon or Hades on the battlefield. *Typhon.* The massive creature had been cast to the deepest trench in the sea, where bindings both magical and not had been used to keep him there...until now. Erebus pulled his arms back and prepared to drench the field in darkness when Poseidon was suddenly at his ear.

"Don't." The god was sweating, breathing heavily, speaking through pressed lips as if he didn't want to be overheard. Erebus turned to him with wide eyes, nearly shaking his head in confusion.

"We can't fuck around—" The god grabbed Erebus's wrist

and lowered it, motioning to the valley with his head. Erebus turned.

There was Zeus, streaking across the battlefield in a beam of crackling electricity. There was chaos to it that made it different from Erebus's or even Nyx's power. Zeus's power felt like a boy trying to ride a horse for the first time, unable to master the strength of the animal; he was headed straight for Typhon.

"He's going to get killed," Erebus snapped his head around and stared at Poseidon. The god's face had calmed down, and there was a firm resoluteness to it as he casually looked away and surveyed the rest of the battle. Some of the titans had been chased away by Erebus's shadows, but others were still engaged in direct combat. No one noticed Poseidon and Erebus watching like sentinels at the top of the mountain.

"Casualties are a fact of war." Poseidon shrugged, examining the end of his trident as if it were the most interesting thing in the world. Erebus sat there for a moment, his mind whirring, until something clicked into place.

"Poseidon, did you let Typhon out?" Erebus didn't wait for the answer as he spun back around and watched Zeus leap into the air and crash into Typhon's chest. Poseidon said nothing, now examining the cuffs on his wrists with cool indifference.

"I may have dangled a carrot in front of Zeus's ego."

Erebus barely avoided laughing out loud in a state of equal parts shock and amusement. *This was their plan.* He mused as he looked for Hades, finding him engaging easily with titans on the battlefield. *I guess his job is keeping up appearances. They released Typhon into the mix, who Zeus couldn't possibly defeat, to act as their murder weapon.* Erebus flexed his fingers and released shadows onto the battlefield once more to keep up the illusion that he was engaged in battle and not the spectator sport in front of him.

They watched as Zeus crashed into the great sea monster,

again and again, electricity writhing like additional arms all over Typhon's body. Nothing seemed to slow him down. Zeus was already looking exhausted; his nose was bleeding and there was a wound on his leg that looked serious. The god took a few steps back, letting out a great shout as bolts of lightning came down from the heavens and shook his body. He stood there, nearly on fire, as waves of electricity pulsed off him. The other gods and titans took notice, nearly every fight stopping as they turned to look.

"What's he doing?" Erebus looked over to Poseidon, whose expression had turned grim.

"Fuck," Poseidon hissed, uttering a line of curses as he nearly stamped his foot on the ground. "He's turned himself into a conduit."

"A what?" Erebus sounded incredulous. It was something they had never seen the god do before. They watched as Zeus's entire body grew obscured, invisible in the waves of lightning that kept coming from the sky. Typhon reared back and with a tremendous shout, leaned down and picked up Zeus with a hand that covered the god's whole body.

Erebus watched in morbid fascination as Typhon's entire figure was lit up with electricity, waves of sparks cascading over him as he convulsed wildly. He looked like a fish trying to breathe on dry land. The monster heaved, dropping Zeus with a shout like he had grabbed a burning torch, which, in a way, he had. Poseidon was still cursing up a storm next to him as Erebus watched Typhon collapse... and not get back up.

The entire battlefield fell silent. A few harrowing moments passed, and as soon as the gods were sure that Typhon wasn't getting back up, they cheered. Kronos and the rest of the titans retreated once more, and the gods didn't bother giving chase. They were too busy rushing towards Zeus, Apollo and Ares picking him up off the ground, dusting his clothes and helping him walk off. The great carcass of Typhon gave a morbid twitch every once in a while as the last of the lightning shuddered through it.

Suddenly, Hades was beside them, shaking his head and wiping blood from his arms. It likely was not his own blood. He nodded once at Erebus and clapped Poseidon on the back.

"Did we come up with a plan B, brother?"

Nyx wasn't sure how long she sat with Thanatos, who said nothing in return. He simply waited. When she felt like her soul had been excised, and the greatest of bleeding wounds had been staunched, he stood. He walked off in no direction and disappeared, heading to wherever he was needed next. Someone always needed Thanatos, and he needed to *be* needed. Nyx didn't take any offense to it; she knew that was his nature. It was the only way that he knew how to help.

She sat there for a little while longer, digging her toes into the black dirt of Tartarus, watching as the shades slid by in peace. It looked like a ghostly dance, some of them greeting each other, but never stopping. They would move as if they were floating on water, in perpetual motion, until they, too, had spent out their demons and were ready to reemerge.

Finally, Nyx was ready. Her heart no longer felt like it was being ripped out of her chest, and her body didn't feel on the verge of collapse. There was a persistent ache in her mortal bones from the stress of managing both the powers of night and darkness, but in that pain, there was strength. The strength of softness, of her heart that bled for her lover, but a soul that refused to stop. Nyx had accepted that she would always love Erebus. She wasn't going to waste any more time, secretly furious with herself that she *didn't* hate him for what he'd done.

The light around her got brighter, and Nyx realized she didn't remember leaving Tartarus. She had dissolved into the sky and surrendered, her primordial form stretching out over the Underworld like she had just awoken from a nap.

"Nyx." A soft voice caught her attention, and she recognized Hecate. The goddess often used her witchcraft to let her voice find Nyx, wherever she was, in times of crisis. It took only a moment for Nyx to materialize in the courtyard of Hecate's home, where she was already waiting.

"I see you're at least getting used to greeting the immortals *outside.*" Nyx couldn't help but smile.

"I have had to redo my kitchen at least three times in the recent weeks." Hecate rolled her eyes and waved her hand in the kitchen's direction. "Which maybe it needed it one time. Not three." Nyx crossed the courtyard as her legs materialized underneath her, moving like she was walking on water.

"Why do you call?"

"You need to see what's happening." Hecate's voice was serious. "There's more than Zeus's game afoot. I hear things."

"What things?" Nyx's voice dropped as she leaned in, studying her friend's face for the answer, but Hecate shook her head.

"A battle is starting. Prometheus is dead."

"Prometheus? The titans killed one of their own?"

"The whispers say that he attempted to broker peace, and the titans thought he was an official envoy from Zeus, but he went on his own." Hecate chewed on her lower lip, a habit that she only took to when she was excessively nervous.

"Go. Hide in the shadows, if you must, but watch the battle closely, Nyx. I fear for all of us if you're not there." There was a severity in her tone that Nyx knew she shouldn't take lightly;

something had spooked Hecate, a woman who by definition was very difficult to frighten.

"I'll go." Nyx nodded and Hecate's face caught in surprise. She hadn't expected the primordial to go so easily. Nyx nodded in acquiescence as if she read her friend's thoughts. "I trust you. You would not ask me to go unless you had concerns."

Hecate nodded, grabbing Nyx's hands and pressing a kiss to them.

"Be careful."

Nyx tossed some of her hair over her shoulder. "It is them who should be careful. There is nothing above or below that could surpass me."

Hecate let out a long breath.

"That's what I'm concerned of." There was a wariness to her as if she had already felt the tremors of Erebus losing his grip on himself that very morning. Nyx said nothing, breaking eye contact with Hecate for a moment before she began to dissipate.

"I'll be careful," Nyx promised.

Hecate's face lightened slightly at the promise. She watched until Nyx was no more, ascending out of the Underworld and towards the frontlines.

*Oh, Fates.* Hecate rubbed her hands together. *Protect us all.*

))) )

NYX CLOAKED her presence as she got closer to Mt. Olympus, the sight of it alone making power furl out from her. She struggled to reign it in, knowing that it was in everyone's best interest if they didn't know she was there. For now. The valley at the mountain's base came into view, where Nyx got her first glimpse at what was going on between these gods and titans.

She stopped, slipping down into her mortal form like water. She knew that it would be harder for Erebus to detect her if she was in her corporeal body. She had picked an olive tree on a hillside overlooking the valley, where she was able to get a full view of both sides. There was a loud shout and the ground shook with the movement of armies, Nyx's gaze sharpening as she looked out over the chaos.

Kronos had started moving, and all the titans were advancing on the base of Mt. Olympus.

*Where are the gods?* Nyx felt her pulse pick up as she scanned the valley for any sight of them. She breathed a sigh of relief when they came into view, rushing down into combat with weapons raised. There was a sickening sound of bodies and weapons clashing together when the lines met, a sound that Nyx knew all too well from millennia of monsters, gods, and titans at war. It was the sound of first blood of the unlucky—or the lucky—who had fallen at the front. Nyx had never been drawn to weaponry and felt it a barbaric invention of mankind. She preferred all her battles be fought with power.

She studied the line, trying to see who on the gods' side had fallen. It didn't look like there were many; some titans hadn't gotten back up, but the gods that fell were back on their feet. Nyx didn't have time to be annoyed with herself at the small sense of satisfaction that it brought her.

As soon as the gods had rushed forward to meet Kronos, there was a wave of power that rushed through the valley. It was so strong, it nearly knocked Nyx out of her place in the branches. Her hand went to her chest as she tried to breathe through it, but the power caressed her like a lover—like it knew her.

*Erebus.* She breathed, her eyes falling shut as her head dipped back. *Oh, my sweet Erebus.* Nyx had never been without his presence for so long. The tremors of his darkness running over her felt like his hands, caressing and touching every inch of her. Nyx gripped the tree branch harder, fighting to stand up straighter and focus her vision once more.

There was Erebus, standing at the top of Mt. Olympus. Nyx watched in awe as his shadows cascaded down the mountainside, their serpentine movement mesmerizing as it looked like the mountain wept shadows. She studied his face, unable to look away, fighting the urge to explode into her primordial form and go to him. There was something that was ancient, almost elemental, in Erebus when he was surrendering to his power.

The wildness in Nyx clawed at her skin, sending shimmers of starlight and black smoke down her arms. *That* was always the reason that she had never been without Erebus, not because of what he did for her but how he magnified her. Elevated her. Set her free and encouraged her wildness.

As she sat in the tree, fighting to stay in place, she watched Erebus use more of his power than she had seen in a century. It was a magnificent sight. She thanked the Fates that she still had a primordial's vision in her mortal body, unable to tear her gaze from his eyes. They had gone fully black, sweat coating his curly hair at his temples. She trailed down his body as she watched his hands flex and release, flex and release... Nyx wasn't even watching the battle anymore, but her focus was broken when she saw Poseidon.

The God of the sea slid up behind Erebus, getting his attention and breaking him from his trance. He reigned in his power, bottling most of it up. Nyx felt the trailing ends of his power recede from her like silk ribbons running over her skin. She shuddered and bit back a curse at Poseidon. Her frustration was short-lived as Nyx tried to make sense of what she was seeing; the two were in stilted conversation.

The earth heaved, causing the olive tree to shake violently. Nyx's hands flew out to a branch, and she held on, her resolution to stay in her mortal form slipping with every passing minute. Then there was another earth-shaking thud... then another... and another. Nyx turned her head carefully towards Kronos's ranks.

*Oh, Fates.* Nyx rolled her eyes at the sight of Typhon. *How did Kronos find a way to get him out of his trench?* Nyx was merely annoyed that Typhon had been released, her fear nonexistent. *I suppose this is what Hecate foresaw.*

Nyx stood a little straighter, rolling her shoulders back as she prepared to enter the fray. *I guess this whole thing is going to be a little bit shorter than everyone thought.* She paused for only a moment, wondering what kind of fallout she would have to silence from Zeus, but that moment cost her. There was a streaking blaze of light across the valley, and Nyx looked up to see Zeus hurl himself into Typhon's chest.

Her mouth dropped open as she watched the god struggle with the monster, each of them going blow to blow. Current ran over Typhon's limbs and tentacles, but it merely slowed him down; it did not incapacitate him. Zeus was struck twice by the heavy talons on the end of those wicked wings, but he, too, did not stop. Nyx stood to intervene but found her gaze turning once more to Erebus across the valley. She saw it. His shadows were still pouring out of him, but they were less powerful. Poseidon and Erebus were watching Zeus intently.

*Curious.* The wheels in Nyx's mind started turning as she watched Zeus struggle. *Very curious.* None of the gods seemed to be motivated to step in, even the ones on the battlefield. Nyx leaned back against the tree trunk and made herself content to watch. She was utterly unprepared when only a moment later, Zeus had been dropped to the ground only to have scores of lightning start raining down from the open sky. He ran it through his body like an ongoing current, instead of the single strikes she had seen him use, as he waited for Typhon to pick him up. As soon as he did, Nyx knew it was over. The grip of the electric power seized up the monster's muscles. and he fell. Zeus was victorious.

*That's disappointing.* Nyx merely shrugged, logging away for future reference that Zeus had picked up a few new tricks of his own. She could tell by the scene in front of her that the battle had ended; Kronos and the other titans were in retreat. Nyx sighed, her face turning up towards the mountaintop, but she could no longer see Erebus. Her own shadows began pooling at her feet as they disappeared, her body beginning to melt away as she prepared to sink back into the Underworld.

"Going so soon?" Nyx slammed back into her body so quickly, she almost toppled out of the tree. Hermes was perched on the edge of the branch and was grinning ear to ear. Nyx bit back the growl rising in her throat.

"You are not to speak a word of my presence here. To anyone."

Hermes only shrugged.

"I'm not worried about that. I do think there's something that you should know, though." His voice had a singsong quality to it that made Nyx want to shove him off the edge of the branch, if she didn't know he was holding himself up.

"Tell me now and quickly, trickster, or I'll take special care in pulling it out of you slowly."

"Is that a threat or a promise?" Hermes smiled, making Nyx's power flare over her arms in response. He held up his hands in surrender. "All right, all right. Glad to see you're back to your old self."

"Spit it out."

"Poseidon and Hades are plotting to kill Zeus." The words sounded nearly gleeful coming out of Hermes as if he was discussing wine. Nyx's power reacted in surprise, starlight pouring off her shoulders as a tremor erupted from her. Hermes laughed. "Easy, easy. Don't let 'em know you're here, right?"

"How do you know this?" Nyx's voice was clipped as she advanced towards the trickster. If tensions weren't so high, they made for quite a comical sight, both balancing on an olive tree branch.

"The same way that I know everything. I overheard it."

"You overheard Hades and Poseidon discussing that they were planning on killing Zeus?"

"No," Hermes cackled. "I heard Poseidon, Hades, *and Erebus* discussing that they were planning on killing Zeus."

Nyx's heart froze. "Erebus?"

Hermes started fiddling with the belt around his tunic as if he were bored. "That's what I said. Apparently," he said, looking up at Nyx, "that's the only reason he's still here. He was on his way back to you when he found out."

Nyx's heart unfroze, restarted, and damn near melted out of her chest. There were too many things to process at once. First was the idea that two of the three most powerful brothers were planning on killing the third. The third being *Zeus*, of all people. The second was that Erebus had been ready to come back to the Underworld when something swept him up in this plot. Nyx shook her head once to clear it, refusing to succumb to her own feelings.

"Where is Erebus now?"

# PART III

"I thought you'd never ask." The smile never left Hermes's face, but it looked even brighter as he responded. His expression sobered for a moment as he peeked over his shoulder. "I'm sure he's with the other gods now. I'll let him know you're in Greece, okay? We'll have to wait until nightfall unless we want Zeus knowing that you've left the Underworld."

Nyx smiled, a smirk crossing her face with a feline twinge.

"Waiting until nightfall is my specialty."

Hermes looked shocked for a second before breaking out into laughter, nearly doubling over as he placed a hand on his stomach to steady himself. "That was almost a joke, you know."

Nyx winked at him, feeling emboldened and lighter by the minute. Her gaze shifted up to Mt. Olympus as she thought of the packed halls and crowds of aimless immortals gossiping one another to death over wine. In the early days, when gods were cropping up like flies, she had tried to socialize with them, and it had never gone well. Death, darkness, and nightfall were not appropriate small talk topics; Nyx had no interest in tempering herself for anyone.

"How will you talk to him without any of the other gods hearing?"

Hermes crossed his feet at the ankles, balancing on the edge of the branch with hardly any effort. "Don't worry about it. Tricks and messages are *my* specialty." Before she could say anything else, Hermes departed, speeding off as a fissure of light. She watched as the golden blur swept over the now vacant valley, disappearing as it swept up the mountainside.

"You better not be tricking me," Nyx muttered under her breath, letting herself melt into black clouds, dissipating on the wind. There was nothing left to do now but wait.

))) )

HERMES WAS a trickster with a heart of gold, but he wasn't a fool. There was no doubt in his mind that Nyx was preparing a back-up plan in case he was double crossing her; the god found himself surprisingly keen to garner favor with Nyx. He had watched her in Hecate's kitchen as their worlds had imploded, and seeing that kind of true heartbreak, genuine pain, didn't sit well with him. Hermes was more than willing to condemn or jest those whose egos were on the line but never their hearts. As he rounded up towards the great hall, he kept searching for his target. Poseidon or Hades would do as well as Erebus. Yet, as he landed, he saw that the gods had formed a jostling crowd at the doorway.

The gods were at least in high spirits, cheering and responding to something happening inside. Most of them were holding chalices of wine, and he spotted Dionysus collecting money, taking bets and encouraging the partygoers.

"What's happening?" Hermes turned to him, nodding his head in the direction of the door.

"The gods are blowing off some steam." Dionysus laughed, his permanently red cheeks getting even ruddier. Hermes eyes got wide—that could mean a very large number of things and some of them weren't good. Hermes turned away and pushed himself to the front, sending a sharp kick to someone's ankle and an elbow to Apollo's ribs to get through. He wasn't prepared for what he saw when he finally shoved through.

"Oh, for *fuck's* sake," Hermes hissed, clapping a hand over his face in tragedy-worthy dramatics. The reason that so many gods were crowding the doorway was because the center of the hall had been cleared out. The rest of the immortals lined the walls, spilling out into the crowd that Hermes had jostled his way through. In the middle of the room was now a chalk outline in the shape of a circle. Ares and Hephaestus stood off to one side, with Erebus standing next to them. His arms were crossed, and shadows had wrapped around his arms like bands. In the circle were Hades and Zeus, circling each other slowly, their knees bent as if they were ready to pounce. Both gods were utterly nude.

"Wrestling? Really? Now?" Hermes cursed under his breath, squeezing his way towards the wall so he could make a beeline for Erebus. He walked past everyone, cheering at the right times and moaning when the rest of the crowd did. Before long, Hermes was standing up against the wall right behind Erebus.

*"Darkness."* The messenger god used his power to drop into Erebus's mind. To the primordial's credit, he didn't react outwardly when he heard Hermes.

*"Yes?"* It wasn't a time to mince words.

*"Nyx is waiting for you."*

The sound of the gods cheering as Hades flipped Zeus to the ground drowned out the sound of Erebus yelling.

"Where?"

))))

THE REST of the day passed torturously slow. Nyx was unable to stray far from Mt. Olympus, her eyes fixed on the horizon. Not long after Hermes left, she got a grip on her emotions long enough to retain her mortal form; it was still in their best interest to keep Zeus guessing as they waited for him to slip up. She had no further conversation with Hermes. The only instructions were to wait until nightfall. When Nyx caught a glimpse of Helios's chariot nearing the edge of the horizon, she couldn't sit still for another moment.

Nyx sprung forth from the hidden edges of the valley, racing up into the sky like a comet. The hem of her tunic turned into clouds the color of the evening dusk, becoming a train of outstretched purple, blue, and black behind her. Her features began to fade away as they were edged with starlight, until she exploded like a starburst. Nightfall spewed out from her and blanketed Greece, waves of her power rolling over the land like the tide. Nyx threw her arms out wide and evaporated entirely into her primordial form, spreading her body out over the world as it sunk into the blackness. She felt herself twisting in the sky, her outline only distinguishable by gray clouds, tossing her arms out above her as she floated in repose. The moon wrestled itself from her stomach and took up its place in the sky as the final dance began.

As the goddess prepared to chase away dusk with the final knell of nightfall, she threw her shoulders back and took a deep breath. This was usually Erebus's job, bringing forth the final curtain of darkness that cemented Nyx's hold over the world. She felt calmer than she had in days, burying any confusion that she may have over Erebus and surrendering herself to her power — power that could handle both night and darkness. She flexed her fingers and felt that building wave within her. There was a solitary moment before she unleashed, where in a dance of the balance of her own totality and emptiness, Nyx surrendered.

She let go of the feelings of frustration, confusion, and love, and gave everything over to the night. Each argument that she had, the way she had screamed at the Fates, attacked Hades, whatever would happen tonight with Erebus, none of it mattered anymore. Her mind was blissfully blank as she closed her eyes and settled in to do what she had created herself to do. Nyx felt her body slowly beginning to electrify, a sensation that swept up her phantom legs. She tossed her head back and let go, darkness pouring out of her like a flood. It dripped from the sky and began to cover Mt. Olympus, chasing away the evening dusk. It drank the last drops of light from the horizon as it made way for the moon and stars.

Nightfall began moving over Greece, still pouring from Nyx's body, when she suddenly almost fell out of the sky in surprise. There was another wave of power rushing up to meet her, covering her body with its own. It wrapped her up completely and held on tight, buoying her as the sudden combined strength doubled the potency of the darkness. It started coming from every pore, cascading down from the heavens, and covering the earth in a dance.

"Nýchta." Erebus's voice was rough, nearly dropping to a heady growl as it broke the silence. He had followed Hermes's instructions to the letter, waiting until the sunset and then joining Nyx in the heavens.

"Erebus." She tried to keep her voice even, but there was too much between them. Even now, both in their primordial forms as their power licked at one another, the feel of him caused her chest to seize. She knew that she would always love Erebus, but she hadn't been prepared for the feeling of his working alongside her—to be reminded of what it had felt like for thousands of years to push and pull in such a way that they made the earth turn each night. She should've known

that Hermes wouldn't have orchestrated a simpler meeting
when they were both in mortal forms. She couldn't think of
that now as another dark wave of Erebus's shadows flicked
over her, the last remaining spots on earth succumbing to it.

"I've missed you." Erebus's words were simple, but they
were potent. Overcome with the dizzying effect of nightfall
once more, Nyx leaned her head back and sighed. Erebus was
next to her, similarly affected. When she looked over at him
and met his gaze, she saw an expression that she rarely saw on
Erebus's face. He was nearly drunk on her power. Both were.
The heady presence of their powers working together, caressing, touching, sliding over one another, was causing the lines to
become blurred. Nyx felt hot all over, a great heat rising in her
wherever Erebus's shadows licked at the lines of her phantom
body.

Erebus was similarly affected, feeling intoxicated on the
sweet scent of her. It was like waves of jasmine and poppy,
threatening to hold him down and drown him in it. His body
began to tense as sweat broke out on his brow and chest. The
loose, black chlamys that he wore slid back down to earth and
turned into smoke. Nyx rolled over on her side to face him, the
last of her own celestial coverings falling away. They laid there
in their primordial forms, throttled by the overwhelming
feeling of being pressed up against each other, unable to find
words. There was so much unspoken between them, but it was
fighting against millennia of togetherness. Erebus leaned
forward until he bent down and covered Nyx, his lips just
barely grazing against hers. His body shook with the willpower
to not throw himself upon her, but he waited.

It was that hesitation amidst the headiness, the patience.
Even when they were threatening to rip the sky apart with a
forgotten need for each other that bordered on bloodlust, he
waited.

Nyx didn't.

She tilted her head and kissed him, capturing his mouth

with hers as her arms immediately went around his neck. As soon as Erebus felt Nyx, he responded on instinct. He tangled his hand in her hair as he wrapped an arm around her waist, made of waves of moonlight. His dark shadows curled around her moonlit body, cradled in the heavens, and the contrast drove him nearly insane. Here was Nyx, in all her heavenly glory, painted against the nighttime sky—and here was Nyx, curled up in his shadows and relishing the pushback as she ground her hips up against him. Their embrace grew more frantic as Nyx bit at Erebus's lower lip, her hands moving to rub over his broad shoulders. Erebus growled, flipping them over and covering her body with his. Her head fell back against the clouds, starlit hair spreading out across the sky. Nyx fit perfectly in between Erebus's shoulders, his body caging her in such a way that she felt *free*.

"I've missed you," Erebus said again, and Nyx nearly moaned out loud at the sound of his voice, breaking the steady sound of their breath. His chest was heaving as he picked up his head and looked down at her, his hand cupping her face. "Could you ever forgive me?"

His voice was tinged in regret, a deep sound that seemed to reverberate in Nyx's bones. She felt her heart slow down just a beat as her hand bent his head back towards her, and she nestled her face in the crook of his neck. They stayed there for a moment, breathing each other in like it was the last thing they would ever remember. Erebus let out a low moan, his hips bearing down on hers, his arousal heavy between his legs. Nyx pulled back; her eyes were wild as she spoke.

"Don't ask me questions right now, Erebus." She was nearly panting, struggling to keep her eyes from rolling back into her head as shadows licked up her legs. "Just fuck me."

Erebus stopped, and she saw the flicker of worry on his face. That this was another fleeting embrace, a mistake, something that they were falling into out of habit and lust. Nyx looked into his eyes, and she saw the devastation of a man possessed, whose heart was churning in his chest at the thought of her rejection. There were no words, in Greek or any language she had ever known, to cry out to him how much she loved him. Nyx loved Erebus, but there were too many questions, perceptions of her own rejection that she had suffered at his hand, in memories that were too recent. All she could offer him was this moment, right now, nestled in the starlight as their bodies stretched across the heavens. He hesitated.

"Please…"

Erebus's expression contorted to one of almost rage as he kissed her, his movements dominating and possessive. His hand wrapped around her throat, and his grip tightened, sending Nyx's hips canting up on their own volition as her eyes fluttered closed.

"Look at me," Erebus growled, bearing more of his delicious weight down on top of her. "If this is what we have, then *look at me,*" he said again, the command in his voice impossible to ignore.

Nyx opened her eyes and met his stare, slid her arms down, gripped his back, and held on. Erebus's other hand went to her hip and wrapped one of her legs around his waist. He stayed there for a moment, poised at her entrance, and Nyx whined. She was drowning in the heat and power radiating off his body, the ache between her thighs pulsing to the point of pain.

Erebus was no better off, feeling throttled by her scent and the sweet, divine feminine starlight that she was made of. It had him preparing to sink Greece into the sea if someone looked at her the wrong way. Nyx opened her mouth to beg to him to move, but the words died on her lips. Erebus thrust forward and sheathed himself in her entirely in one movement as Nyx's head fell back in a silent scream.

The last barriers of control that they had were gone and Erebus's movements were wild. He set a merciless pace as he drove into Nyx again and again, her hands scrambling for purchase at his wide shoulders. She left scratches in her wake as their passions fused, pouring everything into one another until they were breathless. The heavens began to shake, and stars dropped from the heavens as Erebus hit that blessed spot inside of her again, and again, and again. Nyx's release came so suddenly, so intensely that she wept comets, dazzling streams of starlight pouring from the panes of her body as she convulsed.

Erebus fucked her through the throes, his pace losing his rhythm as his movements became wild and manic. He leaned down and bit at Nyx's shoulder to keep from bellowing like an animal as he finished; shadows blanketed the earth in its entirety.

For a moment, the world was plunged into utter darkness as he collapsed against her. When Erebus picked his head up, he nearly screamed in agony as Nyx's celestial body dissipated beneath him, like sand blowing away on the wind.

Erebus was alone.

Erebus had to breathe slowly and fight the urge to go hurtling after Nyx. They both knew that he wouldn't, even though there was no place on earth that he couldn't find her. She needed space. He would respect that, above all else. His need for her was strong but not nearly as much as his need to please her, respect her. It was a line he had crossed once, and he wasn't ready to do it again. The night sky was thick around him, both of their powers still bleeding into one another. Erebus waited until it was the earliest hours of dawn, unable to move without running towards Nyx until their powers had started to ebb.

When the first hint of light crept up on the horizon, the stranglehold that her scent had on him started to lighten. Erebus dropped back down to the earth, materializing in his mortal form as he landed in a cloud of shadows. He stalked out of the fog, shadows curling over his shoulders and around his ankle. The world was quiet as he crossed the valley with one destination on his mind. He bent down swiftly, picking up his chlamys without stopping and drawing it up on his shoulder. Once he was adequately dressed, he pulled his shadows back into him, masquerading his appearance once more. As Erebus's features dulled and lost their immortal edge, he let his power dim in his eyes.

The gates were slowly filling with traffic, even this early in the morning, as Erebus looked around. There were great cracks in the ground surrounding the city's wall; trees were uprooted, and scores of earths were black as if they'd been badly burned. Erebus cursed under his breath as he looked around, blending in with the crowd as they walked under the stone arch. Inside, the city itself wasn't looking much better. Some of the houses were leaning to one side, pools of water flooded out parts of the road. Only half of the market carts still stood, the other half lying in piles of kindling. Erebus knew that he was looking at damage from the gods' war; anytime they clashed like this, using power with abandon, it sent tremors out into the physical world. Each crack, every broken door and burned strip of land, could be attributed to Ares's spear or Artemis's arrows. Every time an immortal drew blood, the earth responded in kind. Fractured.

*This is what Nyx wanted to prevent.* The self-loathing bubbled up again in his chest. *No matter who wins in a gods' war, mortals lose.*

The deeper that Erebus got into the city, the less damage there seemed to be. The buildings grew closer together and the alleyways and roads were tighter, so it was only through luck that the aftershocks didn't do extensive damage to the interior of the city. *Although, the Fates would be livid to hear me say that it was in part due to luck.*

Erebus kept a watchful eye on the street as he maneuvered it, taking note of each person. No one seemed to be in excessive peril; they moved about as though this was to be expected. It got more desolate as he got to the city center, his mind made up as he made a beeline for his final destination. Since there was no one around, Erebus picked up speed a little, hitting a pace too fast for a mortal man and stopped when he finally reached the door that he was looking for. He knocked once, remembering to smile at the last minute as to not upset delicate mortal sensibilities.

Makaria answered, a look of stunned surprise on her face.

"Isn't this a fortunate day." She breathed out slowly, nervously looking over her shoulder back into the temple behind her. Erebus knew that his guess had been correct.

"Would it be all right if I came in?" Erebus asked delicately. It was a loaded question, one that inquired about the receptiveness of the goddess inside the temple. Makaria nodded in response, her expression unintelligible. Erebus stepped through, ducking his head under the low door as he stepped through. He followed the priestess, and when he walked into the main hall of the temple, it took everything in him to not fall to his knees.

Nyx was in her mortal form at the head of the room, her back towards him. He knew that she would have sensed his presence from a block away, but she made no move to acknowledge him. She was studying the sculpture of her likeness, her head turned to the side. While Erebus had disguised himself as a mortal when he walked amongst men, Nyx shared no such concerns. Her hair was still trimmed with starlight and there were dark clouds at her feet. When she took a few steps to the side, they moved with her as if she couldn't touch the ground.

"I'll let you two talk." Makaria's voice was nearly melodic as she stepped away, closing the door behind her.

They were alone once more. Erebus said nothing, quietly walking around the edge of the room. He couldn't keep his eyes off Nyx, who still had not yet looked at him. There was a soft music coming from somewhere, and the incense was lit, filling the entire room once more with the scent of rosemary. She was glancing back and forth between the statue and the ground, like she was fighting not to stare at him.

She was fighting the urge to keep off Erebus. She felt his presence as soon as he turned on the street, let alone stepped into the room. Every muscle in her body was telling her to abandon these false pretenses and return to him, to stay resolute in the idea that whatever it was, they could figure it out. The atmosphere was quiet and peaceful around them although she felt anything but. Erebus continued to wait for her to speak, slowly taking laps around the great hall as if he had all the time in the world, which she supposed he had. Finally, Nyx broke the silence.

"I heard about Poseidon and Hades."

Erebus's heart stopped for a second as he looked up at her, eyes quizzical.

"Oh. We're not going to talk about what has just happened." It wasn't a question. Nyx held her breath, the tension between them starting to calcify. It was like every time they spoke these days, it only managed to put distance between them. Erebus had stopped his pacing and was closer to her now, but when Nyx finally spoke, she ignored his statement.

"Do you want to tell me what you know of Hades and Poseidon's plan?"

Erebus sighed, but he relented, not wanting to push her anymore. They were both hurting—that much was clear. He took another step closer to her, however, hedging his luck. Nyx took a deep breath, eyeing the way that his shadows trailed out from behind his feet as if everywhere he stepped became scorched earth.

"All I know is that they told me they have been plotting to kill Zeus. It was the only reason that they were keen in the first place to side with him."

Nyx hummed in agreement. "I suppose I found it a bit odd that Hades agreed to join in."

"They only told me last night, and they've been planning this from the beginning. I had no idea what Poseidon had pulled with Typhon."

"That was Poseidon?" Nyx turned on her heel and glared at Erebus, her temper flaring. "I assumed that Kronos found a way to get him out. You're telling me that Poseidon *set that monster free?*"

Erebus nodded, watching as the anger on Nyx's face morphed to shock and back again.

"They figured that he was stronger than Zeus, but Zeus's ego would compel him to take on Typhon anyway. For glory."

Nyx scoffed. "Yes, yes, men and their glory." She had begun pacing in small circles around the statue again, studying it as if she was confused.

"Do you not see a resemblance?" Erebus asked her gently, nodding in the direction of the marble face. "I nearly fell to my knees when I saw it for the first time. Of course, I was missing you terribly... I suppose I still am."

Nyx felt her resolve slip a little as a sad smile crossed her face. "I've missed you, too." There was something sad in her voice, something final, that forced Erebus not to press the issue. They were both quiet as Erebus started slowly walking around the statue, too, both subconsciously beginning to mirror one another's body language. It was relaxed, open even if they couldn't vocalize it to each other. Nyx found herself staring openly at Erebus for a second too long, causing her to clear her throat and break the tension.

"Are they planning anything else? It's incredibly dangerous and foolish to let monsters loose in Greece and *hope* that they go where you want them to."

"I'm fairly certain they thought it through more than that." Erebus shrugged, running a hand through his hair. "They sent Typhon straight to Kronos, who was able to convince him to join the side of the titans. He didn't just luckily appear on the battlefield."

"I know. Still. This is too dangerous for mortal men, Erebus." Nyx began pacing around the statue once more, not realizing he had stopped moving and she was getting closer to him. "When immortals start playing these games... *oof!*" Nyx was cut short as she walked into Erebus, his hands immediately coming out to her shoulders to hold her steady. They stayed there, eyes locked on one another, and Nyx felt that telltale heat begin to consume her. Erebus's thumb gently rubbed over her skin in small patterns like a honing beacon, and Nyx fought the temptation to collapse into his chest. This time, it was Erebus who exhaled a shaky breath, stood a little straighter, and let her go.

"When immortals start playing these games, it's men who get hurt." Erebus finished for her, a sick feeling settling in his stomach. It's what Nyx had said when she had to save her acolytes from Hera's priests. The only way that she knew how to save them had been to send them to their deaths, quickly and painlessly.

"Exactly." Nyx shook her head, pausing for a moment like she couldn't believe what she was about to say. "But... Zeus is a problem. On a good day, he only poses a mild threat to mankind."

"What are you saying?" Erebus scowled, looking over at her in confusion. Nyx's attention was lost in the rafters again as she moved away from him, her expression flittering from awe to confusion. It was as though being in a temple dedicated to her was something terrible and flattering all at once. She wasn't facing Erebus when she spoke.

"I'm saying... we stay. We help Poseidon and Hades. I'll need to stay out of this for now, so Zeus doesn't get spooked —" Erebus was stuck on Nyx's word choice.

"We?" There was so much hope in his voice, it crushed Nyx, but she didn't trust herself to answer.

"I don't know." Her voice was quiet, but she looked up at him, staring at him directly from where she stood, but Erebus shook his head.

"The prophecy, Nyx. What about what Hecate said? If you fight in this..."

"I know that we need to do this. We're... *our* power is

better together. It's a fact. We can't escape that now, whatever arises because of the prophecy, we'll face it."

"If Zeus knows that we're working together, he'll be too guarded."

"That's why we won't let him know. Tell no one that I've arrived in Greece."

Erebus looked confused.

"Not even Hades and Poseidon?" The silence between them moved from comfortable to deafening as Nyx's expression hardened. He was once more staring at the ancient, primordial being.

"I don't trust anyone, Erebus. You shouldn't either." Erebus only nodded in response and Nyx continued. "We stay. We hope for the best when it comes to the prophecy. We defeat Zeus. We'll work together when we must... It's the only way." There was a moment before Erebus responded, unable to keep himself from asking the question.

"And after this?"

Nyx was quiet, turning away from him once more and walking towards the door. Erebus thought that she was going to leave without saying anything, but she stopped in the doorframe. Without turning around, he heard her answer.

"I don't know."

## ❧ 33 ❧

Erebus had nothing else that he needed to say. Nyx would find him when it was time or they needed to regroup. He stared at her once more, drinking his fill as if it was the last time, and quietly left the temple. He didn't see Makaria on his way out, but he heard her voice in the great hall as he stepped outside. The sun was high in the sky now, and Erebus blinked, sticking to the walled sides of the street in the shadows. His own shadows followed him, trailing up his calves when he stepped too far out into the sun. It took only a few confused glances from men until Erebus realized he was still dimming his power, therefore looking like a man with shadows acting bizarrely around him. He couldn't help but smile to himself, gently shaking his legs as if he had dirt on his shoe. The shadows disappeared as did his brief reprieve.

The walk back to Mt. Olympus would've been shorter if he had shed his facade, and instantaneous if he went in his primordial form. He needed the time to think. They were all now playing a dangerous game—one that couldn't be won through power alone. If all they needed was raw strength, there was no one more powerful than Nyx. The hierarchy was simple. That method would cause irrevocable damage to the mortal world, however, which they wanted to avoid at all costs. If they openly went against Zeus, while it sounded like Hades and Poseidon had allies, Zeus had his own. Even if everyone stepped aside, it would open a whole new power struggle for Mt. Olympus. Zeus wasn't officially king yet, but he was acting like it, and no one seemed to be objecting. There were politics to consider now. With so many gods and a near never-ending number of immortals, monsters and titans—assassinations used to be so much easier.

It took the whole day to walk back as a mortal. When Mt. Olympus finally came into view, Erebus let his mortality slip away, and the glimmer of power returned to his eyes. He still took the long way up the side, using the gods' path, refusing to turn into his primordial form. Even his shadows stayed hidden away. He didn't want to admit to himself that he was still haunted by what he and Nyx had done that morning; sliding back into that same form, his most powerful one, that had tasted her again would leave him breathless. As he neared the top, he lent his ear towards the great hall, listening on the perimeter of the mountain's precipice. It seemed as though all the gods were gathered there once more, and while it didn't sound like any wrestling matches had commenced, wine had begun flowing.

He turned his back to the pantheon and started walking away, staring at the rows of houses and buildings set up for the gods. Once the noise of the gathering was out of earshot, he slowed his pace. Dusk was settling. He looked up to the sky, a dull shade of gray as it waited in the in between. *Is she going to call for me again?* Erebus wasn't sure. Almost as if she had heard him, the night sky began to darken. It shifted like a watercolor in front of his eyes, going from the lightest of blues to the darkest of orange and purple hues. The prettiest sunsets always happened when Nyx was in a good mood, and she stopped to chat with Helios; it always made for the best colors.

Erebus let a soft smile cross his face as he looked up at the clouds. *Now, you're just showing off, my darling.*

The sky began to darken another shade, and he heard it. The sweetest of melodies, a song that stirred his blood and made him stand up at attention. Nyx was calling for him.

Erebus immediately transcended into his primordial form, all previous hesitations abandoned, and met Nyx in the sky. Their job was more efficient this time, there were no distractions, and nightfall happened quickly and succinctly. It was a welcome change, the proper balance of darkness and night bringing proper balance to life and death—but it was clinical. They were working together the way that they always had, except it was like all their passions and lust had been drained out of them that very morning. Well... not drained but dormant once more.

It was a bittersweet moment when Erebus landed back down on the top of Mt. Olympus, eyeing all the torches that had been lit around the pantheon. In the time it took him to usher in the night, the party had evolved. *Perhaps devolved is a better description. How many torches do they need? Who keeps letting Dionysus set the agenda* and *provide the wine?* Erebus rolled his eyes and began walking again, content to spend the rest of the night in solitude. He needed one night without plots or politics. He missed the silence of the Underworld and all that it encompassed.

Erebus only made it a few steps away when he felt someone behind him, a crackling electricity denoting their power. His shadows sprung to life, curling up around his arms and legs, some shooting out across the ground towards the intruder. Erebus turned around, fighting to keep the sneer off his face.

"Zeus." His voice was barely more than a growl. The god stood there, a few paces away, his arms crossed over his broad chest. He was wearing a simple tunic, but the belt at his waist was gold as was the band around his forehead. Erebus noted it with a frown of distaste. "Didn't take long for you to literally start wearing a crown, I see."

"What can I say? There was a... popular vote." Zeus's voice was full of mirth, but there was something darker to it — more sinister. Erebus took a step towards Zeus, keeping his shadows at bay, even though Zeus kept one eye on the phantom limbs.

"I'm sure that you didn't coerce any of the voting, either. Interesting, I didn't think that the gods were a democratic lot."

Zeus only shrugged. "You would be correct about that." There was a second meaning in his answer, one that Erebus knew meant that quite a bit of coercing had happened behind the scenes.

"What have you come to say to me?" Erebus cut straight to the point, mimicking Zeus's posture as he took another step toward the god. He smiled internally when he saw the god struggle for a moment to not take a step back. Zeus didn't say anything, his mouth now set in a tight line, but he clasped his arms behind his back. He started to walk in a slow arc around Erebus, who backed up to keep facing the god as he moved. Erebus didn't appreciate how he was trying to corner him like prey. He remained quiet until Zeus spoke. When he did speak, it was with a cold, calculating tone and a cruel smile.

"It's interesting... how adept you think that you are."

"I'd love to hear more of your thoughts on the subject."

Zeus began pacing once more. "Did you really think that no one would notice what happened in the sky last night?" He looked up at the heavens, now flickering with starlight. Erebus's breath caught in his chest, and he knew that they'd been found out. *No matter. I guess we're doing this the violent way then. More for me.* Erebus couldn't exactly say that he was frustrated with the outcome. It was too easy for him and Nyx to overpower Zeus and any of his supporters; yes, there would be some collateral damage, but it was better than all the politicking.

"If you're jealous, you can say so." Erebus's face split into a warm smile as he tipped his head to the side, teasing Zeus. He let his shadows spill out a little more, flickering over the cobblestones and even crawling up some of the columns of nearby buildings. They were spreading out and circling around the two immortals, trapping them in a web of Erebus's design. Zeus didn't notice.

"You've reunited," Zeus said simply, shrugging his shoulders as he continued to walk with his hands behind his back. Erebus raised an eyebrow and studied him, both seizing each other up like predators. Except Erebus was a very, very different kind of predator than Zeus.

"We did." Erebus was careful with his wording. If Zeus noticed, he made no comment on it and continued.

"I take it that means that Nyx has taken a side. Surely, she is distraught with how much peril it brings to the mortal realm. I know she cares deeply for them."

"You're acting very removed for someone who spends a lot of time in the mortal world himself." Erebus raised an eyebrow in challenge. Zeus only rolled his eyes and let out a huff of laughter.

"What can I say? I do, but I can't say that it means a lot to me."

Erebus shook his head. "How unfortunate, knowing what discord that causes your wife and by extension... everyone else."

There was a beat of silence as the men moved a little closer to one another. Erebus could see small currents running from Zeus's fingers, across the folds of his tunic and down into the ground beneath him. He had been practicing; Erebus had to give him that. His own shadows were smoothing themselves out over every crack in the ground; Erebus felt them drinking up Zeus's power as it ran into the earth. The tension between them was growing palpable like two dogs on the end of their leashes.

"That's part of being married to a powerful woman. You would understand that, wouldn't you?" Erebus ignored the obvious attempt to rile him up and forced himself to stay calm. Distaste rose in him when he heard the way Zeus chewed on the words *powerful woman* like it was an unsatisfactory quality.

"You said it yourself. You heard it last night. It sounds like you know very well what I do with a powerful woman. Whether you can do the same remains to be seen." Zeus flashed an agitated glare at him, which only encouraged Erebus to go on. "Maybe that's why you prefer mortal women, Zeus," he hissed. "Do you feel like the king of the gods when they succumb to you because they're afraid?"

Zeus growled, turning and snapping at Erebus. "Don't concern yourself with me, Darkness."

"But you seemed very concerned about me and my bed. Are you hoping to join? We haven't done that before, but maybe after a few millennia, it's time to try." His light tone succeeded in pushing the last of Zeus's buttons. Zeus stalked forward, crossing the gap between them as lightning fell from his fingers like a forge. Erebus didn't blink as he released the grip on his shadows, letting them surge forward and start to drown out Zeus's lightning.

Zeus screamed as the shadows traveled up the bolts of power and gripped onto his arms and legs. He flailed about like he was stuck in tar, pulling his arms and legs in any direction he could to release himself.

"It's no use, Zeus," Erebus growled, stalking forward and leaning down until he was in Zeus's face. Zeus stood immobilized, the shadows snaking around him and holding him in place. "Yes. Nyx and I have reunited. She has not chosen your side. That's all you need to know. Do we have any other problems here?"

Zeus struggled again, and Erebus's gaze flickered down to the shadows and lightning that were curling and uncurling around the god's limbs. He couldn't help but smile at the sight, the darkness swallowing up each flicker and spark that came out of Zeus.

"No," Zeus gritted out through clenched teeth, his hair falling into his face as he struggled. "We don't have any problems." Yet, he struggled again, and Erebus kept an eye on the bonds that were holding him.

"Then what was the point of this?" Erebus hissed, staring Zeus down as he stepped closer in intimidation. "You know you can't beat me." Erebus felt something going off in his head. This wasn't right. Zeus *did* know that he couldn't beat Erebus. Why had he attempted to corner him in the dark? On Erebus's own terms? Zeus's face lit up in a dark smile, the gold across his brow glittering with sparks of lightning like a twisted conduit.

"To distract you."

"You what—" Erebus was cut off with a guttural scream, falling to his knees in front of Zeus. In an instant, it was the God of lightning who was towering over Erebus. There was something cold and heavy that was sitting around Erebus's wrists, sending freezing shockwaves over his body. A horrid emptiness spread in him, and Erebus realized that he couldn't feel his shadows. It sent him to near madness in the blink of an eye. His face contorted in rage and pain as he twisted around, eyeing the heavy metal around his wrists. He could barely hear Zeus laughing behind him as he looked up, staring at the god who had thrown the chains on him while his back was turned.

"Hermes," Erebus growled, his voice sounding murderous. He was still struggling wildly against the bondage, sweat breaking out on his brow. His very, very *mortal* brow, he realized, as he was now in the form that he took when he went to hide amongst mortal men. Hermes was standing a few feet away, with an impassive look on his face.

"It's not his fault." Zeus boomed with laughter, and Erebus turned around. "Like I said. There was a vote. It sounds like

Hephaestus told you of the little *project* that he was working on for me."

"What in the hell are you planning?" Erebus hissed, lunging for Zeus even while he was on his knees. Zeus took one step to the side, and Erebus hit the ground, sending the God of lightning into another round of laughter.

"I was glad to hear that you and your lovely consort had made up." Zeus wiggled his fingers and watched the lightning dance across them. "I wonder if she'll come for you."

Erebus's face twisted as he began to laugh. "You'd try to use me as *bait?* For Nyx?" Zeus's expression only faltered for a minute, but Erebus continued. "You are going to die for this."

Zeus waved his hand in the air in nonchalance. "That's something I'm always prepared for. We'll see what happens when things start getting worse for the mortal world. We know that she'll do anything to stop that." A sick realization settled in Erebus's gut.

"You don't care at all about defeating Kronos, do you? This has been about primordials all along." He spat at Zeus's feet, who only smiled in response.

"There we go. I was wondering when you'd catch on, but then again, you were so *eager* to pick up arms to defend Nyx's honor. It was admirable, really, which meant that we had to keep up the charade a little longer. Kronos is a problem, but he'll be easily dealt with. The real prize is tossing you two away with him."

"This won't end well for you, Zeus," Erebus hissed, his head growing dizzy the longer he went cut off from his shadows.

"Maybe." Zeus shrugged. "But death is inevitable." He leaned down, getting close to Erebus's face as he slapped his cheek a few times. "Even for a primordial."

## ❀ 34 ❀

Erebus had felt a lot of things in his long life. He had felt pain before, and he knew what death felt like; he'd sired it. He had never, in all his existence, known what it was like to be without his shadows. It was excruciating. It was a feeling that made him want to claw at his own skin as if he could rip it open and reveal them. Erebus had passed out on the sidewalk with Zeus in his face, all his strength seeping from him. When he finally came to, he was sitting in a small room, with no bearing as to where he was.

"Fuck…" he hissed slowly, sitting up from a low bench where he had been placed. The room was utterly bare with stone walls, a tiled floor, and one high window he couldn't reach. The door was undoubtedly locked from the outside, but Erebus wasn't even sure that he could stand to go try it. The chains around his wrists were thick and made an abhorrent noise every time that he shifted. He looked down, trying to study them for any weak spots.

*Damn you, Hephaestus. How the hell could you agree to make something for Zeus and then actually deliver?* Hephaestus had delivered. They had the same impeccable craftsmanship which everyone had come to expect from the god. All the metal was so finely fused together that it looked like it was one solid piece. However, they worked. He had to commend the god for his creativity. Instead of making a chain so strong that it would hold a primordial, he made a chain that made a primordial so weak that a chain would hold them. It would be an ingenious idea if Erebus wasn't currently on the receiving end of it.

*I don't know if I've ever been that stupid.* He cursed himself. *I was so damn focused on Zeus—and since when does Hermes not make a blasted amount of noise everywhere that he goes?*

"Hermes." Erebus cursed his name aloud, spitting on the ground. He began muttering under his breath as he ran a hand through his hair, a nervous habit, causing the heavy chain to hit him in the nose. "Gods damn it! I'll kill you for this!" He shouted at the door and into the presumably empty hallway.

It was still dark out, so either he had been out for an entire day or not very long at all. Erebus had too many questions and no abilities to calm himself down to sort through them. The agony of his missing shadows was like a phantom limb; it was clear through his damp clothes that he hadn't stopped sweating since he'd lost the sensation. He leaned his head back against the cool wall, his breath shaky.

*There must be a way to warn Nyx. I don't know how he plans to use me as fucking bait. Does he have another pair of chains? How does he think he'll even get them on Nyx? This is insane.*

"It is insane." A deep, quiet voice broke through the silence of the night, causing Erebus to sit up with a start.

"Who's that? Why are you here?" He normally would have felt his own power rising to the surprise of a visitor, but he felt nothing. *And get out of my head, while you're at it.*

"Your expression looked rather incredulous." The voice answered, coming from the other side of the door.

"Who are you?" Erebus said it again, his temper rising at the sheer weight of his own vulnerability. He had never felt this incapacitated before and wasn't looking to make a habit out of it. There was a heartbeat of agonizing silence before the door swung open and Hephaestus snuck in.

"You bastard," Erebus screamed, jumping to his feet as the chains swung between his arms. He took a step forward but faltered, falling to his knees as he hissed out another long string of curses. "Do you have any idea what you've done?"

Hephaestus was as calm as ever, seemingly unfazed by Erebus's reaction. He waited until Erebus glared up at him, expecting a response, before he started speaking.

"I do. Do *you* know what I've done?" There was something in his voice that made Erebus feel like he had missed something. Hephaestus leaned back against the door, crossing his leg at the ankle and running a hand through his beard absent-mindedly. He was wearing his helmet, making it impossible for Erebus to read his expression.

"You made these chains. You made Zeus a weapon that could contain immortals. Why would you do that?" Erebus shook his head in bewilderment as he sat down on the floor, coming off his knees. Hephaestus nodded slowly as if he was dissecting this new information.

"I did do that. It's not the only thing I did."

Erebus started grinding his teeth together in frustration, feeling a growing sense of urgency.

"What... else... did... you do?" Erebus choked the words out slowly, staring up at the god with an angry and tense expression. He couldn't tell for sure, but Hephaestus's head moved in such a way that he thought he might be smiling. It took a second before he answered.

"I made Zeus the chains. It's in my best interest to remain a very... neutral party. I'll take requests, and payment, from anyone."

"That's a coward's way to live," Erebus growled, fighting the urge to leap onto Hephaestus since he knew he didn't have the strength. "You'll take money from all sides in a war, but you won't ever fight yourself? You call yourself a god?"

Hephaestus shrugged, something about him was so resolute that he was unbothered. He stood with his shoulders straight, bright eyes boring a hole into Erebus where he sat.

"You do not know what I do during the ides of war or what I call myself. You are the God of darkness, and Zeus, the God of lightning. Do you know what I am, Erebus?"

Silence.

"I'm the God of alchemy. The God of bottled chaos. They say only women can grow mankind, gestate a god, create new life. Do you know what I can do with metal? With wood? With the things of the earth?"

Hephaestus was met with silence again. Erebus had never heard him speak this way. His voice dropping to its lowest register with a command to it that even Erebus had to admit was impressive.

"Do not ever say that I have done another god's bidding." Hephaestus spat the last word like it was poisonous. "Yes, I created those chains for Zeus. Ask me about them, Erebus." Erebus raised an eyebrow and sat a little taller, his gaze roving over the god.

"Tell me about these chains, Hephaestus."

The god nodded once; all the fire that had been in him seemed to cool back down to an ember. "I made the weapon that could capture any immortal, no matter how strong they are. It uses their own powers against them, it bottles up their power, effectively acting like a seal on an amphora."

"Helpful," Erebus interrupted with a sneer.

"I'm going to ignore that you seem to don't understand I'm trying to help you." Hephaestus quipped back. "They amplify your own powers and keep you from them, but every god has a weak spot. A counterpoint."

"All right..." Erebus looked up at Hephaestus, trying to uncover where he was going.

"Your power is darkness. The chains are bottling up that

darkness and holding it from you. What is your opposite?"
Hephaestus asked a leading question.

"Light, I guess." Erebus shrugged. "It doesn't really work
that way, though, I can summon darkness even during the
day..."

"The chains are not *literally* you." Hephaestus groaned,
getting annoyed that Erebus wasn't catching on. "They won't
work in the daylight."

"What?" Erebus shook his head in shock. "They won't
work?" Hephaestus nodded.

"I've designed them that way. There's a loophole for every
god's power, if they can figure it out." Hephaestus's voice got
quieter. "I'd never make a weapon that held absolute power."
There was something in his tone that made Erebus think this
was something more personal for Hephaestus than he was
letting on.

"Once the sun rises..." Erebus trailed off, almost too
hopeful to say it aloud but Hephaestus nodded.

"You'll be able to break them, and your powers will return
to you. They were put on you under the cover of night, but in
daylight, they won't hold the power." Erebus nodded, a quiet
sense of contemplation coming over him as he let out a long
breath. When he looked up, Hephaestus had opened the door
and was on his way out.

"Thank you." The god turned around, nearly entirely
covered in shadow now. He nodded once, Erebus couldn't be
sure, but said nothing and shut the door behind him. There
was something to Hephaestus that none of the other gods
could figure out, not that anyone had really tried. This
certainly wasn't clarifying anything. At least he knew he had
an out. Erebus just needed to wait.

"I hate waiting."

———

)))

————

IT WAS BARELY dawn when Hades stepped out of his Olympus residence, still fussing with the ties of his chiton. He looked up to see Poseidon already waiting for him, standing outside his door.

"It's a bit early for plotting, don't you think?" Hades asked quietly, falling into step beside Poseidon as they made their way towards the great hall. Most of the gods were now spending all their time there, losing themselves in revelry until they had recharged enough to descend upon the battlefield. Poseidon looked around them, ever cautious that they would be overheard.

"Do you think this is wise?" Poseidon asked Hades without looking at him, his voice low. Hades knew that he was referring to their latest development, following Typhon's fail to kill Zeus on the battlefield. As the pantheon came into view, Hades only nodded in response. The duo made their way to join in the crowd, knowing that it would only seem suspicious if they avoided everyone entirely.

As they approached the steps, a voice called out from behind them.

"Hold on."

Both gods turned around and saw Erebus, looking livid and rubbing one of his wrists absentmindedly. Poseidon raised an eyebrow in his confusion, but Hades only grinned.

"Don't think we didn't notice what you got up to during nightfall." He looked at Erebus as if he was salivating for details. "It seems that you two have made up well. Is the Consort of Darkness going to be gracing us all with her presence?"

"Be quiet about it," Erebus snapped, looking around them

like Poseidon had. "It's best if it's... not known that she's... involved."

Erebus chose his words very carefully, still not even fully understanding himself if he had gotten back together with Nyx. Zeus knew of her presence now, but that seemed moot. Erebus had intended on leaving immediately for the Underworld, but it would be best to stay. His presence would startle Zeus and confuse him. Zeus also wouldn't do anything to jeopardize the hold that he had on the other gods. This included capturing Erebus publicly or admitting that he had petitioned Hephaestus to make a weapon that could hold anyone. Surely, the latter would not spark confidence in Zeus as a ruler of gods.

The three immortals fell into silence as they approached the steps, the commotion inside making it apparent that the gods were still going strong. Hades put his hand on the door when a voice rung out behind them.

"Going inside without me, boys?"

## ❦ 35 ❦

H ecate's voice was mischievous, and when the gods turned around, she had a smile on her face. It was an increasingly rare occurrence to see Hecate out of the Underworld, but there she stood. She was in her full god form, the heads of the crone and the maiden on her shoulders. There was a trail on the ground behind her of glimmering red dust, traces of the power that was running under her skin. She was wearing a large, golden pendant of the triple moon—a symbol that she shared with Nyx. Her hair hung nearly down to her waist while her arms had bracelets that looked like a dog's open jaw encompassed her hand.

Even Hades and Erebus, who had seen Hecate in her full power, were slightly taken aback. Poseidon, who had *never* seen Hecate like this, was unable to keep from openly staring. It was Erebus who took a step forward, offering her a warm smile.

"It's always a delight, Hecate." He reached for her palm and kissed it, giving her a healthy show of respect, regardless of the power hierarchy between them. Hecate gave him a sly smile and breezed past him, walking in between Poseidon and Hades without a second glance at either of them.

"I've decided this was taking too long," she said with a smirk, turning back at the men as she grabbed the door handle. "I've come to speed things up." With that, Hecate tossed open the doors to the great hall, the rush of wind from its momentum causing her hair and tunic to flare out behind her. She stepped into the great hall, and there was a collective gasp before a few of the different gods swarmed Hecate. She was a rarity in Olympus, even more so than Hades, who had the unpleasant responsibility of fraternal relationship with Zeus.

Poseidon, Hades, and Erebus filed in, keeping to the edge of the crowd. Zeus hadn't noticed Erebus yet, but as soon as he saw Hecate, he stepped off his dais and walked over to her. Hades rolled his eyes as he watched it unfold.

"Oh, this is going to be delicious." Hades chuckled, crossing his arms and leaning back against a column.

"Why do you say that?" Poseidon followed Hades's gaze.

"You haven't spent much time with Hecate, have you?" Erebus grinned and Poseidon shook his head in answer. "Then you are going to enjoy this, too."

They all watched as Zeus stepped in between Artemis and Nike, grinning lecherously at Hecate. Hecate took a step back from Zeus, her eyebrows raising. He opened his mouth to say something as Hecate held up a hand to silence him. They couldn't hear what Hecate and Zeus were saying, but watching the scene unfurl before them was no less satisfying. They watched on as Hecate dismissed Zeus with a wave of her hand, turning back around and giving Aphrodite a small smile.

"I think she's secretly in charge of all of us," Poseidon admitted, his eyes wide as he got an idea of what the Goddess of witchcraft was all about. The gods milled about for a little while longer, until there was a great bellowing sound that shook the hall. It sounded far off, and Erebus knew it was coming from the valley.

Zeus stood immediately, and the sounds of weapons being unsheathed and the dull hum of power began to fill the room.

He parted the crowd and stormed out, the rest of the gods following.

"Here we go again," Hades chuckled, magically pulling out his bident once more. Poseidon laughed, a darker sound that Erebus was used to hearing from the god. He cracked his knuckles, summoning the infamous trident out of thin air.

"Come on, boys, I think our luck is about to change." There was a tone to Poseidon's voice that subtly let Erebus know whatever *plan B* was, the brothers had found it. *God help us.*

They filed out, making up the rear of the war procession, finding Hecate waiting for them.

"What are you doing here?" Erebus asked with a raised brow as they fell a few steps behind the rest of the gods. Hecate shrugged.

"I wasn't kidding. I do think that everyone needs to wrap this up. I don't like the havoc it's causing, having gods, primordials, and titans all locked in a confrontation." Erebus studied her face for a moment, noticing that she wasn't making eye contact with him.

"Did Nyx send you?" His voice was dreadfully quiet, almost hopeful, when he asked. His heart skipped a beat waiting for her answer. When she did speak, it was quiet, just for him.

"Yes. She is still concerned about the Fates' prophecy, but she asked me—"

"She asked you to watch after me?" Erebus raised an eyebrow, not offended by the concept but also confused as to how a god, any god, less powerful than him would be of great assistance. Hecate shrugged as if she read his thoughts.

"I think more so there would be someone you trusted out there, Erebus. Not everything can simply be settled by a power struggle." Erebus sighed, the ever-present ache in his chest getting more prominent by the minute.

"I do trust you, Hecate."

The goddess grinned, flipping some hair over her shoulder as she hid her other heads.

"Excellent. Now, let's wrap this up. I left Thanatos in charge of my dogs, but I have a feeling he'll be busier than the rest of us soon." There was a wicked gleam in her eye when she said it, and Erebus knew that as wise as Hecate was, she was not to be messed with. She had a bloodthirsty streak as wide as the rest of them, except hers only came out when it was justified, making it more dangerous.

By the time Erebus had caught up and stared over the precipice of the mountain, no one was prepared for what they saw. Hecate was gone, rushing down the mountainside with the other gods as quickly as she could, vanishing and reappearing in midair. There was a massive mass at the base of the mountain, standing taller than anything in the valley. There was an earth-shattering roar that shook rocks free from the cliff side, sending them down on some of the heads of those below. At the base of the mountain, plucking gods out of the sky, was Hekatonkheires. One of the most feared creatures of Greece, he was stronger than all the gods and all the titans. The giant had over fifty heads and one-hundred arms, all of them moving sporadically. His most memorable trait, however, was the stench—a smell that came from fifty mouths, maws open, smelling of rotting flesh. It carried through the valley and made everything smell like death.

Erebus turned and looked at Poseidon and Hades, both of whom had deadly serious expressions on their faces.

"Are you *fucking* kidding me?" Erebus growled, immediately pulling back his arm and delivering a swift blow to Hades. The god stumbled backward, ichor pouring from his nose. Poseidon stepped in between them with his hands up in a placating gesture.

"Erebus, easy. I know that this seems brash—"

"Brash?" Erebus yelled, shoving Poseidon in the chest.

"You really should just challenge Zeus to combat at this point, if you think unleashing Hekatonkheires was the best *plan B?*"

Hades stood up from the ground, wiping at his nose. "Listen, we've thought this through…"

"We don't have time for that," Erebus snapped, his gaze returning to the battlefield down below. It was already devolving into carnage, and Erebus cringed at the sight of the bodies.

It took one lunge and he was off, diving into the fray. Erebus rolled his shoulders back as he slid down the mountainside, rejoicing in the feeling of his shadows once more. He stopped halfway down, with a great shout and tossed his hands out into the air in front of him, and a wave of blackness unfurled from him. It was like a blanket tumbling down the cliff side, not like veins, but a wave. The darkness consumed everything that it touched and leaving no light behind. It was not like nightfall, no, it was the absence of *everything.* To be within the darkness was to hardly exist at all; it was Erebus at his most primordial, an elemental blackness that things had to claw forth to existence. Erebus's yell shook the heavens in answer to Hekatonkheires, his veins turning black under his skin. His body shook with the strength of his exertion, chest heaving as a raw, unfiltered power was violently ripped from his body at his own command.

Every god and titan down below stopped and turned, seeing Erebus on the side of Mt. Olympus and the rushing wave of blackness towards them. This had surpassed anything that they had seen, even his efforts the day prior. Hecate grinned wickedly in encouragement, using his momentary distraction to drive a poisoned blade between the ribs of a titan. The gods cheered as the blackness rushed down to meet the hundred-armed monster, but only one face was utterly unamused. Zeus.

The God of lightning had been making his way towards Kronos, utterly content to leave Hekatonkheires alone, much to Poseidon and Hades's disappointment. Zeus decided that if a missing Erebus didn't pull Nyx out of hiding, then the monster would. What he did not account for, however, was Erebus. There was a petulant rage in Zeus that was fully unlocked at the sight of Erebus, once more, displaying greater power and authority than Zeus could ever imagine. Zeus's eyes nearly went red with anger as his shoulders tensed, conjuring up a lightning bolt that he gripped in his hand like a sword. The battle had descended into utter chaos around him once more, as the darkness continued down the mountainside, slowly but surely.

Hekatonkheires was distracted by a melee of gods flying around him—most notably Hermes with winged sandals and Helios in a blazing chariot, distracting him with piercing blows at one of his many eyes. The monster didn't see the blackness rushing down upon them. The darkness alone wouldn't kill anyone, but it would greatly inhibit them, rendering them virtually senseless. It was then that Erebus was able to step in, with all his senses intact in the darkness, and end his opponents.

Zeus gripped the lightning tighter and kicked off the ground, launching himself above the fray and up towards Erebus. Poseidon and Hades had already joined in the fighting down below, waiting for Erebus's darkness to descend upon the battlefield in totality. Poseidon caught a glimpse of Zeus, rocketing up toward Erebus with murder in his eyes. The primordial was in deep concentration, required to both wield his power and avoid giving himself over to it completely.

"Erebus," Poseidon yelled out, his voice becoming a booming echo that shook the valley. It got his attention, and Erebus stopped, the shadow on the mountainside stopping its progression. He looked up right at the moment that Zeus tackled into him, the impact sounding like a thunderclap. No one noticed, there were now too many enemies, and the gods were all locked in combat. Ares and Apollo had joined the frays that were throwing barbs at Hekatonkheires, none of which were making a lasting impact. Hecate herself had proved wickedly efficient with short blades and was moving through a line of titans with barely a sweat breaking out on her brow.

Erebus and Zeus rolled until they came to a stop, both now on a short outcropping on the side of the mountain. Zeus stood first, his eyes contorting to an expression of utter madness as he bared his teeth. Erebus stood up and dusted himself off, his black shadows still filling his veins. They began to circle each other once more, seizing up their opponent. There was now a spinning thundercloud that was forming above Mt. Olympus and the entire valley, a dark, ominous vortex that sparked with lightning. Hekatonkheires let out another shout that sent rocks tumbling down the mountainside as the cliff face shook—he was beginning to climb the mountain.

"Zeus," Erebus's voice had dropped, a commanding tone to it that was so powerful, it reminded you that he was one of the first five beings in existence. "You need to think very carefully about what you're doing right now. Do you think the gods aren't watching? Why are you attacking an ally?" Erebus tried to appeal to Zeus's ego.

Zeus only curled his lip, his tunic torn in spots, making him look more like a madman than a king of the gods. Lightning started flashing around the pair as it started to rain, soaking both gods to the bone in an instant.

"It doesn't matter," Zeus hissed. "They'll believe anything I tell them. All that matters is getting you old, ancient relics out of my way!" His voice escalated to a scream as he leaped forward, lightning raised high above his head. Erebus easily rolled out of the way, content to let Zeus tire himself out. As much as he wouldn't mind destroying Zeus, he knew there were still some things that were more trouble than they were worth, and having to stick around Mt. Olympus and clean up that political mess wasn't worth it. If he died in battle, that was one thing; if he died in one-on-one combat with a primordial, it was another.

"Get back here, you coward," Zeus screamed, jumping back to his feet and turning on Erebus like a dog. His appearance was almost completely unhinged, spit flecking his beard and his eyes roved wildly as if he couldn't focus on one thing. His tunic was ripped and bloody, and he only wore one sandal. He slowly crept forward, flexing his muscles like a cat, as electricity sparked over his back and arms. Erebus didn't look much better, although he was infinitely more composed. The dark cloth of his chlamys whipped around in the wind, wet curls now sticking to his forehead. The sky had grown even darker as the rain pelted down around them, lightning and thunder flashing in tandem with Zeus's laborious breath. If it were any other opponent that stared down Zeus, it would be intimidating.

It wasn't any other opponent. It was Erebus, who looked up at Zeus from underneath a heavy, furrowed brow and only smiled. Shadows began dancing up his arms and legs, caressing each part of him like a lover, his veins pulsing.

"I would be very careful," Erebus muttered, looking at Zeus through the rain as the battle waged on below them. There was another bellowing shout that Erebus knew without looking was Hekatonkheires, slowly climbing up the mountain as he dodged attacks from the swarms of gods. "I've been itching for a fight for a long time, and I'd be more than happy to give it to you."

"I've seen your tricks, Erebus—"

"Oh no," Erebus laughed, "You haven't."

At that, Zeus launched himself forward, his hand raised above his head as he descended upon Erebus. The wind and rain pelting at his back made the image that much more threatening, his arm pulled back as a bolt of lightning emerged from Zeus's grip like a hidden sword. There was already a gleam in

Zeus's eye, one of victory, that set Erebus off. Everything felt like it began moving in slow motion.

Erebus reached up and grabbed onto the lightning bolt Zeus was holding, shadows exploding across it like tar. Zeus watched in horror as Erebus yanked it, pulling Zeus down to the ground out of midair. He landed with a sickening crack as the lightning bolt exploded, raining down sparks on both as a chorus of shadows leaped from the carnage. Erebus laughed at the expression of extreme frustration on Zeus's face and felt his shadows running through him, covering Zeus like rope, pushing down and anchoring Erebus to the mountainside itself. There was another tremor, and Erebus knew that the monster was still getting closer.

He grinned, hardly able to hear Zeus's curses over the rain and wind, before leaning down and grabbing Zeus by the tunic. He hauled Zeus up with one arm and walked towards the edge, watching the rage in Zeus's eyes contort to fear.

"This is one of my favorite *tricks*," Erebus growled, leaning in so he was face to face with Zeus. He took another step forward and extended his arm, dangling Zeus off the edge of the mountain. Erebus peered over the edge and saw Hekatonkheires, clamoring and throwing hundreds of fists against the mountainside not fifty feet below them. Zeus was a pleading, crying mess, clawing at Erebus's arm.

"You wouldn't! You can't! Please, listen…" Erebus only rolled his eyes as the thunder flashed behind him, framing him in black clouds of both his and Zeus's creation.

"Even your own thunderstorms listen to me, Zeus," Erebus purred. "They listen to the darkness."

"Erebus—"

The God of darkness let go.

## 36

E rebus watched Zeus drop down into the waiting jaws of the great monster, catching his breath while shadows still danced on the ground around him. Hekatonkheires screamed as he saw the god and reached up, one of his arms plucking Zeus from the sky. The monster released his grip on the cliff and dropped back down to earth, creating an earth-shattering tremor when he landed. Erebus watched in tense confusion as Hekatonkheires didn't destroy Zeus, but gripped him tightly, walking across the valley.

There was still a swarm of gods surrounding him, arrows and blades flying at his many heads and hands, but nothing seemed to stick. He easily batted away every attempt to pluck Zeus from his grip. Erebus watched on, dumbfounded, as Hekatonkheires walked through the chaos and headed straight for Kronos's frontlines. Erebus vanished into the air, reappearing down at the base of the mountain where the fighting had stopped. Every eye was fixed on the great giant carrying Zeus. He materialized next to Hades, who was pulling his bident from the corpse of a titan.

"What did you do?" Erebus asked again, turning to look at the god with a shake of the head. "If you wanted him dead…"

"We do," Hades insisted, "but we had to strike a deal." Erebus looked on as the monster continued to waddle through the chaos at his feet, some gods and titans unable to avoid his step. They were crushed instantly. There was a sudden burst of movement from the ground, a tangling mess of vines shooting up from the red earth. They immediately wrapped around Hekatonkheires's legs and arms, immobilizing more than half of him in a moment.

"Oh, for fuck's sake." Hades hissed. "Fuckin' Demeter."

They watched on as the goddess propelled herself up the greenery, Hera following close behind her as they used the vines as a bridge. The goddesses had swords pulled from the bodies of titans and began decapitating heads of the monster… one by one. Hekatonkheires screamed, sending a shockwave through the valley that had even Erebus and Hades going to cover their ears. They watched in a gross fascination as *heads* fell to the ground, causing the monster's movements to slow down. It looked for a moment that the two goddesses would come out with a victory until both missed one of the many limbs reaching for them. In a second, Hekatonkheires had both Demeter and Hera in his grasp. The vines withered up and turned to ash immediately. He freed himself as he began to move again towards the enemy camp.

"Please tell me this was part of your plan," Erebus grunted.

"No. Only Zeus was."

"I'd love to know the details, Hades." Erebus's voice was growing tense. He was fed up with only getting half of the plan from the brothers. Hades made a sigh that sounded like a relent.

"We bargained with Kronos. He could have Zeus if he left the rest of us alone. We agreed to help Kronos free Hekatonkheires to make it all happen in a way that looked… organic on the battlefield." Hades plucked a piece of tunic from the end of the bident. Erebus let out a low whistle. There was nothing that shocked him anymore when it came to the loyalties of gods, but even he had to admit that this was impressive in its political delicateness.

The fighting had slowed, all eyes still fixed on the giant as he crossed the center of the valley and over to Kronos's side. Kronos stood, wet with the rain, but otherwise unruffled. He didn't even look like he had picked up a sword that day. Hades and Erebus watched on as Hekatonkheires handed over the three gods, Zeus, Hera, and Demeter to Kronos. Kronos stood as tall as the monster, accepting the three gods with ease. Erebus could see the bodies of the gods struggling, throwing their fists against his grip. He could only watch on in devout horror as Kronos unhinged his jaw and tossed all three of the gods into his mouth, swallowing them whole.

"Fuck..." Hades's eyes were wide, and he looked like he had gone a little pale. A moment later, Poseidon appeared next to them.

"All right." His voice had a tenseness to it as he tried to sound calm. "We didn't know what Kronos was going to do, but we knew he was going to kill him."

"Them," Erebus corrected Poseidon although he wasn't sure why. "That wasn't just Zeus."

"Is... is it over?" Hades looked back towards Kronos, all of them waiting with bated breath to see what happened next. There was a sudden, deep sound that they couldn't place for a second... until they realized that Kronos was laughing. He was laughing, a deep, belly laugh that shook the valley almost as much as the roars of his giant. When Kronos finally stilled, he looked out over the carnage, seeing the gods and the titans who were frozen in disbelief and confusion. Kronos turned his head to Hekatonkheires and nodded.

"Go."

The gods couldn't hear him, but they read the command on his lips, fumbling for weapons as Hekatonkheires turned on his heel with impressive dexterity for a monster of his size and charged back into the fray. It was like a switch had been flipped and the battle resumed at full strength. The message was clear: this changed nothing.

"Now what's your plan?" Erebus screamed, staring at the brothers.

Both Hades and Poseidon had the wherewithal to look ashamed. Erebus scoffed, but there was another scream that cut him off. They turned to find Nike in the hands of the giant, dangerously close to one of his gaping jaws. The image shocked all of them to action, determining that there was a time to talk politics later.

Hades and Poseidon were immediately pulled into combat by lesser titans and began cutting their way through the ranks to get to the monster. Erebus dissolved into shadows once more, reappearing high above the valley. It was the best vantage point to dictate his shadows, to send them out like sentient soldiers of his own. He leaned back against the cliff side, catching his breath and calming himself down for a moment. He felt a gathering churning in his gut, his power rising to his call once more, threatening to overtake him entirely. Erebus struggled with the notion to let it *go*, but he knew that there would be nothing left if he did. It was elemental. It didn't know bad or good, right from wrong. There was only power, and he needed to keep a grip on it, so he didn't kill every living thing in the valley when he unleashed.

He felt the shadows taking over his veins like blood, the darkness in the sky and in the thunderclouds deepening in their answer. Erebus screamed, a sound that was lost on the wind, as he rallied his strength one more and prayed that he would stay in control. There was a heartbeat, then two, and suddenly...

"Erebus." A soft voice cut through the utter chaos around him, and Erebus threw his eyes open.

Nyx was standing in front of him, her body barely containing the power within her. She looked like liquid starlight, like fire so hot that it was almost cool to the touch.

Her train was made of comets, and he could see the outline of the moon over her heart.

"Nyx." He said the word and it was reverent, like a prayer. Erebus lurched forward and wrapped her up in his arms, cradling the star to the heart of darkness. There was no hesitation as she tangled her hands in his hair, murmuring something that he couldn't hear. Erebus pulled back slightly, cupping her cheek and rubbing his thumb back and forth.

"What are you doing here? The prophecy—" Nyx cut Erebus off with a shake of her head.

"I figured it out."

Erebus felt his whole body go cold.

"What does that mean?"

Nyx sighed, *"'The night Nyx fights will be her last.' I am* the night, Erebus. Keeping myself from you, the way that we refused to work this out… I was fighting with *myself.* That's what was going to kill me."

Erebus stared at Nyx in utter shock, his mind going a million miles a minute as they stood there. They clutched one another in the pouring rain, the sounds of the war below getting lost on the wind. There was a question building in Erebus's chest and it had been incubating there for a while. He stood on the side of the mountain with Nyx in his arms and found that he couldn't hold back for a second longer.

"Will you still have me, Nyx?" It was the only thing that she could hear. Nyx nodded, and Erebus felt like he might explode as the feeling overtook him.

"Yes," Nyx said it aloud and tears fell from her eyes, mixing with the rain on her cheeks. Erebus gripped her tighter and pulled her to him, crushing his mouth to hers. He kissed her wildly, possessively, with every bit of his power and hers coming crashing together in the skies above them. It was like they were conductors, orchestrating the ripples of their strength in the sky and darkness around them when they came together. It responded to the united front of night and darkness, and ripples of black magic rolled off the mountain.

When Erebus pulled away, the look in his eyes was feral. He realized that it matched Nyx's equally wild gaze.

"It's time for this to end." Nyx's voice had taken on a tone that he had rarely heard from her, one that was both lethal and playful. "I've had enough."

"You know that I love watching you work." Erebus's grin was equally devastating. There was something that crossed between them that was unspoken, nothing that ever needed to be said out loud. Erebus leaned down and kissed her once more, his hand tangling up in her long hair, and when he released her, they both vanished up into the skies.

The battle below was in full force although the gods were making a feeble showing. Hekatonkheires was moving through the lines without hindrance; no blow that seemed to strike him even made him stumble. Even Erebus could see that there was a measly number of gods left. Most of whom were stuck engaged with titans, waiting like sitting ducks for the giant to pick them up and finish them off.

Nyx and Erebus made their way down the mountainside as the powers of night and dark caressed in the sky, making ribbons of dark power ripple through the atmosphere. When they landed in the valley, there was a crack that split the earth. Erebus exploded into shadows as they burst forth from his skin, blanketing the entire battlefield in a blackness that it choked out the senses. He surrendered himself entirely to his darkest core, the strength of universes throttling out the light. He knew that with Nyx alongside him, she would keep him in check. She was the balance. There was no fear of *total* oblivion with her alongside him—just the right amount.

The valley filled with screams of gods and mortals alike as the darkness blinded them. From the crack in the earth, all the spirits and creatures of the night began to claw their way to the top. It was everything that Nyx encompassed, the essence of night, death, and everything in it. The shades of nightmares, the dreams of artists, and nocturnal creatures that only existed in the corner of your vision. They were now only illuminated by pockets of moonlight, as Erebus's darkness only moved aside for the will of night herself. The gods and titans began to blink as pockets of the valley became clear to them. Most of the participants were too stunned to speak although some titans dropped their weapons and fled immediately.

The great crack in the earth expanded once more, and the creatures piling out of it increased. Now there were demons, monsters with a thousand eyes, the darkest things that were in primordial pockets of the earth that have never been seen by God or man. They filed out into the valley and began circling, waiting for their commands. Kronos began shouting something from the other end of the field and Hekatonkheires lurched forward, moving into action as he tried to capture the creatures of darkness. They all evaded his grasp, his many hundred eyes still useless in the light.

Erebus let his shadows go free, wrapping themselves around the giant's arms but not tightening. Not yet. He turned and watched for Nyx, who appeared at the apex of the crack in the earth. She was in primordial form, the outlines of her body made up entirely by constellations. She stood over fifty feet tall, reigning over even Hekatonkheires, her hair rippling like water and shining with the light of a dying star. A black hole spun in the center of her chest, containing the strength of the cosmos, and her eyes had turned entirely white. Purple and blue clouds covered her feet as power crackled in the atmosphere around her.

As the gods slowly began to adjust to the dark, they looked upon Nyx. No one had seen this in a thousand years, and some of the gods began to scream. There was only one voice who laughed and that was Hecate. Erebus turned to find her, and she was standing over the body of a titan, one who had a scaled face, plucking a knife from between his eyes.

The atmosphere began to shift from shock and fear to tense anticipation. Erebus waited for Nyx's command; the monsters and essence of night stood poised to eliminate every threat on the battlefield. Gods held their breath, unsure who Nyx was fighting for. Then there was Kronos, whose face was a stony picture of defeat.

"Ancient one," he acknowledged, dropping a sword down as he stared up at Nyx's form. "We have prayed for your return."

## 37

Even Erebus's eyes went wide in shock as he watched Kronos drop down to one knee. He knew that there was no defeating Nyx, but the titan was dropping not in surrender, but in respect. Erebus turned and looked at Nyx, watching her expressionless face.

"I've heard your prayers, Kronos." Her voice was deep and reverberated throughout the valley, causing every living thing to stand still. Erebus could only stare, wondering what this was about. Kronos was older than the gods, but younger than the primordials. It would make sense that if he had prayed to immortals, it would've been to the ones that were the most ancient of them all. He didn't expect this. Nyx tilted her head to the side as she spoke. "I have ignored them."

There was a flicker through Kronos that looked like rage, but he held it within. He stood up to his full height, unsheathing a sword that he had strapped to his back.

*Oh, he can't be this stupid.* Erebus looked on in shock as Kronos wielded the weapon. *He is this stupid.*

"If you have ignored our prayers, Ancient One, and you come here to subdue us all, I cannot let that happen." Some of the gods around him started to nod in agreement, and Erebus shook his head. He started calling out to them over the sounds of the wind and rain.

"Don't listen to him," Erebus shouted, gesturing to the massive titan who had taken another step towards Nyx. "Do not waste your immortal lives away, she is not here to —"

Erebus was cut off as Kronos charged forward, thrusting his sword into the packs of demons and creatures around him. The blow plunged the entire battle back into chaos, with Hekatonkheires resuming his warpath too. The gods and titans fell on each other once more, but Nyx did nothing. Every creature at her command stayed still, including Erebus's shadows. Erebus waited, his gaze flickering back between Nyx and the giant, who was plucking gods out from the sky left and right.

*"Wait."* It was Nyx's voice in his head.

*"Nyx… we're losing…"*

*"Wait."*

Erebus watched with bated breath as his shadows began to quiver with pent up energy. His muscles twitched as he held the line of darkness, the shadows wrapped around Hekatonkheires but not allowed to squeeze. The giant reached down and grabbed a deity, tossing them back into one of his gaping jaws. Kronos made a loud shout from where he stood, and Erebus turned to see him engaged in combat against both Poseidon and Hades.

*"Nyx…"*

*"Wait."*

Then Hekatonkheires moved closer to the great crack in the earth, stepping through the demons at his feet as if they were wildflowers. No impact could harm them, and his feet went through the monsters like shadow. They dissolved and reappeared where he had stood; no weapon could land a blow against their ghostly hides. Hekatonkheires grew outraged, bellowing a horrendous sound, each of his mouths crying out in sync. He was balanced on the edge of the earth, his arm raised again as it threatened to pull Ares out of the sky.

*"Now, Erebus!"*

Erebus released every ounce of power that he had, and all hell broke loose on the combat field. The entire scene lasted only a few seconds, but to Erebus, it felt like it went on for hours. All his shadows came to life immediately, choking the life out of each of their opponents. The titans ran screaming as the shadows caused by the moonlight suddenly animated, tightening around throats and even cutting off limbs like wire. Each of Nyx's demons sprang into action, all of them turning on their closest opponent, devouring titans whole. There was no limit to Nyx's boundless power as everything she was came to life in the valley and throttled the life out of their enemies. In a flash, it was all over. Nyx had merely blinked and decimated their opponents where they stood.

The only two that were left was Hekatonkheries and Kronos—the latter of whom was still swinging his sword wildly against a demon that looked like a boar. Erebus surged his shadows forward. Each one found one of the giant's mottled necks, and with a flick of his wrist, the shadows tightened. There was a horrendous sound as fifty heads gasped for air, choking, and a hundred hands clawed at their own eyes until they bled. Erebus stood, an ancient part of him fulfilled at the sight, and snapped his fingers. The shadows disappeared and Hekatonkheries dropped.

He was dead.

The sight of his greatest champion falling to the ground, technically without a hand being laid on him, sent Kronos into a panic. He hacked his way wildly through the remaining demons, although they kept multiplying like the heads of the hydra. The remaining gods had slowly backed away from the battlefield and were now standing in a crowd at the mountain's very base. They watched on in horror and awe as Nyx simultaneously commanded the forces of hell and night incarnate, hardly moving as the leagues of titans were gobbled up and destroyed. It only took another moment, and Kronos was the only titan left on the entire battlefield.

Nyx realized this, blinking, and slowly recalled some of her power. The crack in the earth opened a little wider, and all her forces were sucked back into it. It happened so quickly that even Erebus was hardly able to register it, and then the crack sealed itself up like it had never been there. The only remaining thing in the valley was Nyx, staring at Kronos on his knees. Some of her primordial form had faded away, and she slid down into a mortal form like water being poured into a jar. Her eyes were still alight, but her hair turned back to its raven black, and her body found solidity under the folds of a black tunic that glittered with starlight.

She took a few steps forward toward Kronos as if she didn't even realize that all of Olympus was now watching her, holding their breaths. Even Erebus had moved to the base of the mountain and was standing once more next to Hades and Poseidon. Everyone was wiping blood from their faces and dropping weapons to the ground, their arms too tired to hold them up anymore. Yet, as they tried to reconcile what they had just witnessed, they couldn't stop from staring at the scene unfolding before them.

Kronos was utterly defeated, bent on his knees in the center of the valley. Every other opponent had been vanquished. When he had fallen to his knees, now in surren-der, the grass—wet with the blood of his titans—had made a horrid, squishing sound.

"Kronos." Nyx's voice now sounded like silk, running over the earth in waves as she approached him. "You have made a grave error."

Kronos made no response but went prostrate before her as she approached. It made for a powerful sight; Nyx in her nearly human form, with a titan throwing himself to the ground at her approach. She smiled and simply turned her head to the side and looked at the gods.

"Hecate?" she called out, and the Goddess of witchcraft emerged, a matching smile on her face. She seemed to be the only one who had her wits about her and was suffering from a serious case of shock. Hecate seemed to nearly float over the battlefield as she made her way to its center, tilting her head in respect when she made it to Nyx.

"Do you have what I requested?" Nyx asked again, a lilt to her voice that Erebus couldn't place. Hecate nodded, pulling a small satchel somewhere from the folds of her chiton. She handed it over to Nyx with a smile and no further explanation. Nyx turned back to Kronos, Hecate staying by her side, and tossed the small bag at his head.

"Eat it," she commanded, her voice now echoing with authority. Kronos turned his head to the side, and without standing, he grabbed the small bag and tossed it into his mouth, whole. Nyx looked over to Hecate, and she shrugged as if to say, 'That'll work.'

They all watched on as Kronos chewed slowly, grimacing at times. Erebus felt like he was nearly going to crawl out of his skin as they waited, no one clued into what Hecate and Nyx had planned. It took a few more agonizing moments and Kronos swallowed. Almost immediately, he lurched back up to his knees, gripping at his stomach wildly. The transformation from a titan in surrender to a madman was instantaneous. His arms wrapped around his stomach as he banged his head into the ground, screaming out for relief as Erebus imagined the concoction eating him up from the inside.

*That's an... interesting way to go?* Erebus wondered why Nyx had summoned Hecate to do away with Kronos in such an indirect fashion as opposed to handling him on the battlefield a few moments before. Erebus didn't have to wait much longer for the answer to his question. Kronos had hunched back up and had his hands on his knees, retching like an alley cat. The rest of the gods watched on in utter repulsion as Kronos then vomited, the bodies of Zeus, Hera, and Demeter tumbling out onto the ground.

There was a collective gasp as the gods watched on in disgust and surprise. The three gods stood slowly, bracing themselves on one another for support, but looking no less worse for the wear than the rest of the immortals. They looked back behind them and saw Nyx, who nodded in the direction of the base of the mountain. Zeus, Hera, and Demeter picked themselves up and slowly walked to the edge of the valley. They attempted to join the rest of the gods, but they were given a wide berth, Zeus especially.

Everyone turned back to see Hecate walking away, leaving Nyx staring down at Kronos. He had not died but was still coughing and sputtering about on the ground. Nyx turned her head and searched for Erebus, her eyes finding his instantly. He knew what she was asking without even needing to say it, and he gave her a short, nondescript nod. It was over in a second. Nyx pulled a blade of moonstone out of the air, and in one fell swoop, she cut Kronos's head from his body.

No one reacted. The gods all stood, looking at Nyx, the body of Kronos, and at one another interchangeably. The goddess sauntered forward, and the clouds began to clear. The rains stopped, and slowly, by the time she reached them, they were bathed in the soft light of twilight. The group that was left was small, a fraction of how many gods had first gone into battle. They were covered in blood and gore, wet from the rains, and staring at Nyx with expressions ranging from awe to terror to anger. Zeus stood farthest away and closest to the back of the crowd, with enough wisdom to at least appear humbled. Nyx stood in front of the crowd of the gods—at least, those who were left—and addressed them.

"Gods." Her smile was soft, and her tone was placating. "This war is over. There is no more Kronos, and any titan who would seek revenge for him lies dead beside their leader. What-ever you wish to do with yourselves, you may."

There was a collective sigh of relief as Erebus watched her in utter awe once more. It was Poseidon who raised his voice next.

"Might I suggest... everyone retires for the evening. Go home. There are many things that we'll need to discuss, but those can wait until morning."

"Or at least until I'm drunk," Dionysus called out in response, looking utterly put out that he had been pulled into a war and not an orgy. He was a formidable foe, nonetheless, sheathing a wicked blade that Erebus was sure was typically used to harvest grapes. The gods scoffed and let out a quiet laugh, Dionysus effectively diffusing the mode.

The gods turned and took off in all different directions, and Erebus's mind reeled. There were still so many things that they would have to sort out. *What are we going to do with Zeus, who was very much alive? Nyx needs to know that we can't trust Hermes. Do Hades and Poseidon think that their brother is aware of what they tried to pull? Those damned chains need to be dealt with...*

"Erebus." Nyx said, pulling him from his thoughts, and he snapped his head up, seeing her standing in front of him. He smiled, his arm going around her waist and pulling her to him. He looked up at the setting sun.

"We have a nightfall to arrange, my love." His voice was raspy, heavy with the exertion of the day. Nyx let out a soft laugh, leaning into him and running her fingers down Erebus's jaw.

"I have something I want to do first."

## 🦋 38 🦋

Erebus raised a brow as he looked at Nyx. The expression on her face was unmistakable as he studied it, her hands going down to his chest, tracing the edges of the fabric there. She tilted her head in response, only giving him a coy nod.

"Not here," Erebus shook his head, looking around at the valley. A devilish thought crossed his mind, and he grinned. His grip around Nyx's waist tightened. And he took off, her arms tightening around him in surprise. She made no use of her own power, content to let Erebus carry her wherever they were going. There had been enough talking between them for now. She buried her face into the crook of his neck and inhaled, his body still smelling like smoke and power. Nyx's power was absolute, and she had hardly broken a sweat with her display. Erebus was a different story.

When she felt her feet touch the ground, Nyx picked her head up and looked around the room. She felt a rush of heat run down her body and leaned in closer to Erebus; his hands didn't leave her waist as she looked around.

"Oh… that's *dark.*" Nyx couldn't help but laugh as they stood in the middle of Zeus's great hall. All the gods had left, and they were alone. She studied Erebus's face as decadent thoughts went through her mind. "What if he comes back here?"

Erebus shrugged, his gaze predatory as he stared down at her. "I don't mind an audience." Nyx's grin turned wicked as she turned around, walking to the center of the room. She stopped when she got to the massive dais, her chiton flowing behind her as she walked up the steps. Nyx settled herself down in Zeus's throne, spreading her legs as wide as the chair arms would allow her. The folds of the fabric kept her from being exposed but the motion was enough to set Erebus off.

Nyx smiled, licking her lips as she raised a finger and beckoned Erebus closer. "Come to me." Her voice sounded like liquid velvet, and Erebus nearly launched himself at her before she held up a hand. He stopped. "Slow-ly." Erebus watched her tongue move when she uttered the word as his hands twisted at his sides.

He resumed what felt like an impossibly long walk to where Nyx was seated at the head of the room, both drinking their fill. Erebus's hair was wild, the humidity and rain sending his curls in all directions, except for where it was plastered to his temples. Nyx felt tension rising in her belly as she watched him, coming towards her with slow, predatory movements. His black chlamys was open on one side as she got an eyeful of his muscular thigh with every step. The sharp indent of his hips and the muscles of his ribs where visible to her, and Nyx had to fight from grinding down in her seat. Dark hair dusted his chest and arms, and his eyes were alight with adrenaline. She didn't think that he had stopped breathing hard since the battle had ended. Erebus's blood was running hot, full of the ancient power she helped him to release, but every muscle in his body was tight as he approached her.

When Erebus reached the foot of the dais, he growled. "This suits you."

He looked and took in the sight of her sitting on the throne.

Nyx was in her mortal form, a tight band around the waist of her chiton arranging the fabric in such a way that it seemed to hug her skin. Her long, dark hair was trailing down her back, and Erebus wanted to wrap it around his fist and pull. Erebus took one step up, but Nyx shook her head, her lust turning over to a devious expression. She grabbed her hem, pulling it upwards, and Erebus watched as his blood raced, watching as Nyx's shapely legs were revealed, up to decadent, curvy thighs that nearly glowed white. She stopped right before revealing herself entirely to Erebus, and he growled, his whole body tightening like a spring.

Nyx wanted to laugh but felt the ache between her thighs magnify at the sight of him, poised like an animal who wanted to *devour* her. The atmosphere around them was heavy with strums of power and the smell of sweat and blood. She leaned her head back against the chair and dropped her hem, her hands going up to her breasts and squeezing. Erebus made a strangled sound that was somewhere between a growl and a moan. Nyx sighed, her voice breathy as her eyes fluttered closed.

"Worship me, Erebus."

The command in her voice was a green light to Erebus's body, and he launched into action. His hands were rough on her skin, and Nyx gasped, Erebus dropping to his knees in front of her. He pulled her chiton off in one rip, the controlled violence of the action only making Nyx writhe in her seat. Erebus's hands pushed her legs open impossibly wider, pulling one leg up on his shoulder and holding it there. His free hand gripping her other hip and beginning to rub small circles there.

"Darkness—*ah!*" Nyx had started to plead with him, and it turned into a cry, as Erebus leaned forward and licked up her core. Nyx felt the rest of the strength leave her body as it melted across Zeus's throne, legs held open by Erebus as he began to feast on her. She twisted in the seat until Erebus's grip tightened on her, holding her in place as he probed her gently. Nyx made another mewling sound as her hands found his hair, pulling at it and then pushing him closer. He let out a dark chuckle at her urgency that reverberated inside her, stealing her breath.

"I guess this is where they keep the nectar on Mt. Olympus." Erebus smirked, finally starting to fuck her with his tongue. Nyx let out a small scream, sending off ripples of starlight around her. Erebus let go of her waist, his thumb finding her clit and beginning to draw similar circles around it. Nyx was a live wire. The sight of Erebus on his knees before her was almost enough to send her over the edge. He leaned back and Nyx cried at the loss of contact, slumped down in the seat from where Erebus was still holding her leg on his shoulder. He smirked, wiping traces of her off his chin.

"I swear, if you don't—" Nyx didn't get a chance to finish her pleas. Erebus leaned forward and pulled her clit into his mouth. It was all that it took, and Nyx's whole body was arching off the throne as she came. She was white-hot, her veins pulsing with nothing but lust and moonlight. When she fell back against the back of the chair, she was possessed —all she wanted was to be filled with Erebus, she wanted his shadows to consume every part of her. They had been apart too long, and it was never going to happen again. Every particular in their bodies was singing out for its counterpart, a desperate, ancient force destroying any defenses they had built up against one another. Erebus sat on his knees, his hand rubbing soothing ministrations on her leg.

Nyx pulled her leg off his shoulder slowly, standing up on shaky feet. She took a deep breath and stared at Erebus, her expression leaving no room for debate.

"Sit." She growled, and once again, Erebus moved like it was compulsory.

He traded places with her, sitting down on Zeus's throne. As he shifted in the seat, the chlamys moved, revealing his hard length to her. At the sight, Nyx felt her muscles clench around nothing, and she hissed. Erebus laughed, enjoying the sight of her so flustered over him. It was a sight that he would never take for granted—that the most powerful woman in the universe was reduced to this at the sight of him. He made her this wild. It stroked part of his ego, and he preened, unable to contain his pride at pleasing her.

He sat up a little straighter, ripping the chlamys off and sending the brooch that pinned it at his shoulder flying across the room. Nyx was on him in a second, straddling him and holding herself right above Erebus. It was his turn to growl in frustration, as he could practically feel the heat radiating off her. Nyx threw her arms around his neck and leaned forward, kissing him hard. Erebus's hands went to her hips to steady her, letting Nyx take charge of the embrace. It was filthy, all tongues and teeth, and she pulled back, biting his lower lip until she drew blood. He was covered in sweat and dirt from the battle, and the overwhelming scent of *male* was driving her to her base instincts.

Erebus wasn't faring much better. He couldn't keep his hips from thrusting up, teasing Nyx across her folds as deep sounds came from somewhere in his chest. She was nearly glowing, a stark contrast to her raven hair, every inch of her dipped and curved like she was designed for him.

"Please." Erebus's voice turned into a whimper as he looked at her. "Nyx…"

She only nodded, unable to keep herself off him for another second. Nyx's hand dropped down, and she gripped him, guiding him into her as she sat down fully. Erebus nearly shouted at the feeling of her around him, hot and wet. Nyx's head fell back as she reveled in the sensation of him. As soon as she was seated, starlight began shooting off her skin and shadows started licking up their bodies. Their powers danced over their skin like hands, caressing, pulling, and licking, sending them into a delicious sensory overload.

"Nýchta," Erebus crooned, licking up her jaw until he was

whispering in her ear. "Fuck me on this throne." Nyx moaned and started to move her hips, rolling on top of him until they were both a mess. She set a merciless pace, her thighs burning as she rode him until she started to feel pleasure building somewhere deep in her belly. She was so desperate for him, falling out of the rhythm that she had set for herself.

"Use me." Erebus wrapped his arms around her body and pulled her even tighter to him. "Fuck me, Nyx. Take whatever you want from me." His words were like gasoline, and Nyx ground down on him, picking up her pace until they were both shouting. Erebus knew that she was close from the way she tightened around him, his hand slipping from her waist as it pulled back, delivering a sharp slap to her ass.

The sudden sensation sent Nyx over the edge, her sudden release sending her body into spasms. She collapsed on top of Erebus, putting her head on his shoulder. Erebus held her with one arm around her waist, fucking up into her through her orgasm as he chased his. Nyx moaned and turned her head, biting down on his neck. It had the same effect on Erebus as he thrust up into her, shaking her whole body as she came with a shout.

They both sank back down, breathing heavy and unable to move. Erebus didn't know how long he sat there, but even the events of that day wouldn't have been enough to move him in that moment. He finally slid out of Nyx, kissing her face when she whimpered at the sensation. She resettled, moving her legs so she was sitting in his lap instead of straddling him. Her head fell to his chest, and Erebus occupied himself by running his hands through her hair. Nyx breathed him in deeply, everything about this feeling *right*. There was nothing that would ever feel more complete to her than Erebus. When they had both caught their breath, Nyx looked up at him.

"I know that you had your motivations." Her voice was quiet, and Erebus looked down at her in surprise. "I didn't... agree with them. I felt rejected." There was a tone in her voice that Erebus had never heard before. He squeezed her tighter as she continued. "It took me a while to see that fighting with you was like fighting with myself. I know that you weren't rejecting me."

"If anything, I was rejecting how I felt the world was treating you."

"It feels like it was forever ago. So much has changed." Nyx was right. It seemed like eons ago that they had their first disagreement about Erebus joining Zeus; how he had been so consumed with the idea of being in the light, of bringing her honor. The war had unfurled so many different motivations, plots, and schemes. They never would have guessed that it would have ended with a fratricide plot and Zeus's scheme to lock both Erebus and Nyx away forever.

"It has." Erebus bit his lip, taking a deep breath before he continued. "What about us, Nyx? Have we...changed?" The silence was deafening for a few moments, and Erebus was preparing to cut his heart out and leave it at Nyx's feet.

"No." Nyx shook her head, looking up at him with a soft smile on his face. "We haven't changed, Erebus. I might change. You might change. But *us*, *we*...we will always be better together."

Erebus leaned down, pulling her into a kiss. When they finally broke apart, the glint in Erebus's eye was infectious.

"Do you think we should tell Zeus what happened in here or let him figure it out?"

## ❧ 39 ❧

The next day, the gods gathered in Zeus's great hall and immediately devolved into chaos. Kronos was gone, but they had to deal with the fallout of Zeus's deliberate attack on Erebus and the shambles that the mortal world was in. Erebus wanted to exile Hermes. Poseidon and Hades were desperate to determine if anyone had discovered their failed plot, and Nyx really wanted to go back to the Underworld.

They were all standing together in a circle, shouting, with the throne sitting empty behind them. Some of the deities hadn't returned, deciding to return to their responsibilities without any care for how they worked out the politics of it. One of these was Hecate, who had simply slipped back into the Underworld and decided she would have no part of this. Between those who didn't choose to return and those that they had lost, there were only twelve gods in the room.

And they were all talking at once.

"I don't see why it matters…"

"Someone needs to be in charge —"

"Not you."

"Certainly not —"

"Stop talking." Nyx's voice cut through the din. She raised a hand up in silence, and all the gods quieted down. They had seen what she had done the day before, and no one was going to challenge her. "I am correct in assuming that you are the only gods left —"

"There are more, but they've chosen to not be a part of this...council," Hermes interrupted Nyx and stumbled over the word choice.

Erebus felt his temper flare as he stared at the god, a murderous look in his eye. Hermes looked sheepish, and Erebus didn't know if it was out of guilt or fear.

"Do not interrupt me," Nyx said evenly, and Hermes nodded exuberantly as if it was an impulse that he was trying to contain. She took a deep breath and continued. "Then I am correct. You are the gods who have remained to sort out this mess you've found yourself in."

There were nods all around. Even Zeus nodded his head, keeping his eyes downcast. He had the air of a whipped dog about him, and Erebus took special glee in it. Even if he couldn't stop flicking his eyes over to the dais, feeling hot all over again at the memories of what they had done atop it the night before. Nyx took in everyone's agreeable expressions and resumed, her voice sounding bored.

"Zeus, step forward."

The God of lightning stepped forward, a few paces into the center of the circle that they found themselves in.

"Hephaestus, you, too, please." Nyx looked over to the god, who didn't seem surprised or concerned as he came forward. She took another slow breath as if this was taking all her patience and kept speaking.

"Zeus, is it true that you plotted to imprison both Erebus and me? And you brought Hephaestus into it by soliciting a weapon that would contain any god?"

Zeus's eyes got wide as the chorus of gods erupted around him. The shouting carried up to the rafters, and Erebus chuckled to himself. Nyx had exposed not only Zeus's attempts to imprison them, but she revealed his plan to have a weapon that would control *any* immortal. Even if no one care that he had gone after them, they will certainly care that he was interested in a weapon that could control them.

"N-no, that's not..." Zeus attempted to defend himself, but Hephaestus raised a hand politely. Nyx held her arms up for silence, and all the gods quieted. She nodded at Hephaestus to speak. He cleared his throat, his eyes shining with something unknown from behind his helmet.

"I'm happy to corroborate that. It's true. Zeus engaged Kronos as a distraction to take down you, Nyx, and Erebus. He was after absolute power as *king of the gods,*" Hephaestus said the words with a sneer, "and knew that it would be easy to consolidate power with yours out of the way."

"Out of the way," Nyx repeated and raised her eyebrows as she hummed, playing with the chains in her hands. "You agreed to make these chains for him?" Hephaestus nodded without hesitation.

"I did. I made them with a loophole. Any god would have a way to get out of them if they were clever enough."

"Why did you do this?" Nyx pressed again, and all the gods were on edge as they stared at Zeus and Hephaestus. Erebus could've sworn that he saw Ares crack his knuckles a few times. Poseidon and Hades were fighting to keep their anxiety off their faces, wondering if Nyx was going to call them forth to atone for their sins. Hephaestus seemed to be choosing his words very carefully, and when he spoke, it sounded personal.

"Choice matters." His voice was rough. "I'll never create something that renders absolute power or takes away someone's choice."

Nyx took in his answer and saw Aphrodite shifting uncomfortably in the background. There was a story there for another day when her patience with the gods wasn't completely spent.

"Thank you, Hephaestus. You may go." Nyx gave him a thousand-watt smile, and Hephaestus stepped out of the circle before turning his back and leaving the room entirely. He wanted to be back under the mountain like Nyx wanted to be back in the Underworld. She turned to Zeus and the smile on her face vanished.

"What do you have to say for yourself? To your brothers and sisters?" Nyx gestured at the gods standing around him. "You propelled them into this war with delusions of grandeur and made yourself a king. How did that go for you?"

Zeus said nothing, staring down at the ground. Nyx shook her head and pushed him again.

"I'm going to need an answer, Zeus. How did that work out for you?" Erebus stood off to the side, wondering what was wrong with him that he found the sight of Nyx taking Zeus to task so *hot*. Zeus coughed, shaking his shoulders and picking his head up.

"I failed."

"That's right!" Nyx clapped her hands together. "You did. Then you got Erebus involved, which got me involved, and now I'm here ironing out your mess. Do you think that's what I want to be doing right now?" Nyx pressed again, and Zeus shook his head.

"Out loud, Zeus."

*Fuck.* Erebus was a few seconds away from having to adjust himself. *Yeah, I don't want to know why that's doing it for me.*

Zeus coughed. "No, I do not think that you want to be doing this right now."

"You are correct," Nyx nodded, turning to look at the other gods. None of them raised any objection, and she knew that she would not be defied. "Zeus, as a punishment for your scheming and treachery, I'm going to give you exactly what you wanted."

There were gasps of shock from all the gods, but no one dared challenge Nyx, and even Erebus's head snapped up in surprise. Poseidon and Hades tossed him a confused stare, but he held his hand out at his side as if to convey 'wait a minute.' Nyx waited for a heartbeat, letting her words sink in before she continued.

"Zeus, you are welcome to the title of 'King of the Gods.' Of course, that means you will be burdened with all the responsibilities of a king... with some stipulations of course." Erebus had to bite his lip to temper his smile as Nyx spoke. "Ask me what they are, please."

"What are they?" Zeus choked on the words, his face red and enflamed.

"You are to remain imprisoned on the mountain for the rest of your days, no matter how many they may be. A king should never leave his throne or abandon his subjects. Everyone will speak for an eternity of how Zeus ruled from Mt. Olympus."

She made a motion to the dais behind them, and Erebus tried to subtly pull at the folds of his chlamys. Zeus's eyes got wide in shock, but he dared not open his mouth to speak. Nyx leaned forward, her voice taking on a deliciously wicked tone as the true nature of her verdict came through.

"Tell them whatever they want. Spin whatever myths about yourself that you would like. Whatever you want to do to help you sleep at night, do it. At the end of the day, you and I will both fall into our respective beds at night, and we will all know the truth. You will be a prisoner, a mock king."

There was a beat of silence, and the other gods' expressions ranged from impressed to stunned, yet there was not a voice raised in dissonance. Nyx began walking in a slow circle around Zeus, sounding positively melodic.

"I suppose I'll offer you some conditions, of course. Once a year, you'll be allowed off Mt. Olympus for one day, but you must not go as a god or in your mortal body. You'll have to sneak off this mountain as a beast, as a bird, as an animal. I don't trust you to not get in too much trouble otherwise."

There were a few more moments of silence, and Erebus

watched as Zeus's face got redder and redder. The other gods all now shared the same expression, one of contentment. No one was speaking up for Zeus. Finally, the tension cracked, and Zeus spun on his heel and looked at Nyx.

"Is that all?" His voice was angry, but Nyx only smiled.

"Yes, that will be all with you. You're dismissed. I will speak to the rest of your brethren without you."

There was a stunned moment of silence before Zeus stormed out of the room, nearly taking a column with him when he went. After another second, Hera scurried out of the room after him. *Probably for the best,* Erebus mused, *she likely knew that her own transgressions would come up if she stayed.*

Nyx turned to the remaining gods, her smile now gone but a passive look on her face. "For the rest of you, I have no qualms. My only request is that you go out into the mortal world and repair the damage that was done. The aftershocks of yesterday were carried throughout Greece."

"What will you have us do?" Artemis spoke up, a respectful note in her voice. Nyx shrugged, coming over to stand next to Erebus. His arm slid around her waist.

"Do whatever you do best. Demeter, head to the fields that have been destroyed. Poseidon, call back the rivers that have overflowed. Hades, to my Underworld, please. The management has been lax." Nyx waved her hand in the air. "I don't need to dictate the rest of this. Go forth, the twelve of you, the gods of Greece."

Nyx's tone was so final, it was a declaration. There were nods of acceptance and a few smiles of encouragement. Hades and Poseidon seemed relieved, Hades giving Erebus an all-too-charming smirk on his way out. One by one, the gods left until only Hermes was left. Erebus let out a low growl and felt Nyx's hand run down his back.

"Easy, Erebus. Hermes and I had a conversation." Erebus scoffed, staring at Hermes for an explanation. Hermes held his hands up in surrender as he took a step forward.

"It's true. I knew about the loophole in Hephaestus's chains. I only volunteered to help Zeus trap you—"

"As a friend?" Erebus couldn't help but shake his head and smile at the trickster.

"Yes!" Hermes nearly shouted in glee, clapping his hands together. "I volunteered to trap you as a friend. Besides, you should see Ares when he gets his hands on…"

"That's enough." Nyx shook her head with a smile. "Go on, Hermes. I'm sure you have trouble to stir up."

Hermes didn't need any other encouragement, disappearing in a ball of light that streaked out of the great hall. Erebus and Nyx were alone.

Nyx turned to Erebus and sighed, leaning her head against his shoulder. "Can we go home now, please?"

"You don't want to stay? I must admit," Erebus growled and bit Nyx's ear playfully, "it was quite the sight watching you take Zeus to task."

Nyx pulled back, humming slightly as she looked up at him. "Is that so?" Erebus nodded in response, and she laughed. It was a full sound, something that Erebus's wanted to bottle up.

"Then yes, let's go home." Nyx cast a fleeting glance at the dais. "We'll need more room this time." Erebus nodded, pulling her flush to him once more as he leaned down and kissed her soundly. Both began to disappear in a cloud of dark smoke and clouds, the quiet, expansive fields of Tartarus the only thing on their minds.

"Home is right next to you." Erebus kissed her forehead as their bodies dissolved into shadow. He felt Nyx's laugh through the ether as they plummeted back down to the Underworld.

"Don't you ever forget it again."

# EPILOGUE

Aeëtes leaned back and inhaled deeply, the smell of sea and saltwater flooding his senses. His shoulders visibly relaxed, and he exhaled slowly, letting the sun wash over him and warm his tired bones. Aeëtes had been inland for far too long. He had been visiting Colchis, but his heart had yearned for Heraklion, with its bustling port and the sun that never seemed to set. The chaotic sounds of ships loading and unloading, of gulls and men haggling, all of it only served to relax him.

Aeëtes was the Crown Prince of Colchis, so he supposed that he should call it home, but he had been raised in Heraklion and that was where he wanted to stay. The king and queen of Colchis weren't even his parents; they had adopted him when he was left on their doorstep. He stayed in Colchis for a few years and was sent to Heraklion to live with their court and train. It was a common enough practice for royal families of the Greek empire to send their sons off to be raised by strangers. You were never too young to make political alliances.

This was where he grew up. All his memories were here, his friends, the places where he had earned his scars and bruises—even if he did stand out here. Aeëtes stood nearly a foot taller than most men, barrel-chested with long limbs. His skin was bronzed from a lifetime spent in the sun, with warm lines that appeared around his face when he smiled. Even his hair was different, the color of chestnuts with gold streaking through it, and he kept his beard cropped close to his face. He had broad features, a wide nose and a jaw to carry it, which made his whole face light up when he laughed. His clothes were always simple, never indulging in finery, and everywhere he went, he went barefoot.

He was the opposite of everything a prince should be, but… Crown Prince of Colchis was only one of his titles.

Aeëtes was a god. He wasn't really the god of anything, nor did he think that he was particularly special in any way. He was, however, immortal. As a gift for raising his son, Aeëtes's father, Helios, had also bestowed immortality on his human foster parents. Aeëtes figured that it was as good of a thank-you as any, and it also saved him from ever really needing to prepare to take the throne. Not like his father listened to that logic.

*"Immortal men die all the time."*

*"Don't think that you're going to get out of your destiny, Aeëtes."*

*"The gods gave you to us for a* reason. *You will take over this throne, and I don't care if it takes centuries to make you."*

Aeëtes shook his head as if he could empty it of thoughts of his father. He figured that it was a bit cliché, a crown prince on the run from his destiny. He couldn't help it. He had no desire to rule over a kingdom of men—all he cared about was freedom. That was mainly due to his mother, an oceanid, whose name he never learned. Aeëtes had never spoken directly to his father, but if he ever did, that would be the first question that he asked.

He stared out over the horizon, sitting down on the dock and slipping his feet into the cool water. The sun was starting to set on the horizon and Aeëtes watched, wondering if his

father could see him as he pulled the chariot over the orange
sky. Aeëtes looked like he was barely a thirty-year-old man. In
actuality, he was well over two hundred by mortal standards.
Gods didn't count in the same way: you were either immortal
or you weren't. Aeëtes figured it was time to stop wondering
when dear old dad would make an appearance. The gods did
whatever they wanted.

Aeëtes included.

Which is what brought him here, back to his beloved
Heraklion, knowing that it was the last night that he was going
to spend in the city. It was time for Aeëtes to do the one thing
that he figured most crown princes knew how to do best—run
away.

———

STAY TUNED for Hecate and Aeëtes's story in *Lost to Witchcraft*.

# ALSO BY MOLLY TULLIS

## The Romanov Oracle

### Prologue

*"I hate purity, I hate goodness! I don't want virtue to exist anywhere. I want everyone to be corrupt to the bones." - George Orwell*

While memories of revolutions heavily focus on the fire and ash, let us not forget the humble spark. It's the incendiary device that rips fabric from the seams, pulls hearts from their chests, and babes prematurely from their mothers.

Before the fires and the firing squads, before the wretched rumors and the gossip that tore a dynasty apart — the smallest of sparks, the brightest of flames, brought 300 years of history and divine rule to its knees. Yet, it was not bombs or bullets that provoked a revolution and toppled the gold-drenched domes of Russia.

It was but two people who fanned a spark that became a flame; one that lit the match that burned down life as they knew it; all while the couple danced in the center of the fire's afterglow and kissed the ash from one another's cheeks

♔ ♔ ♔

St. Petersburg was a haven for the rich, the mighty, and the occult. In 1901, she was a glistening whirl of parties, balls, masques, rituals, sacrifices, and holy baptisms — all baking together under fur trappings and operatic arias.

The Romanov dynasty had been in effect for over 300 years, bringing about the belief of a god-divined right to rule Russia. Which, in turn, created a passive view towards their positions as totalitarian rulers. It bred the rationalization that God found them worthy to rule over the country, which meant, whatever happened to Mother Russia had to be His will. Why else would their lineage have stayed in power through the decades?

Tsar Nicholas II believed their only responsibility was to keep up the iron fist under which eighty percent of the country suffered; the Romanovs had increased in power and decreased in commitment. Famine stretched as far as it did wide, and a shortage of firewood plagued the poor — while the wealthy hosted dinners that displayed caviar purely for the aesthetic and held celebrations where half the food prepared was wasted.

But all that glitters is not gold.

In reality, something far more sinister lurked underneath the silver plating and rough-cut gemstones. It was a front that disguised old-world rituals that had been in effect for centuries.

There was an innumerable amount of secret cabinets, courts, and committees — all with one tie to some religion or another or some secret lord of the state — turning the political subterfuge in the Winter Palace into a melting pot of black magic and Latin recitations of the Lord's Prayer.

Every dance held midnight incantations where saints walked the halls of the Winter Palace like shadows, every song was a prayer played backward, and every jewel was cursed; when there was a masque, there was hardly ever not a hidden priest or khlyst devotee behind it.

The Romanovs' increasing paranoia and grip on the edge of their dynasty's gilded seat caused them to seek counsel in the arms of the *dvoryanstvo*, the nobility, and, more secretly, their priests. A delicate balance between money and religion rocked the family into two separate directions, the Tsarina clinging to her priests as the Tsar did to his nobles.

It was this whirling family portrait of fanaticism and opulence that Anastasia Romanova was dropped into, carrying the last of her father's family magic, which her mother had prayed against, and her father had exorcised.

At her fingertips, she held the beginnings of a spark that would incinerate everything around her, leaving behind nothing but ashes that would give way to only two names that rang through history itself: Rasputin and Anastasia.

# ABOUT THE AUTHOR

Molly Tullis would have picked the Phantom of the Opera over Raoul and named her French bulldog Jean Valjean. She only believes in black clothing, red lipstick, and never turns down an iced coffee or tequila. She enjoys writing fantasy, romance, or any genre with an opportunity to insert a dark-haired, morally grey man. Her debut novel, *The Romanov Oracle*, was inspired by a love of history and a simultaneous desire to rewrite it with more magic.

When not identifying as an author, she identifies as a woman with bangs, finger tattoos, and a nose ring, who can tell you what planets are making you sad.

Her DMs are always open on Instagram and Patreon (@thebibliophileblonde), and you can get information on all upcoming projects at www.thebibliophileblonde.com.

Printed in Great Britain
by Amazon

82213838R00190